DAEMONHAMMER

More great Warhammer 40,000 fiction from Black Library

EISENHORN: THE OMNIBUS
by Dan Abnett
(Contains the novels *Xenos, Malleus, Hereticus* and *The Magos* plus several short stories)

RAVENOR: THE OMNIBUS
by Dan Abnett
(Contains the novels *Ravenor, Ravenor Returned* and *Ravenor Rogue* plus two short stories)

LEVIATHAN
A novel by Darius Hinks

• VAULTS OF TERRA •
by Chris Wraight

Book 1: THE CARRION THRONE
Book 2: THE HOLLOW MOUNTAIN
Book 3: THE DARK CITY

• DARK IMPERIUM •
by Guy Haley

Book 1: DARK IMPERIUM
Book 2: PLAGUE WAR
Book 3: GODBLIGHT

• DAWN OF FIRE •
Book 1: AVENGING SON
by Guy Haley

Book 2: THE GATE OF BONES
by Andy Clark

Book 3: THE WOLFTIME
by Gav Thorpe

Book 4: THRONE OF LIGHT
by Guy Haley

Book 5: THE IRON KINGDOM
by Nick Kyme

Book 6: THE MARTYR'S TOMB
by Marc Collins

Book 7: SEA OF SOULS
by Chris Wraight

Book 8: HAND OF ABADDON
by Nick Kyme

Book 9: THE SILENT KING
by Guy Haley

DAEMONHAMMER

DARIUS HINKS

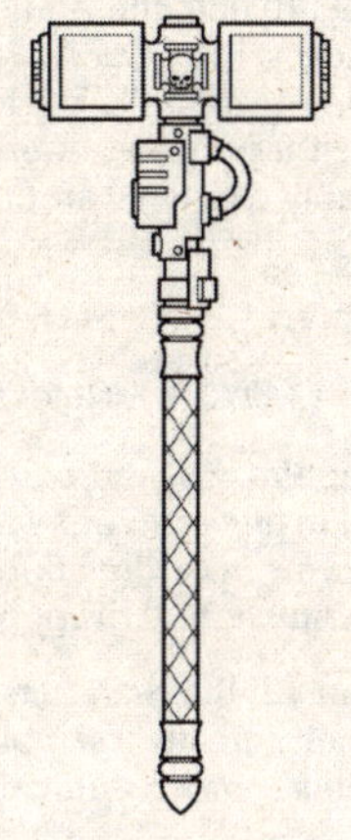

BLACK LIBRARY

A BLACK LIBRARY PUBLICATION

First published in 2024.
This edition published in Great Britain in 2025 by
Black Library, Games Workshop Ltd., Willow Road,
Nottingham, NG7 2WS, UK.

Represented by: Games Workshop Limited – Irish branch,
Unit 3, Lower Liffey Street, Dublin 1,
D01 K199, Ireland.

10 9 8 7 6 5 4 3 2 1

Produced by Games Workshop in Nottingham.
Cover illustration by Nathaniel Himawan.

A CIP record for this book is available from the British Library.

ISBN 13: 978-1-80407-702-3

Printed and bound in the UK.

For more than a hundred centuries the Emperor has sat immobile on the Golden Throne of Earth. He is the Master of Mankind. By the might of his inexhaustible armies a million worlds stand against the dark.

Yet, he is a rotting carcass, the Carrion Lord of the Imperium held in life by marvels from the Dark Age of Technology and the thousand souls sacrificed each day so his may continue to burn.

To be a man in such times is to be one amongst untold billions. It is to live in the cruelest and most bloody regime imaginable. It is to suffer an eternity of carnage and slaughter. It is to have cries of anguish and sorrow drowned by the thirsting laughter of dark gods.

This is a dark and terrible era where you will find little comfort or hope. Forget the power of technology and science. Forget the promise of progress and advancement. Forget any notion of common humanity or compassion.

There is no peace amongst the stars, for in the grim darkness of the far future, there is only war.

Anamnesis

That which proceeds from Him cannot be false.

The Emperor's face is dark with blood. It swells over his eyelids and weeps down his cheeks. Of all the things I've seen today, it is this that finally threatens to break my will. I am barely ten years old, but I have given all I have to this statue, polishing the ancient stone and reading the inscriptions, committing every line to memory. To see it defiled fills me with rage. I stare into the Emperor's eyes and recite the words in my mind, steeling myself with the familiar cadence.

He is truth incarnate. That which proceeds from Him cannot be false. That which does not proceed from Him is a lie.

Killers move closer. Screams follow. People are dying outside. Gunfire rattles, bodies burn, and smoke curls lazily from beneath the door, blurring my vision.

Awful sounds try to lure me from my vigil, try to make me look at the shapes on the floor, but I lock my eyes tighter to the Emperor's gaze.

We are the heirs of Terra. Blood of the Throne. The adamantine spirit of man. The light in the abyss.

Footsteps rush towards the door, and it bangs open.

'Torquemada!' I recognise the voice of a temple guard. 'They're coming! Arm yourself!'

A knife clatters across the floor towards the foot of the statue.

'There's nothing you can do for them! Leave!' The guard waits, panting, then rushes from the shrine, leaving the door squealing on its hinges.

Fury quickens my pulse. The chapel-master did this. *His* weakness is to blame.

More footsteps approach the open door. Slower. More considered.

I glance at the knife, then lock my eyes back on the statue. The Emperor *will* hear me.

There is a rattle of guns being raised.

He walketh in fire and blood.

He walketh in judgement.

Light flashes in the Emperor's eyes. A less devout soul might dismiss it as firelight, bouncing from the surface of a raised gun, but I know the truth. It is an answer.

A *promise.*

I wipe away the Emperor's tears. 'The Emperor of Holy Terra knows your name and He sees your sin.' As I speak, I adopt the steady tone that my father used in sermons. 'He is the light that burns.'

Armour-clad fingers settle on triggers. Booted feet move closer.

He that cleaves to the Throne shall abideth.

'Hold.'

The voice is low and heavily accented. It rings across the old stones.

Curiosity gets the better of me, and I turn to face my executioners.

I expect a feverish rabble, but they are soldiers, dressed in lustreless black, faces hidden behind masks. These people are not idolators. They are well armed, and they stand in disciplined, well-drilled lockstep. The leader is a tall, heavyset brute with black hair cascading down over his shoulders, but the most striking thing about him is his armour. It is unaccountably beautiful – an ancient suit of golden ceramite.

He studies me in silence.

I glare back, and then I look, finally, at the shapes on the floor. The bodies are so mutilated they make no sense. They are a hideous puzzle. My strength fails. I fall to my knees, reaching out to the remains, fingers hovering above ruined faces.

The stranger comes closer. 'Your family?'

I manage to nod.

'And this?'

'The chapel-master.' My voice cracks. I think of what his *kindness* has wrought on my brother and sisters, father and mother. They did nothing wrong. It was the chapel-master who took pity on the idolaters. It was the chapel-master who refused to condemn them without a trial. And this is where his tolerance led. They carved their idols into my family.

Into them.

I want to claw at my face, but even through my despair, part of me is intrigued by the stranger. 'Who are you?' I ask.

'Lord Inquisitor Laredian.'

The man's title means nothing to me, but his demeanour is impressive. The screams outside have reached a desperate pitch, but Laredian is unafraid. He is calm.

He looks at the pieces of my family. 'Do you know why they died?'

'Because the chapel-master showed mercy.'

Laredian raises an eyebrow. He seems surprised by the speed of my answer, by my confidence. 'Exactly.' He touches the chapel-master with his boot, squeezing blood from the rags. 'Mercy. The mother of heresy.'

He comes to my side and looks up at the statue. Then he removes his gauntlet and places his hand on the ancient stone.

'You are not a heretic,' I whisper.

Laredian touches the spot where I wiped blood from the Emperor's eyes. 'Neither, I think, are you.'

CHAPTER ONE

The room was seventy feet long but seemed smaller due to the mess. Banks of cogitators teetered on top of each other, rattling against bulkheads and spooling parchment onto the floor. There was a row of tables down one side that looked like sarcophagi, covered in corpses and surgical equipment. The walls were obscured by wires and duct piping, and there were servitors buried under the equipment, murmuring and twitching, hunched over runeboards. They were monofunctional wretches with scab-encrusted heads, wasted arms, and tails of knotted cabling where their spines should have been. As Lord Inquisitor Torquemada Coteaz entered the chamber, the servitors showed no sign of recognition, sucking mindlessly on the nutrient pipes sewn into their mouths.

'My lord,' said a voice. It was an inorganic rasp, crackling from an emitter in the ceiling.

Coteaz looked around the room. 'Albaro.'

Cables undulated and birthed a pale object: the head of an elderly man covered in engine grease. He blinked away some of the gunk and smiled at Coteaz, revealing gleaming yellow teeth. As the cables settled, it became clear that the head had no body. Beneath its jaw, where a neck should have been, there was a plastek collar connecting it to a cluster of pipes. Albaro stared at Coteaz, his disembodied head swaying. Then he looked past the inquisitor to a group of retainers following in his wake. Albaro was chewing tabac, and black spit oozed between his teeth as he smirked. He spat a treacly gobbet on the floor.

The nest of cables shifted again, carrying Albaro's head higher, until his eyes were level with Coteaz's. Wires lifted from the wall, acting as his arm, and he pointed towards the back of the chamber. 'She has been oiled and sanctified.' He sneered at the retainers again, as though challenging them to speak, but they said nothing. The cables swallowed his face, then he re-emerged at the far end of the room, sprouting like a scornful bud. 'Should be less painful this time.'

Coteaz and the others picked their way across the room, stepping carefully around machines and blank-eyed servitors, heading over to the space Albaro had indicated. Some of the tables had been shoved aside to make space for an iron chair, big enough to resemble a throne but less ornate. It was a simple metal frame, like a scaffold stuffed with wires and capacitors and draped in plastek tubes, each filled with dark fluid and tipped with a copper syringe. There were straps on the arms and a cowl at the back, placed where a head would go. More straps lay around the base, to restrain the sitter's legs, and the whole thing was bolted and riveted with such brutality that it looked more like a weapon than a piece of furniture.

Coteaz's face was lined with age, and there were only a few wisps of grey to soften the lines of his brow, but he moved with the speed of a younger man, striding up onto the pedestal and sitting down with a clang. As he sat, words rose from his memory, words from his childhood. *Blood of the Throne. The adamantine spirit of man. The light in the abyss.*

Albaro's head resurfaced, covered in more engine fluid. 'You need to remove the armour, remember,' he said. 'Ceramite dampens the currents. Restituta don't like it.'

Coteaz stood, arms raised in readiness, and for the first time that morning, he actually looked at his retainers. Only three were present. Standing directly before him was Korov, a bull-necked colossus who dwarfed even Coteaz. He was shrouded rather than dressed, wrapped in sheets of filthy sackcloth bound with synthleather straps. Every inch of the sackcloth was covered in writing – furiously scrawled pleas for absolution and forgiveness. In some places, Korov had simply written the word *Sinner* over and over again, the letters growing frenzied and distorted in places, overlapping and spiralling around each other. In place of arms he had dozens of vulcanised rubber tendrils that ended in claws, grips and drills, and his face was almost entirely hidden – the top half buried in a grubby hood and the rest encased in a stained plastek muzzle. Only his eyes were visible, furtive and restless, looking everywhere but at Coteaz. The sound of heavy breathing growled through his muzzle.

Standing beside him was Turcifel. The two of them could hardly have looked more different – where he was grubby, she was immaculate, with flawless pale skin, flowing white robes, and glossy black hair combed in a centre parting so severe it looked as if it had been painted on. She stood erect, with her hood thrown back and her chin raised, her fingers locked around a long string of green prayer beads. But like Korov, she avoided Coteaz's gaze, staring into the middle distance. This was, no doubt, hard for them to watch.

Standing a few feet behind the other two was Captain Malevich, dressed in the smart black carapace uniform of Coteaz's

Scion companies. As High Protector of the Formosa Sector, Coteaz had almost limitless resources. Entire armies were at his disposal. But the Scions were his elite troops, some of the most seasoned veterans in the entire sector, and Malevich was amongst the best of them. He stood with rigid, military bearing: shoulders back, chest out, hands clasped behind him. He was a tempered weapon, forged by the same schola drill abbots as Coteaz; a compact man with skin the colour of rosewood, a clean-shaven jaw, streaks of grey at his temples, and an oiled pencil moustache. Unlike the other two, he was looking directly at Coteaz, taking in every detail. He was sharp and neat – sleek as a blade.

As Coteaz studied his acolytes, hooded serfs rushed from the shadows and began removing his armour, cradling every filigreed plate with reverence, wrapping the golden ceramite in cloth, and whispering to the pieces as they carried them away to be oiled and polished. The suit was a priceless relic, intricately detailed with thousands of holy sigils. Illuminated scrolls fluttered from the greaves and gilded reliquaries clattered at the belt, objects so sacred worlds had died to preserve them. The armour was rumoured to be even older than Coteaz's flagship, the *Pilgrim's Wrath*, and legends claimed that it had been forged in the Sol System, within sight of Holy Terra itself. The sun that shone on the God-Emperor might once have warmed this armour. Its value was impossible to quantify.

Once the armour had been removed, the serfs cautiously lifted Coteaz's warhammer, their eyes straining ecstatically. It took four of them to lift it, and Coteaz gave them a warning glance as they carried the weapon away and wrapped it in his crimson cloak. The daemonhammer was a conduit of his faith, anointed by the Holy Order of the Sacred Throne and able to harness the violence of his prayers. Over the years, he had poured so much of his belief into it that if it were damaged, he was not sure his mind would endure the shock of separation. But the risk was worth it. The daemonhammer was so innately holy that even the monsters of the empyrean quailed before it.

At Albaro's prompting, the serfs also removed the quilted garments Coteaz wore under his armour until he was naked apart from a loincloth. The light in the chamber was brutal, revealing the whorls of scar tissue that covered the inquisitor's muscles. There was a time when he knew the cause of every wound, but after so many years, they had become too numerous to track. As a youth, he had considered them badges of honour; now they felt more like a warning.

What was it Laredian used to say? *Time has no antidote.* Coteaz shook his head, irritated by his cowardly turn of thoughts. *He that cleaves to the Throne shall abideth.*

'Begin,' he said, settling back against the cold metal as the serfs strapped him into the seat.

Once the straps had been fastened and checked, Albaro ordered everyone to step back. Then his face slid back under the pipes, and viewscreens flickered into life around him. Coteaz resisted the urge to close his eyes as the chair stirred. A motor growled behind him. Cogs rattled and bellows hissed. Cords slid across his face, binding him tighter as vials dropped from the ceiling. As the tubes slid into position, Coteaz lost sight of most of the room. Only Turcifel's face remained visible. She was whispering prayers and gazing into the distance, looking at places no one else could see.

Pain scuttled up Coteaz's arms as needles punctured his skin, linking him, through tubes, to the glass vials. Data scrolled across his retinal overlay, reporting incisions and rates of blood loss. There was a whirring sound as something burrowed through the cables and pressed against his chest. Something cold and metallic. Pain flashed across his ribs, followed by numbness as morphia shots took hold. For Coteaz, pain was a constant, so to suddenly feel its absence was oddly disorientating – as if he had lost one of his senses. He could still feel the object against his chest, though, and after a few seconds it sprouted barbs, hooking tighter.

'Out with the old,' rasped Albaro, as the engine noise shifted in pitch, becoming a thin whine. The pipes fixed to Coteaz's right arm shivered as his blood rushed out into them. 'In with the less old.' Coteaz's left arm juddered as cold liquid was forced into his veins. Pumps gasped, servos whined, and the stink of ammonia filled the air. The process was demeaning but not, he thought, impious. The Emperor willed this machine into being. And that which proceeded from the Emperor could not be a lie.

He continued looking at Turcifel, wondering idly where her mind was, and from her, his thoughts turned to the other members of his retinue – not the legions of agents he employed across the sector, but the small group that travelled with him on the *Pilgrim's Wrath*. All of them were impressive in their own way. Unique, even. But they were trusted servants, nothing more. Even after all these years, he had never found an acolyte with whom he could share even a tenth of his knowledge. The idea troubled him more than the blades that were cutting into his scalp. After all these decades, there was still no one but him.

He noticed that Turcifel was frowning at him.

'Albaro?' said Captain Malevich. Coteaz could not see him, but his clipped tones were unmistakeable.

'It's nothing.' Albaro no longer sounded like he was smiling. 'Give me a minute.'

The chair was shaking more than usual. Coteaz felt warmth rush from his chest and begin pooling in his lap. 'What is it?' he asked.

'My lord,' said Albaro, sounding unnerved. 'I just need a minute.'

Coteaz no longer felt numb. Pain bloomed behind his ribs, and his veins were burning, hammering fitfully. This was worse than usual.

'Get him out!' ordered Malevich as scuffling sounds filled the room. 'He's haemorrhaging.' Coteaz heard things being shoved and pulled, then the sound of breaking glass. The pain was now all over his body. It felt as though something was trying to emerge from his cranium.

It was only when his heart stopped that Coteaz realised he was dying.

His breath stalled in his chest and, unexpectedly, an image filled his mind, a memory he had long fought to suppress. The scene was as vivid and awful as the first time he saw it. He saw the Golden Throne engulfed in flames. It was nothing like the crude chair he was dying in; it was a grand edifice, the work of centuries, gilded and armoured like a battleship. The figure at its centre was a pillar of blue flame, and heaped around the throne room lay thousands of dead. Coteaz looked around in horror, as if he were truly there, and saw that the walls of the Imperial Palace had toppled and the world outside was aflame. But it was no ordinary fire. It was a fire that lived: grinning and writhing, moaning ecstatically as it dissolved walls, flesh and air. The flames climbed higher, engulfing the stars, consuming the heavens, and leaving a maelstrom in their wake. He knew it was a lie, but it grew more vivid every time he went under Albaro's knives.

'No,' said Coteaz, as his life ebbed away. 'No!' he roared, lurching to his feet.

'Stop!' cried several voices at once.

Skin tore from Coteaz's arms. The engine wailed.

Coteaz was blind with pain and something buckled behind him. Agony exploded in his head. Then the strength went from his legs, and he fell.

His head hit something hard.

Then there was nothing.

CHAPTER TWO

The chapterhouse on the *Pilgrim's Wrath* radiated Imperial power. It was a grand, twelve-sided room dominated by a towering column at its centre that supported a domed ceiling. The column was carved in the shape of a capital 'I' with three horizontal bars framing a circle at its centre. The circle contained an enormous rockcrete skull that glowered down at the twelve thrones placed around the edge of the room. This stylised 'I' was the sigil of the Emperor's Holy Inquisition, the institution that had defined every aspect of Coteaz's life for decades. But his attention was fixed on the single, large doorway that led into the room. When Coteaz had taken possession of the ship from his disgraced predecessor, Lord Laredian, the Ordo Malleus had seen fit to make alterations to its livery and architecture. They claimed the redesign was in tribute to its new master, but Coteaz knew the truth: it was to remove the stain of the old one. Thanks to him, Laredian had died under a cloud – a cloud that the Ordo was keen to disperse.

Over the subsequent years, Coteaz had become blind to most

of the ship's architecture. The vessel was over three miles long, and he rarely visited more than a few decks. But he saw the doorway to the chapterhouse almost every day, and over the years he had become obsessed by it. The imposing, moulded arch had been redesigned to incorporate an hourglass, surrounded by a nest of dying serpents. At its centre was an intricately carved grain of sand, falling but not falling, frozen in place for all eternity, defying the passage of time. As he looked at it, his mind slipped back across the decades and he pictured Laredian's face, recalling how he reacted when Coteaz accused him of heresy. He could remember every detail, even after all this time. It was the fulcrum on which his life had turned. Laredian had been old by then, much of his physical strength gone, and when he realised what Coteaz had done, how he had turned his own methods against him, Coteaz saw fear in his eyes. He had never seen Laredian look afraid before that. It was terrible to witness.

Traitor.

Laredian had whispered the word, lips quivering with venom. Coteaz knew it was untrue. Whatever Laredian had done for him, his ultimate loyalty was to truth and the God-Emperor. But he had never forgotten the rage and hurt Laredian forced into that single word. Laredian believed Coteaz was a traitor.

How?

Footsteps echoed into the chamber accompanied by the clank of a broken bell. Coteaz looked down from the architecture, drawing his thoughts back to the present, adjusting his position in his seat. It was days since his heart had stopped in Albaro's device, but pain still gnawed at him as he shuffled in the throne. Though he had been leeched, sewn and cauterised, the cuts were still raw. New pain merged with old. Every movement drew fresh torrents of agony.

As Coteaz shifted position, so did the raptor perched at his side. Thula was a Glovodan psyber-eagle – a genetically engineered miracle with glossy tawny plumage that turned to white around her two proud heads. Her beaks were as gold as Coteaz's armour and her eyes flashed as she looked up, studying the doorway with cool disdain. She was magnificent, over three feet tall, and if she were to spread her wings, they would stretch to nearly seven feet. At the sound of the footsteps, she turned one of her heads to Coteaz, a question in her eyes. He shook his head and gently stroked her, tracing the shape of the rivets under her feathers.

Hooded figures swept into the chapterhouse, whipping up dust from the flagstones with long scarlet robes. The Ostiarii were Coteaz's personal order of sacristans. Keepers of his relics and guardians of his faith. They approached him, as always, as if they were approaching the God-Emperor Himself, heads bowed and faces hidden deep in their cowls. Some carried gilded reliquaries while others cradled bones on embroidered cushions, holding them up to him like offerings. One carried a banner made from scraps of preserved skin, crowded with lines of tiny sigils: a collection of holy texts understood only by the senior sacristan, Salmasius.

Salmasius himself was at the head of the group, moving with all the speed his ancient legs could muster. Like the others, he wore thick, voluminous robes, blood red and embroidered with gold-threaded images of the Inquisitorial rosette and the key-shaped symbol of the Ostiarii. Salmasius was older even than Coteaz and clearly struggled to walk, but there was a quiet dignity to his movements. He had a polished femur in one hand and a cracked bell in the other, and after every fourth step, he gently tapped the bone against the bell. He paused before the inquisitor and performed a stiff bow, then walked slowly to his allotted throne, to the right of Coteaz. The rest of the sacristans bowed, then withdrew from sight, standing in a recess behind Salmasius' throne.

Salmasius did not speak for a moment, sitting rigidly in his chair as he waited for his breathing to settle. Finally, the old priest pulled back his hood and turned to face Coteaz. His face was painfully gaunt, and his skin was the same colour as the bone in his hand. His eyes were deep-set and clouded with cataracts, and his face was so lined that it took Coteaz a moment to realise he was scowling. When Salmasius spoke his voice was a whisper, but the acoustics of the chapterhouse amplified it, revealing the concern in his tone. 'My lord. You let Albaro live.'

Coteaz nodded.

Salmasius curled his thin lips. 'The man's a heretic.'

Coteaz did not deign to answer.

Veins of colour crossed the old man's cheeks. 'You could have died in that chair.'

'If it wasn't for Albaro, I would have died a long time ago. His contrivances are the only reason I endure. The restituta worked perfectly on the previous occasions. The problem is not Albaro. The problem is that I ask too much. I ask the impossible.'

'*Nothing* is impossible with the will of the God-Emperor.'

Coteaz looked at the hourglass again, staring at the frozen grain of sand.

Salmasius followed the direction of Coteaz's gaze. He softened his tone. 'You're still in pain.'

Coteaz could have laughed. *Still in pain.* He was a patchwork monster. His body was a mess of transplanted organs, powercells, bionics, and offcuts from cadavers. He wore a suit of borrowed flesh. All he knew was pain, and every ache felt like nature screaming at him, demanding that he yield – that he accept the inevitable. But, of course, he shared none of this with Salmasius. Besides, he cherished the hurt. It told him he was still alive; that he still had time to do the Emperor's work.

'I am healing,' he said. 'Which is why Albaro is being mended rather than executed. I need him, Salmasius. I need him to find new techniques of preservation. If the restituta fails, he must find another method.'

Salmasius looked unconvinced. 'I just wish you could find a less repulsive chirurgeon. Heretic or not, Albaro's corrupt. And I'm not talking about his body. The man has no decency.'

'He has faith in the Emperor. And the Emperor has faith in him. Why else would He have granted him such genius?'

Salmasius shook his head but said no more.

A moment later, they heard the sound of others approaching the chamber.

Turcifel entered first and stared eagerly at Coteaz, taking in his polished battle plate and his upright posture. 'My lord,' she said, her relief plain. 'You are well.' She bowed and headed to her throne.

Korov stomped into the chamber and knelt before Coteaz. 'Blood,' he said, his voice low and rough, 'of the Throne.' He did not seem to be addressing anyone in particular, but Coteaz answered him, repeating the phrase. Korov made a thin rasping sound, as though struggling to breathe. Then he rose and dropped heavily into a chair.

Captain Malevich arrived next, flanked by black-armoured Scions. They saluted Coteaz, then Malevich ordered them to stand guard in the hallway outside while he took the seat to Coteaz's left.

As Malevich sat down, another figure entered the chamber. Sixtus was emaciated and crook-backed, dressed in similar robes to Salmasius. But Sixtus' robes were unfastened from the waist up to accommodate the logic engine sewn into his chest. It looked like a brass, rune-inscribed clock face adorned with many smaller, concentric dials and clockwork mechanisms. The left side of Sixtus' head was unaugmented, with the features of a normal, if malnourished, man, but the right side was a hollow mass of pipes that snaked up from the device in his chest and fed into his skull. Unlike most servitors, he had vestigial traces of humanity that allowed him to follow the subtleties of a conversation. Where his right eye should have been, there was a crystalflex lens, whirring and clicking as he focused it on Coteaz.

'Lord Coteaz,' he said, his voice gurgling like a water whistle. Rather than taking a seat, he hobbled over to the chapterhouse's central pillar, unclipped one of his cerebral implants, and connected it to an input in the rockcrete.

Finally, a slender, regal-looking man entered the chamber, wearing an embroidered, emerald-coloured dress coat and black breeches. Voltas had flawless skin, golden, shoulder-length ringlets, and a drowsy, half-lidded gaze. He reminded Coteaz of an expensive automaton, polished and elaborately decorated, with a head that seemed slightly too large for his narrow shoulders. Everything about him spoke of confidence and privilege. Aside from his luxurious clothes he carried mastercrafted weapons that glittered as he sauntered into the room. He had an ancient, monosteel power sword at his hip – an elegant, rapier-bladed relic with a knuckle guard like silver gossamer. And at his other hip he wore a pair of matching laspistols that were just as ornate – ivory-coated duelling pieces with gems running down their fluted barrels. Such conspicuous wealth might have looked gauche on someone else, but Voltas wore it with a nonchalant swagger. He paused to give Coteaz a languid bow, then took a seat near Turcifel.

Coteaz watched the group as they settled in their seats. He had thousands of agents at his command, and entire armies stood ready to march under his banner, but only these select few would ever be admitted to this room. With a blink of his retinal overlay he slammed the doors. The chapterhouse was warded by high-level privacy fields, and with the doors closed, everyone present could feel at ease to discuss all but the most sensitive subjects.

'Sixtus,' he said.

The servitor wheezed and turned to face the column. There was a musical ticking as he adjusted dials on his chest. Then the suspensor lumens died, plunging the chamber into darkness. There was another clicking sound and the cosmos swam into view, filling the room with spectral planets and stars that hung in the air, turning slowly around the column. The hololith was projected from the eye sockets of the skull at the centre of the pillar, and as the image rotated, it washed a rainbow of colours over the seated onlookers. The image was distorted by static, glitching and fragmented, but when Sixtus made a few more adjustments to his chest, the planets became vivid and jewel-like.

Coteaz studied his domain as it danced before him. There was no corner of the Formosa Sector he was unfamiliar with. Some regions were veiled by warp storms, others were uninhabitable, but he knew them all by name. As far as he was aware, there was no sector in the entire galaxy that had been so accurately mapped, save Sol, perhaps. He leant forward to look closer, but as he did so, pain lanced into his chest. He bit back a curse, conscious that everyone in the room was watching him.

'Malevich,' he said.

Captain Malevich marched across the flagstones to stand in the stars with Sixtus. 'My lord,' he said, saluting. 'Good news from Syrens.'

As Malevich spoke, Sixtus adjusted the display, zooming in on a particular star system – five planets orbiting an aged red sun.

'Your informants were correct,' continued Malevich. 'The source of the heretical propaganda was the Chartist Captain, Valerios. He resisted arrest and died at the scene. Your suggestion that we investigate the Chartist Guild was insightful. Several Chartist vessels are now impounded and being investigated by the local law enforcement operatives. It would appear that Valerios was an idolator, as you suspected.'

'Throne preserve us,' intoned Salmasius.

'Throne preserve us,' echoed Malevich.

'Keep a close watch on the other guilders,' said Coteaz. 'And have one of our operatives talk to a man called Vitus Angra in the Ilheos Munitorum offices.'

'Angra?' Malevich turned to Sixtus.

Sixtus wheezed and fiddled with the discs on his chest, rotating them a few notches. A new image blinked into view, dwarfing the planets of the Syrens System. It was a blurry pict capture of a plain-looking, bulbous-nosed youth, dressed in the ill-fitting robes of a junior Munitorum scribe.

'I have minimal information on Vitus Angra,' burbled Sixtus. 'Escrivano. Skilos class. Nineteen Terran-standard years old. Perhaps twenty. The census records in Ilheos are incomplete and unsatisfactory.'

'Find him,' said Coteaz. 'I'm reliably informed that he was in contact with the Chartist Captain and involved in the production of the propaganda material.'

Malevich indicated that Sixtus should remove the pict. 'The news from the Lucar System is less pleasing,' he said, proceeding to describe an investigation that had been floundering for several months. For the next hour, Malevich gave status updates from around the area of the Formosa Sector he was responsible for. He barely moved the whole time, keeping his chin raised and addressing Coteaz as if he were speaking to a battalion of stormtroopers. He was occasionally wrong-footed when Coteaz revealed unexpected information, but each time, he maintained his composure and thanked Coteaz for the new names without asking where they had come from.

When Malevich had finished, Coteaz waved him back to his seat. 'Interrogator Voltas,' he said, turning to the man with aristocratic bearing.

Voltas strolled over to Sixtus and took out a sheaf of papers, but before looking at them he gazed languidly at Coteaz. 'My lord. Does the name Agent Krasner mean anything to you?'

Coteaz was impressed. Since making Voltas his interrogator he had placed dozens of systems under his care, and the man had somehow picked one incongruous name from billions.

'None of your operatives are called Krasner.' Coteaz kept his tone flat.

Voltas studied Coteaz from beneath hooded eyes. There was something reptilian about him, and his speech was so ornate that the words slurred into a ripple of elongated vowels. 'Forgive my presumption in raising the matter, High Protector, but you have deployed an agent called Krasner to a planet called Novalis, in the Ixos System, which I believe falls under my jurisdiction.'

Coteaz realised that he should have expected this. Voltas was *fiercely* intelligent. He doubted anyone else in his retinue would have unearthed that name. But the interrogator was displaying a surprising lack of tact for someone raised amongst Formosa's highborn. This was not something Coteaz had wanted to share with the entire group, and Voltas could have anticipated that.

Behind Voltas, Sixtus was bringing a new image into view, showing a different cluster of planets as the interrogator continued talking. 'I was surprised to find that we had a presence on such a seemingly forgotten backwater,' he said, 'so I did some research. Novalis was considered a dead world until a few centuries ago. After several failed attempts, a mining colony was established, despite the harsh conditions. It has not been a very successful enterprise. There are less than a dozen mines still operating, and they are not expected to last more than another decade. Average life expectancy for the colonists is even lower than Imperial-standard for this kind of world. Slaves and indentured workers rarely live past their mid-twenties. Records indicate that the population is down to no more than a few million inhabitants. But there are several valuable seams of thullic ore, and the rewards are considered worth the investment.'

Coteaz could feel Salmasius looking at the side of his face, and Thula shuffled on her perch, glaring at Voltas and flexing her talons. He stroked Thula and remained quiet, keen to know how much the interrogator had learned, and possibly shared with others.

'Thullic ore is prized by the fleet,' Voltas went on. 'But my instincts tell me that is not what Krasner was sent to investigate.' He continued gazing languidly at Coteaz, but when he saw there was no answer coming, he glanced at Sixtus. 'Show the Vespertinus primary hub.'

'Show the primary hub,' responded Sixtus, echoing the words in a dull monotone. He adjusted the hololith, zooming in on the surface of Novalis. The image was not as clear as the preceding ones, hazed by static and jagged lines of pixels. He burbled, fiddling with his cogitator, but the image remained blurry. 'Chromatic aberration. Pollutants in the mesosphere. Seventy per cent of the archival plates are distorted.'

Blurred as the image was, it still revealed the peculiar nature of the planet. The entire surface resembled congealed blood.

'How old is this image?' asked Voltas.

Sixtus turned the dials on his chest. 'How old is this image? The image is nine hundred and fifty-four Terran-standard days old.'

Voltas nodded and ordered Sixtus to close in on a cluster of hazy shapes. 'At some point before this image was taken,' he said, 'a Glovodan Adeptus Mechanicus explorator fleet entered the Ixos System. Under the leadership of Magos Xylothek, they have established a mobile research facility. It is currently operating just to the south of this mine.'

Sixtus shook his head and burbled in disagreement, seeming agitated. 'There are no records of such a–'

'No records,' interrupted Voltas. 'Precisely. No permission was requested or given. Reason enough for concern.' He was still studying Coteaz. 'Is that the reason we deployed Agent Krasner?'

Coteaz relaxed. The interrogator had unearthed some basic facts, but Krasner had kept the important information obscured. 'Magos Xylothek has flouted protocol, so I considered it worthwhile keeping an eye on her,' he replied. 'If my contacts in the Vespertinus hub had not alerted me to her arrival, I would have had no idea the Mechanicus was there.'

'You have contacts in that *particular* mine?'

'I have contacts wherever people draw breath. Krasner is a skilled agent. If you intercept any of his reports, treat them extremely sensitively. And ensure I see them immediately.'

Voltas thought for a moment, then handed something to Sixtus.

Sixtus slotted the object into his chest, and the discs rotated, clicking into a new configuration. The Formosa Sector was extinguished, plunging the chapterhouse into darkness. Then a new hololith swam into view – a blind woman's face, cowled and half thrown into shadow. She was pale and emaciated, with sutured scars where her eyes should have been. She looked panicked, her head tilted sideways at an awkward angle, but the image was frozen and the only sound was a hiss of static that poured from the emitters overhead.

Coteaz was tiring of Voltas' theatrics. 'What's this?'

'A message from Agent Krasner. Intercepted by the orbital relay at Cabral. The astropathic chorum experienced great difficulty in extracting it. The chorister you see here suffered a cranial bleed, but before she lost consciousness, she managed to visualise some of the message and relay it.'

Voltas knew things that he did not. The thought did not make Coteaz happy. 'Show me.'

The image of the astropath's face was dozens of feet tall and slashed by static, and when it flickered into life, her voice was a distorted howl that rang out across the chapterhouse. She was shaking violently. *'These were his words,'* she gasped, glancing over her shoulder. *'It is here. They have found it. Lord Coteaz, you were right. It* does *exist. And it* is *on Novalis.'* The woman paused, gripping her temples. *'But you must move fast.* She *is here too. Sato. And she knows. Come quickly. I have had no option but to tell her that–'*

The woman's face froze, mid-sentence, the image flickering in and out of the darkness.

'Play the rest,' said Coteaz.

'Play the rest,' mumbled Sixtus. 'Impossible. There is no more to this recording. The file is not truncated. That is the entire message.'

'That was all the astropath could relay,' said Voltas. 'The head chorister was concerned. He said there was a deliberate attempt to suppress the message, as if someone on Novalis didn't want it to be heard. The relay's hexagrammatic wardings were compromised, and he was forced to shut down for several hours.'

'And I am only hearing about this now?'

'I was only informed two days ago, my lord. And you were still recovering. If I had known who Agent Krasner was, and that his work was important to you, I would have passed the message on sooner.'

Coteaz wondered if the interrogator was trying to make a point. Was he playing games? If so, he would regret it. 'Two days,' he muttered, talking more to himself than Voltas. 'And the message would have taken a long time to reach the orbital. Krasner must have sent it weeks ago.'

No one said anything for a moment, and the only sound was the static from the flickering hololith. Then Captain Malevich spoke up, his expression even more rigid than usual.

'My lord, is the message referring to *Interrogator* Sato?'

Everyone in the room looked at Coteaz. Even Korov glanced up, breathing heavily into his muzzle.

Voltas frowned. 'Sato? Wasn't she someone in your employ?'

'One of my retainers,' said Coteaz. 'Before your time. She was a disappointment. She is not to be trusted.'

'Is she a threat to Agent Krasner? Do we need to–'

Coteaz held up a finger to silence him. 'I must think on this.' He looked over at Sixtus, who was still bathed in the light of the hololith. 'Examine the message. Contact the astropathic relay. Find out exactly how many weeks have passed since Krasner said those words.' He rose to his feet. 'The rest of you, return to your work. We will reconvene tomorrow.'

Voltas remained silent as Coteaz marched past him and headed for the doors with Thula swooping after him. This had not gone as he planned. He should have briefed Coteaz in private.

'Session dismissed,' said Coteaz, catching the eagle on his wrist as he left the room.

Korov slouched to his feet and lurched after Coteaz as the sacristans, led by Salmasius, followed at a statelier pace, banners and bones held aloft as they shuffled across the flagstones. Sixtus deactivated the hololith and headed after them.

Captain Malevich started off across the chamber, then paused and headed back to Voltas. 'Forgive me, interrogator, but why did you withhold that information?'

Under normal circumstances, Voltas would have ignored such an ill-mannered question from a soldier, but Coteaz had given the captain extraordinary powers of command. He clearly placed great trust in the man. It might not be wise to make an enemy of him.

'Lord Coteaz was fighting for his life,' he answered. 'He was in no fit state to receive messages.'

Malevich continued staring at Voltas. 'You could have brought the matter to my attention.'

'Are you *accusing* me of something, captain?'

Turcifel approached. 'Captain Malevich. I was not aware that Lord Coteaz had instructed you to deputise in his absence.'

Malevich's expression remained impassive. Only a slight tensing of his jaw gave away any hint of emotion. 'Forgive me,' he said. He nodded to Turcifel, saluted Voltas, and marched away, leaving the chamber.

'How peculiar,' said Voltas. 'Throne knows how that man achieved high rank with such clumsy manners.'

'He's unnerved by what happened to Coteaz in Albaro's machine,' said Turcifel. 'As is Korov.'

'Korov? The man's a simpleton. He's barely sentient.'

Turcifel gave Voltas a look of amused condescension. She slowly rolled one of her prayer beads between her fingers. 'Do you think the Lord High Protector likes to surround himself with simpletons?'

'But Korov's a brute. Little more than a combat servitor.' Voltas pictured the rag-bound savage, wondering what he had missed.

Turcifel inclined her head, as though observing the charming, naive behaviour of a child. 'Have you heard of Salomon Korov?'

Voltas' mind swam with facts – detailed images of the military essays he had read in his father's libraries. 'The officer in charge of the Militarum regiments during the second Valhalis Campaign. Well regarded. Inventor of the Adiantum Manoeuvre. Picked the wrong side during the Moortgat Affair. Executed along with all the others.'

'Executed by whom?'

Voltas leafed through imaginary pages. Then he felt a shock of recognition. 'Inquisitor Coteaz.' He laughed. 'Korov used to be *General* Korov? Fascinating. What a miserable fate, to become such a mindless brute. It would have been better if he *was* a servitor – at least then he would be oblivious to his fall from grace. Why did Coteaz let him live? The man obviously had no grasp of politics.'

'Coteaz has little interest in politics. He cares about what's in a man's soul. Korov made no attempt to evade justice. The other conspirators tried to bribe their way out of the situation, but Korov saw he had made an error of judgement and handed himself over to Coteaz. There was no way he could retain his rank and position, but Coteaz saw his worth. The fact that Korov has no head for politics only made Coteaz like him more. The subsequent years have changed him immeasurably. I doubt he remembers anything of his old life. But when all else is forgotten, he will remember his debt to Coteaz.'

Voltas thought of how Korov acted around Coteaz – protective and unquestioningly loyal. It made sense. Coteaz had not only spared his life; he had given him a chance to redeem himself.

'So he's a penitent?' he asked.

Her expression hardened. 'I have said too much. It is not my place to analyse Coteaz's decisions.' She turned to walk away without replying, seeming to have grown bored of the exchange.

Voltas grabbed her hand. 'Wait.'

She stared at her hand in his.

Cold radiated from her palm. It was so intense it became painful, and he released his grasp.

Her tone was as cold as her skin. 'Tread carefully.'

Voltas had met Turcifel several times before, but this was the most she had ever spoken to him.

'Coteaz values loyalty above all,' she continued. 'If you are loyal to him, he will be loyal to you. He'll defend you to the hilt. But if he thinks you are not completely trustworthy, then you're nothing.'

'Why might he think me untrustworthy?'

She was looking up at the vast skull on the pillar. 'Why *didn't* you tell Captain Malevich about Agent Krasner?'

'Why would I confide in a common soldier? My allegiance is to the lord inquisitor. Besides, why is any of this a matter for such concern? Agent Krasner is under Coteaz's protection. The Mechanicus would not dare harm an agent of the Ordo Malleus.'

'It is not the tech-adepts that concern Lord Coteaz, it is Castra Sato.'

'Really? A failed acolyte? There must have been many of those over the years.'

'She is unusual. Voidborn. Birthed on the deck of a freighter, like all of her ancestors. But the ship was travelling through the warp when she drew her first breath, and that makes her even stranger than her kin. She was shunned and persecuted for much of her life, but Coteaz saw that she had value. Her faith is pure. He has made sure of that. And the nature of her birth has given her a link to the warp.'

Voltas glanced at her hand. 'Is that what you…?'

'My skills lie in another direction. And, in truth, I know little about Sato's abilities. I only know that Lord Coteaz valued her enough to make her an interrogator, and even considered making her an inquisitor, right up until he decided to execute her.'

Voltas had planned his route to power many years ago. Even as a child he knew he would escape the docile masses, and joining the inquisitor's retinue had shown him how. He would prove his worth to Coteaz and would be made inquisitor. Then, one day, he would become lord inquisitor. And after that? Well, Coteaz would not always be the High Protector… So he was keen to know how his predecessors had failed. And Turcifel was hesitating, as though willing to say a little more.

'*Why* did he decide to execute her?' he asked.

'She betrayed his trust,' said Turcifel. 'Shared his secrets. Became disloyal. That would usually mean a death sentence, but Coteaz rated her so highly he gave her a chance to repent. He said he would consider sparing her life if she came back to him and told him everything she had done. But instead of trying to atone, she left. And she's never been seen since. Until you mentioned her name, I think he thought she was dead.'

'What kind of secrets did she share?'

'They returned from a mission that only they know the details of. Both of them were wounded, and Coteaz no longer trusted her. That's all I know.'

'And now he thinks she is pitting herself against him? Threatening his agents?'

Turcifel shook her head. 'I must go,' she said, crossing the chamber and heading for the door.

As Voltas watched her leave, he considered how odd her manner was – candid one moment and cold the next. She could be a useful ally, he decided, if he worked out how best to play her.

He drove her from his thoughts by recalling the words of Agent Krasner's message, wondering what had prompted Coteaz to cut the meeting short. There was something no one had acknowledged. Before mentioning Sato, the message referred to something else.

They've found it, Lord Coteaz. You were right. It does exist. And it is on Novalis.

Found what? This was the thing Voltas had expected Coteaz to take interest in, but the inquisitor had conspicuously not mentioned it. Why? Why had he glossed over that point? That was the real secret here. The real *opportunity.* As he marched from the chamber, he could focus on only one question.

What was on Novalis?

CHAPTER THREE

Skulls swayed over Coteaz's head – hundreds of them, draped in vast garlands from the ceiling. He paused to look up at them, making the sign of the aquila and whispering a prayer. The sacristy was one of the largest chambers on the *Pilgrim's Wrath*. It was the spiritual heart of the vessel, the home of the Ostiarii, and here, in the company of Salmasius, Coteaz could think clearly. It was a bone chapel, crowded with human remains, so heavily ornamented that no trace of the ship's superstructure was visible. Every arch and pillar was clad in skulls or even entire skeletons, giving the impression of a lifeless host, twitching in the candlelight.

A colonnade bisected the hall, running down its centre, an avenue of ossified columns that soared up into the darkness, their capitals barely visible as they merged with a distant, vaulted ceiling. The skeletons along the walls had been positioned in such a way that they appeared to be worshipping sculpted slabs of stone, which had been placed at intervals along the walls. The slabs were called cadaver tombs – grand monuments to death, decorated with life-size effigies of the people interred behind the stones. The carvings did not show the deceased in their prime but in a decomposed state, skin shrivelled and decayed, peeling from the bones, the stone carved so cunningly that it looked as if it would be soft to the touch. The candlelight came from ornate candelabras, gripped by skeletons on the walls.

Rather than finding the sacristy morbid, Coteaz found it invigorating. It was here, in the company of the dead, that his mind felt keenest; that he felt he was seeing things as they truly were. Down here, in this flickering light, he could marshal the torrent of dates and facts that hounded him and see the truth that lay behind them.

Salmasius and the other sacristans were walking behind him, spreading censer smoke and whispering prayers, but Coteaz marched through the hall, taking deep gulps of the dank air. Thula flew ahead, gliding through the scented haze and on into the next chamber. The grand hall led to a series of smaller chapels. These too were populated by the dead, but here the corpses were newer. Some were still being worked on by sacristans, preserved and worshipped and placed in attitudes of reverence. Most of the deceased in these smaller rooms were known to Coteaz. He had sent many of them to their deaths, and he could still recognise their faces – loyal, inspired servants of the Throne who had given their lives in his service. Given their lives so that the monsters of the warp would never claim dominion over the material realm. It was the weight of their sacrifice that gave him his purpose. He bathed in it, reinvigorated by the ferocity of their faith. So much had been given by so many.

The final chapel was the smallest, a sanctuary that was rarely entered by anyone other than Coteaz and Salmasius. The corpses on the walls had their hands outstretched, and each mouldering fist gripped something incredible – relics of every kind, from ancient force weapons to locks of hair. There were chests placed around the room's circumference and a table and chairs at its centre.

Thula had already settled on her perch, and Coteaz was about to take a seat when he noticed a new corpse: a Throne agent called Vasari. Vasari had approached Coteaz a few weeks earlier, revealing a shameful secret. He had confessed that a blemish under his arm had taken on a peculiar shape. It was a face, as yet unformed, eyes still closed, but unmistakeably daemonic. Even though he was in Coteaz's employ, Vasari knew little of Chaos. Only a fraction of Coteaz's retainers understood the true nature of the enemy. But Vasari knew corruption when he saw it, and he knew he was damned. He had begged Coteaz to execute him before his soul was lost. Coteaz had embraced the man and, before he took his life, had sworn to him that in death he would be renewed. In his final moments, Vasari had wept with relief.

His corpse had been placed near Coteaz's seat, and Coteaz sensed Salmasius' hand in that. The old man knew him well. He knew how to give him ballast. Coteaz stepped up to Vasari's corpse and pressed his hand against the cold skin.

'Emperor preserve us,' he whispered.

'He will,' replied Salmasius, entering the room and slamming the door. 'But He expects us to do all the heavy lifting.'

Coteaz caught the amused gleam in the old man's eye. He sat down in his chair and waved Salmasius to the other one. 'He has concerns of His own.'

Salmasius poured them both some wine, studying Coteaz over the rim of the cup. 'Do you think he's right? Agent Krasner, I mean. Do you think he's really found it?' He was trying hard to sound nonchalant.

'You know Magos Xylothek as well as I do,' Coteaz said.

'*Nothing* drags her away from Glovoda. But she's left the safety of her forge world and made the perilous journey to Novalis, risking her life on a toxic world. Only soul glass could have drawn her out of her lair. My contacts on Glovoda tell me it has become even more of an obsession for her. It is now all she thinks about. But, for her to have travelled to Novalis, she must be *sure* it's there. There have been rumours for decades but she has never done anything as rash as this.' He removed his gauntlets and flexed his fingers, looking at the scars across his knuckles.

Salmasius stared at him, his head quivering. 'Agent Krasner's message could have been sent weeks ago. If there really *is* soul glass on Novalis, Xylothek's tech-priests could have found it by now.'

Coteaz shook his head. 'I have been tracking them since they arrived, long before I sent Agent Krasner. They have very little to go on, in terms of location. Krasner knows more than they do. I made sure of that. And that planet is not easy to explore. No, it is not Magos Xylothek that concerns me.'

'Sato? What could she do? One woman. No authority. No operational support.' He grimaced. 'And a voidborn into the bargain. She will be rightly shunned. What can she hope to achieve?'

'She is *alive.* And she has crossed countless systems to reach that mining colony. Think about that. Consider the scale of her achievement. To travel so far without being under my aegis. She left here with *nothing*. And now, after all my years of searching, she has reached the soul glass before me. Despite all my resources, she did what I could not. If she can achieve that much, what else can she achieve? Who's to say she won't reach the soul glass before Agent Krasner?'

Salmasius grimaced. His face was so heavily lined that, in the flickering light, he was almost indistinguishable from the cadavers looming over his shoulder. 'That kind of power *must* not fall into the hands of someone like her.'

'I should not have let her live.'

'You are human, Torquemada. Fallible. And in all the years I have known you, it was the first time your instincts led you awry. Giving her a chance was a reasonable thing to do. Anyone who truly wished to serve the Imperium would never have dreamt of leaving your service.'

Salmasius was right, of course, but Coteaz had often thought of the strength she had shown, turning away from him. Turning her back on the Ordo. It was the same strength that originally drew him to her. He pictured rats lying dead on a bloodstained deck. She was an exceptional individual. He shrugged the thought off.

'She was borderline radical when she left me,' he said. 'I dread to think where her allegiance lies now.'

Salmasius made the sign of the aquila across his chest. 'It may be that she was a heretic to begin with. The Enemy is subtle, Torquemada.' He drank more wine. 'Who will you send? Interrogator Voltas?'

'I intend to go myself.'

Salmasius put his cup down and sat back in his chair. 'What about the conclave on Varoth? If you turn the *Wrath* around now, you'll be weeks late. Months, maybe. The other inquisitors may already be arriving.'

'They can wait.'

Salmasius licked his lips. 'They can wait, yes. And every second they wait, they can talk. And the more they talk, the more chance that Inquisitor Zamorin will guess you've laid a trap for him. People know you've lost faith in him. It won't take much for him to realise you called the conclave to denounce him. He knows Varoth is where you accused Laredian. If you take the *Wrath* to Novalis, Inquisitor Zamorin might flee before you arrive. You'll miss your chance.'

'I do not plan to take the *Pilgrim's Wrath* to Novalis. You know how closely watched I am. Taking the *Wrath* would risk alerting others to the presence of the soul glass. No one must know. I will not draw undue attention to that planet. I will take the *Purity of Faith*. I can travel in secrecy with a small group of retainers, leave the *Wrath* on her current course, and rejoin her when she drops into high anchor over Varoth. I will send word to the conclave that I am delayed. I have plenty of people there who can ensure Zamorin does not leave.'

'I'll come with you.'

'Novalis is too toxic. You heard what Voltas said. The place is a hell.'

'But the soul glass. Think what it will mean to you if it really is there. This is momentous. But it might also be a test of your faith.' He waved to the skulls leering down at them. 'You won't have this place to guide you. Let *me* be your sanctuary.'

Coteaz shook his head. 'I need you here. I'll take Korov and Malevich. And perhaps Turcifel.'

'And Voltas?'

'Perhaps. I am starting to think he has reached the limit of his usefulness. But taking him to Novalis might be a way to answer my questions about him.' Coteaz looked at Vasari, studying the corpse's clouded eyes.

Salmasius noticed the direction of his gaze. 'You bought that man salvation. Thanks to you, he still serves the God-Emperor. And now he marches in the Emperor's Host. The veil has fallen from his eyes. He resides in the presence of divinity.' The priest leant closer, lowering his voice. 'He fights at His side. As will all of us who hold true. Our battles in this life are nothing to the struggle that awaits us. Mortal life is the least significant part of our service to the Emperor – an island surrounded by an ocean.'

Coteaz cherished these moments with Salmasius. 'Your faith is an inspiration,' he said.

'I see the God-Emperor's hand in everything. How could humanity have lasted this long, against such determined foes, if He wasn't guiding our every step?'

Coteaz pictured a corpse, blackened and twisted at the centre of the Golden Throne, drenched in flames. The image had haunted him since his heart stopped in Albaro's rejuvenat machine.

Salmasius frowned, looking at him closely. 'We should pray.'

Coteaz emptied his cup, still staring at Vasari's corpse. 'Aye.'

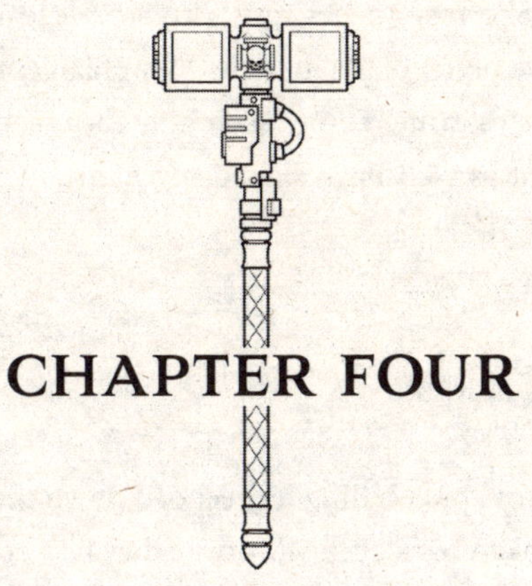

CHAPTER FOUR

The cell was in darkness, but Sato's nightscope had brought it to life, painting the walls with washes of luminous green. She was on one knee, hunched over a corpse with her chain-sickles embedded in the skull. Blood washed over her legs as she levered the hooked blades, splitting the bone.

'For Throne's sake,' she cursed. 'There's a piece stuck in there. Lodged behind a metal implant. I can't get it.'

Khull's face loomed towards her, muzzle quivering.

Sato carefully levered the bone apart, spilling more blood and revealing the pallid mass underneath. 'A piece of my blade is lodged in his brain.'

Khull moved closer, breathing heavily, staring at the body. Then she looked away. 'Someone's coming. Adepts. Lots of them. Throne, these people stink. Do they sweat oil?'

'How long do we have?'

Khull backed away into the darkness, hooves clattering across the wire mesh floor. 'They're already here. We'll have to stand our ground.' She began unfastening the weapon strapped to her back.

Sato rocked back on her heels, staring at the corpse. 'No, we have to go.' She rose to her feet. 'But I can't leave it like that. There's a piece of my blade in there. Monofilament. Xenos-made. They'll know it's mine. You've seen how they pick these corpses apart. I might as well have signed my name.'

'I could eat it.'

'The blade?'

'The head.'

Sato stared at Khull.

Khull shrugged.

The sound of approaching feet echoed down the corridor outside. Sato looked back at the doorway they had entered through and the ladder outside that led back up to the rest of the facility. 'Can you get him up through the access hatch?'

Khull crouched next to the corpse and slung it easily over her massive shoulders. Blood washed down her horns and onto her muzzle. She licked it, baring dagger-sized teeth.

The footsteps were close now, and Sato nodded to the ladder outside the room. 'Back the way we came.'

Khull raced up through the access hatch, despite the weight of the corpse, and Sato rushed after her. They emerged in a narrow corridor with no doors. There were strip lumens running down the centre of the ceiling, and Sato touched the goggles of her helmet, killing the nightscope.

'Quickly,' she whispered, rushing off down the corridor with Khull thudding after her.

They had almost reached a T-junction when she heard shouts of alarm coming from the room they had just left. Seconds later, klaxons started barking. Sato ran on, taking a left at the junction and waving Khull to follow her. The corridor rose gradually until it reached the facility's ground level. Sato mag-locked her billhooks to her armour and took out her pistol, edging slowly out into a larger corridor, signalling for Khull to wait out of sight. She could hear booted feet clattering in the opposite direction, and the klaxons were still howling, but there was no sign of anyone approaching. She raised her pistol, adjusted the settings, and fired at the strip lumens overhead, plunging the corridor into darkness. Then she clicked her nightscope back on and headed out into the darkness.

They passed closed doorways and piles of empty void-crates, then reached another junction. Sato shot out more lumens and studied the corridor. She blinked a schematic over her retina and compared it to the view ahead.

'We could reach the loading doors on the east side of the complex.' She scrolled through another schematic. 'And from there we could make it to the aircars.' She looked back at Khull. 'No. That won't work.'

Khull's face was now entirely drenched in blood, and she looked delighted about it. 'What's wrong with heading for the aircars?'

'The tech-priests will be watching the exits.' Sato shook the corpse. 'And I don't think this will pass unnoticed.'

Blue light split the darkness. It slammed into the wall near Khull, kicking her sideways across the corridor. She snarled as fingers of electricity danced over her skin.

Sato whirled around and, without thinking, fired her pistol, spitting superheated plasma back down the corridor. There was a thud as someone fell to the floor.

'Are you hit?' whispered Sato, rushing over to Khull and helping her to her feet.

'I'm fine.' Khull gestured to the man Sato had just shot. The body was heaped in a revoltingly unnatural pile. '*He* might not be.'

'Pick him up,' snapped Sato, before marching off down the

corridor, pistol raised, towards the corpse. It was a Mechanicus adept, and he was missing half his face. 'We'll have to drag them both out.'

Khull shook her head. 'If you really don't want a fight, we've got to move fast. That won't happen if we're dragging two bodies.'

'We can't leave them here. I told you, there's a piece of my blade in one of them.' Sato blinked the schematic back across her retina. Some of the details were obscured by columns of Mechanicus Techna-lingua, but she could just make out a second layer of shapes, superimposed over the corridors. 'Waste disposal,' she said, 'just a few more feet down that way. We can drop the bodies in the chute.' She grabbed one of the corpses, while Khull grunted and threw the other one over her shoulder.

The access code for the hatch was on the schematics, and she punched it into the runeboard. To her relief, the hatch clattered open, creating a circular hole in the wall. Together, they began cramming the bodies into the chute. To her dismay, they both remained there, lodged at the opening, limbs lolling out into the corridor. The approaching footsteps were close now and she could hear someone howling, summoning more tech-priests.

'Get rid of them,' she demanded.

Khull leant on Sato's shoulder and gave the bodies a kick. With a slow, screeching sound, they finally dropped down the chute.

Sato clapped Khull on the shoulder then looked back at the corridor. There was a trail of blood leading to the waste hatch. The corridor was still in darkness, but most tech-priests had some kind of optical implant. Besides, once the lumens were fixed, the blood would be impossible to miss.

Khull made a low growling sound, took a chainaxe off her back, and dropped into a fighting stance.

Sato lowered herself to one knee and took out an object that looked like a small lantern. She placed it on the floor, then looked around at the corridor. She triggered the device and a timer flickered into life on its side, counting seconds.

'In there,' she said, gesturing to one of the doors that led off the corridor.

They dashed into a storeroom, and Sato slammed the door shut. They were crushed close together in the darkness, and Khull looked down at her with a disgusting leer.

'Keep back from the door,' said Sato. A second later, brilliant light flashed outside. She waited a moment, then risked a look out. There was smoke billowing back and forth, but all trace of the blood had vanished. Figures were rushing out of the gloom, so she gently closed the door. Khull continued wearing the same, obscene grin as she and Sato listened to tech-priests running past their hiding place. Sato glared up at her. Khull licked her lips and smiled even wider, revealing the troubling size of her teeth. Sometimes, if dressed in heavy robes, Khull could just about pass as a normal human, but like this, close up, there was no mistaking how monstrous she was.

They stayed like that until the sound of footsteps had died away. Then Sato slowly opened the door.

She examined the schematics again. 'We're not far from our rooms.' She waved her gun at the corridor opposite. 'Let's see if we can get back without killing anyone else.'

Khull stomped through the darkness after her, making no effort to hide her disappointment.

CHAPTER FIVE

Voltas hurried through the darkness, following the light of his lumen. He was in one of the abandoned maintenance levels that yawned between the *Wrath*'s lower decks. It was a cavernous space, but he sensed he was the first person to have entered in months, perhaps years. There were parts of the ship that had never been seen by the current crew, known only in rumours and songs, and he guessed this was one of them. Dust billowed around him as he stepped between abandoned void-crates and rusting promethium drums, his light flickering over mounds of unrecognisable refuse. The lumen's thin beam seemed, if anything, to make the darkness more oppressive.

Something moved past him, not far from where he was walking. He halted and whirled around, but his lumen revealed nothing except the remains of a rusty gantry, crumbling in the darkness like a leviathan on a seabed. Voltas peered into the gloom. The spaces between the ship's decks were not considered safe. Crewmen told fanciful tales of creatures that lived down here in the darkness, entire species that had evolved during centuries of warp travel, thriving in the forgotten regions between the enginarium and cargo holds. Voltas checked the pistol at his belt. He gave no credence to the stories of humanoid rats and ferocious predators, but there could be deserters hiding out down here, or stowaways – people who might attack if surprised. He waited for a moment, listening out for other sounds, but there was nothing, and after a while he headed on.

As he walked, he took out a data-slate and checked his route. The schematics that mapped the level had long been thought lost, but within weeks of arriving on the ship, Voltas had unearthed them, digging out records that even the captain had no knowledge of. Voltas did not consider it strange that he knew more than anyone else on the ship. Since childhood, he had understood more than anyone else about pretty much everything. Before he could speak, he had beaten one of his tutors at a game of crowns, causing such a stir that he could still remember their shocked faces. His mind worked at a different speed. He had the ability to study two seemingly unrelated pieces of information and spot causality that others missed. His tutors called him a savant. His parents named him child prodigy. But Voltas thought it was simpler than that – he simply knew how to look. Everyone else saw what they expected to see, rather than looking at what was there.

Since coming aboard the *Pilgrim's Wrath*, Voltas had delineated regions of the ship that were considered unmappable and also located several ancient, abandoned cogitator stacks – information nodes that he could use to monitor every logic engine on the vessel. The stacks had been wired in the forges of Mars, by enginseers who had long since died, but Voltas had been able to decipher their peculiar Mechanicus cant, and in the last few days, he had accessed the logic circuits used by Lord Coteaz himself. Voltas knew the dangers inherent in what he was doing, but he felt no doubt. He had to know everything. If there was information to be had, he had to seek it out. It was a kind of addiction, he supposed, but it had served him well so far. *Be bold*, said a voice from his past, and he nodded in answer.

Voltas heard the sound again. Something *was* with him in the darkness. He drew his sabre and depressed the power node. Energy splintered down the blade as he held the sword aloft, throwing more light across the rubbish-strewn floor.

'Who's there? Speak.' His voice was swallowed by the gloom.

He wondered if he should head back. It would be a frustrating delay, but he had to be careful. He was a skilled swordsman and could deal with most threats, but he could not risk being seen. He was spying on the spymaster.

He looked back the way he had come, then back towards the cogitator stack. It was only a dozen yards or so ahead of where he was now standing – a column of blackness darker than the rest. He sucked his teeth, trying to remember the sound, trying to work out if it could have just been one of the overgrown rats that lived down here. He quickly discounted the possibility, recalling the sounds of rats he had heard before. He was able to summon the memories with absolute clarity and the noise was not the same. Then he noticed a flake of rust tumble from a nearby girder. Probably nothing more than that, he decided – a scrap of metal falling from the distant ceiling. He killed the sabre's power, slid the weapon back into its scabbard, and hurried on, keeping his lumen fixed on the hulking shadows up ahead.

After a few minutes, his lumen picked the stack out of the darkness, flickering over its ornate panels. There were dozens of similar structures nearby, and this one seemed to be nothing more than another support column. Voltas knew it was much more than that, though.

He took a battery pack from his belt. It was no bigger than his fist and looked like it had been salvaged from a burnt-out groundcar, but it was incredibly valuable. Thanks to his parentage, Voltas had never had to worry about the value of things, yet he handled the battery pack with care. Such relics were hard to come by, even for the very wealthy.

He worked at a hidden panel on the side of the stack. It was rusted shut, but he managed to lever it open with a knife. The metal let out a screech of complaint as it yielded, the sound cutting through the darkness. The mechanisms inside were inscribed with binharic and Mechanicus runes. He opened the panel the rest of the way, then, taking a ring of keys from inside his coat, he began fixing the battery to clasps inside the stack. He tightened each bolt with care, listening to the clicks as he rotated the keys, knowing the exact configuration prescribed by the original template.

As Voltas turned the final bolt, there was a hiss of escaping gas, and a needle flickered in a gauge. Then there was a rattling noise as blue lights blinked into life up the side of the column. Lenses clicked, rolled, and then filled the air with luminous holoscript. A storm of glowing binary whirled around him as the stack pulled information from the ship's logic network. He watched the drifting lights, translating the symbols in his mind until, after a few seconds, he was no longer looking at zeros and ones but names and reports. He wiped down some rune keys with his sleeve and began to type, reconfiguring the data.

At first, Voltas only saw refuse management records and manifest reports. Then he progressed to reports logged by deck officers and even aides to the ship's Navigator. Finally, he reached what he was looking for: encoded communiqués from Coteaz's agents.

He scrolled through the holoscript until he found entries from Agent Krasner. There was nothing from his time on Novalis. The astropathic plea for help must have been his first attempt at contact. So Voltas looked further back, tapping at the runeboard and filling the air with a new storm of data. There was a lot to read. Krasner had clearly been in Coteaz's employ for many years. Voltas shook his head, intrigued to see some of the things Krasner had done in the inquisitor's name. Much of it seemed counter-intuitive, deranged even. Krasner had helped prop up wayward dictatorships, encouraged insurrections, aided narcotics dealers, and even hindered the work of other Ordo agents. It was a catalogue of political disruption and criminality, but Krasner was acting, always, under Coteaz's instruction, reporting every murder and plot to his master.

Voltas heard another sound and looked away from the cloud of numbers. Again, there was nothing. When he looked back at the binary, it was as if his vision had cleared. That brief pause was enough for him to refocus. Now, when he looked at Agent Krasner's crimes, Voltas began to untangle the layers of complexity. Whenever Krasner had hindered the work of an inquisitor, the inquisitor was later revealed to be dangerous – either misguided or outright heretical. Wherever he had aided a coup, the local government was later revealed to be hiding a shameful secret. Voltas laughed to himself. He had unlocked the code. He studied Coteaz's method of work; through the actions of Agent Krasner he saw a mind of beautiful intricacy. Everything was linked. With this one agent, Coteaz had built a political web of such complexity that the events he engineered appeared to be random. Krasner would never have seen the full picture – all he knew was to trust Coteaz and do as he was ordered.

Voltas' head reeled as he considered that this was the work of only *one* agent. Coteaz had operatives and informer networks scattered across the entire sector. If each was working to a plan as intricate as this... Voltas struggled to pursue his line of thinking, awed by what Coteaz had achieved. He had created a sprawling, operatic masterpiece. Some of the connections were obvious, but others were incredibly subtle. It must have taken decades. He was seeing Coteaz's life's work, rendered in dazzling binary. Then, another thought occurred to him. Coteaz's work was impressive, but it was also fragile. It was a house of cards. If one agent died here, a world could fall there. If an arms dealer failed to deliver his goods, a coup could fail and a disaster, on the other side of the sector, would be unleashed. If Coteaz's grip slipped, entire systems could fall. Millions of people could die. It was a work of genius and madness.

For a moment, Voltas forgot why he had come to the cogitator stack. Then he shook his head and recovered, diving back into the binary. He was searching for a link between Agent Krasner, Coteaz, and the mining colony on Novalis. Why had Coteaz sent Krasner there? He doubted it was just to spy on the Mechanicus, given the complexity of Coteaz's plans. The Mechanicus. The thought of the tech-priests reminded Voltas of another name: Magos Xylothek. He tapped at the runes again and stood back from the holoscript, his pulse hammering as he saw the link. Coteaz, Krasner, and Xylothek had one thing in common. They had all looked into something called soul glass.

He reconfigured the data, looking for every mention of soul glass. Dozens of restricted reports filled the air, all concerning heretics. There were cults scattered across the sector and even in other parts of the galaxy, that had built entire religions around the concept of soul glass. They were resurrectionist cults – deranged, radical individuals who believed the God-Emperor could be reborn into a new body, but only if his current, ruined body was destroyed. They advocated the dismantling of the Golden Throne. The word *transmigration* came up repeatedly, used to describe the process of removing a soul from a dying body and using the soul glass to place it into a young, healthy body.

As Voltas scoured the data, he realised that Coteaz had personally obscured every reference to the soul glass. He had also dealt with many of the cultists himself. The reports were horrifically detailed. Coteaz had acted with unflinching brutality. *He wants the soul glass for himself,* thought Voltas. *He doesn't want anyone else to find it because he needs it.* He thought of the complex network Coteaz had built. Of course. Coteaz had to find a way to continue, to endure. He *had* to stay alive. And with the soul glass, he could place his spirit in a new vessel.

The most gruesome account Voltas read was nothing to do with the death of a cultist. As he absorbed the grisly details, Voltas realised he was reading about the death of one of Coteaz's own agents – a man who had served the inquisitor for many years. The agent had acted in a manner that Coteaz considered disloyal, and that was enough for the inquisitor to sentence him to death.

Voltas immersed himself in the data, feeling as if he was diving into an ocean of fascinating, shocking knowledge, and he gradually lost all sense of time. It was only when he stumbled, slumping against the column, that he realised he had been there for a very long while – hours perhaps. His head was hammering, and he felt dizzy. He staggered away from the stack, lurching backwards so suddenly that he nearly fell.

As he moved, Voltas heard the sound again. A rustling noise. He whirled around and splashed light over a shape perched just a few yards from the cogitator stack. Four eyes glinted back at him.

Coteaz's eagle.

Voltas whipped out one of his duelling pistols and aimed at the bird. It did not flinch, continuing to stare at him. He tightened his finger on the trigger, but as he looked into the eagle's eyes, he felt as though he was looking directly at Coteaz himself. Shooting the eagle would be like shooting its master. He lowered the gun, still looking at the creature. It watched him for a moment longer, its eyes full of disdain, then spread its vast wings and launched itself, silently, into the darkness. Voltas kept his lumen pointed at it, but it was soon out of sight.

Voltas recalled something he had just read – the horrific description of how Coteaz dealt with people who betrayed him. 'No,' he said. 'He values me too much.'

He quickly removed the battery and closed the panel. The sound of hissing gas died, and the pillar sank back into darkness. Then he strode back the way he had come, skirting crates and scraping his shins on pieces of rubble. As he ran, he processed what had happened. The eagle could not speak. It could not *tell* Coteaz what it had seen. But he knew it was more than a pet. It was a psyber-eagle, created by the Adeptus Mechanicus as a gift. The inquisitor and the eagle shared a bond, that much was obvious just from watching them together. But an eagle could not read. It could not know what he had seen in the holoscript.

He reached some ladders, clambered up to an access hatch, and emerged onto a hab-deck. A few ratings saluted him as they hurried past. Voltas ignored them and strode in the opposite direction down the passageway, heading back towards his own berth. The inhabited levels of the *Pilgrim's Wrath* were nothing like the place he had just left. The architecture was heaped with ornate relief work and intricate mouldings, and there were sconces every few yards, cradled by winged saints and holding lumens that spilled warm, flickering light across the deck plating.

He eventually reached a passageway that was in darkness, but as he marched down it, lumens blinked into life before him, revealing thick, faded tapestries draped over the bulkheads. It was only as the final lumen lit up that he saw Korov, standing in front of the door to his berth. The man was so large he had to stoop in the confines of the passageway. His mouth was hidden, as always, by his plastek muzzle, and when he spoke, his words were muffled.

'Recant.'

'What?'

'Coteaz,' said Korov. 'Go to him.'

Voltas tried to ignore the images of torture that filled his thoughts. This meant nothing. There could be dozens of reasons why Coteaz wanted to speak with him.

'Where?' he asked.

Korov tilted his head back, and Voltas caught a glimpse of his feverish eyes. He marched past Voltas, gesturing for him to follow and heading back down the passageway.

Ten minutes later, they were standing outside the door to a room Voltas had never seen before. It was more ornate than the others nearby, and the surface had been inscribed with the barred 'I' of the Inquisition. Korov stomped away without another word.

Voltas dusted down his dress coat, raised his chin, and rapped his knuckles on the door.

Mag-locks clicked and the door slid sideways, revealing a long, empty antechamber. Voltas crossed the room and walked through a doorway on the opposite side, entering a spartan-looking chamber. There was a table at the centre and Lord Coteaz was seated at it. The room was devoid of any other furniture, and the absence of decoration made Coteaz appear even more striking than usual. He looked like a work of devotional art. There was a single lumen, embedded in the table, lighting the inquisitor from beneath and throwing angular shadows across his face. The filigree on his armour glittered as he gestured to an empty chair.

Voltas was unsure how to gauge the situation, so he simply

nodded and took the seat. His attention was so consumed by the presence of Coteaz that it took him a moment to realise there was someone else in the room or, rather, some*thing*. The psyber-eagle was on a perch at the back of the chamber, watching him with the same intensity as Coteaz.

Coteaz said nothing so Voltas broke the silence. 'My lord?'

Something flickered in Coteaz's gaze. Anger? Amusement? Voltas struggled to tell. Then the inquisitor reached down to his belt and unclipped an hourglass. It was as big as Voltas' forearm and clasped within an intricately inscribed frame. Coteaz turned the hourglass over and placed it gently on the table.

Voltas stared at the sand as it fell through the glass neck, filled with outrage. He was familiar with Coteaz's hourglass. Everyone on the ship had heard of it. Coteaz had never failed to extract a confession before the sand ran out.

'My lord,' he asked, '*why* did you summon me here?'

Coteaz remained silent, his eyes cold. He might have been a corpse. Only a faint movement of his nostrils revealed that he was still drawing breath. His face was devoid of emotion.

Memories flooded Voltas' thoughts. He remembered the day Coteaz recruited him. It had been the crowning glory of his young life. Not just an inquisitor but an inquisitor lord and the High Protector of the entire Formosa Sector. It was the recognition he had waited so long for. When his mother told him the news, she had wept. Her unique genius of a son had found his way to flourish, his route to power. It was the prize he had always known he deserved. And he would not let it slip away now.

He held Coteaz's gaze. 'Why am I here?'

Coteaz looked at the hourglass. Voltas was shocked to see that two-thirds of the sand had already flowed into the bottom half of the glass. More images crowded his thoughts, so vivid that he could barely see the inquisitor any more. It was as if he were experiencing a waking dream. He saw a blade approaching a staring eye, organs still beating as they were removed from a chest, fingernails splitting as they were torn from cuticles. All of it horribly vivid. He was breathing so fast that his head was spinning, and his vision started to grow dark. His muscles went into spasm, and he realised that he could not open his hands. They lay like hooks in his lap. Somehow, without speaking a single word, Coteaz was breaking his will. The only part of the room he could still see was the hourglass. Everything else was in darkness. The upper half was now almost empty. Where had the time gone? There were only a few grains of sand left to fall.

'I only wanted to better serve you,' he said.

Coteaz continued looking at the hourglass. The last grain of sand was about to fall.

'Stop this!' said Voltas. His pride was crumbling. His voice trembled.

Coteaz seemed fascinated by the final grain, his eyes following it as it bounced and circled the drop.

Then, as if they had decided to form themselves, words poured out of Voltas. 'I needed to know how I could assist you. I needed to know what you wanted on Novalis. So I accessed your cogitation network and I saw it. I saw what you need. I saw the soul glass.'

Just as the last grain was about to fall, Coteaz took the hourglass from the table and returned it to his belt. When he finally spoke, his voice was calm.

'What else?'

'I saw everything,' admitted Voltas. 'I saw what you've built. I saw how it works. Links and fulcrums. Weights and counterweights.' His fear diminished as he remembered it. 'It's beautiful.'

'Beautiful?'

Voltas saw his chance. Coteaz was intrigued by his choice of words. 'I think the same way as you,' he said, speaking quickly. 'I understand what you have built. I thought I was the only one whose mind worked like that. I see your logic. If you continue enabling Governor Karasou's addiction, he'll never deal with the problem on Melfis. And if he never deals with that problem, the Attican Twelfth will always require munitions from Sostra. And as long as Sostra's running arms to the Attican Regiment, he'll always need information from Agent Cherso. And as long as Agent Cherso is in his employ, he'll–'

Coteaz raised his hand for silence. 'And the shipments to Somnium?'

'A distraction. While the Navy are kept busy dealing with that problem, you have room to manoeuvre on Megaluda. If they knew your agents were there, it would cause an outcry. They'd never understand that you were only–'

'You understood all this from one glance?'

'When I look at data it sings to me, Lord Coteaz. I hear its voice. A melody. I can see what you have done, but no one else ever would. And that's why you need me.'

'*Need?* I have servitors and logic engines to process data.'

'They can process numbers, but that is not the same as understanding what lies behind them. It is not the same as understanding your *intent.* No one else could actually grasp your schemes as I do, my lord. I could help you harness all that information. There are so many actors on your stage. So many threads. But I could help. I'm more than a savant. You know I am. I spent my youth in the great houses. I have the respect of Formosa's greatest leaders. And the only reason I have been seeking out knowledge is to better serve you.' He waved at the doorway behind him. 'I know why you seek the soul glass. I know what it's capable of. You could transmigrate your soul into–'

Coteaz raised an eyebrow.

'Of course. I understand. No one else must know what lies on Novalis.' Voltas leant closer to Coteaz, lowering his voice. 'But you're going there. You'll need to be sure that only *you* lay hands on it.'

'If I took you to Novalis, how would you help me find what I seek?'

'I can decipher the Mechanicus techno cant. It would take a little time, it will be heavily encoded, but I've never found a code I couldn't crack. And I'm sure, even though they can't see it, the Mechanicus will have all the information we'd need to unearth the location of the... of the thing you seek. Besides which, I can defend you with my life. You know how skilled I am with these weapons. I am worth ten of your Scions.'

Coteaz glanced at the eagle, and Voltas sensed that something passed between them. Then the inquisitor leant back in his chair, looking intently at Voltas. 'You saw the way I work. I have allowed idolators and blasphemers to live.' He spoke softly. 'Why?'

'Because the ends justify the means. Because you are–'

'No!' It was the first time Coteaz had raised his voice.

Voltas realised he was not yet in the clear. 'Then why...?' He shook his head. 'I thought I understood. I thought you were allowing lesser evils to go unpunished so that greater evils could be averted.'

'You understand *nothing*. Nothing goes unpunished. Nothing is forgiven. To act against the Imperium, to act against the God-Emperor, is unpardonable. It is heresy. That is incontrovertible fact. I might play out the rope, but I *always* tighten the noose. There can be no tolerance. No sympathy. No compromise. No cracks in the dam.' He waved at the walls. 'This means nothing. Ships and weapons. Armies and fleets. All of it could be swept aside by a single unpunished act of heresy. You think you understand, Voltas, but you have no idea. No idea of the things that watch us from beyond the veil, waiting, searching, hunting for a crack in our armour, an act of misguided leniency that could open the door between us and the warp.'

'I *do* understand. And the more I know, the more I can help. Even if the soul glass transmigrates your life essence into another body, a younger body, the old you might be lost. Your knowledge might be lost. All those things I saw…'

The light faded from Coteaz's eyes. 'I have to reach the soul glass before anyone else. Castra Sato means to take it before I can. I think it was her that tried to scramble Agent Krasner's message to the relay station. I have to stop her.' He took a long, slow breath. 'And perhaps you may be of use to me in that.'

'That's *all* I desire, Lord Coteaz. I just want a chance to show you what I can achieve.'

Coteaz unclasped a reliquary from his belt. It was a small, scrimshawed box, inlaid with gold. He opened the lid, took out a coin and looked at it closely, before handing it to Voltas.

Voltas received it with reverence, holding it over the table lumen and turning it gently between his fingers. The coin had an hourglass engraved on one side and, on the other side, an image of a man's head. One side of his face was young and healthy, his expression triumphant, framed by a halo of sacred light. The other side was a skull with flesh hanging from the bones. The thing was beautiful and grotesque. Voltas had a suspicion that it might be real silver.

'Do you know what it is?'

'A memento mori. A reminder that we die.'

'Why might such a reminder be useful?'

'So that we use our time well. So that we don't waste what we have.'

'Exactly. We have so little time. And so much to achieve. But life is a drug. We become addicted to it. We lose ourselves in it.' Coteaz narrowed his eyes. 'But this coin could remind you of other things. For example, when you look at the young face, you see the future we could grant humanity if the Ordo holds true, if we prosecute the Emperor's will without flinching, if we never let fear or vanity stay our hand. But the other half of the face, the rotten one, shows what will become of humanity if we falter, if we are weak, if we are tolerant, if we show *mercy.*'

Voltas understood the significance of the gift. He knew, from his research, that Coteaz had given similar coins to other retainers, but only those he trusted with *particularly* important work.

'I won't fail you,' he said.

Coteaz touched the coin, tapping the decayed half of the face. 'Pray that you don't.'

CHAPTER SIX

It was only as he neared the end of his life that Elias Jode found his courage. He had never considered himself a brave man. He thought that, like his parents before him, he would die unnoticed in the mines without leaving a trace. He worked at the seams with the same bleak humour as everyone else, waiting for death to take him. Counting the days. He watched his skin gradually crystallise, taking on the same bloody hue as everything else on Novalis, and he had felt his breath weaken with every passing year. But then, not long after he turned twenty-one, his lover, Elzevyr, grew ill. There was a natural order to things on Novalis. If you were unable to work the seams, you were unable to earn your rations. Death usually followed soon after. The thought of his own death was insignificant, but the thought of losing Elzevyr was too much to bear.

It was around then that his courage came to him. It spoke to him in a voice so clear he assumed someone was talking aloud. It took him a while to realise no one else could hear it. It told him of a cavern, and a lake, in a pinnacle far from the seams, where scavenger engines never drilled, ruins where overseers never went. It told Elias that there was a way to escape death – a way to *cheat* death.

He was afraid, at first. He had heard tales of murderers who killed their kin, believing they were possessed by spirits and dark gods. But, when Elzevyr came close to death, he could not bear to let her go. He had no choice. The voice told him how to take Elzevyr to the cavern in the forgotten place and, even more incredibly, of secret routes to grain stores and storage warehouses. The voice had asked only a small favour in return, and since then, Elias had found the courage to do many things he would never have dreamt of.

Elzevyr did not wake as Elias moved the curtains aside and entered the cavern. She was sleeping on a pile of thick synthwool blankets – the kind that were reserved for only the most senior overseers. There was a bio-lume in a niche, not far from where she was sleeping, and in the golden light, Elias could almost imagine her skin was still a natural colour, as it had been when he first met her. In sleep, she seemed to be free of pain. He crept slowly towards her, studying the lines of her face. She looked tired and thin but at peace. The pump that drained the fluid from her lungs was wheezing a gentle lullaby, and he thought he could see the trace of a smile on her face. He crouched next to her and carefully disconnected the pipes from her chest. He took the canisters to the other side of the cavern and emptied the bloody liquid. Then he reconnected the pipes to her chest.

'You should be asleep,' she said, smiling without opening her eyes.

'So should you.'

She opened her eyes and lifted herself up onto her elbows to kiss him. 'I feel a little better,' she said, through a yawn. 'I don't know what you're feeding me, but it's doing something.'

She was still smiling but there was concern on her face. 'What *are* you feeding me?'

He held her for a moment, then kissed her head. 'I told you. I found a way into another storeroom. It's where they keep the good stuff.'

She still looked troubled. 'So good it cures disease?'

He raised his hands in mock outrage. 'A simple "thank you" would suffice. Are you worried about the overseers missing a meal?'

She tried to keep smiling, but he could see it was forced. 'I wish you'd tell me the truth.'

'I am. The overseers have so much food they can't even keep track of it.' This part was true, and the idea made him want to rage. 'They don't know what they've got stashed away. We survive on corpse starch and vitgruel while they leave crates full of meatslabs to rot. Their records are such a mess there are entire storerooms full of food that would have been wasted if I hadn't liberated them.'

She shook her head. 'You're just a miner, Elias. How can you know so much about what the overseers have or don't have? How can you know where to find things even they can't?'

Elias tried to sound flippant. As Elzevyr's health improved, she had started asking difficult questions. And he knew she would not like the answers. 'They leave things lying around. Consignment dockets listing every shipment from Port Gomera. They're idiots. Do you expect me to feel bad about it?'

She looked at him in silence as he gave her a cup of water. Then, after drinking, she grimaced in pain and lay back, struggling for breath.

'You need more food,' he said, stroking the facets on her cheeks.

She shook her head. 'I can't eat anything else. I couldn't. Not yet.'

'Then sleep.'

She closed her eyes as he pulled the sheets up to her chin and kissed her forehead.

'I brought you this,' he said, hanging a delicate chain around her neck. There was a medallion dangling from it, wrought of golden metal.

He turned to leave, moving quietly because he thought she was already asleep, but just as he reached the curtains she spoke, her voice husky. She was looking, with half-lidded eyes, at the medallion.

'Elias. Don't do anything *bad.* Not for me. Don't be like them. Don't turn into one of them. Stay true.'

'Of course,' he whispered, sneaking out of the cavern. But something about her words troubled him. *Stay true.*

He crawled down into a narrow passageway and picked his way through the rocks, heading back to a larger cave near the surface. Helk and Sturm were waiting, silhouetted by the red glow pouring in through the cave mouth. He was so surprised to see them that he reached for the autopistol hidden under his envirosuit.

'Relax,' laughed Sturm, holding up his hands.

Elias loosed the gun and shook his head. 'What are you doing here? I told you I'd meet you back at the refinery.'

'We thought you'd want to hear the news,' said Helk. Both of them had the unmistakable crimson colouring of a miner. There were crystals forming around their tear ducts and at the corners of their mouths, like glittering scabs, but there was a vigour to them he had never seen before. They were still hollow-cheeked and haggard, but they stood straight and their eyes shone. The last few weeks had transformed them in a way that was subtle yet profound. They wore identical yellow envirosuits, branded with the red circled 'V' sigil of the Vespertinus mine, but other than that they looked nothing like each other. Helk was squat, broad-shouldered with blocky features and a thick beard, whereas Sturm was wiry, gaunt and stooped, with a bald pate and hooked nose.

As the two men stared at him, Elias saw how eager they looked. 'What?' he demanded, stifling a laugh. 'Why do you look so pleased with yourselves?'

Sturm grinned.

'Shall we show him?' said Helk. 'Maybe that's better?'

'Yeah,' said Sturm. 'You need to see this, Elias. Words don't do it justice.'

Confused, Elias thought back over the day. His courage had spoken to him, just after he finished his evening shift, telling him of another forgotten storeroom. He had been keen to see Elzevyr, so he had sent Sturm and Helk to find it and investigate.

'What is it?' he asked again. Their excitement was infectious. 'Bigger than the others? Better food? What? Stop grinning like idiots and tell me.'

'Ya gotta see it,' repeated Sturm.

Elias felt a rush of foreboding as he looked at the eagerness in his friends' eyes. Where was this all leading?

'What is it?' asked Sturm, noticing his troubled expression.

He hesitated, unsure how to explain. Then he gripped their shoulders. 'Promise me something,' he said.

'Anything,' replied Helk.

'Promise me that, whatever happens, we will never become like them.'

Sturm frowned. 'Like who?'

'Like the overseers.'

Helk snorted. 'What are you talking about? How could we ever be like those self-serving maggots?'

They both stopped grinning as they saw how serious Elias was.

'Promise me that we'll always do the right thing,' he said, holding out his hand to them. Suddenly, he felt afraid, as though something important hinged on their response. 'That we'll stay true.'

They both gripped his hand. 'Stay true,' said Helk, matching Elias' serious tone.

'Stay true,' echoed Sturm.

Elias removed his hand. He felt somehow lighter. 'Come on, then,' he said. 'Show me what you've got.'

The two men grinned and headed out of the cave, waving for him to follow. As they stepped into the rain, the three of them lifted the hoods on their envirosuits and fastened the rebreathers. The rain on Novalis rose rather than fell, bleeding constantly from the rocks and rushing up to the clouds. It was hot and red, like everything else: the rocks, the clouds, even the sky. It looked like boiling blood. The perpetual shroud of smog made it impossible to see the sun, but as the rain hissed skywards, it created a ruddy heat haze on the horizon, promising a dawn that never came. They had emerged onto the side of a colossal tower of crystal that soared hundreds of feet up before disappearing into the clouds, and below them, the view was identical – the column plunged out of sight, vanishing into a sea of fumes. Around them, they could see hundreds more of the columns, like a forest of emerald tree trunks. The columns were natural formations known as pinnacles, and they covered the entire surface of Novalis. There was no ground, as such, just jagged spurs that knifed up from the planet's core.

On the nearest pinnacles, small shapes were visible, scuttling spiderlike across the surface or flying across the abyss, carried on whirring metal wings. From this distance the scavenger engines looked like insects trailing spindly legs, but they were, in fact, big enough to hold tons of equipment, and the legs were actually drill cables, powerful enough to punch through even the hardest rocks.

'This way,' said Helk, stomping off through the fumes. The path was old and well cut, but they all knew to tread carefully. It was dangerous to be outside for long, but rushing could be fatal. The crystal was unpredictable. In some places it was several feet thick and formed on ancient rockcrete, but in other places it was only a thin crust that could easily give way. They said no more as they stumbled up the path. The rebreathers made it possible to travel without choking but did little to stop the rad-poisoning. And the more the men spoke, the more pollution they would drag into their mouths.

It took them nearly half an hour to reach the next cave mouth, and Elias was growing impatient to know what they wanted to show him. Images played through his mind of the glorious banquet that was awaiting him. Meatslabs, he guessed, or maybe something even rarer. Real meat, perhaps. Or real fruit. He had heard of such things. Elias began to salivate as he climbed, and he whispered thanks to his courage, amazed yet again by how much it had helped him.

They reached the cave mouth and climbed inside, removing their masks and hoods as they headed down rough-hewn steps into a deep, gloomy chamber lit by a single, blinking bio-lume. There were empty storage crates scattered around and pieces of broken equipment, but other than that the cave seemed devoid of interest. Helk and Sturm rushed past the crates, still grinning as they approached the opposite wall.

Sturm pointed out a narrow crack in the surface. 'It's exactly like you said. Come and see.' He squeezed through a gap that seemed impassable and vanished from sight. Helk laughed and followed.

Elias paused, looking at the hidden entrance, then squeezed in after them. The passageway was narrow, and the crystal grew hotter the deeper they went. Elias triggered the lumen fixed to his collar and the others did the same. He could see their lights bobbing up ahead as they struggled through the tight space. Other routes spurred off to the left and right, and he realised there was a whole network of tunnels up here that none of the other miners knew about. They squeezed and clambered through increasingly narrow passages, sweat pouring down their faces, until Sturm and Helk finally came to a halt and looked back at him.

'You're not gonna believe this,' laughed Helk. Then the two men dropped from view, climbing down into a hidden chamber.

Elias rushed after them, but as he reached the opening and saw what lay beyond, the strength went from his legs. He had to sit before he fell. As the three men looked around, their lumens washed over a collection unlike anything Elias had ever seen. Even in the thin beams of light he could sense the scale of what they had found. There were huge piles of weapons, enough to supply an army. Stacks of shotguns sat next to hundreds of lasguns and grenade launchers, and in the surrounding gloom, he could even make out large ordnance weapons, the kind of things used by Militarum regiments to break sieges and level buildings.

'Sweet Throne,' he whispered.

'Wait,' said Helk, rushing over to the wall. He pulled a lever and hundreds of bio-lumes hummed into life, flooding the chamber with light. It was only then that Elias realised how big the room was. It was like a vast warehouse, and the whole space was heaped with weapons. There were even vehicles draped in tarps that looked to be armoured transports and personnel carriers.

Elias climbed slowly down into the chamber, shaking his head. 'I don't believe it.'

'But you sent us here,' said Helk. 'You gave us the exact location. Didn't you know?'

He shook his head. 'I thought it would be food.'

Sturm walked over to him. The smile was gone from his face. '*How* did you know about this place? How did you know about any of them?'

Elias ignored the question and picked up a lasrifle, checking the mechanism. It looked like it had never been fired: oiled and lethal. 'There's so much here. What could the overseers possibly want with all this stuff?'

Helk grinned. 'They don't even know it's here. That's the joke.' He waved at a pile of crumpled parchment. 'It's a balls-up. A Munitorum department on Actoris keeps answering a requisition that was fulfilled centuries ago. Someone *did* once request some munitions, but only one delivery. And the idiots on Actoris keep sending more.' He grabbed one of the scrolls and waved it around. 'The overseers used to try and fix the problem. They sent messages to Actoris, but the logisticians never saw them. They're probably buried under piles of paperwork. So Munitorum adepts kept answering the same requisition over and over again. Throne knows how long it took for them to stop. But it was before Governor Aldrov's time.' He waved to a pair of vast doors. 'Those things were locked away decades ago. Maybe centuries ago. And no one knows this is here.' He looked at the tiny opening they had crawled through. 'Until you told us about that.'

Elias felt drunk. He was still struggling to grasp the scale of what he was seeing.

'It all makes sense now,' said Helk, staring at him. 'This is what you've been leading us to. This is why we've been painting those symbols and hammering those icons.' He took a medallion from under his envirosuit. It was crudely hammered, but the symbol was simple enough to be recognisable: a sun with wings of fire spreading from its sides. 'Novalis will rise.' He whispered it like a prayer, gripping the icon.

'Novalis will rise,' repeated Sturm. The humour had gone from their faces. They looked at him like he was a saint.

Elias felt as if he were teetering on a precipice. He was on the brink of something terrible, but there was still a way back. He could leave this room, block up the entrance, and swear the other two to secrecy. But he could see an image in his mind. He saw it as clearly as the gun he was holding. It was Elzevyr, lying in stolen sheets with pumps sucking fluid from her lungs.

'Novalis will rise,' he whispered, gripping the gun tighter.

Anamnesis

He that cleaves to the Throne shall abideth.

I am familiar with death. We are close. Travelling companions, you might say. My journey to deliverance began with the slaughter of my family. Then, when Laredian left me at the Santuosso Schola, the curriculum granted more opportunities for me to watch people die. But though I am nearly twelve, this is the first time I have observed the rite of the sepulture. It is considered so sacred that children are rarely permitted to watch.

As I climb the steps of the Vachori Basilica, keeping close to Inquisitor Laredian's side, I am acutely conscious of my appearance. Like all progena, I wear the simple grey robes of an orphan, yet despite my young age and my humble clothing, the nobles on the steps can barely meet my eye. I am a ward of the High Protector. An unassailable member of Inquisitor Lord Laredian's retinue. Even the most entitled princelings are cowed. I hold my chin high. They are wise to be afraid. Laredian has taught me an invaluable truth. Real power does not come from a family name. Real power does not come from material wealth. Real power comes from knowing more than everyone else.

The lords of Galamiel resemble wading birds, elegant and slender, draped in hoary furs, breath pluming as they loom over me and greet Laredian. Galamiel has two seasons: a brutal winter followed by several weeks of even colder weather. Snowflakes whirl behind me as the basilica's great doors slam shut. Cold knifes through my orphan robes, but I refuse to let it show. I wipe ice from my face and look up, impressed by the majesty of the building.

Laredian laughs at me. He is a savage-looking man, so heavily muscled that his gilded armour struggles to contain his bulk. He has the stance of a fighter, a blunt, blocky face, and hair knotted in a plait that hangs down his back like a lash. But there is more to him than meets the eye. It has been less than six months since he removed me from the schola, and he has already taught me far more than the Santuosso drill abbots. Laredian uses his ferocious appearance as a smokescreen. People are afraid of him but not afraid *enough*. They fail to grasp his true strength. He looks like a brute but his mind is subtle and quick. He is everything I would wish to be. Everything I *mean* to be.

'Set dressing, Torquemada.' Laredian taps one of the statues that line the nave, summoning a cloud of dust. 'The Emperor does not live in pieces of granite. Salvation does not spill from a sculptor's chisel.'

We reach a balcony and I see the ritual taking place below. As with most obsequies on Galamiel, the first stage is to remove the deceased's skin. I sense Laredian watching me, so I keep my expression neutral as the priests work, swallowing the bile that fills my mouth. The floor around the dais is covered with scented silver petals, and as the body is taken apart, the archdeacon's blood tinkles musically on the metal. After removing the skin and placing it in a metal casket, the priests begin removing organs. As they work, the sound of the choir fills the chamber and most of the mourners fall quiet, mouthing silent prayers.

'One day you may be taken apart like this,' says Laredian. 'If your end is considered worthy and your body is still intact, your organs will be burned in incense and your bones will be cleansed and used to decorate a mausoleum. And in that moment, there will be a reckoning. The echoes of your life will outlive you. Where you have sown doubt, it will fester. Where you have sown fear, it will cripple. And where you have planted faith, it will empower. While we live, we tend our fires, but once we die they run free, Coteaz, for good or for ill.'

I do not wish to appear foolish in front of my master. Laredian has given me hope when hope seemed beyond reach. But I struggle to understand his meaning. 'When we die, we die. What can I do about things that happen after I'm dead?'

'Nothing. So we must live, always, in the shadow of our death.' Laredian nods to a man on the opposite balcony. He is dressed in the braided uniform of a Militarum officer. He looks agitated and distracted. 'The Lord Marshal Vaqueiros was one of the archdeacon's closest friends. They worked together for years, always seeking to further each other's careers. They had a plan that they hoped would elevate Archdeacon Razeen to the status of cardinal. They permitted insurrection to grow in the town of Mugello. They let heresy go unpunished. And it was so that they could eventually crush it in a manner that would be advantageous to them. The archdeacon was planning to draw the gaze of the ecclesiarch himself. They knew the ringleaders, and the archdeacon had information that would have allowed them to anticipate the insurrectionists' first attack. They began a dangerous game.' Laredian's tone hardens. 'Which has forced me to make a hard choice.'

I am unnerved by my master's tone. *What* choice? I look down at the corpse. 'The archdeacon was a heretic?'

'He intended to crush the insurgency, he just wanted to do it when it would be to his advantage. And, in truth, his motives were honourable. Half the cardinals in the synod are frauds. So he spoke to his friend, the lord marshal over there, and they agreed to let the heretics continue plotting until the time was right. Then, in the midst of their scheming, the archdeacon died. Now the lord marshal is left with only half a picture of what's happening in Mugello. Murders have taken place and books have been stolen, and he's unable to act. He dare not approach the Ministorum priests because he doesn't know which of them were in the archdeacon's confidence. And he can't admit he knew about all of this weeks ago without looking like a heretic. He knows there will be another attack soon but not where or when. He can't do *anything* without damning himself. He could have sought me out. He could have confessed his failure. But he chose a different path.'

I watch the Militarum officer with a growing sense of horror. 'Are you going to arrest him?'

'I will deal with him. But because the archdeacon has taken secrets to the grave, the revolution has festered and grown into something of significance, something neither of the conspirators imagined. Which makes my job harder than it needed to be. There will be *many* deaths. Deaths that could have been avoided. Mugello will have to be destroyed. Left to their own devices, the insurrectionists have stumbled across proscribed texts.'

'You would burn an entire town because people have read forbidden books?'

'There is *nothing* more dangerous than a book. Perhaps by burning a town I will save a world, but perhaps not. We may be talking billions of deaths rather than thousands.'

'Because a man died?'

'Because a man died without finishing what he began. Because he refused to consider his own mortality. Because people go through life refusing to accept that it will end. They're so afraid to face their mortality they squander the time they have.'

Laredian studies me. 'But you are different. I thought it the moment I found you in that shrine. And you have proved me right in the Schola Progenium trials. You fought with such passion, such *faith*. Whatever lit that fire in you, you should be grateful.'

Grateful? I picture the mutilated bodies of my family, their bodies cut with runes that hurt my eyes. I can still taste the pain of it. Over the years, my grief has hardened into hate. Mercy has robbed me of so much.

Laredian looks out at the gathered crowds. 'The architecture *does* look beautiful. And the congregation seem so handsome and dignified. But they are adrift. All of them. On the inside, where it matters, they have lost control. Their lives are in tatters. None of them have the ballast you have. There are mistresses and confidants in here who will be left terrified by the archdeacon's death. He convinced them to make bold plans. He promised to be their patron. Their protector. And now he's gone they have nothing to cling to. The ripples of his death will spread and spread. Unless I stop them.'

Laredian gives a signal. It is little more than a flick of his fingers, but I recognise it. Black-armoured figures respond, taking up positions throughout the crowd. Laredian's stormtroopers, Ordo Scions – veteran warriors armed with advanced weaponry and an absolute faith in their inquisitor lord.

I am determined to live up to the trust the inquisitor has placed in me. I stand tall and keep my expression neutral.

Laredian looks at me with pride, and I am so humbled I can almost forget the horrors that are about to ensue.

Later, as we leave the basilica, a flurry of snow whips up around Laredian, bathing him in gold and silver, framing him like a figure in a painting. He looks so vivid. So timeless.

Within, the sound of gunfire rings out, followed by a chorus of panicked screams.

The congregation tries to flee.

No one makes it to the doors.

Laredian does not pause to look back as he waves me on. 'We have work to do.'

CHAPTER SEVEN

The *Purity of Faith* was the smallest voidship in Coteaz's fleet. She was insect-like when compared to the *Pilgrim's Wrath*, little more than a skiff, with just a few dozen crewmen and a Navigator. But she was equipped with the warp drive and navigation sanctum required for interstellar travel, and she was outrageously fast, fitted with plasma drives that could have served a ship ten times her size. She was a sleek black dart, with none of the buttresses and ramparts of her larger siblings, and her capacity to evade detection was enhanced by an ancient obfuscation field that enabled Coteaz to enter planetary orbit unannounced.

Like the rest of the vessel, the *Purity of Faith*'s observation deck was cramped, and as Coteaz approached the circular oculus that dominated the space, the rest of the onlookers had to move aside to make room. The display bathed him in ruddy light as he drew near.

'Did the augur returns make any mention of warp storms?' he asked.

'Any mention of warp storms,' droned Sixtus, clicking dials on his chest. 'No. There were no mentions of warp storms. No records of any empyric disturbances in-system. This anomaly is recent. It has emerged since we translated back into realspace at Volo. The deep augurs showed nothing unusual. And that was less than a hundred hours ago, ship time.'

Four other people were crowded into the chamber along with Sixtus: Voltas, dressed as finely as ever and standing as though posing for a portrait; Turcifel, loitering in a corner, toying with her prayer beads; Korov, glowering in his hood as his mechadendrites snaked around him; and Captain Malevich, standing to attention at Coteaz's side. They were all looking at the oculus. Most of the display was taken up by the vast crimson sphere of Novalis. It looked like a dying sun, but none of them were focusing on the planet; they were all watching a light that was rippling towards them through the void. It was a maelstrom of different colours, spiralling from the darkness like ink.

'Solar wind?' asked Voltas. 'Hitting the planet's magnetic field?'

Coteaz looked over at the interrogator. Since receiving the memento mori he had become even more confident than before. Coteaz did not necessarily see this as a flaw. It was Voltas' confidence that had enabled him to ascend so quickly to the rank of interrogator. But there was still a question hanging over him. What exactly did he want? Was it just to serve, as he claimed, or something more?

'Sixtus,' Coteaz said. '*Could* it be solar wind?'

Sixtus made a burbling sound. 'Could it be solar wind? No. The disturbance is too far from Novalis' atmosphere. And it is approaching the *Purity of Faith* in a manner that appears deliberate.'

'I have studied Novalis at length,' said Voltas. 'I examined

Astra Cartographica records dating back to the earliest days of the Imperium. But I saw no mention of this phenomenon on any of the star charts.'

'My lord,' said Turcifel, emerging from the shadows. 'The light sees you.'

If anyone else had spoken to Coteaz in such a cryptic way, he would have dismissed them out of hand. But he had learned not to ignore Turcifel. She rarely spoke, and when she did, it was usually worth listening. Pressing her to speak with more clarity tended to make little difference. The maelstrom of light was approaching at incredible speed, already starting to block out the view of the planet.

'It *knows* you,' she said.

Everyone was looking at her, but Coteaz noticed that Voltas was regarding her with particular intensity. The man had an almost pathological desire to know everything. He was obsessed with pinning things down. Coteaz could imagine an enigma like Turcifel becoming a dangerous distraction for him.

Turcifel's eyes widened. Before she could speak again, the colours in the chamber changed – or rather, they faded, leaving everything stark and monochrome, like a grisaille painting.

'Coteaz…' she began, then stopped as the temperature in the chamber plummeted.

'Turcifel,' warned Captain Malevich. He gripped his pistol and glanced at Coteaz.

Turcifel was standing still, apart from her head, which was shaking. Her eyes had rolled back in their sockets.

'Is she having a seizure?' Voltas asked. He stepped towards her, then halted, staring at the floor around her feet. It was rippling, as if it were boiling.

'Lord inquisitor?' Malevich had taken his pistol from its holster.

'Turcifel,' said Coteaz. Even from a few feet away he could feel the cold radiating from her. 'Turcifel,' he repeated, gripping the haft of his hammer. 'Listen to me.'

'Novalis will be reborn.' Her voice was flat and lifeless. 'Novalis will rise.'

The floor undulated and the temperature continued to drop. Shapes appeared near Turcifel's feet. They were vague and unformed, but Coteaz began to recognise the outlines of inhuman faces.

'Lord Coteaz?' said Malevich, raising his gun.

'Wait.' Coteaz gripped his hammer tighter. Light shimmered in the metal as he mouthed prayers, summoning the Emperor's fire through its ancient scrollwork.

Turcifel stiffened, arching her back. The floor boiled with even more ferocity. The smell of rotting meat filled the room.

'Turcifel!' cried Coteaz, holding the hammer aloft. The metal blazed.

Malevich took aim at her head.

Turcifel's eyes rolled back into place, and she slumped against the wall. The shapes vanished. The floor became stable again. Colour bloomed back across the room and the temperature returned to normal.

Coteaz lowered his hammer. 'What did you mean? You said "Novalis will rise."'

She paled and shook her head, touching her prayer beads.

Coteaz saw the wary look in her eyes and understood it. He had struggled to guide her. Something had come between them. She had almost slipped from his grip. Which placed her in a dangerous position.

'What can you remember?' he said.

She stared at the floor, still shaking her head, then masked her fear, adopting her usual neutral gaze. 'I remember the light growing too bright. Then nothing.'

Coteaz looked deep into her eyes, searching for any trace of deception or change. He could see nothing. And their bond was such that he was sure he would know if there was any trace of corruption in her. But he was still troubled. This was not a controlled use of her power. Something had worked through her.

'Lord Coteaz,' said Captain Malevich, lowering his pistol. 'Look at the oculus.'

The light had vanished and the *Purity of Faith* was approaching high orbit over Novalis. As they flew closer, satellites drifted into view – a glittering cluster of orbital anchorages, guide-tugs, and transport ships floating across the blood-red sphere. Further out, there were larger ships – clippers and freighters ten times the size of the *Purity of Faith*.

'Chartist Captains,' said Voltas. 'They dock here so they can ferry ore from Port Gomera, down on the surface. Some areas of the processing hives are still functional.'

'Contact the officer in charge of Port Gomera. He's called Kraeling.'

'Actually,' said Turcifel quietly, 'I *do* remember something.'

Everyone turned to look at her.

'Hate. *Unbridled* hate.' She looked at Coteaz. 'Directed at you.'

CHAPTER EIGHT

Coteaz's shuttle dropped towards the surface of Novalis, buffeted by storms. He looked out through a viewport in its fuselage, scouring the mountains of chem-fog, trying to understand the scenery unfurling beneath him. It consisted entirely of crimson stalagmites – crystal deposits so massive they could be seen from low orbit and so numerous that it seemed the planet was bleeding up into the atmosphere. It was as if a pool of blood had been raked by claws and the strands were still hanging in the air.

The shuttle was rattling and jolting, and the pilot was battling with the controls, but everyone on board endured the turbulence in silence. Coteaz was seated at the front, beside the pilot. Beside him was Korov, barely able to fit in the cockpit. Behind them, in the passenger compartment, was Captain Malevich, Turcifel, Sixtus and Voltas. And, at the rear of the shuttle, rigid and grim-faced, sat ten of Malevich's elite, black-clad Scions. Thula had endured the indignity of being placed in the cargo hold with the weapons and void-crates.

As they circled lower, Coteaz began to make out some details through the clouds. Port Gomera was a grand name for what was effectively a jumble of mooring spars attached to the side of a mountain-high stalagmite. There was a comms tower and some hab-blocks but little else. It looked like a nest on the side of a dead tree, lashed by wind and clinging to the rocks. The surrounding landscape showed remnants of industry – refineries, warehouses and chimney stacks, but they were all broken, dark and corroded, abandoned long ago to the elements. There was a pair of bullish-looking orbital lifters moored to one of the port's spars and a few shuttles at another, but there was no one to be seen on the storm-whipped landing pads.

The shuttle settled on the pad with a roar of retro-thrusters. Fumes whirled around the vessel. Coteaz waited for a few moments, then, when he realised the haze was not going to clear, ordered the pilot to open the landing hatch. As he left his seat and stood at the hatch, Coteaz was surprised to find that the air was warm. It was not the warmth of a summer's day but the clammy heat of an enginarium. It was so stifling that he thought, for a moment, that the atmosphere was not breathable. Then he realised that it *was* possible to breathe, just hard, requiring several deep breaths where one would normally have sufficed.

'Inquisitor Lord Coteaz!' called a voice through the whirling clouds.

Coteaz marched down the landing ramp towards a group that had assembled to greet them. There were a dozen colonists, all clad in bulky yellow envirosuits branded with red 'V's. The suits were filthy and had clearly been repaired many times, and the faces he saw through the visors looked tired and drawn. Their skin also seemed to be discoloured. It was hard to make out details through their grubby visors, but they looked sunburned.

The man who had spoken was a few paces ahead of the rest. He dropped to one knee as Coteaz approached, gesturing for the others to do the same. 'What an honour,' he called out. 'To meet an agent of the most holy God-Emperor Himself. I am Port-master Kraeling. I'm delighted to have a chance to assist you.'

The man was lying. No one was delighted to meet an inquisitor. But Coteaz noticed that he spoke clearly and without panic. This was unusual. It pointed to either strength of character, mental instability or heresy. It would be an easy matter to decide which.

Captain Malevich and the others were emerging from the shuttle and gathering on the ramp behind him and the port-master stood, waving at the entrance to a hab-block. 'Quickly. Inside.'

The two groups hurried across the landing pad towards the nearest building. It was a simple, ugly blockhouse, with none of the ornate stylings of Imperial architecture. Everything in the port conveyed an air of transience. Nothing here had been made to last. The rockcrete was covered in the same red crust that coated everything else on the surface, and Coteaz got the impression that Novalis was gradually subsuming all evidence of human habitation.

They passed through a vacuum-sealed chamber that resembled a void-lock on a starship, then entered a long, gloomy mess hall. The ceiling was low, with a single humming strip lumen running down the centre, and the tables were all empty. There were fuel drums, sacks, and void-crates scattered around, and a pict-feed was being projected onto the far wall, showing flickering, silent footage of pilgrims marching on Terra, massed in their thousands as they made their way past statues of saints and primarchs. Coteaz imagined the projector did not usually display recordings of such a pious nature.

Kraeling hurried over to the projector and killed the power. The images spooled on for a few seconds, becoming fragmented and nonsensical, then died.

'Forgive the mess,' he said, hurrying back over. 'We rarely have visitors.' He laughed nervously. 'We *never* have visitors.' He unfastened the hood of his envirosuit and removed it. The others did the same and Coteaz frowned as he saw their faces. They were not sunburned. They were covered in a layer of red crystal. It looked exactly like the surface of the stalagmites outside.

Kraeling raised his hands, looking panicked. 'It's just a side effect. Of the ore, I mean. It's not mutation, lord inquisitor.'

Coteaz glanced at Sixtus.

'A side effect of the ore,' droned the servitor. 'Not a genetic mutation. Quite possible. Probable, in fact, due to the nature of thullic ore. It would explain the low life expectancy of the colonists.' Sixtus was able to follow the factual content of conversations, but the idea of tact was beyond him. It would not occur to him that mentioning the reduced longevity of the colonists, while standing in front of them, might be in poor taste.

Kraeling picked at the crystal on his face and peeled some of it away, revealing pale skin underneath. 'We're still under here, I promise you. This stuff grows on everything. It's like mould.'

He seemed on the verge of saying more about the mutation, then changed his mind and spoke in more neutral tones. 'Our facilities are basic, Lord Coteaz, but you're welcome to take my quarters. Would you like to recover from your journey? Or can I help you with something else?' He paused, glancing at Coteaz's gun.

Coteaz shook his head. 'We won't need rooms. I'm here to see Magos Xylothek.'

Kraeling visibly relaxed as he realised Coteaz had not come to see him. 'The Mechanicus facility moves around,' he said, 'but the last time we heard from them, it was positioned to the south of the primary hub, Vespertinus. Near one of the abandoned processing hives. They call their facility Domus Alpha. As far as I'm aware, Magos Xylothek is still in command. They keep to themselves. Tech-priests have visited Vespertinus in the past and maybe some of the smaller mines, but I've never spoken to any of them myself. They docked their landing shuttles here when they first arrived, but they didn't want to speak to me.'

'What is the best way to reach them?'

'Flying's the only option on Novalis. Even if we had the resources, we could never build a transitway. There's no ground.' He waved at the door. 'The pinnacles have no bottom. They just keep going. Unless you have a mining rig, the only way to reach Domus Alpha is to use your shuttle. We've not had any word from Vespertinus for nearly a month, though, so the storms must be pretty bad up there.' He thought for a moment, then slapped his yellow suit. 'You'll need some of these. They're not much use, but they're better than nothing. Don't get caught out in the weather, though. The suits buy you an hour, at most and I–' He had to pause as a deep, whooping cough shook his chest. Then he shrugged. 'This place is poison.'

Anamnesis

The ship sings as it dies – a keening dirge that groans through the bulkheads as the hull collapses, ravaged by the void tide.

I block out the din, picking my way through the bodies, looking for life amidst the death. Stablights flicker across the deck, picking out faces so distended they have become inhuman. Every chamber is filled with the same thick, charnel stink, but I am not ready to abandon my search.

'Malevich?'

The vox crackles in my ear. *'Nothing, Lord Coteaz. Only more of the dead pilgrims. No sign of any survivors.'*

'*Someone* triggered that beacon. Someone wanted us to board this vessel.' I consider the roll-call of enemies who might lure me to an abandoned ship. 'When was the *Light of Vengeance* last sighted?'

'No one has seen this ship since it left its moorings on Ophelia VII, well over a century ago, headed for the Sol System.'

Scions move forwards, stalking through the darkness in silence, but I pause, crouching next to one of the bodies. It is moving, its chest rising and falling, despite the ruined state of its skin. There is only one way a human body can draw breath after enduring such terrible disease. And yet… I sniff the air. The stink of putrefaction is overwhelming, but I do not detect anything else. After so many years of serving Lord Laredian, I have been taught how to harness my Emperor-given powers – how to single out the reek of heresy. Even in the carnage of a battlefield, with the dead heaped in mounds, I can taste the presence of warp spawn; *feel* it on my skin. But today I feel nothing.

'This was not a plague of unbelief.' Several of the pilgrims are still gripping reliquary boxes and holy books. I whisper a prayer. 'They died with their souls intact.'

I reach down and gently move the pilgrim who is still breathing. 'Can you hear me?'

The skin comes away under my gloved hand, sliding from the bones like slow-cooked meat, revealing rotten, fibrous layers beneath. As the body collapses, the movement is explained: rats scatter and the remains crumple to the floor, becoming still.

'Lord Coteaz. I am outside the chapel on Astrum Deck. Bio-scans indicate that there might be someone alive in there.'

I stand and cross the chamber, gesturing for the Scions to follow.

'How many?' I ask when I join Malevich and the rest of the Scions outside the chapel.

'Impossible to say.' Malevich's eyes are cold behind the lenses of his rebreather. 'If someone *did* attack the ship, they might have tracked our approach and holed up in here. This could still be an ambush.'

'If there *are* heretics in this chapel, I want them alive. They can tell me nothing if you butcher them.'

The Scions salute in silence.

'The lock has been disabled from the other side,' says Malevich.

I step back from the door. 'Take it down.'

When the dust has settled, I step up to the smouldering hole, my bolt pistol raised. At first glance it looks just like the previous chambers. There are dozens of dead pilgrims piled in a heap. It is a pitiful scene. Some took their last breath while cradled in each other's arms; others died reading from their holy texts, praying, to the very end, for salvation. But as Malevich and the other Scions spread out, taking up positions around the edge of the chamber, I notice something interesting. I glance at Malevich and silently draw his attention to the base of a pulpit. Separate from the dead pilgrims, there is a smaller pile of remains. Rat bones. Gnawed until they split and still wet. Fresh kills.

I spot a trail of blood that is brighter than the rest, leading away from the rats to the heap of human remains. I follow it, keeping my pistol raised. 'Show yourself.'

There is movement beneath the bodies.

The Scions lift their guns to their shoulders.

'*Show* yourself.' I lend my voice power, using psychic techniques Laredian taught me.

A hissing sound comes from the bodies.

I step closer and see a patch of flesh that is paler than the rest – bone-white amidst the bruise-dark. For the first time since boarding the *Light of Vengeance* I sense something besides death and disease – something *other*. It is unlike anything I have experienced before. It does not make my skin crawl in the way a creature of the warp might.

I place my finger over the trigger.

A figure leaps from the corpses and attacks, racing towards me.

The Scions take aim.

'Hold your fire!' I cry.

The figure is not what I expected. Rather than a traitor Guardsman in defaced battle gear, or a cultist draped in talismans, it is a tall, gangling youth.

'Stand still!'

The figure halts, straining and spitting and reaching out towards me.

'Xenos?' says Malevich, his finger hovering over his trigger.

The figure is strange, but human – a young woman, perhaps only in her late teens. She is long-limbed, dressed in mouldering rags, and she moves in such an odd way that I understand why Malevich might be confused. My voice has stopped her approaching, but she continues moving – rolling her shoulders and knotting her long arms in a peculiar, fluid manner that makes her look like she is suspended in liquid. She is gripping a makeshift weapon – a kind of hook, made from a piece of broken metal. The hook is wet with blood and clogged with scraps of fur. The rat killer.

There is something hypnotic about the girl's movements, and her skin is so colourless she looks more dead than the corpses. Her eyes are also unusual, devoid of any hue, pinprick pupils with no irises. But these are not the things that draw my attention. It is her expression. Her face is twisted by a ferocious determination. While everyone else on the ship has died, she has clung to life.

She is too furious to die.

She finally overcomes the force of my command and lunges, drawing back her hook to open my throat. I grip her wrist and lift her from the floor. She convulses as I hold her, spitting and hissing, kicking at my armour.

Something about the scene feels oddly significant, oddly familiar. At first, I struggle to understand why. The girl is strange, but there is more to it than that. I feel as though I have lived this moment before. Then I realise what it is – the dead pilgrims, the bloodstained altar; it reminds me of the day I first met Laredian. The day I was saved.

'Who are you?' I ask.

The girl looks surprised by my calm tone. The hate in her eyes merges with curiosity. She stops struggling and I lower her to the floor. She crouches like a cornered animal, looking from me to the row of guns that are trained on her.

'What is your name?' I say.

She rolls her head on her shoulders, writhing and coiling.

When she tries to speak, the word is so hoarse she has to repeat it.

'Sato.'

CHAPTER NINE

'High, ah, Protector.' Magos Xylothek scuttled insect-like towards Coteaz. 'How old you, ah, have become.'

The landing platform at Domus Alpha was larger than the one at Port Gomera: a broad semicircle of latticed metal jutting from one of the stalagmites like an enormous spider's web. Where the port was jury-rigged and ramshackle, this was sturdy and well engineered. It was encased in an enviro-baffle that looked like an enormous sheet of hessian, but was actually made of something strong enough to resist the fury of the storms that snapped and ripped around the facility. Coteaz and his retainers were standing at the foot of the shuttle's landing ramp, looking across the platform to an imposing building. The Mechanicus complex resembled a cathedrum, with sweeping buttresses and thick, blocky embrasures, and there was a broad colonnade leading to a pair of grand entrance doors. Outbuildings and arcane machines stood in ranks beneath the snapping canvas: drill rigs, comms devices, winged, bird-like flyers, and other contraptions that would only be recognisable to a Mechanicus adept. Beneath the platform, leaking blue light up through the grilled metal, were enormous engines and bundles of claw-like landing gear. Further below, half a mile beneath the facility, there were glimpses of abandoned industry – the fossil-like remnants of ancient towers and processing plants, crumbling slowly into mounds of crystal.

From the waist up, Magos Xylothek appeared to be a normal woman in her seventies, with dark, heavily lined skin and close-cropped white hair. From the waist down, however, she was entirely bionic. Her Mechanicus robes sported a skirt of metal protrusions that acted in place of legs and extra arms – hinged, needle-like rods that jerked and clicked as they propelled her forwards and probed the air around her, like feelers. She was followed by a huddle of red-robed tech-priests, many of whom were even more mechanised than she was, and there was a broad, heavy-set priest at her side whom Coteaz remembered from the last time he had seen the magos. Genetor Glycon was Xylothek's most trusted advisor. Behind them, waiting near the doors to the compound, stood a perfectly square phalanx of Mechanicus soldiers: masked, titanium-legged skitarii, armed with radium carbines.

Xylothek attempted a smile as she reached Coteaz, but it looked more like a grimace. 'It is, ah, good to see you again,' she said. The Mechanicus rarely had need to speak out loud, having developed more efficient ways to converse with each other, so her words were hoarse and clumsily formed. Up close, he saw that her face was not simply more lined than before – there had been a more significant change. Her eyes had been discarded and replaced with spheres of what looked like ebonised wood. They were scored with rings of binary that rolled constantly, clicking and swivelling. Her eyelids had also been removed, and the skin around the orbs was raw and red. Several of her mechadendrites ended in lenses, and it was these, rather than her eyes, that focused on Coteaz.

They studied each other in silence for a moment. Coteaz had been anticipating the meeting, wondering how she would react to his arrival. Now that he saw her, he had his answer. She was not going to admit that she was here looking for the soul glass. He could force the information out of her, of course, but that would be a mistake. A feud with such a senior prelate of the Martian priesthood would draw all eyes towards Novalis. Besides, she was a devoted servant of the Imperium. He would avoid harming her if he could. He would play her game and avoid mentioning the glass. He could simply tell her he had come looking for Agent Krasner.

Before he could speak, however, she said, 'Your, ah, acolyte is eager to converse with you.' One of her mechanised limbs gestured to a figure who had just emerged from the doors to the facility.

'Krasner,' said Coteaz, relieved to learn that the man was unharmed.

Xylothek conferred with Genetor Glycon in silence, transferring data through methods Coteaz only dimly understood. Their mechanised tendrils rippled as they leant towards each other, adding to Coteaz's sense that he was standing with a pair of metal insects. Glycon seemed agitated, and Coteaz sensed that something was wrong. He was about to ask Xylothek for an explanation when the figure approached and he understood.

It was Castra Sato.

He rested his hand on his bolt pistol as Sato strode towards him. She had shaved her head and her face was networked by fresh scars, but she was otherwise unchanged: unusually tall, deathly pale, lean as a canid. She was clad in black carapace armour – moulded, close-fitting armaplas, similar to the plate worn by

Captain Malevich – and a pair of repulsive weapons sat mag-locked to her thighs: slender, scythe-shaped pickaxes, like narrow-bladed billhooks dangling chains that ended in metal weights. Coteaz had seen similar weapons before – chain-sickles of xenos manufacture. She wore them brazenly, making no attempt to hide them. But there was something about her appearance that Coteaz found even more offensive than her proscribed weapons. There was a metal sigil embedded in the breastplate: a gilded, Inquisitorial 'I'.

Coteaz was still gripping his gun, but he gave Malevich and the others a warning glance, indicating that they should follow his lead. Then he strode towards Sato, nodding at her rosette. 'You have no right to wear that.'

She ran her finger around the outline of the rosette. 'Perhaps I should introduce myself,' she said. 'I am Inquisitor Sato of the Emperor's Holy Inquisition. My mentor is Inquisitor Zamorin.'

Coteaz was rarely surprised, but for a moment he was unable to speak. Sato had put herself beyond his reach. For now, at least. Even he would not denounce another inquisitor, unless it was done formally, as part of an Inquisitorial Conclave.

Magos Xylothek shook her head. 'Who were you, ah…? You were expecting to meet another?'

'He came for Krasner,' replied Sato.

Genetor Glycon leaned in to Xylothek. His hood shifted and Coteaz saw his face, or at least, what remained of his face; it had mostly been replaced by circular lenses – domes of green crystal, like a cluster of insect eggs – though there were a few scraps of his original flesh puckered around them, like waxy grey petals. He spoke aloud, the words emerging from an emitter sewn into his throat. 'Venerable magoss.' His voice was a white-noise hiss. 'Krasner iss with the otherss.'

Xylothek made a whirring sound then turned to Coteaz. 'Krasner is dead.'

Coteaz gripped his gun tighter. Krasner was his route to the soul glass. 'Agent Krasner was under my aegis.'

'I was unaware, ah… I was not cognisant of this fact. I did not know he was in your, ah, employ.' Xylothek spoke in bland tones. 'He did not divulge his affiliation to the Holy Ordos.'

Coteaz glared at Sato and she met his gaze confidently, staring back at him with her colourless, ink-dot eyes. There was a time when he could guess her thoughts, but now he struggled to read her expression. Had she killed Krasner to strike back at him? Did she despise him *that* much? Or had she killed Krasner so she could get her hands on the soul glass?

'Take me to him,' said Coteaz.

As they marched across the platform, Coteaz processed the new information. Agent Krasner was dead. Sato was now an inquisitor, and she had a powerful inquisitor lord as her patron. In fact, she had surpassed the need for a patron. She had been afforded all the power and privilege that came with the title of inquisitor. The situation was more precarious than he would like. Everything hinged on secrecy. No one must know he was here. And now he was potentially in conflict with another inquisitor. He would have to proceed with care.

It was only as they reached the doors to the facility that Coteaz noticed the figure waiting just inside. The person was roughly human in proportions, but her face was deformed, with a muzzle-like protrusion at its centre, featureless black eyes that were unnaturally large, and humps beneath her hood that looked like growths of some kind. She was broad-shouldered, heavily muscled, as tall as Sato, and gripping a chainaxe that looked like it could split a Land Raider. Her legs were a peculiar shape, too. It was hard to tell under her fatigues, but they looked bent back below the knee while her boots seemed suspiciously like thick, pitted hooves.

'Packmaster Khull,' said Sato. 'Sanctioned abhuman, approved by the Dictates Imperialis and permitted by the Register of Proscribed Citizens to be employed by an Ordo agent. While she is under my aegis, she is free to go wherever she likes.' She looked at Coteaz, as though daring him to disagree.

'Transgressor,' snarled Korov into his muzzle. He strode forwards, weapons growling into life, but Coteaz held him off with a warning glance. They were on Mechanicus soil and Sato was an inquisitor of the Holy Ordos. Coteaz imagined what it would be like to flout the law – to gun the two of them down, despite Sato's Inquisitorial rosette. Even as a fantasy, the idea did not appeal. Some rules could be bent or overlooked, but not that one. If the sanctity of the Holy Ordos was dismantled, it would be the beginning of the end.

'You have begun down a dangerous path, Inquisitor Sato, and we both know where it leads.' He locked his gaze on hers. 'Tread carefully.'

She seemed on the verge of replying, but then she simply shrugged and headed inside, Khull thudding after her.

The inside of Domus Alpha was a mess. The hexagonal corridors were narrow and crowded with exposed cabling and rattling cogitator banks. There were blue strip lumens running along the ceiling, but every dozen paces or so there was a pane of armaglass that spilled a column of infernal light into the gloom.

'I did not, ah, expect to see you again,' said Xylothek as she scuttled and lurched down the corridors. Her words were stiff and automaton-like, but Coteaz sensed vestiges of humanity beneath the surface. Perhaps she had not entirely forgotten their bonds of friendship. Perhaps, in her own way, she was even pleased to see him. And there was something else. Humour, he thought. Perhaps she was enjoying their game of cat and mouse.

'Can't a man visit an old friend?' he asked.

She made a clicking sound that might have been an attempt to simulate laughter.

Her adepts led the way through chambers that were crammed with machines and cowled priests. Finally, they stepped back out into the eerie quiet of the dome, with the crystal tower looming overhead, assailed by silent storm clouds. They crossed a cloistered courtyard and Coteaz dismissed most of his entourage, ordering Malevich to do a reconnoitre of the facility while Interrogator Voltas secured their rooms. Sato and her companion stayed nearby, and he wondered what reason she had given Xylothek for her presence on Novalis. She was not foolish enough to mention the soul glass.

He followed the adepts back into the complex on the other side of the courtyard, and a few minutes later, they passed through a set of heavy, armour-plated doors into what looked like an abattoir. It was a large, rectangular room and the walls were lined with corpses – five of them, hanging upside down, suspended on cables that were fixed to winches on the ceiling. The bodies were in a pitiful state, their bones broken and organs removed, but Coteaz could tell, by how augmented they were, that they were tech-priests. Each corpse was being worked on by a bristling mass of servo-arms and automated saws. The machines were picking at the dead like carrion birds, pecking and tearing. The bodies were bloodless and waxy-looking, and the flesh gleamed white in the harsh light of strip lumens.

Coteaz and Xylothek stepped into the centre of the chamber, looking around at the frenzied dissections.

'The first adept to die was working on digs near the Vespertinus mine,' said Xylothek. 'The mortality rate is high in the mines, due to falls, cave-ins, and the toxicity of the air, so the death did not seem anomalous. But then there was another death.' She nodded to her genetor. 'I instructed Glycon to investigate, and he found that the deaths were not accidental.' She waved at the mutilated corpses. 'We have lost two tech-thralls, two enginseers and a lexmechanic.'

Glycon hissed through his throat grille. 'I surmised, at first, that it might be local fauna, but then I devised a superior theory.' He looked at Xylothek, who nodded for him to continue. 'During my time at the Vespertinuss mine I was witness to great unrest. The indentured workers know that other mines have collapsed or been abandoned, and as a result they have become discontented. The close proximity of the ore shortens their lifespanss and leads to various psychoses. From analysing the frequency of violent deathss I learned that the situation has recently grown worse. One of the miners even attempted to attack *me.* After disabling her I performed a rudimentary autopsia cadaverum procedure. The results confirmed my suspicionss: the indentured workers are in a state of mental degradation which is resulting in aberrant behaviour.'

Coteaz noticed something. 'None of you have the red crystal forming on your skin.'

Xylothek shook her head. 'The symptoms you describe stem from a respiratory condition. We of the Cult Mechanicus are less susceptible to such weaknesses of the flesh. Few of us rely on anything as inefficient as lungs.'

Sato raised an eyebrow.

Coteaz almost asked her for her thoughts, as he would have done years ago. Then he remembered that she was no longer *his.* He looked over at her, and the abomination at her side. He still thought it possible that *she* was behind the murders. She displayed clear signs of radicalism, consorting with abhumans and sporting xenos weapons, but she was also a sanctioned operative of the Ordo. He could not accuse her of anything without proof.

'Magos Xylothek,' he said, pretending to accept Glycon's theory, 'how have you dealt with these insurgents?'

'We have, ah, limited resources, High Protector. A single skitarii maniple. Forty troops. We are a research facility, not an explorator fleet. We are not equipped to suppress revolutions. I attempted to contact Governor Aldrov, the official in charge of Vespertinus, but there has been no, ah, reply. The mine is currently at the centre of a violent storm, so I will not take the facility there. The radiation is highly concentrated in the mines, and I will not have our work disrupted.'

Coteaz nodded at the bodies. 'It has already been disrupted.'

Xylothek's eyes rotated, making the strange clicking sound again. 'The problem is more severe than you know.' She clattered across the floor on her needle-legs and pointed out another pair of corpses at the far end of the room. They were more intact than the others and there was still blood flowing from the wounds. 'These two were killed here, in the ruins beneath Domus Alpha. Someone, ah, breached our security cordons and attacked adepts working in the abandoned processing hive.'

'Where is Agent Krasner?' Coteaz looked around at the different bodies.

'He told us he was working for the Chartists,' said Xylothek, leading the way to a final corpse.

Coteaz had to look hard before he could recognise the man, and in the end it was only the ident tattoo on his shoulder that made him sure. Krasner's head had been destroyed. Hacked apart. To see him like this, strung up like meat, filled him with outrage. He recalled the last time they spoke. Krasner had grasped his hand, swearing to find the soul glass. Coteaz wondered if he ever did.

The wound patterns looked familiar. Coteaz studied Sato through Thula's eyes. His bond with the eagle enabled him to see what she saw, as a kind of peripheral vision, but if he desired it, he could look directly through her eyes. To everyone in the room, it looked as though Coteaz's attention was still fixed on the corpse, but he was actually examining Sato's xenos weapons. As he suspected, the blades were the right kind of shape to have made Krasner's head wounds. Sato noticed Thula looking at her, but if she guessed what was happening she hid it, saying nothing, her expression impossible to read.

As he looked at Sato through one set of eyes, Coteaz continued examining Agent Krasner, taking a lens from his belt and leaning closer to the body.

Glycon gripped his arm. 'We have not had time to properly examine this particular body yet.'

Coteaz looked at Glycon's hand in disbelief.

'Withdraw,' said Xylothek.

Glycon hesitated, then loosed his grip and backed away.

Coteaz held the lens to the pulpy mess that used to be Krasner's head. The wounds were not, as he first thought, the result of a frenzied attack. The skull had been levered apart with care. It had all the hallmarks of Sato's work. She was always precise and neat with her kills.

Coteaz adjusted a control on the lens' casing and it rotated, bringing the pulverised mass into sharper focus. The skull had been carefully opened to reach a certain part of Krasner's brain. Coteaz used the lens to take pict captures of the incisions. If he examined Sato's chain-sickles, he was sure they would match the cuts. He considered demanding that she hand them over, then decided against it. He could not be sure exactly what game she was playing. It could be that there was a bigger picture here that he was missing. It was better to let this play out for a while.

As he recorded the pict captures he saw that some of the brain's external membrane had been sliced. He removed one of his gauntlets and used his finger to gently fold it back. Examining the soft ridges underneath, he noticed something odd. Some of the shapes were angular and inorganic. They had been imprinted deliberately on the brain. They were so faint they could easily have been missed, and they were only depressions, so he had a suspicion they might fade in a few days.

'What have you found, ah, High Protector?' asked Xylothek, stepping to his side.

Coteaz put his lens away, wiped his fingers on a cloth, and replaced his gauntlet. 'Nothing yet,' he lied. 'I will need to examine him in more detail. Have this body taken to my chambers.'

Xylothek's expression hardened, and Coteaz thought, for a moment, that she might end the pretence – that she might admit she knew something about why Krasner had died, and why Coteaz sent him to Novalis. But then her features became blank again. She nodded. 'Genetor Glycon will show you the way.'

Tech-thralls unfastened the body, laid it on a gurney, and wheeled it through the doors. Coteaz was about to follow them, but upon reaching Sato he paused.

There was defiance in her eyes but something else, too – hurt, perhaps? She studied the scars on his neck and face. 'Another rebirth, Torquemada? The joins are starting to show.'

She had never used his first name before. It sounded awkward in her mouth.

'Come to me in an hour,' he said. 'Bring the truth.'

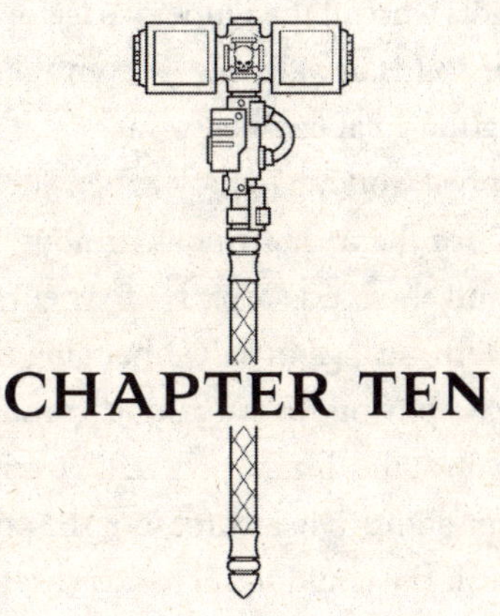

CHAPTER TEN

'The past is a lie.' The priestess looked down from her lectern, gripping its sides as it clambered through the bloody light on mechanised legs. 'As is the future.'

The miners were hunched and gangly, limbs shaking as they drilled, their crystal-coated skin visible through their goggles, but the priestess' skin was untainted. Her arms were plump, pale and strong. Instead of a hollow-cheeked grimace, she wore a proud, confident smile, and beneath her yellow envirosuit, Elias saw glimpses of luxurious red robes. 'The only thing that matters,' she continued, smiling at the toiling workers, 'is now. This moment. This is real. Your work is real. Every stone you crack is a tribute to the God-Emperor. Every bead of sweat is a prayer. And He sees all of it. He knows of your sacrifice. He feels your devotion. Even amongst all the multitudinous heavens, He sees your strength and faith.'

Elias was further up the face with Helk and Sturm, their drills hammering against the rocks, filling the air with dust and noise, but the priestess' words rang out over the din, amplified by an emitter in her lectern. 'Perhaps you wish you could serve on the front lines of a great army, that you could join the ranks of martyrs and saints who fill the Emperor's legions, but let me tell you this – your toil is as valuable as even the greatest martyr. You are fuelling the great engine of war.'

Elias had stopped working to look at her. She was surrounded by overseers, all of them clad in flak armour and armed with shock mauls, and there was a pack of cyber-mastiffs padding around the lectern, strings of saliva hanging from their metal jaws, but she was oblivious to everything, consumed by her own oratory, staring up at the distant cave ceiling, gripped by rapture. No one was responding to her words, but she nodded happily as she cried out, as if she could hear crowds cheering her on. 'You *are* martyrs! Offering strength and sweat so that He can continue His great work. So that He can protect those within His reach and search out those who are not. Be brave. Be strong. Never forget that everything you do is in His name.'

Elias waited until the moment his courage had specified, then he held out his drill and dropped it onto the rocks. It clattered loudly on the ground, causing people to look up in surprise.

'Feel your breath as it fills your lungs!' cried the priestess, lost in her oratory, heading closer to Elias. 'These are the lungs granted to you by the God-Emperor. Feel your muscles as they work, bringing the...' Her words trailed off as she noticed a commotion around the base of the lectern. Some of the overseers had seen that Elias had stopped working.

'You!' cried one of them, pointing his shock maul at Elias. 'What are you doing? Get back to work!' His cyber-mastiff jolted against its lead, shaking its mechanical head and growling, spraying spit from its metal teeth.

Elias said nothing and remained motionless. Helk and Sturm dropped their drills and stood next to him, their expressions resolute.

'What in the name of the Throne are you doing?' cried the overseer, his face flushing with colour. He was too shocked to move for a moment, then he lowered his shock maul and took a laspistol from his belt. 'I'll teach you some respect.' It was rare that the overseers had a chance to flex their muscle, and Elias could see how excited they were at the prospect of making an example of him.

'The Emperor sees your sin!' The priestess' lips were trembling as she turned to the nearest overseer. 'Punish him!'

The overseer sneered as he fired. The blast tore through Elias' suit, passed through his chest, and exited from between his shoulder blades in a crimson spray.

'Novalis will rise,' said Elias calmly, staring at the overseer. There was no pain. It was exactly as his courage had told him it would be. The las-fire had no effect on him. If anything, the hole in his chest felt good, as if he had removed an annoying scab.

'Blasphemer!' cried the priestess. She stared at his wound, incredulous. 'This is witchcraft! Shoot again!'

The overseer said nothing, staring in shock at the hole in Elias' suit.

'Kill him!' cried the priestess.

The overseers overcame their surprise and rushed forwards, hate in their eyes and electricity dripping from their mauls. They were only a few feet from Elias when they noticed the other figures appearing on the ledge, above the lumens.

'What's this?' grunted the senior overseer, lowering his maul in confusion. The figures had been hidden until that moment.

Elias raised his fist and the figures stepped forwards into the light – thirty miners, the entirety of the next shift. But they had not come to mine. They were dressed in flak armour, similar to the suits worn by the overseers but newer and cleaner, and they were holding gleaming military-issue lasguns that were all pointed at the overseers.

The overseers were massively outnumbered and most dropped their weapons, but the leader held on to his gun and glared at Elias. He rushed forwards, raising his maul to strike. 'There's more than one way to kill a filthy–'

His words were cut off as a barrage of las-fire ripped into him, shredding his armour and kicking him back in a cloud of blood. He landed heavily on the rocks, tried to rise, then collapsed and lay still, a crimson pool spreading around him. The few overseers who were still holding their weapons dropped them and put their hands on their heads. The dogs howled and strained at their leashes, but the overseers held them back.

'Wait,' gasped the priestess as the miners turned their guns on her. Her face was ashen as she stared at Elias' wound. 'What have you *done*? What do you want?'

Elias broke the seal of his envirosuit, took out his pistol, and walked slowly towards her, stepping over the overseer's still-smoking corpse. 'We want to live. So we are turning our back on your God-Emperor.' He flipped his gun and held it towards her. 'Which means you finally have your chance to fight for him and become a martyr.'

She stared at the gun in horror, then at the bloody hole in his chest, shaking her head. His skin was blistering and already knitting itself back together.

Elias held the gun out for a moment longer then shrugged and took it back. 'Strange. I thought, from your sermons, that you would relish the opportunity.' He spoke to the miners, who were gathering around him, glaring at the priestess and the overseers. 'Take their weapons. Put restraints on them. And on the dogs.'

'Where are you taking us?' whispered the priestess, wide-eyed.

'You could stay here, in the mine.' He waved at the red crystals. 'With the rock that you value so highly.'

The priestess screamed at the overseers. 'Do something! He's a witch!'

The overseers looked at each other but refused to move, keeping their hands on their heads.

'You have damned yourself for all eternity,' whispered the priestess, shaking and clutching at her suit. 'You will *burn* for this!'

Elias could hear his courage, telling him what to do next, where to go and what to say. He smiled, picking absent-mindedly at the scab that had been a gunshot wound just seconds ago. 'I don't think we will.'

CHAPTER ELEVEN

Coteaz thought of another time he had executed an inquisitor: the day he killed Laredian. There had been no secrecy on that occasion. Coteaz had been careful to act in full view of his fellow inquisitors. It was the largest conclave ever summoned on Varoth. He had made sure of that, keen that everyone should learn from Laredian's mistake. They needed to see that even the mightiest among them could fall. Laredian had damned himself as surely as the most pitiful cultist. All eyes had been on him as he strode down from the auditorium's galleries and walked through the stalls to the stage. But when Coteaz smashed the crystal that proved his master's heresy, only he and Laredian saw the face that flickered in the broken shards. Only they saw the daemon Laredian had struck his bargain with. Coteaz had never forgotten it.

'Sato is approaching.' Malevich's voice crackled in Coteaz's vox-bead. *'She has come alone.'*

Coteaz checked his chronograph. She had waited exactly an hour, as he had ordered. He closed a door, hiding Krasner's shrouded corpse, and took a seat in the small room Xylothek had set aside for him. 'Inform the others that I am busy. No interruptions.'

'As you command, Lord Coteaz.'

Coteaz killed the vox-link. Malevich was good at masking his emotions, but there had been a hint of frustration in his voice. The captain probably considered this an unnecessary risk, meeting Sato without Scions on hand. It would bother him that he could not be there to protect his lord. But Coteaz needed to see her alone. One way or another, he needed to be sure.

'It is time,' he said.

Korov was kneeling a few feet away. At Coteaz's words, he finished his prayer and stood up. His sackcloth hood fell back, revealing the grey, sutured mess where his face used to be. He said nothing, but Coteaz sensed a question in his eyes.

'I may have no choice,' he said, looking at the daemonhammer lying before him on the table. He was speaking to himself, more than Korov. 'Executing her without a trial *is* a risk, but unless she reveals something I've missed, it will be my only option. The evidence is damning. She was present at Krasner's death. Her blade marks were all over his skull. The most likely explanation is that she killed him. Which means she probably killed the Mechanicus adepts too. Her motives are unclear, though. She may have come here looking for the same thing as me. Her lord, Zamorin, would give anything to possess it. Perhaps the adepts had information she needed. Or perhaps they were close to uncovering the soul glass, and she wished to stop them.'

Korov continued staring at him. 'Transgressor,' he said.

'Perhaps. Stay out of sight and keep your weapons ready.' Coteaz glanced at the hammer. 'It's important that this goes smoothly.' He nodded to Korov's array of tools. 'If I *do* kill her, dispose of the body immediately. It must not be known that she died at my hand. And we must ensure there is no evidence linking me to her. I will *not* give Inquisitor Zamorin ammunition to use against me. It could hinder my plans for the conclave.'

Korov lifted one of his filthy bindings to his mouth, kissed the word *Sinner*, then backed out of the room.

There was a tap at the door and Coteaz opened it. Sato stood in the doorway looking at him; then she looked at the hammer lying on the table. He sat down and waved her to the other chair, but she hesitated, shifting her weight from one foot to the other, still looking at the hammer. Finally, she nodded and sat down. He poured them both a cup of amasec. He was surprised to realise that he wanted to give her time. He wanted her to prove him wrong.

She looked at her drink dubiously.

He raised an eyebrow. 'I am not a poisoner.'

She swapped the cups and drank from his. 'How *did* you intend to kill me, then?' she asked, tapping the rosette on her chest. 'Before you saw this?'

'I didn't come here for you. I came for Agent Krasner.'

'You abandoned your conclave and crossed half the sector because one agent was in trouble?'

'Nothing has been abandoned. I will still reach Varoth in time. The conclave will proceed as planned.'

She took another sip of her drink, her eyes flicking from side to side. She fiddled with her hands, folding them, bending the fingers back and cracking her knuckles. She was just as he remembered: always in motion, crossing and uncrossing her arms, bending her joints, drumming her feet on the floor, performing an endless, fluid dance. It required a conscious effort to remember that he was not facing his most promising protégé, but a dangerous enemy. She had probably murdered Agent Krasner.

And who knew what other crimes she had committed to get this far. So why was he staying his hand? What was he waiting for?

She looked up at him and her expression hardened, as if she had read his thoughts. 'What did you find in Krasner's head?'

Coteaz took another sip of amasec. 'Do you think I summoned you here so I could share information with you?'

She rose from her seat and began pacing the room, reaching back to grab her shoulder blades as she walked. 'If we *were* to share information, I know things that might interest you.'

Coteaz looked at his hammer, still wondering why he was prolonging this. But he could not help taking her bait. He nodded for her to continue.

'I've been here for months,' she said, flexing her joints and rolling her shoulders. 'I've examined the bodies of adepts.' She leant on the table, looking directly into his eyes. '*Before* Xylothek's tech-priests examined them. Before they obscured the evidence.'

'Why would they obscure evidence?' he asked.

She sat back in the chair, then stood and resumed pacing. 'We both know what's on this planet, Coteaz. And I knew it before you did. I know what you've come for. I know the real reason you're on Novalis. And it isn't to see an old friend.'

'You know nothing of my motivations.'

'You must think I'm a fool,' she said. 'But then I suppose you consider *everyone* a fool. Tell me this – how much have you shared with your new interrogator? I can answer for you: nothing. Because you don't trust him.' The words sounded rehearsed, and Coteaz sensed that she had waited a long time for this moment. 'Does he know the real reason you're on Novalis? No. Because if you *did* trust him, if you stopped hoarding your knowledge, he might *surprise* you. He might become the protégé you *pretend* to be looking for.'

He realised that she wasn't the only one who had been waiting for this chance to speak. 'You are living proof of why I need to be careful,' he said.

She waved the insult off. 'You don't want a protégé. You never did. Perhaps you *think* you do, but it's the last thing you want. Imagine if you really did put your trust in someone. Imagine if you *confided* in them. Think what it would mean. If you allowed someone to know even half of what you know, you would no longer be irreplaceable.' She splayed her long, elegant fingers, staring at them. 'And actually, I think it's more than that. I think you're afraid that if someone knew the things you know, they might be a threat. I *understand* you, Torquemada.'

'All you understand is your own ambition. And all you want is power.' He placed his hand on the daemonhammer. 'And your allegiance to Zamorin proves you don't care how you acquire it.'

'We could find the soul glass, Torquemada. Consider that. If you confided in me, if we worked *together,* we could find the thing you have sought all these years. Or we can waste our energy fighting as others close in on the prize. We have an opportunity. You need the soul glass and you need *my* help if you don't want Xylothek to take it back to Glovoda.'

'Xylothek? She doesn't know where the soul glass is. If she did, she would *already* be on her way back to Glovoda. She wants me to halt these murders. That means she is not planning on leaving yet. She has not found the glass. And I am disinclined to believe she is murdering her own adepts.'

'So you think *I'm* your rival,' she said. 'You think I'm the murderer. Even though I'm asking to work with you. Xylothek has more to do with this than you realise.'

'You think she is killing her own adepts?'

'Perhaps. The deaths are part of a ritual. I don't have all the details yet, but I am close. It's something to do with finding the soul glass. So, obviously, she can't share her methods. Who knows how the Mechanicus sanctify their work? I imagine it's not unusual for them to spill a little blood. They place little value on it.'

'It's not her,' he said. 'There is someone else.'

Her eyes flashed as she saw that he was preparing to share information.

'I agree with your logic to a certain point,' he continued. 'The marks on Krasner's corpse were precise and, as you say, ritualistic. Inflicted with care. Intended to achieve something very specific.'

She nodded eagerly. 'That story about disgruntled miners is a decoy. We both know it. Perhaps Xylothek's not behind the murders, but she's definitely not sharing the truth. I *know* what you saw on Krasner's brain, because I've seen the same.'

She took a black card from her armour and unfolded it into a data-slate. She triggered the device and showed him an image. It was a jumble of angles, circles and lines, very similar to the shapes he had discovered inside the agent's skull.

'I examined some of the corpses before the tech-priests got to them,' she said. 'They all had these symbols pressed into their brain tissue.'

When he saw the first pattern, as he studied Krasner, Coteaz had formed a theory, but it was only now, seeing three of them side by side, that he realised he was right. 'Do you realise what they are?' he asked.

She shook her head, clearly irritated. 'Designs for Martian circuitry?'

'No. These are not Mechanicus designs.'

'Letters of some kind, though. A ritual, written in some form of xenos language?'

Coteaz felt a flicker of disappointment that she was so wide of the mark. 'They are pieces of a map.'

She frowned. Then her eyes shone with recognition.

'A map that draws itself,' he continued. 'A map created by the death pulse of a human mind.'

She was nodding now. 'Like the one we uncovered on Zullo IV. Yes. I remember. These circles are locations. What did you call it? A Tabella Mortem.'

'A quietus tablet, yes. The one we found on Zullo IV was the first I had ever seen outside of pict footage. They are profoundly dangerous relics, forged by sorcery and idolatry. They are prized by traitors and heretics, but they are often overlooked by grave robbers because they are so plain – sheets of thin, dull, hammered metal, until they are used.'

'Used *how?* You never explained. You warned me that they were dangerous, but you never explained why.'

'They are not as inert as they appear. Their makers use sorcery to imbue them with enticing secrets – often a map of some kind, leading to a seemingly wonderful reward, and then they hand the tablet over to an unwitting prey. The tablets *will* reveal their secrets, but only if the user abandons themselves to heresy and unbelief. Death is the catalyst, you see. Ritual murder is the key. Anyone using the tablet is dragged into a spiral of bloodshed and witchcraft. They *think* they are merely revealing a map, but in reality they are performing a ritual whose purpose they could never guess at.'

Sato adjusted the image to show how neatly the three shapes fitted together. 'Someone's murdering the adepts to awaken the quietus tablet. To reveal a map.'

'A map to the soul glass.'

'It could lead to anything. What makes you sure it's the soul glass?'

'I cannot be sure. But Tabella Mortem technology originated on Mars, in the dark ages before the Imperium, in exactly the same forges as the soul glass. They were even created in the same period of prehistory. The same *decade.* That seems quite a coincidence.'

'It *could* be a coincidence.'

'Events rarely dovetail by accident. Like attracts like. In a sector as vast and varied as this, it is unlikely that something invented on Mars, at exactly the same time as the soul glass, is being recreated here, on Novalis, and being used to kill people who are looking for the soul glass. There is a connection.' He peered at the lines on her data-slate. 'But there's no grid reference, no geographical features. The few tablets I've seen pict captures of were very detailed.'

'But they were relics,' she said. 'This one's new. It's still being drawn. It's incomplete. The rest of the details will emerge when the map is finished. Then it will look just like the others.'

'When more people die.'

'When more people die.' She leant back in her chair. 'We could finish the map. You and I.'

Coteaz raised an eyebrow.

She waved her hand dismissively. 'I'm not talking about ritual murder. I mean we could combine the images I have with the images you took from Krasner's brain. We could start to draw the map.'

'Have you heard a word I said? A quietus tablet is *profoundly* heretical. Drawing that map, or even trying to grasp its shape, would corrupt us both. The tablet masquerades as a treasure map, but its true purpose is far darker. It is a talisman. A weapon of the Ruinous Powers. If we studied those lines long enough, they might lead us to the soul glass, but by the time we found it we would be wretched, craven things.'

'Then what do you suggest?' she asked. 'What is your plan? I *know* you have one.'

She finally noticed that his hand was locked around the daemonhammer. She gave him a cool glare. 'I am an agent of the Throne.'

He took his hand off the hammer and sat back in his chair. 'You have given me much to consider. I will talk to Magos Xylothek. I may be able to unearth some of her secrets.'

She stared at him. 'So where does this leave us?'

He thought for a moment, then reached into his armour and held out his hand. There was a coin in his palm – a memento mori, identical to the one he had given to Voltas. 'I imagine you disposed of the last one,' he said.

Her expression hardened. 'I'm not here to grovel. I just think we need to work together. I didn't come to beg for a second chance.'

'Begging wouldn't help.'

She laughed bitterly and showed no intention of taking the coin.

Even now, he could not be sure of her motives. Rejecting him could mean many things. He needed more time to consider the matter. 'It might be that you can be of use to me,' he said. 'I will think on it.'

She rose to go, pausing at the door to look back at him. 'One of us will be judged, Torquemada, but it may not be me.' There was no anger in her voice now. She sounded almost sad. Then she closed the door and was gone.

Coteaz looked down at the coin, still sitting in his palm. What had made him offer it? It had not been part of his plan. It bothered him that his thoughts regarding Sato were so ill-defined. He stared at the coin for a few moments. Then he stood up and locked the hammer to his armour.

'Korov.'

Korov's eyes were blazing as he entered the room. He managed to drag words from his throat. 'She… lies.' He was shaking with anger as he stared at Coteaz.

Coteaz placed a hand on his shoulder. 'And, like all good liars, she dresses deceit in layers of truth. She's told me more than she realises.' He pictured her face, trying to untangle the mystery behind those monochrome eyes. 'And if I had executed her, I would never uncover what it is she's hiding.'

'Blood of the Throne,' said Korov, sounding reassured.

'Blood of the Throne,' agreed Coteaz. He opened a vox-link to Malevich. 'My suspicions were right. Send my message to the *Pilgrim's Wrath.* Use the encryption codes I gave you.' He opened the door and strode off down the corridor, heading towards Xylothek's chambers. 'The situation is worse than I feared.'

CHAPTER TWELVE

Magos Xylothek's sanctum was plain and utilitarian, but she had a small table and some chairs and she poured him a drink as they talked. To an observer, it might have seemed like they were simply two old comrades reminiscing, but they both knew Coteaz was not there to talk about the past; he was there to find out what Xylothek knew. His usual ploys, however, had so far come to nothing. Xylothek had so little humanity left in her that it was like trying to outwit a cogitator. They had been close, once. It was Xylothek who gifted him Thula as a sign of gratitude. So he felt a flicker of sadness at the fact that she now seemed almost a stranger.

After nearly an hour of brittle, unproductive talk, Xylothek crossed the chamber and approached a workbench. It was covered with pieces of ephemera arranged in neat rows. Lumps of meat floated in jars. Fragments of dismantled weaponry nestled next to works of religious poetry. Mouldering ledgers propped up copper-plated skulls.

'I found something that made me, ah, think of you,' she said, in her odd, droning voice. She rummaged through drill bits and stacks of vellum, feeling her way with gleaming tendrils. 'In a crypt on Glovoda. There have been humans there since the days of the, ah, Great Crusade. Since before the coming of our explorator fleets. There were colonies near the equator, where the temperatures are, ah, less extreme. They were gone by the time my forebears arrived, but we still unearth ruins.' She lifted up a skull, no bigger than her fist, studying it for a moment, before placing it carefully to one side. 'Let me find it,' she said, opening chests and unscrewing bottles.

Coteaz went to her side, intrigued by the collection of relics. These were the things she had considered so important she would risk bringing them all the way to Novalis. He noticed spaces on the desk where some objects had been recently removed. They would be the treasures she knew he would disapprove of – nothing overtly heretical, of course, but contentious in some way, perhaps linked to xenos cultures or remnants of forbidden technology. She would not have hidden them through shame, more out of respect for his role and to spare them any awkwardness.

'Here it is,' said Xylothek, picking up a fragment of lichen-covered stone. It was small, only the size of his index finger, a piece of broken rockcrete, but she held it with reverence. 'Do you see the inscription?'

He took it from her and peered at the characters carved along its length. The letters were an archaic form of High Gothic, so stylised that it took him a moment to decipher the words. Once he had translated them in his mind, he recited them aloud. '"All that is acquired will be lost."' He looked at Xylothek, wondering if he had translated it correctly. And wondering why those words should be significant to her.

The black spheres rolled in her eye sockets, clicking as the circles of binary realigned. 'It was part of a lintel, over the, ah, entrance to a tomb. There were many warnings carved there, warnings from the dead to the, ah, living, but this one in particular made me think of you. I researched the origin of the phrase. It is Terran. A fragment of an old religious tract.' She noticed Coteaz's suspicious glance. 'Nothing heretical. The meaning is simple and, ah, profound. Whatever you accrue during your life, whether it be knowledge, wealth or power, you lose it when you die. It is a warning we should all heed.'

'All that is acquired will be lost.' Coteaz repeated the phrase, and this time he felt the weight of it. It reminded him of things Laredian had taught him when he was still a youth. But he could not understand why it struck a chord with Xylothek. 'You will never die,' he said, looking at the sections of her body that had been replaced with machinery. 'Not through any natural means, at least.'

'There are different ways to die.' One of her mechadendrites reached up, touching the scars on his face. 'We are in the endgame. The final act. We have collated. We have waited. But now the waiting must, ah, cease. We must employ the weapons we have forged. I trust you, Torquemada.' A little humanity crept back into her voice. 'I always did. With you as High Protector, Formosa has endured. But when you are gone, who will, ah, take your place? You *will* die. And if you do not appoint a successor, others will, ah, appoint one for you. There is great danger in that.'

Coteaz saw a glimpse of the Xylothek he knew many years ago. She had identified his weakness and tried to exploit it. She knew that losing control of Formosa was his greatest fear. She was attempting to distract him from his purpose in coming to see her. And it had almost worked.

He smiled. 'I forget how long you've known me and what good friends we were.'

'We are *still* friends.' She placed the stone back on the table, being careful to return it to exactly the same position. 'What do you intend to do next?'

'Fly north. To the mines.' Coteaz lied without compunction, knowing he was being lied to in turn. 'I believe your genetor is correct. I think these murders are an act of insurrection. And I intend to root out the instigators and make an example of them.'

'An end to the murders would be beneficial.' There was no trace of emotion in her voice, no way to know what she thought of his deceit.

He examined her scored eyes, trying to discern her true feelings. Was it possible that she *had* killed her own adepts in an effort to find the soul glass? Was it possible that she would employ something as heretical as a quietus tablet? Had she changed so much?

He thought of another way to probe her. 'What if there *was* a way for one to live on? A way to achieve immortality. What would that be worth, do you think? Would it be worth taking risks for?'

'Risks?' She sounded reticent. 'What kind of, ah, risks?'

'Lord Coteaz.' Malevich's voice crackled in Coteaz's ear. *'There's another body. A fresh kill.'*

'Hold your position.' Coteaz blinked schematics across his retina, quickly locating the glyph that denoted Malevich. 'I can be with you in less than a minute. No one is to approach the body.' He switched the vox to an open channel. 'I will meet you there.'

He rushed out into the corridor with Xylothek racing after him. She did not demand an explanation, and he knew that her adepts would already be briefing her. There was no need for her to vox or call commands. The Mechanicus were linked to each other in ways that made such crude forms of communication unnecessary. But as they ran through the facility Xylothek droned to herself, using the same indecipherable argot he had heard her use before. Then she scuttled past him with surprising speed.

Coteaz slowed, then stopped. He watched her go. When she was out of sight, he turned and headed in the opposite direction.

CHAPTER THIRTEEN

As Inquisitor Sato ran through the facility, she wondered why Coteaz had used an open vox-channel. Nothing Coteaz did was accidental. It could have been intended as a sign he was starting to trust her, but somehow she doubted it.

Khull was at her side. 'Coteaz will be there. No chance to do any digging.'

She gave the abhuman a warning look as they turned a corner and saw a pair of open doors leading out into the storm. The enviro-baffle was visible through the opening, snapping and billowing.

Interrogator Voltas appeared from another direction, and Sato heard the clatter of boots and metal feet as Scions and Mechanicus troops approached down other corridors.

Voltas reached the doorway and looked disdainfully at her. Then the three of them stepped over the threshold. The weather slammed into them as they edged out onto a metal-grilled walkway that circled the facility's engines.

Captain Malevich and another of Coteaz's Scions were hunkered down a few feet further along the walkway beside not one, but two corpses. Both were Mechanicus adepts. The first was sprawled across the walkway. Her crimson robes billowed around her, and her head had been opened in the same manner as the previous victims. Sato knew, if she examined the corpse, she would find more traces of the map imprinted on the brain. The second adept had suffered greater indignities. He was nailed to the side of a gantry, his arms spread and skin peeled back to resemble wings. Blood rained down as the corpse shook in the wind.

Magos Xylothek clattered onto the walkway, flanked by skitarii as she rushed over to the corpses. It was the first time Sato had sensed any kind of emotion in her. The clues were subtle, but Sato had been trained to read signs others might miss. Xylothek's face remained impassive, but her posture had changed – her shoulders had dropped and her head was swaying slightly. She seemed genuinely saddened by the deaths of her adepts.

'Take him down,' the magos said.

Malevich raised his chin. 'They are not to be moved. By order of the Emperor's Holy Inquisition.'

'This is Mechanicus territory.' Xylothek's tone was cold. 'These are my adepts. You will do as I say.'

Malevich and the other Scion gripped their lasguns. 'Magos Xylothek,' said Malevich. 'I take my orders from the High Protector.'

'Who's not here,' breathed Sato, looking around for Coteaz. Suddenly, it occurred to her why he might have chosen to use the open vox-channel. Perhaps he wanted everyone to gather here so he could be unobserved somewhere else. He had mentioned that he was going to try to find out more about Magos Xylothek. Perhaps he was ransacking her chambers. This thought led to another, more troubling one.

'We must get back to my rooms,' she whispered to Khull as she turned and ran back down the walkway.

* * *

The lock had been cut from the door. The metal was still glowing as Sato shoved it open and revealed her room. Furniture had been overturned and the contents of her void-crates had been tossed across the floor. Coteaz was seated at the centre of the mess with the hulking, shrouded figure of Korov at his side.

'How dare you!' said Sato.

Khull snarled and stepped past her, gripping her chainaxe.

'Recant!' Korov exploded into action. His tendril-like limbs lashed onto Khull, tightening around her chest and arms. He lassoed her throat and slammed her into the wall. 'Transgressor!' She hit the wall with such force that her chainsword fell from her grip. Khull was massive, but Korov carried her like a child, smashing her repeatedly into the rockcrete.

'Stop!' Sato drew out her chain-sickles and dropped into a fighting stance.

Coteaz nodded.

Korov loosed his grip but continued looming over Khull, who was breathing heavily as she slid to the floor.

'You have no right to invade the sanctity of an inquisitor's chambers,' said Sato, glaring at Coteaz.

'We will discuss your rights in a moment.' Coteaz held up a small object between his finger and thumb.

Sato gripped her chain-sickles tighter, wondering if the time had come when she would have to fight or die at his hand. He was holding a piece of the quietus tablet.

'Did you make this?' he asked.

She glanced at Korov. He was a monster, but they had fought together enough times for her to know his weaknesses. He fought without skill or accuracy, relying on brute strength and savagery. And he was too heavy to move fast. She could outmanoeuvre him. Then she realised how absurd she was being.

She might defeat Korov, but Coteaz was a different matter. Besides, he was wrong about her.

'Of course I didn't make it.' She lowered her weapons. 'I got it from Krasner.'

'How?'

'He came to me on the night of his death. He was going to search Xylothek's laboratoriums. He gave me that and made me swear to protect it if he did not return.'

'Krasner knew better than to give something so dangerous to one such as you.'

'One such as me…' Sato shook her head. She crouched next to Khull and examined her wounds, helping her to her feet. The abhuman looked more humiliated than hurt, and she glared at Korov. 'Krasner took me into his confidence long before he brought me that fragment,' said Sato. 'He trusted me, as a fellow Ordo agent. We uncovered some of the bodies together.'

Coteaz studied her in silence. She thought, again, that she might have to fight for her life, but then he softened his tone. 'I received an astropathic message from him. It was only a fragment, but it did imply he had shared something with you.'

He tilted his head to one side as a vox message crackled in his vox-bead. 'Then let them remove the bodies,' he replied. 'But tell the magos that you will stand watch over the remains until I can examine them.' The signal died and he looked back at the fragment of quietus tablet. 'Where did Agent Krasner find this?'

'In the brain of a murder victim.' She stepped closer, itching to snatch it from his grip. 'You know what I could do with it,' she said.

He looked at a rope of knotted parchment that was looped at her belt. 'I have never found another voidborn who can do what you do.'

'And there is significant empyric residue,' she said. 'I could track the maker. I knew it the moment Krasner handed it to me. The person who made the tablet was *consumed* by hate. I can't be sure if the maker is also the person committing the murders, but it's a clear trail. I *could* find them.'

'But you have chosen not to. You have waited here instead, watching tech-priests die. If Krasner *did* trust you, he made a mistake. He died and you did nothing.' Coteaz leant forwards, cold fire in his eyes. 'Why have you let these murders continue? If you saw a route to the mapmaker, why didn't you follow it?'

'Because the mines aren't safe. Krasner told me that when I arrived and Genetor Glycon confirmed it. The place is a powder keg. And for weeks no one has heard anything from them. And finding the person who made the weapon wouldn't necessarily lead me to the killer.'

'There's more to it than that. This is exactly the kind of lead you would usually follow. Why have you waited here?'

She sighed. 'I sensed more than just the mapmaker when I touched that thing. There's something *powerful* behind these murders. There is more than just human hate at work here. That's why I knew Glycon was wrong about the problem just being the fault of rioting miners. I sent word to Inquisitor Zamorin, requesting more troops, but I can't reach him because he's crossed the sector for your conclave.'

'Does Zamorin know about the soul glass?'

'No. I told him I was keeping an eye on Xylothek. I know what he is. You're not the only one who can recognise people's flaws.' She tapped her rosette. 'He was a means to an end. I *did* want him to send troops, but getting word off this planet is impossible. Nothing gets in or out. I knew *you* would come, though. And I knew that with Malevich's Scions we would have enough firepower to deal with whatever's happening in Vespertinus. So I waited.'

'Vespertinus?'

'That's where I think they are – the one who made the quietus tablet. The psykanic trail leads in that direction.'

'You are a liar. You had a chance to tell me about this fragment and you said nothing. You speak of trust between fellow agents, but I had to ransack your room to uncover the truth.'

'Trust? You came to Novalis to *kill* me. Do you think I don't know? You can't think me *such* a fool. I left you. You would never forgive something like that. And now you're looking for an excuse to justify revenge. A way to reassure yourself that murdering me is a rational act rather than a vengeful one. Of course I kept this secret. What other defence do I have than secrets?' She noticed that his hand had fallen to his pistol.

'What will you do with that?' she said, speaking quickly and nodding to the fragment of tablet. 'You tell me that trying to understand the map would be too dangerous. So what use is it without my inner sight? If I die, it's just a piece of lead. But *with* me, it is the key to everything. It can lead us to the mapmaker. We *have* to work together.'

There was a long silence. Coteaz looked her up and down, glaring at the sickles she was wearing and then looking at Khull, his eyes lidded.

'I lied because that fragment was my only chance to stay alive,' she said.

'Always the survivor,' he said.

There was another long pause. Then he nodded and rose to leave, gesturing for Korov to follow. 'I have things to prepare. I will summon you soon.' He handed her the piece of quietus tablet as he left. 'Have the coordinates ready.'

The door rattled shut and the sound of their boots receded down the corridor.

Once their footfalls had faded, Khull turned to Sato and raised an eyebrow. 'How long until he works out you don't have the coordinates?'

'I *will* have them.' She sat in the chair Coteaz had just vacated and stared at the piece of tablet. 'Soon. I just need one last attempt.' In truth, she was surprised Coteaz had bought the story about her wanting to wait for him.

Khull limped to another chair and sat down heavily, rubbing the back of her head and then looking at the blood on her palm. 'And then what?'

Sato was trying to concentrate on the tablet, but something about Khull's tone grated on her. 'And then I will be a step closer to finding the soul glass.'

'And this soul glass, it's incredibly powerful.'

'Get to the point.'

Khull shrugged. 'When you told Coteaz you wanted to work with him, it sounded...' Her lip curled, revealing an enormous, chipped canine. 'Convincing.'

'I need him. How can I survive up there without him?'

'There's more to it than that.' Sato had never seen Khull like this. She was trying to look as scornful as usual, but it was an affectation. Her voice was taut. Her eyes were shining. 'You *do* want to help him. You still trust him. You're still his servant.'

'He's just another tool for me to use.' She waved the piece of tablet. 'Just like this. Just like you.' Sato regretted the last comment, but Khull was being infuriating. 'He's blinded by faith, just like half of the Ordo. Their eyes are so full of religion that they can't walk straight.'

'But not you.'

'No. Not me. I have no desire to martyr myself. I mean to *survive.*'

Khull shrugged, clearly unconvinced.

'Do you know where I was,' said Sato, 'when Coteaz found me?'

'A schola?'

'Buried under a pile of corpses. The corpses of my family, my friends, everyone I knew. They starved and choked on disease, every last one of them, and do you know what? That's not even the real tragedy.' Sato could hear that she was almost shouting, but rage was rising up from her chest in waves. 'The real tragedy is that they never, not for one minute, stopped *believing*. They *believed* that the God-Emperor was testing them. They *believed* that whatever the galaxy threw at them, they would eventually reach Holy Terra, even if they had to die to do it. But while they prayed, I hunted. While they wasted away, beaming at imaginary saints, I ate insects. I caught rats. I *survived*. Their mindless faith will *not* kill me.' She paused for breath and lowered her voice. 'And that's how Coteaz found me. With rat blood under my fingernails and bile in my veins. He thinks he *saved* me. He thinks he lifted me up from that charnel house.' She looked at the blood on the wall, left by Khull's head. 'But I'm still there. Still feeding on rats. Still surviving.'

Khull seemed on the verge of pressing the matter, but then she decided against it. She nodded to the piece of tablet. 'Try now.'

Khull was right. Sato's pulse was hammering in her veins. This could be her chance.

She took a cincture from her belt and tied it around her head. It was made from streamers of knotted parchment, all of which were crowded with text too small to be read by the naked eye. She pulled the parchment so tight that it pressed her eyes into her sockets. Then she gripped the piece of tablet, forcing the corners into her skin, turning it between her fingers. She murmured the mantra, an incoherent jumble of sounds. Her pulse thudded in her eyes in time with the mantra, and it became the sound of a great ocean, breaking on an endless shore. The smell of burning filled the air, and she felt ash settling on her skin. Then, as the throbbing in her eyes became more painful, she began to see lights flickering across her vision. She saw slender columns of rock rising from darkness. It was working. She was seeing a route across Novalis. She was rushing north towards buildings – one of the old processing hives. She wanted to cry out. It was *working*. But she maintained the mantra. She needed to see the mapmaker. She needed to know exactly where they were.

Traitor.

The word filled Sato's thoughts, obliterating everything else. Darkness fell and her inner sight failed. The voice was horrific. It was inhuman and it caressed her skull, grotesquely pervasive, like a cowl of worms, probing and gnawing at her thoughts. Then she realised there was something in the darkness. A shape, coming slowly into focus.

It was a face.

Sato snatched the cincture from her head, throwing it to the floor and jumping from the chair.

'No!' she cried, whirling around, looking for the face, half expecting to see it in the clouds of ash that were floating around her.

Khull leapt from her seat and gripped Sato by the arm. 'What happened?'

'I don't know,' muttered Sato. The memory of the face was quickly fading, and she could not remember the word that had invaded her thoughts. But she could remember the violent nausea it had induced.

'Do you have it? Do you have the coordinates?'

Sato thought of how close she had come before the vision was extinguished. 'Almost.'

Khull frowned.

'It's enough for now,' said Sato. 'It will have to be.'

CHAPTER FOURTEEN

Elias paused at the threshold, waiting for the others to catch up, wanting to see the excitement in their faces. With the help of Helk and Sturm he had freed nearly two hundred workers in a single day. It was incredible. The impossible had become possible. And the speed of change had left him feeling drunk. As he watched the miners climbing through the ruins towards him, he saw their eyes widen with joy. He had brought them to a pinnacle that none of them had ever visited before. It was home to a processing hive called Taphos, and it was cursed. Or, at least, that was what they had always been taught. Taphos was, allegedly, a place filled with ghosts. And, of all the old, abandoned hives, it was the most irradiated. Elias had never heard of *anyone* coming here. So, as people felt the clear air and saw rocks that were free of crystals, they cried out in shock. There were even traces of new life – lichen, moss, and flowers nestling in the cracks and potholes. People grasped his hand and slapped him on the back as they reached the entrance to the ancient tower at the centre of the ruins. Their excitement only grew as their eyes adjusted to the fierce glare of the lumens fixed to the walls. Every surface had been worked and carved until the chamber resembled the inside of a grand palace. Imperial architecture merged seamlessly with unfamiliar motifs.

'Why does it look like this?' gasped Sturm, gazing up at the arches overhead. 'Why does it look beautiful?'

Elias smiled. 'When the Chartists first colonised Novalis, they had grand dreams. They thought they were going to terraform parts of the planet and build a permanent base of operations here. With so much thullic ore to be mined, they wanted to make sure they staked their claim. They soon learned that the place was too toxic for any of that, but when they built the Taphos mine they were still under the impression that this was going to be a long-term operation. They were still aiming high when they converted this pinnacle.' He laughed, bitterly. 'By the time they started work on Vespertinus, they knew they would be lucky to keep the mines going for more than a few decades. So they were less concerned about ornate pillars.'

Helk shook his head. 'Governor Aldrov always said Taphos was the most polluted of all the abandoned mines.' He waved at the walls. They were age-worn, clearly incredibly old, but free of crystals. 'But it looks better than anywhere I've ever seen. How's that possible?'

'It's something to do with the planet's ecology,' said Elias, lying smoothly, replying exactly as his courage had instructed him to. 'There's chem-fog everywhere else in this demus. Governor Aldrov's right in that sense. But here, around the old tower, the air has gradually cleared.' He grinned, thinking of something else his courage had told him. 'Look at this.' Elias threw back the hood of his envirosuit and removed his rebreather. Then he took a deep breath, holding it in his lungs while still smiling at Helk and Sturm, before exhaling with a satisfied sigh. He could still taste fumes, but where before they had been harsh and painful, they now felt like a tonic, flooding his muscles with vigour and sharpening his mind. 'I don't know how it's possible, but it's true. And every time I come here, I feel better.' He tilted his head to one side, showing them the side of his neck.

Sturm reached forward to touch the skin, eyes straining with shock. 'No crystals.'

'They've started coming away,' said Elias. 'It's nothing I've done. I haven't been picking at them. Just coming in here is enough to make them go.'

Helk and Sturm cautiously removed their hoods and took deep breaths. Their eyes shone, and they grinned. 'Feels incredible,' said Helk, filling his lungs again and balling his hands into fists. 'I feel strong. I feel *good.*'

Elias laughed. 'Come and look at this.'

He led them through the crowd of workers, many of whom were following his lead and removing their masks, laughing as vigour flooded their frail bodies. At the back of the entrance hall, there was a magnificent doorway that led onto a smaller chamber with passageways running off it. Elias guided his friends along one of the corridors and into another grand room. There was a long table running down the centre and it was clearly intended as some kind of mess hall. People were dashing back and forth, unloading void-crates and sacks, spilling mounds of food onto the table.

Sturm and Helk had been involved in most of the raids that secured the food, but this was the first time they had seen it all in one place.

'Incredible,' whispered Sturm, staring at the table. As well as the standard fare, like ration packs and cans of corpse starch, there were cuts of real cured meat and even dried fruit.

'No,' laughed Elias, leading them down the length of the

room. 'That's not what I wanted to show you. Look who's here.' He waved to a woman who was hurrying back and forth, directing the people carrying the food.

Helk and Sturm frowned in confusion, then Helk shook his head. 'Elzevyr?'

Elias nodded, grinning, before hurrying over to embrace her.

'How did it go?' she asked, hugging him back.

'Well. Very well.' He nodded back to the doorway. 'Come on. Come and see.'

'What's happened to you?' said Helk as he and Sturm approached her, shaking their heads.

She blushed, but turned on her heel for them, showing how much of her skin was free of the crystals. 'No more tubes in my lungs,' she said. She no longer showed any misgivings about what Elias was doing, which made him all the more certain he was on the right path.

'It's a miracle,' whispered Helk.

Elias felt the two men staring at him, looking at him with the same, almost religious devotion he had seen before. It made him feel uncomfortable. 'Come on,' he said. 'Let's introduce Elzevyr to the new arrivals.'

They did not have to walk far. The crowd was already exploring the palace and people began spilling into the mess hall. As they saw the mounds of food, some of them rushed forwards, but Elzevyr intercepted them, raising her hands. 'Wait at this end of the table. Sit down. There's plenty for everyone, but we don't want a feeding frenzy.' As people did as she asked, she handed them plates of food.

As Elias moved through the crowd he touched as many people as he could, patting shoulders and shaking hands. His courage had told him this was the quickest way to spread strength and health among the others.

Sturm and Helk eyed the plates hungrily, and Elias laughed. 'You've earned some of that. Join the others. I have someone I need to talk to.'

Neither of the men needed convincing, and Elzevyr had already forgotten about him, busy coordinating the people who were flooding into the hall, so Elias took his chance to slip away, patting and hugging people as he went. He crossed the far end of the hall and left the room, heading down a smaller corridor that looked like it had been built for menials or victuallers. Here, cracks marred the mosaicked floors and crimson stains striped the walls. At some point the palace had been as polluted as the rest of Novalis. The red rain had obviously seeped up through the floor of all the rooms until, at some point in the recent past, for some unknown reason, it had stopped.

As he hurried on down the corridor, he wondered how long it would be before his friends demanded an explanation. They seemed to have accepted his earlier comment about changes in the environment, but surely someone would soon guess that there was more going on? He pressed on, too excited to concern himself with matters he could do nothing about. The vigour he could feel in his body was so wonderful that it had to be right. The corridor became steps, cut deep into the pinnacle, and after a while, the sounds of the crowd faded along with the light. In these subterranean parts of the tower, most of the lumens were still lifeless, and the steps gradually sank into darkness.

Elias unclasped a pocket lumen from his envirosuit and clicked it on, splashing a ray of light across cracked floor tiles and stained walls. There were still a few mouldering tapestries hanging from the ceiling, and as his lumen splashed over them, it picked out distorted faces from the rotten cloth: warriors who should have looked heroic but were grotesque instead.

Gradually, as he headed deeper underground, the palace began to lose its shape, its structure crumbled in many places and indistinguishable from the original rock faces. There were no traces of Imperial influence in these lower levels. There was even more lichen and mould down here, and spores drifted around him as he walked. He paused, looking back to make sure he hadn't been followed, then turned left through an opening that was barely recognisable as a doorway. These chambers had lain hidden for so long. The tales of Taphos' polluted air meant that, before Elias, no one would have dared look here. The thought made him feel incredibly privileged.

He passed through an antechamber, then entered another huge hall. This one was entirely in darkness, so Elias had to pick his way carefully over the rubble that littered the floor, flicking his light back and forth as he made his way to the large shape at the centre of the room. The space was so vast that it took him a few minutes to reach his destination: a broad plinth supporting an enormous stone bowl. The structure resembled a chalice but was big enough that broad steps circled the plinth. Elias hurried up them and looked down into the bowl of the chalice. It was a circular bathing pool, surrounded by tiered stone steps that led down to dark, oily-looking water. The water was stagnant; the first time he came here, Elias had gagged on the stench, but since then he had grown used to the smell. It was rich and earthy, but he now found it oddly comforting, like the musk from an old, familiar piece of furniture.

The pool in the chalice was not where Elias' courage had first spoken to him, but in recent weeks, it had been the only place he could hear the voice. The voice had explained that this chalice was its route into the real world from the realm of gods and spirits. Elias had not entirely understood, but he knew that the chalice was a sacred, important site. He glanced back into the darkness, checking for signs of Elzevyr or the others. As far as he was aware, they knew nothing of the bathhouse or the chalice, but he felt nervous all the same. There were no telltale flickers of light, so he sat cross-legged at the edge of the pool.

He had known, for a while now, that he was going insane. It was impossible for him to have learned the things he had learned. To have done the things he had done. For a while he had struggled with the obvious lunacy of what was happening to him. He had even considered talking to the overseers and begging them for help. But then he started to see what he was achieving through his madness. The voice in his mind had enabled him to help those who never expected to be helped. The voice had shown him hope. Hope! Who would ever have looked for such a thing in the mines of Novalis? Then, as the wonderful vigour began to fill his body, he stopped questioning the source. He felt more alive than he had ever done before. If this was madness then he no longer wished to be sane. He was starting to think that he really could cheat death. And then, as his excitement grew, and he visited the bathhouse more often, he had even begun to *see* his courage.

'Why did you let the guards live?'

The words rose from the water and reverberated through the darkness: rich, powerful, full of warmth. In the beginning, Elias had only heard the voice in his head, but as he grew stronger and healthier, it had begun leaking into the outside world.

'There was no need for them to die,' he replied, gazing down into the liquid. 'They weren't going to put up a fight. They're our captives now, but in time I think many of them will come round to our way of thinking.'

As Elias' eyes adjusted to the darkness, he saw a deeper gloom, beneath the surface of the pool. He had seen it before and it fascinated him. He thought he understood what it was now: it was him – him as he would be if he stayed true, if he followed the path his courage had laid out for him. The shadow was human-shaped, but much larger than a normal man.

'You are a good man, Elias.' The figure shifted position, drifting through the darkness. ***'But do not judge others by your standards. You have taken a risk allowing those guards to live. If one of them were to escape, they could tell people you are here in this tower. And you are not ready. Not yet.'***

Elias peered at the shape in the pool, trying to discern a face, but the shadow was as mobile and intangible as smoke. 'They're well guarded,' he said. 'And once they realised we didn't plan on killing them, most were keen to understand what we're planning. They're just as unhappy as the rest of us. They're all dying too.' He smiled. 'Or, at least, they *were* dying, until we brought them up here into this wonderful air and gave them some real food. That was when they really started to show an interest in our plans. I don't want to be like them – not the worst parts of them. I want to be better. I want us all to be better.'

The voice laughed, but not in mockery. It was a compassionate, happy sound. ***'I keep underestimating you. Keeping them alive was the kind thing to do. They are just as oppressed as everyone else. Just be sure to watch them closely.'***

Elias nodded. 'That's what I wanted to ask about. I… It's just…' His words faltered. When the voice first spoke to him, he had found it comforting, like revisiting a happy memory, but now, now that so much was at stake, he had become afraid. What if he angered the voice in the chalice? What if he said the wrong thing? What if it went away? So many lives were now in his hands. So many people were relying on him.

'The wheels are in motion. But you have to tread carefully now. You have weapons and you have people, but you do not have an army.'

'An army? Is that what we will become?' Elias shook his head. 'Capturing a few overseers is one thing, but we can't start a war.'

The voice did not sound angered by Elias' doubt. Its tone remained sympathetic and humorous. *'You have only seen a small piece of the puzzle. You are not alone. All across the Formosa Sector, people are standing up against oppression. People are refusing to accept short, brutal lives while others grow old in luxury. Why should people die at all? We can be reborn and renewed, over and over. You have tasted immortality, Elias. And what you see here in these mines is one thread of a vast tapestry. All you need to do is ready yourself. You need to keep yourself safe until your brothers arrive and lift you from your hellish prison. And on that day, Novalis will rise. And it is all thanks to you. You, who have completed every task without hesitation. Do you remember the first thing you did for me?'*

Elias nodded. The memory was incredibly vivid. 'You showed me how to find that sheet of lead.' He pictured the unremarkable piece of metal. His courage had spoken of it in reverential tones, calling it a 'quietus tablet', but it had seemed like a piece of useless junk to Elias. 'And how to score those symbols across it.' Elias smiled. 'And everything stemmed from that.'

'It did. And the quietus tablet was not simply a way to cure your illness. It is a beacon, Elias. Even now, as we speak, my friend is using it and it is starting to kindle. Soon, its flame will reach out into the stars. A signal. A cry for help. And trust me, Elias, that cry will be heard. Thousands will rush to answer it. You are not alone. Your strength and bravery has bought you a position of power.'

Power. The voice could not have used a more potent word. Since his earliest childhood memories, Elias had been tormented by his lack of it. The first thing he could remember was working in the darkness of the mines, trapped and powerless to act, watching people die young, knowing that he too would soon die. He had no interest in wealth, but he dreamt, constantly, of how it would be to choose his own path in life, and to have the ability to save the wretched souls who worked with him.

'So what do I need to do now?' he asked.

'One small thing. The beacon will soon be lit, but there is a final task for you to perform.' A coldness had entered the voice that Elias had never heard before. *'Someone is coming to Taphos, Elias, coming to these ruins, to this very tower. His name is Coteaz, and he means to do you harm. He means to end what you have begun. If he's not stopped, he will take everything you've worked so hard to achieve, and he will send you back to the darkness. The health you have given to your friends will be stolen.'*

'No,' whispered Elias, picturing Elzevyr as she was before he brought her to Taphos, before she had food and medicine. 'That can't happen.'

'It won't.' The voice was calm and compassionate again. *'If you prepare things exactly as I describe, this will be the final hurdle, Elias. Once Coteaz has been dealt with, your path will be clear.'*

'Who is he?' Elias pictured Elzevyr's face again, her eyes full of concern. 'Who is Coteaz?'

'He is the last obstacle, Elias, but you need not be afraid. Everything is in hand. The moment you created the talisman, you made sure of that. Coteaz can do nothing to stop us. As long as you trust in me.'

'Yes,' he said, nodding quickly. 'I understand. What must I do?'

'Bathe with me, Elias. As a final act of fealty. Join me in the pool and I will explain everything.'

Elias studied the black, viscous water. He felt a flicker of doubt as he considered how ancient it must be, and how foetid, but it was a fleeting hesitation. It was like a memory of fear rather than the genuine emotion. His whole body was shaking with excitement. He felt so powerful. So alive. And all because of the voice. How could he fail to trust it? Besides, the smell wafting from the pool was oddly enticing, calling to him like a warm bed at the end of a long day.

He climbed down the steps and found, as he sank into the water, that it was wonderfully warm. He paused, with the water halfway up his chest, and began to laugh. Then he sank beneath the surface.

CHAPTER FIFTEEN

'Vespertinus.' The pilot gestured through the viewport. 'The central hub. It's the largest of the old processing hives. One of the few with mines that are still operational. No mistaking it.' He had to raise his voice or the words would have been drowned out by the flyer's wings, thrumming around the fuselage. Voltas peered through the crimson-stained armaglass, trying to make out the distant shapes. The view was blurred by the rising rain, but he saw that the nearest pinnacle was covered in a sprawling mass of man-made structures: manufactoria, drill rigs, and eight-legged vehicles that lumbered slowly across the crystal. They looked tiny, trailing fumes from smoke-stack crests, but he could tell from the figures near them that they were huge.

Voltas turned to look at Sato. She was seated with Coteaz, near the pilot. At the pilot's words she took out a noose of vellum streamers and tightened it around her head, blindfolding herself. Voltas was close enough to identify some of the sigils on the vellum. They were rites of warding – prayers designed to protect the wearer from warp entities. She was gripping something in her fist, but he could not see what.

'Quiet,' she said, despite the fact that everyone had fallen silent.

She turned the object in her hand, rolling it across her fingertips like a conjuror with a coin. Voltas found it hypnotic to watch. Sato's fingers undulated in a way that seemed quite unnatural, folding and wrapping around each other. She was murmuring something behind the strips of parchment. Voltas noticed then that something was happening to her skin. A fine dust was rising from her hands and her complexion was growing darker. The acrid smell of brimstone filled the cabin, and Voltas coughed as some of the dust hit the back of his throat. It was only as he tasted it that he realised it was ash. Clouds of it began to blossom around Sato as she continued muttering to herself.

Voltas had read texts on prognostication and sympathetic magic, and what he was seeing looked suspiciously like sorcery. But Coteaz, that most puritanical of puritans, seemed content for it to continue.

Sato stopped murmuring and sighed, secreting the object back in her armour. The clouds of ash immediately began to disperse. 'Not here,' she said, removing her blindfold and tying it back to her belt. Coteaz was about to speak, but she held up her hand. 'This *is* the right direction. We are following the right river. But its springs lie further north, beyond Vespertinus.'

Coteaz looked at the pilot that Magos Xylothek had provided. 'What lies to the north of here?'

'Chem-wastes, lord inquisitor. Irradiated rock. Like the rest of the planet.'

'And after that?'

The pilot frowned. 'Taphos, if you go far enough. Another processing hive. One of the earlier ones, abandoned decades ago. I don't know the details I'm afraid, my lord.'

Voltas leant forwards. 'I studied the original colonisation plans, Lord Coteaz. Taphos housed the first mines to be built and the first to be abandoned. The name Taphos predates the hive. The ruins are an ancient site of worship. They date back to the time when man first left Holy Terra and began to explore the stars.'

The pilot shook his head, clearly unnerved by where the conversation was going. 'It's not possible to land there, my lord. The pollution's even worse than here. Vespertinus has an array of chem-screens. They shield us from the worst of the radiation. There's nothing like that at Taphos. And there are terrible storms. Even in an envirosuit it would be very dangerous to stay out there for any length of time.'

'How far?' said Coteaz.

The pilot swallowed hard. 'Thirty miles.'

'Then continue heading north.'

Voltas was just about to ask the pilot a question when the shuttle leapt sideways with a scream of breaking metal.

The engines stuttered and died.

There was an ominous quiet as the flyer dropped, turning as it fell.

The fumes were so thick that it took Voltas a moment to see that the pilot was dead, knocked sideways in his harness, blood rushing from a hole in the side of his helmet.

'Lasweapons,' said Malevich. 'Took out the fuel line.' He grabbed the control yoke from the dead man's hands and tried to right the shuttle, but with the engine damaged, it failed to respond.

Voltas strained to look out through a viewport. 'We need to glide.' He had studied the vehicle's schematics and he scanned through them in his mind. 'Lock the pitch,' he said, gesturing to levers on the control panel.

Malevich flicked the levers and the wings snapped into a

horizontal axis. The shuttle flipped again then steadied as the Scion leant over the pilot's corpse, grappling with the flight stick. Wind screamed through the holes in the fuselage and klaxons began barking from the control panel.

As Malevich brought the shuttle into a stable dive, a wall of rock rushed at them through the smog. Voltas saw details on the rock face as it hurtled towards them. With a final wrench Malevich managed to change the flyer's trajectory so that it was approaching the rock at a shallower angle, but they were still only moments away from impact.

Coteaz twisted in his seat, looking back through the fumes at Turcifel. She looked coolly back at him.

'We'll die,' said Coteaz over the vox-network.

She stared at him with what seemed to be defiance, then she closed her eyes and nodded.

'We only have seconds before we hit,' said Malevich as the surface of the pinnacle rushed towards them.

Suddenly the temperature in the cabin cooled, dropping so quickly that Voltas almost cried out in surprise, feeling as though his skin was covered in frost. His tried to demand an explanation but no sound emerged. Then he realised there was no sound coming from anywhere. Silence had engulfed the shuttle. Light blossomed from Turcifel's prayer beads, spilling through her fingers and blinding him. The tattoo that spiralled down from her eye seemed to come alive, twisting and coiling over her cheek. Coteaz was staring at Turcifel and they were both praying, mouthing words in unison.

The light was too bright to see anything, but Voltas was sure they should have hit the surface by now. The cold grew so intense that Voltas felt like his blood was freezing.

Enough, said Coteaz. The cabin was still silent, and Voltas realised that the inquisitor's voice was only in his mind.

The cold vanished. Sounds returned: heavy, panicked breathing, the rain outside, the blaring of alarms.

The flyer was motionless, lying at a peculiar angle, its fuselage oddly distorted. The metal had bloated in some places and sagged in others. Voltas unfastened his harness and climbed hesitantly to his feet, gripping his seat. The whole structure of the vehicle had been altered, and there were spurs of red crystal jutting up through the floor like the branches of a dead tree.

Voltas saw that behind the passengers, the shuttle was open to the sky. Crimson rain poured up past a gaping hole in the fuselage.

'Quickly,' said Captain Malevich. 'Whoever fired on us is still out there. And we're exposed up here.'

They unfastened their harnesses and began clambering to the rear of the flyer.

'High-calibre laser,' said Malevich, putting his finger in the holes in the fuselage. He peered at the damage. 'Rapid fire. Probably a multi-laser. Militarum issue.'

As Voltas reached the opening behind the seats he saw that the shuttle was cradled in a stone claw at the end of a long, spindly limb. It looked like a geyser had burst from the crystal and solidified on contact with the shuttle. And that was not the only strange thing about their landing. Pieces of the vehicle's hull filled the air – fragments of plasteel were hanging, motionless around the vessel. It looked like a pict capture of an explosion. And some of the pieces had been transformed into hybridised matter – part metal, part red crystal, and part solidified smoke. They looked like fragments of a discarded painting. As Voltas followed the others out into the cloying rain, it was like stepping into a work of abstract art, surrounded by drifting vertices and planes. He looked at Turcifel with new-found respect. Coteaz must be *very* sure of himself to include such a dangerous weapon in his inner circle.

'Fasten your hood,' said Malevich. 'And the rebreather.' They were all clad in black, rubbery envirosuits supplied by Magos Xylothek. Apart from Coteaz. As everyone else fastened their hoods, he donned a golden ceramite helmet that was as beautiful as the rest of his antique armour.

Rain lashed against Voltas' suit as he stepped out onto the limb of rock. It was a strange experience, having rain drumming against the underside of his chin, rather than coming down onto his head. He looked over the side of the narrow bridge Turcifel had summoned, staring down into a dizzying abyss. It was disorienting watching the banks of red rain hurtling up towards him from the darkness, and he stumbled.

He walked over to Turcifel's side. 'You have incredible power at your command,' he said, staring at the shapes hanging suspended all around them. In some places, the air itself seemed to have bulged, like bubbles in glass, distorting the view.

She gave him a suspicious look and he noticed that she was running her beads through her fingers in a frenzied manner, her hands trembling as they moved.

Captain Malevich ordered his troops to spread out along the slender bridge; once in place they all kneeled and put their lasguns to their shoulders, looking out into the storm. He waved everyone else on with his pistol. 'Onto the rocks. Find cover.'

As he hurried along, Voltas glanced back at the shuttle. From the outside, the distortion was much more noticeable. Only the cabin had remained unchanged. The wings and the fuselage were unrecognisable. The metal seemed to have melted, or dissolved into the air. Whorls of plasteel stretched upwards like spun sugar, making it hard to distinguish the wreckage from the rain. They had become a single glittering mass.

'Quickly,' said Malevich, hurrying them on.

They reached the end of the bridge Turcifel had created and

dropped down onto the ground. The stalagmite was vast, larger than any mountain Voltas had seen. Some of the ledges on its sides were many hundreds of feet broad and were littered with the remnants of old processing plants and rail tracks. The expanse they had stepped out onto was networked with similar pieces of rubble – engine parts and scraps of architecture so old and crystallised they seemed like the fossils of long-dead leviathans.

Coteaz had paused and was talking to his psyber-eagle, but he looked up at Malevich's words and nodded. 'Keep moving,' he said, waving towards the hulking remains of an old building. 'Head for that refinery. Follow Thula.' With that he launched the bird into the air, and it pounded off through the rain.

Captain Malevich split his Scions into two groups. One raced ahead, sprinting after the eagle, while the others remained at the rear of the group, scanning the plateau through their gunsights.

Voltas followed Coteaz's lead and began running through the storm, shadowing Coteaz and the Scions. It was hard to see anything with the rain washing up over his hood. The shapes ahead became ruddy smears, and he had to keep wiping the visor to see even that much. It was a dangerous situation and Voltas was pleased to be in combat with the High Protector. Every fight was a chance to prove his worth.

'Hostiles at two o'clock!' Malevich's voice snarled over the vox. 'Drop!'

Voltas sensed, rather than saw, people falling to the ground. He did the same, gripping a pistol in one hand and carefully drawing his power sword with the other.

'A Sentinel,' said Malevich. 'Mars pattern. Armed with a multi-laser. Probably the one that took out the shuttle.'

Voltas squinted through the rain. There was no sign of Captain Malevich or anyone else. He knew that Turcifel could only be a few feet or so from him, but even she was hidden by the jagged, teeth-like ruins that covered the rocks. But over near the ruined warehouse, he saw a gangly, bipedal shape stalking silently through the gloom. Malevich was right. It was an Astra Militarum combat walker – an armoured, two-legged vehicle used to scout out combat zones.

'There are no Militarum regiments on Novalis,' he whispered over the vox as the shape moved closer, swinging its weapon from side to side as it hunted for prey. 'Where did it come from?'

'The governor has vehicles and ordnance,' replied Coteaz over the vox.

'And he's using them against an inquisitor?' said Voltas.

'Perhaps he thought we were an enemy,' suggested Malevich.

'Our callsign was clear,' replied Coteaz. 'As were our markings. These men might not be loyal to the governor. This could be linked to the insurrection Glycon described.'

The vehicle was still pacing across the rocks in ominous silence, moving slowly towards them.

'Malevich,' said Coteaz. 'How many shots to take it down?'

'They're only lightly armoured. Korov could probably take out the driver with one shot if he uses his lascutter. He would need to get closer, though. This rain is a problem. And if we miss, that thing will bolt.'

'You won't need to move closer,' said Coteaz. 'It's headed our way. No need to break cover.'

Something was troubling Voltas about the situation. 'Lord inquisitor,' he said. 'I have studied tactical treatises concerning the deployment of Scout Sentinels. They are designed for subterfuge. Enemy forces rarely see them until it is too late. But this walker is making no attempt to conceal itself.'

'Understood,' replied Coteaz. 'Malevich, scatter your troops. This could be a trap.'

'Fan out!' snapped Malevich. 'Take your–'

The world became blue-and-white fire. Voltas fell back as rocks and metal exploded all around him, hurling shards and dust. He rolled through clouds of debris and tumbled into a ditch, clamping his hands over his head as Turcifel dropped down next to him. The din was horrendous. The thundercrack of discharging lasers pounded his ears, and the ground lurched.

They both hunkered down as flames bloomed overhead and metal clattered across the ground. Voltas risked a glimpse over the top of the ditch and saw that the explosion was the work of Korov. He was stomping through the smoke, heedless of the gunfire, using all of his mechadendrites to cradle a lasweapon so large it looked as if it had been ripped from the turret of a personnel carrier. Embers whirled round him as his gun spat light through the gloom, and he howled with every shot: 'Recant! Recant! Recant!' There were Sentinels everywhere. Voltas guessed there were dozens of the things. One turned and ran towards Korov, but he blasted its legs, sending the cockpit crashing down onto the rocks in another ball of flames. 'Transgressor!'

Behind Korov, Captain Malevich and his Scions had fanned out in a circle. Coteaz's warning had been in time to save them. They had all dropped to one knee, and as Malevich bellowed commands they calmly aimed lasguns, taking precise shots, tearing the walkers apart one by one.

There was a howl from behind him, and Voltas turned to see Inquisitor Sato advancing beside her abhuman. The thing was in a frenzy, trailing drool from her muzzle as she ran towards a Sentinel, swinging her chainaxe. The Sentinel came to a halt and the driver fired at Khull, but the creature just grinned, weaving from side to side and dodging the gunfire. Then she gave another roar and leapt at the walker, jamming the chainaxe through its legs, shredding cables and armour plating.

There was a shower of sparks and hydraulic fluid and the Sentinel toppled sideways, hurling Khull through the air. The cockpit hit the ground, and while Khull was still tumbling across the rocks, the Sentinel's driver emerged and aimed a pistol.

A chain snaked through the air and lashed around the man's neck, jolting him towards Sato, who was vaulting up the side of the Sentinel. The chain was attached to one of her sickles, and as the driver grasped at his throat, struggling to free himself, she sliced the other blade into his skull.

The driver dropped to the ground, dead, as Khull staggered to her feet and saw what Sato had done. The creature threw back her head, bellowing into the rain and pounding the handle of her chainaxe against her chest armour.

Voltas leapt from the ditch and opened fire at the nearest Sentinel, targeting a weak point in its leg armour. The machine staggered and fell, smashing to the ground. He dropped another one the same way. Then, as he looked around for a new target, he saw a flash of light that was different to the las-fire. It came from the direction of the warehouse – a dazzling white nimbus, as if a star had fallen onto the rocks.

Turcifel leapt from the ditch and raced off through the battle towards the light.

Shots kicked up the ground at his feet as he sprinted after her. 'Turcifel!' he called, but his voice was lost in the din.

A figure lurched towards him through the smoke. The fumes confused him, and he thought at first that it was Turcifel returning to look for him, but as the shape loomed closer he saw that it was one of the Sentinels' drivers – a gaunt, crook-backed man in a ragged yellow envirosuit. He was holding a lasgun that dripped rain as he pointed it at Voltas.

Voltas dropped and rolled, dodging the shot. Then he flipped gracefully up onto his feet and slid his rapier through the man's respirator.

The man stood rigid for a moment, his hood filling with blood, before he slid from the blade and hit the ground, his gun clattering across the rocks.

Someone roared behind Voltas and he turned to see Khull standing over another yellow-clad corpse, her chainaxe grinding the man's head, spitting blood and bone. The abhuman stared hungrily at her kill then leered at Voltas, licking blood from her muzzle.

Voltas felt a wave of disgust and wished he could gun the thing down. He watched as Khull snorted, then loped off through the rain, howling and laughing.

Shots whined from every direction, slicing the fumes like razors, and Voltas ran on, looking for Turcifel. He saw the flash of white light up ahead again and sprinted in that direction, wiping his blade clean as he went.

As he neared the ruined warehouses he saw tall and narrow openings, just wide enough for the Sentinels to have emerged from. The light was blinking from the mouth of one of them. He advanced cautiously, duelling pistol in one hand, rapier in the other.

A yellow-clad mob had gathered at the entrance. All of them were armed with Militarum weapons: lasguns, pistols, swords and shock mauls. He guessed there were over twenty, but, heavily armed as they were, they were struggling to hold their ground against a single attacker. As Voltas saw Coteaz he stumbled to a halt, shaking his head. The inquisitor's hammer was bleeding light, turning the rain silver and igniting a halo around Coteaz. Despite the brutality of his blows, the High Protector seemed set apart from the violence. He reminded Voltas of a saint in a fresco, descended from the heavens. Prayers thundered from his mouth with as much force as his hammer, and his eagle circled him, tearing faces and ripping throats.

Voltas' weapons dropped to his sides as he watched, transfixed. It was not Coteaz's strength or skill that gripped him but something harder to explain. He had seen it several times before. There was a power that shone from him. Voltas thought of the mind he had glimpsed in the cogitator stacks. Coteaz's obsessions and risk-taking made sense because he was *unstoppable.* Voltas had grown up in a world of duplicity and politicking, where most decisions were driven by a need for protection. But here was a man who needed no one. Voltas felt a kind of hunger. This was what he needed to become. This was what he *would* become.

Turcifel appeared at his side. She tried to look aloof, but her eyes were bright with emotion.

Coteaz had climbed up a piece of rubble and raised his hammer, howling litanies to the storm as enemies crumpled around him, clutching wounds and staring up at him in terror.

Voltas realised which fresco Coteaz reminded him of. 'He looks like an image of the Emperor.'

Turcifel gave him a surprised look, as though he had unearthed a secret.

'I should help,' said Voltas. Coteaz was clearly in no need of help. He had already crushed half of the colonists and the others were trying to flee. But Voltas wanted to join him. To fight at his side. He approached slowly, trying to quell his excitement, pistol raised, loosing off shots with methodical precision.

If Coteaz noticed Voltas' skill he gave no sign of it, dropping back onto the ground and continuing to pummel the crowd. By the time Voltas reached him, most of the colonists were dead, lying in a heap around the warehouse entrance, but one of them was trying to crawl, despite terrible injuries. He was straining to reach a lascarbine that had fallen a few feet away.

Coteaz approached the crawling man and grabbed him by his envirosuit, lifting him from the ground.

The colonist was bleeding heavily and his hood had been torn off. He should have been dead, but instead he grinned, lashing out with a knife. Coteaz turned the weapon away with ease and stared at him.

The man landed useless punches on Coteaz's chest and head, and was still grinning as the inquisitor dragged him towards the warehouse.

'Wait,' said Coteaz, directing his words at Voltas. Then he hauled his captive into the darkness. As he vanished into the shadows, he was unfastening the hourglass from his armour.

Voltas looked back the way he had come and saw that the fight was almost over. Every one of the Sentinels had been toppled, sending plumes of promethium smoke into the rain. Captain Malevich was leading his Scions towards the ruined buildings, picking off survivors, with Korov and Sixtus following close behind. The abhuman was hunched over a dead driver, tearing at the corpse until Sato ordered her to move away.

A panicked scream echoed out of the warehouse. Voltas looked back at the opening but saw nothing. There was another desperate howl, then silence.

Coteaz re-emerged into the rain, fastening the hourglass to his belt. His hammer was fixed to his back and he looked calm, but before the rain cleaned them, Voltas saw that his gauntlets were dark with blood.

'Was he insane?' asked Voltas. 'Why was he smiling?'

Coteaz did not reply. He was holding something. It was a piece of jewellery – a metal disc, dangling at the end of a chain.

Voltas and the others stepped closer as Coteaz held it up. It was crudely made but looked vaguely like a winged sun. Voltas trawled his memories for a likeness.

'Heliocultists,' he said. 'They used this kind of symbol, until it was deemed heretical. They believed the sun was an incarnation of the God-Emperor.'

Coteaz still said nothing, secreting the necklace in one of the reliquaries locked to his belt.

Voltas persevered. 'If the colonists follow a proscribed faith, that would be reason enough for them to shoot down the shuttle. They would be panicked by the arrival of an inquisitor.'

'*Two* inquisitors,' said Sato, emerging from the rain, folding away her chain-sickles and mag-locking them to her thighs. 'But how could they know we were in there?'

Voltas shrugged. 'Perhaps they have a way of tapping into Mechanicus logic networks?' he said. 'Or perhaps they received word of us from Port Gomera?'

'We can't stay out here,' said Coteaz. 'Xylothek said the suits will protect us for an hour, maybe a little more, but only if we avoid the rain.' He led them into a ruined building.

'We'll have to call for transport,' said Voltas. 'Xylothek had aircars.'

Coteaz shook his head as they headed into the ruins. 'It would take too long.'

'You might not get through to them, anyway,' said Sato, waving at the rain outside. 'The vox-channels on this planet are next to useless. Most of the frequencies are unreliable even when it's *not* raining. It's hard to reach someone who's only half a mile away. You might as well shout.'

'We could try Vespertinus,' said Voltas. 'I saw drill rigs as we came down. Scavenger engines and smaller machines. We can't be far from the hub.'

Sato shrugged. 'You could try. I doubt you'd reach the hub in time, but you might get through to one of the scavenger engines.' She nodded to the corpses outside. 'But the miners don't seem pleased to see us.'

Voltas replied to Coteaz rather than Sato. 'Genetor Glycon said there was trouble up here. But he didn't say *all* of the miners were dangerous. I managed to access some of his reports while we were at Domus Alpha.'

Sato looked impressed. 'You broke into their records?'

Voltas continued speaking to Coteaz. 'Glycon's reports were heavily encrypted, even by the standards of the Mechanicus, so I have yet to extract all the details, but they referred to a dangerous minority rather than wholescale insurrection.'

'They're still sending ore to Port Gomera,' conceded Sato, 'which does imply at least some of the miners are still loyal. There's been no word from them for the last few weeks, but Magos Xylothek told me that's normal. Either way there's a risk, though. If we send out a distress call, who's to say we won't end up attracting the wrong kind of attention?'

She looked at Coteaz and everyone else did the same.

'We have less than an hour,' he said, 'before your envirosuits start to fail. If we get caught in an ambush, we might still be out here fighting when your rebreathers stop working. Sixtus, plot a route from here to the governor's compound.'

'From here to the governor's compound.' Sixtus made a burbling sound behind his visor. 'We are close to the governor's compound and several maintenance trenches are still passable, but it will be a steep climb once we leave this plateau. It will take us two point three hours to reach the gates of the governor's stronghold at the centre of the mining hub, if we move as fast as possible, running whenever we are not climbing.'

'Check your envirosuits,' said Coteaz. 'We leave now.'

'Lord inquisitor,' said Voltas, as the others busied themselves examining their suits for damage and checking the seals. 'The suits last an hour. And the journey is over two hours.'

Coteaz held his hand out into the rain. The psyber-eagle soared into view, shrouded in crimson mist. She hovered, pounding her enormous wings, then landed on Coteaz's outstretched arm. He spoke quietly to her as she shuffled up and down his arm, heads tilting and swaying. Coteaz took a strip of parchment from one of the reliquaries fixed to his armour, wrote on it, then folded it and sealed it with a ring on his finger. The eagle waited calmly as he opened a small hatch under her chest feathers and placed the message inside, then she launched herself back into the storm in a flurry of wings and rain.

'Thula will take word to Governor Aldrov,' said Coteaz as he checked the seals on his helmet. 'He will send aircars to meet us as we make our way to the mining hub. Follow Sixtus to the maintenance trench. Once we reach it, Malevich and I will lead with half of the Scions. The rest will take the rear.' Malevich and the other Scions saluted.

Rain lashed up over them as they broke from the ruins, weapons raised, and ran after Sixtus. Voltas struggled to see clearly as he followed. The rain glooped up over his visor and his breath steamed the inside, giving him the unpleasant sensation he was swimming through blood. Most of the rain rose in thin streams, but in the distance he saw great geysers, hissing as they belched up from the rocks and ruins. He squinted at the corpses as he ran past them, keeping his pistol trained on their forms in case they moved, then Sixtus called out and led the group into a narrow channel cut into the rocks.

There was less light in the trench but more cover. The walls of the man-made crevasse were sheer, unclimbable rockcrete and they were hundreds of feet tall. No one could scale down and attack them. And if anyone was waiting in ambush, the way was too narrow for more than a few people to approach at once.

Captain Malevich made a hand gesture, indicating that it

was safe to advance, and all the Scions triggered lumens on the barrels of their guns, picking out the way ahead.

'Warn me before we reach anything of interest,' said Coteaz, his voice sounding metallic and harsh through the mouthpiece of his helmet.

'Anything of interest,' replied Sixtus. 'There is an opening. Half a mile from here. The ruins of an abandoned comms tower. Oval in shape. Most of the tower is gone, but we will pass through the centre of the ruins and be exposed at that point.'

Coteaz hefted his warhammer, testing its weight as he glanced back at the group. 'Be ready. The Emperor is watching.' With that, the group moved on.

'Interrogator,' said a voice in Voltas' ear. He turned to face Inquisitor Sato. She was walking at his side, keeping her voice low. 'What is your name?'

'Voltas,' he replied. 'The ninth son of House Voltas.' Sato gave no sign that she recognised the name, which told him that she was disingenuous. The Voltas family were one of the largest mercantile dynasties in the Formosa Sector. Their crest was emblazoned on everything from corpse starch to the hulls of voidships.

'And what do you do, Voltas? What are your skills? Other than dressing so beautifully.'

'Courtesan,' growled the abhuman.

Voltas refused to acknowledge the creature.

'I presume, by the way you *intoned* your family name, that you are well connected,' said Sato. 'You could still get away.'

'From what?'

'Coteaz. He'll be the death of you. Either physically or...' She glanced back at Korov. 'Spiritually. Either way, you're fuel for his fire. And by the time you realise what's happening, you'll have forgotten that you were ever anything other than one of his appendages.' She looked at Turcifel, who was whispering to her prayer beads as she climbed the path.

Voltas could not believe the idiocy of the woman, slandering Coteaz to one of his own retainers. 'My faith in Inquisitor Coteaz is constant, unlike your own. He is my lord,' he said.

'But you are *nothing* to him.' She waved at the others in the group. 'He will hold you tight, but only until he disposes of you.'

The woman was bitter and tragic. Voltas almost pitied her. He wondered what had led to her schism with Coteaz. How had she fallen so far from the High Protector's favour? Again, it occurred to him that it might be useful to know how she lost Coteaz's trust.

'What do you want?' he asked.

Something flashed in her eyes, as if she sensed that he was judging her. 'Whatever you think you're going to get out of this relationship, you'll be disappointed. You're just grist to his mill.'

'All I desire is a chance to serve.'

'A chance to serve. A chance to achieve.' She did a peculiar thing with her arms, knotting them around each other. 'That's what he guards most jealously.'

Voltas thought of the things he saw in the abandoned cogitator stacks, back on the *Pilgrim's Wrath*. He felt a surge of pride as he realised how different he was from this peculiar, voidborn woman. 'If Lord Coteaz never took you into his confidence, after all the years you spent with him, perhaps you should ask yourself why,' he said. 'Perhaps he had good reason to keep you in the dark.'

'He's probably fed you some scraps, but don't delude yourself – he's only showing you a fraction of the bigger picture. Did he tell you why he's here?'

'He did.'

She looked surprised, but before she could ask him anything else, the group came to a halt.

'The opening is up ahead, lord inquisitor,' said Sixtus.

Coteaz peered down the trench. 'Magnoculars,' he said, holding his hand out to Captain Malevich. Malevich handed the device to him and Coteaz looked through the gloom. The air was still filthy with smog and Voltas doubted the inquisitor could see much, even through the lenses. 'Is there another route?' Coteaz asked. He handed the magnoculars back to Malevich.

'There is no other route,' said Sixtus, fiddling with the discs on his chest.

'Malevich,' said Coteaz. 'Scout ahead.'

Malevich saluted and nodded to two of his Scions. They gripped their lasguns and moved forwards, keeping their heads low as they edged out into the opening.

'Nothing,' voxed one of the stormtroopers after a few moments had passed.

Coteaz nodded and moved ahead, gesturing for the rest of the group to advance. They all fanned out as they entered an open space littered with rubble. The ruins of the tower were so worn by the rain that they looked like innards, red and glistening in the fumes.

Coteaz paused, drumming his fingers on the haft of his warhammer. 'That smell.'

Voltas felt a rush of nausea as he caught the stench of putrefied meat.

Coteaz signalled for one of the Scions to advance down the trench as it continued on the opposite side of the opening.

The man returned a short while later. 'Blocked. There's a pile of rocks a few feet down the trench.'

Coteaz gripped the daemonhammer in both hands. 'Then ready yourself,' he said. Silver light rippled through the metal as he dropped into a fighting stance. 'This is a trap.'

There was a rattle of weapons being raised, then the only sound came from the wind, howling overhead.

The seconds ticked on.

'My lord,' began Malevich, 'I can–'

The ground cracked near the centre of the open space, kicking up crimson petals of mud. It looked as if a shell had landed.

They backed away, training their guns on the pillar of dust that had sprung up from the ruins.

A man slowly hauled himself into view, dragging his limbs from the ground. Flies billowed from wounds that covered his body. The stench worsened. His eyes were dark and featureless, like a pair of blood blisters. He was wearing an obscene grin.

Coteaz opened fire, tearing the man's head away with a single round.

All across the clearing figures rose from the ground, shrugging off rock and crystal and firing lasguns. As they lurched into view, the sweet, cloying odour grew thicker.

A Scion fell backwards and crashed into Voltas. Blood sprayed from his neck. There were groans and the cough of gunfire as dozens of yellow-clad figures dragged themselves up from the rocks, all firing.

Voltas shoved the dead Scion away, drew his rapier, and strode into the fight, dealing out lethal cuts. Malevich barked commands and Scions rushed through the rain, but he doubted the miners would pose much of a threat – they were moving in clumsy staggers and they were deformed by disease. They looked half-dead. Voltas had dropped several of them by the time he reached the opposite side of the opening. Then he turned and began again, lunging and slashing, sending miners stumbling in every direction. It was satisfying work.

Then, to Voltas' surprise, he saw that the last man he killed was rising to his feet. Voltas had opened the man's throat with a backhanded slash. Tendons hung down the revenant's chest like a wine-drenched beard, but he grinned as he lurched back towards Voltas.

Voltas dodged clear, plunged his rapier into the man's chest, and triggered the current.

A ragged hole opened between the man's ribs, but he was still smiling. As he aimed a pistol at Voltas, the wound on his neck looked like broth boiling in a pan; saffron-coloured discharge rushed from the hole.

Voltas landed a flurry of cuts on the man's head and chest. Wounds closed as quickly as they appeared while others festered and swelled. And as they did so, the stench grew worse, causing Voltas to gag as he fought. He snatched out his pistol and fired into his foe at point-blank range.

The man lurched forwards again. As the wounds healed, Voltas saw that he was leaking more pus, yellow-green strings that hung down his suit.

Voltas backed away and looked around. All of the miners he had killed were lumbering to their feet. He fired again, knocking some of them down, but they were all grinning, oblivious to their injuries.

A wave of heat rushed past Voltas, causing him to back away, shielding his eyes.

'The light that burns!' roared Korov as he stomped past, drenching the miners in flames.

The man Voltas had just been fighting fell and finally lay still, a charred heap, smouldering on the ground.

They were a more interesting foe than Voltas had expected. These people were not just simple criminals, they were cultists, so corrupted by dark worship that it had transformed them physically – carrying a disease that filled them with grotesque vigour. He hacked at his next opponent, triggering flashes of current down the rapier's blade, until the man was little more than piles of meat. Voltas had been trained by the greatest swordsmen in Formosa. This simply gave him an even better chance to prove his worth.

He looked around for another target. The combination of smoke, smog, and rain made it hard to see clearly, but none of the shadowy figures seemed to be near him. There were more shouts and flashes of light. A fresh gout of flames lit Korov's hulking frame, and then, on the far side of the ruins, Voltas saw the same silver-white glow he had seen earlier as Coteaz reared up from the fight, hammer blazing as he pummelled grasping figures. Each blow ignited the miner it landed on, leaking the white glare into their limbs and turning them into pillars of energy. Unlike Voltas' rapier, Coteaz's warhammer was lethal with every blow. Each attacker he struck down, stayed down.

'Interrogator!' cried a Scion from behind him.

Voltas turned on his heel, bringing up his blade in time to parry a slab of rusty metal. The miner gripping it was a mess. His head had been torn open and his face was a mulch of shattered bone and shredded muscle. He was shouting as he drew back his club, but his mouth was pulverised and the words were unintelligible.

Voltas stepped away and fired, disintegrating what was left of the man's skull. His target stumbled, seemed on the verge of attacking again, then dropped to the ground.

The fighting grew more frenzied, and Malevich stumbled as a shot hit his leg, but Voltas was pleased to note that he had cleared one half of the ruins almost single-handed. He was about to join Coteaz and the others when pain flared in his chest and his vision grew dark. He had the odd sensation that he was floating, then he found that he was lying on the floor.

It took Voltas a moment to realise that some time had elapsed without him knowing. Coteaz was no longer on the far side of the ruins but leaning over him, with the rest of the group gathered behind him. The fighting was over. Only a few Scions lay dead, but there were piles of dismembered heretics everywhere he looked.

Malevich dropped to one knee and turned Voltas' head, examining his envirosuit. 'Torn,' he reported.

'Get him up,' said Coteaz.

Malevich gave a hand signal and Scions helped Voltas to his feet. He swayed and his thoughts swam wildly, refusing to focus. He looked around at the mangled remains of the miners. Some of them were barely human. Their wounds had healed over in the most peculiar ways, distorting their limbs and faces. The corpse nearest to him had a grotesquely elongated head and eyes that seemed to be melting into each other, forming a single enormous orb in the centre of the man's brow. Some of the dismembered parts were still moving, trying to crawl across the rocks.

Sato, who was standing nearby, cleaning her chain-sickles, spoke up. 'Magos Xylothek sent adepts up here. It seems odd that they heard no mention of something this extreme. They would recognise these symptoms.' She looked at Coteaz. 'They would know these people are Chaos worshippers.'

'We must move,' replied Coteaz. 'The interrogator's suit is torn. He will die if we don't get him to clean air.'

'We need to go anyway,' agreed Malevich. 'The psyber-eagle might have already reached Governor Aldrov. If we are still down in this trench when they send out a search party, we might be missed. We need to be out somewhere that they can see us.' He examined the tear in Voltas' hood. Then he waved one of the Scions over. 'Patch it.'

The Scion took out a med-pack and did as he was ordered, but Sato shook her head. 'You heard what the tech-priests said. He's going to die.'

Voltas heard what she was saying, but he was so light-headed that he struggled to take anything seriously. He felt as if he was trapped in an alcohol-induced dream. He was still staring at the body parts crawling back towards each other. It was almost like they were dancing. He massaged his scalp, trying to focus.

'The mines…' he managed. His pulse quickened as his memory cleared for a moment. 'Surrounded by supply depots. Built in a circle. Small… Unmanned… There would be… envirosuits.'

Coteaz looked at Sixtus.

Sixtus fiddled with the dials on his chest. 'Circling mining hubs with supply depots. Common practice. And we are near the circumference of the circle. We would simply need to continue on as planned, then double back on ourselves once we leave this trench.'

Sato shook her head. 'That takes us even further from civilisation. We're wasting valuable time.'

Coteaz studied Voltas a moment longer, then he stood. 'We make for the depot.'

Sato's expression hardened but she said nothing.

Malevich saluted and signalled to his men.

There was an explosion from further on as the Scions cleared a route through the next stretch of trench.

Two of the troopers took Voltas' arms and helped him hobble after the rest of the group as they headed into the smoke. A few minutes later, the group climbed up from the trench and emerged onto another plateau. The rain rose with renewed vigour and the fumes were thicker than ever, making visibility extremely poor. Voltas could only see a few feet in either direction, and the little he *could* see was twisted into madness by a series of disturbing hallucinations.

The group turned, clambering down a sprawl of fallen gantries, and Voltas struggled to keep track of time. He was unable to tell if they had been running for hours or minutes. Every now and then, a face swam into view, peering into his eyes, but he had no idea which were real and which were imaginary. Soon, he could no longer feel the Scions gripping his arms and he began to glide up with the rain, floating and rolling, feeling his body disperse. He realised, in a vague, confused kind of way, that he might be dying. The idea was incredible. Impossible. He had known, from an early age, that he was fated for greatness, that he would bring glory to the Voltas name. To die now, dissolved by toxic rain, would be absurd. He battled. He summoned the memory of Sato's sneering face and used it as fuel. If he died, Coteaz might be forced to consider *her* a viable replacement. He could not let that happen. If anyone was to follow in Coteaz's footsteps, it had to be him. No one else could hope to understand what the High Protector had built. Formosa's future was in the balance. The thought filled him with determined rage. He fought the waves of delirium, cursing and praying, but slowly, despite all his efforts, the gloom deepened. Slowly, it consumed him.

Voltas saw corpses in the darkness – blackened and broken, heaped in mounds. At first, he thought he was seeing the dead miners again, but then he realised this was a much earlier memory – a memory from his youth. He was standing in a high tower, gripping the embrasure, looking out across the Voltas estates. It was dawn and smoke was rising from pyres, cowling the trees in ash. Nearly a thousand people, half the royal household – all of them dead. All of them sinners. Many of them were people he had known since childhood. Many were his friends. But he had been right to condemn them. Whatever happened next, he knew he was right.

He heard movement behind him. His mother. Her eyes were red-rimmed as she moved to stand beside him and took his hand, staring out at the dead.

Voltas could not look at her. 'When will it happen?' he said after a moment.

'What, my love?'

'My execution.'

His mother stiffened, tightening her grip on his hand. Then she gently turned his face to hers. He realised that, rather than grief, she was crying with happiness.

'What is it?' he asked.

'Lord Inquisitor Coteaz did not come here to execute you. He came to save you.'

'Save me?' Voltas laughed.

She hugged him. 'He told your father that he believes *you. He believes every word you said about those people. He says your reasoning is sound. He said, and these were his exact words, that such courage could only have come from the Emperor of Mankind Himself.'*

Voltas shook his head. 'But the other royal houses... They demanded my head.'

'They can demand nothing now. They would not contradict the will of the lord inquisitor. And if they tried, it is they who would be executed.'

Voltas stared out at the charred host, studying the horror he had wrought, and he was unable to believe what he was hearing. The High Protector of Formosa had come here, to see him.

'Am I to meet him?' he asked.

'More than that, my love. You are to leave with him.'

'Why?'

She laughed. 'He's an inquisitor. He does not have to explain his motives. But the answer seems plain to me. I think he intends to make you his servant. To train you. It all makes sense now. This was meant to be. This is why you were never destined to succeed as a priest. This is why you could not lead the Voltas trade enterprises. You could not settle because you knew you were right – you knew you were meant for something greater. You saw that, Nicolas, when we could not. And now, here it is. This is your purpose!'

Voltas' parents had said similar things before as he struggled to find his true vocation in life. And each career had come to a more ignoble end than the last. Their latest demand had been that he join a local Militarum regiment. Voltas had considered this the worst of all their plans. How could he, the son of a great house, the greatest mind in the entire system, join the numberless hosts? How could he become just another Imperial Guard officer? But to join the entourage of an inquisitor… That was a goal he had sought his whole life without knowing – an opportunity to be at the burning core of the Imperial machine. This was his chance to shine. This was his route to power.

He gripped his mother's arms. 'I will never fail you.'

'Be brave, Nicolas,' she whispered, her voice trembling with pride. 'Be bold.'

CHAPTER SIXTEEN

Elias held his hands out at shoulder height, palms down, catching the rain. The liquid bubbled up between his outstretched fingers, warm and tacky, then rushed up towards the clouds. He was standing on a derelict landing pad, looking out at the storm. The wind was shoving him back and forth, but he felt no fear. He felt powerful and full of life. He had never dreamt it was possible to feel this way. He was standing near the entrance to the Taphos ruins. They must have been beautiful, once, but rain and time had rendered the place monstrous. The saints above the door looked hunched and wasted, and their faces were contorted by hate.

Elias no longer needed an envirosuit. He could taste the impurities in every breath he took, but they only made him feel even more vital, even more potent. He drank in a few lungfuls, savouring the bitter taste.

As Elias watched the rain, he felt an itch in the corner of his left eye, next to the tear duct. He rubbed at it absent-mindedly and noticed that there was a lump there. To his surprise, something wriggled. The sensation was odd, but not unpleasant. Elias tugged gently, and it slid from behind his tear duct, dropping a string of mucus onto his cheek. He held the shape up and peered at it. It was a fat, pale grub. It coiled and rolled as he dangled it in front of his face. Elias was aware that he should be disgusted, but instead he found it amusing. He laughed, then, realising he sounded hysterical, stopped himself. He could not help finding the incident funny, though. He recalled something Sturm had mentioned earlier in the day. He had told Elias that he had heard back from the other, smaller mines. They were keen to join the attack on Vespertinus and even seemed to have anticipated the call. They had already overwhelmed their overseers and seized weapons in readiness. But the thing that caused Elias and Sturm to laugh was that the miners had said they were turning into grubs. They had not seemed particularly concerned about it, and Elias and Sturm found that hilarious. As Elias watched the maggot writhing between his thumb and forefinger he started to laugh again, but then reminded himself that he had work to do and headed into the tower.

His courage had given him clear instructions, but Elias took his time as he descended into the structure's bowels, keen, as always, not to fail the shadow in the pool. He was starting to think that the courage was a vision of his future self. The shadow had asked him to perform many favours, starting with the creation of the slate with the symbols on, but Elias sensed that, as long as he did not falter, the vision he saw in the pool would come true. He was going to ascend. He did not know the names of the old gods, the ones who lived beneath the tower, but he knew they were on his side.

He reached what appeared to be a blank, featureless wall. He dragged his finger over the surface, drawing the same seven-pointed shape he had scored into the metal map, months earlier.

After a few seconds, he saw the shape start to appear on the rocks as lines of smoke that hovered just above the surface of the stone, glowing faintly. Then, with a rumble he felt in his guts, the rock slid aside, revealing a broad, smooth-sided corridor. There was no light, so he clicked on his lumen and headed inside. The thin beam flicked back and forth as he walked slowly forwards, treading carefully as the path began to descend.

There were more dead ends, and each time, he had to draw a slightly different version of the symbol, touching the stone in seven places to open doors that had clearly been closed for centuries. The heat had been growing as he went lower, and as he entered the final room, Elias was glad he was only wearing a thin tunic and trousers.

'Beautiful,' he whispered as he took it in. The space was like nothing he had ever seen before. It was clearly not designed by the same architects who made the mines above. Rather than classical pillars and colonnades this place resembled honeycomb, filled with loops and whorls of slender stone, spiralling around each other in a way that made him feel dizzy. It was a strange mixture of organic and manufactured, as if the rocks had been grown and nurtured rather than hammered and chiselled. The light he needed to see by was coming from the rock itself, radiating from every contorted limb; even after so long in the darkness, it did not hurt his eyes. His courage had not told him who made this place, describing them only as *the ones who came before,* but Elias could not help wondering if they might have been xenos. There was a time when the very idea of such creatures would have filled him with terror, but since bathing in the pool he struggled to fear anything. He felt invincible.

'Who were they?' he whispered.

'They were men, such as you.'

Even now, Elias felt a rush of excitement when the voice spoke to him. The words created a physical reaction in him, causing his pulse to quicken and his thoughts to clear. It was a kind of love, he realised.

'Men?' he said, looking around at the strange shapes. 'But this looks nothing like any architecture I have ever seen.'

'These people had no association with the Imperium or your God-Emperor. You have been lied to, Elias. Cruelties have been inflicted on your flesh, but even worse than that, your leaders have robbed you of your own past. Humankind crossed the stars long before the birth of the tyrant who sits rotting on the Terran throne. There was a time when people still had hope and freedom. Can you imagine that, Elias? Once, long ago, your ancestors were not bound by superstition or fear. If they had courage and conviction they could strike out into the stars and make a life for themselves. When humans first came to Novalis they lived like kings. They paid no tithes and they worshipped no gods. They chose their own way, and they lived long, fulfilling lives.'

It would not have occurred to Elias to doubt the voice. It was *his* voice, after all, talking to him with wisdom he would acquire in the future. 'Then what happened?' he asked.

'They lived in peace for a long time. And they created wonders. I wish you could have seen them. They developed medicines so powerful they could alter the bodies of their unborn children, protecting them against illness and age, so that they lived long lives, free of disease or infirmity. And they developed machines that could build anything they desired. Machines that could think and learn. There was no need for work and toil. Men like you lived in luxury, with mechanical devices tending to their every need. I don't mean those grotesque, mind-wiped abominations you call servitors, I mean sentient wonders able to do everything that their human masters desired. Everything that makes your life

miserable was consigned to the past: work, illness, oppression – the people who built these rooms knew nothing of such things.

'But there is evil in the galaxy, Elias. Most people are like you – given the chance, they will try to do good. Given safety and dignity, people will usually try to give others the same. Kindness begets kindness. But there are a few exceptions, those souls who crave power above all else. When the God-Emperor rose to power, he was drunk on ambition. He had conquered an entire world, but even that was not enough for him. He wanted more. Conquest was all he had ever known. He wanted to rule the entire galaxy. But when he looked at the stars, he saw people that had no need of him. Novalis was not the only place where people were happy. All across the galaxy, humanity had used science and technology to thrive. And the Emperor knew that if people were content, if they were free of hardship, they would be content to exist without him. Content to exist without an Emperor. Or a god.'

For the first time Elias could remember, the voice sounded bitter.

'So the Emperor denounced science,' his courage continued. *'He called it heresy. He denounced the very thing that had elevated your species from suffering. Then he massed his armies and sallied forth into the stars at the head of a great armada. And, whenever he reached worlds like Novalis, where people had used science and technology to improve their lives, he waged war, dismantling wonders that could never be remade. Wonders he did not even understand. He crippled humanity. He robbed it of hope. And then, when your ancestors were at their lowest ebb, lost and afraid in the darkness, unable to defend themselves from the galaxy, the Emperor welcomed them into his fold. He offered them protection. But only, you understand, as his slaves. He brought humanity to its knees. And now, because they are denied the truth, because they do not know their own, tragic past, they pray to him. They worship the source of their ruin.'*

Elias' bond with the voice was so intense that he could feel its pain. Tears welled in his eyes as he considered the countless tragedies he had seen in his short life. He pictured all the mine workers he had seen die while still young, praying as they toiled, begging the God-Emperor to watch over them as he worked them into the grave. 'But I am going to save us,' he whispered.

'You are, Elias. And we will soon pass the final obstacle.'

'Coteaz.'

'He is cunning. And he has stopped people like us before. He does not blindly serve the Emperor, as you have done. He understands what he's doing. He knows that he's a tyrant's lackey. He's as evil as the Corpse-Emperor he serves. But he's also as greedy as the Emperor. He's hungry for life. Where people like you would be happy to live a normal, healthy span, Coteaz wants to live forever. He has come here seeking immortality. What could be a better example of the Imperium's inequity? While most people die young, toiling in manufactoria and mines, he wishes to prolong his privileged existence for all eternity. But his greed will be his downfall.

'I have brought him here. He doesn't know it, but I have enticed him. There are treasures in these rooms that you have opened, Elias – relics of your ancestors' technology. They foresaw their doom, you see. In their wisdom, they knew that the Emperor's brutal crusade was on its way to destroy them. So they took their greatest inventions and buried them, deep beneath the ground, in these very vaults. The rest of their civilisation has been burned away by countless wars, but down here, some of their crowning achievements have survived, and one of them, the soul glass, is the thing Coteaz most desires. He has been searching for it for many years. He thinks if he can lay his hands on it, he could live forever. He thinks he could spend an eternity serving his Corpse-Emperor.'

'And could he? Would it work?'

'The thing is many thousands of years old. Until you threw those doors open, it had been hidden down here, preserved by the artifice of its makers. Coteaz hopes it will work and that is enough to bring him to us. You have opened the vaults, and he will now be free to seek his prize. The effort will consume him. And as he focuses on that task, I will rise and strike him down.'

'But will you need help? Shall we tell the others?'

'I will have help. The quietus tablet is almost complete, and once the final point has been added, my friends will rise from the storm and join me as I strike Coteaz down. We will end his reign. We will free Novalis.'

Elias nodded, reassured, as always, by his courage. He looked around at the marvellous architecture, vaguely aware that there was something wriggling behind one of his fingernails. 'Let them come.'

CHAPTER SEVENTEEN

Voltas was coughing, spraying blood onto the inside of his visor, but Coteaz's attention was focused on Turcifel. 'You are in the hands of the Emperor,' he said. 'He *will* preserve you.'

She nodded but still looked troubled. Most of the group were exploring the depot, looking for traps or signs of another ambush, so Coteaz was alone with Voltas and Turcifel. The former was lying on a gurney, dazed by morphia and a cocktail of other meds, while the latter stood near the door. The medicae room was tiny, barely large enough for Coteaz and Turcifel to fit next to the gurney, but the strip lumen in the ceiling still worked and the shelves were crowded with syringes and med-packs. Whatever had happened in the mines, this place had been left intact.

'Where are we?' mumbled Voltas, his words slurred as he lifted himself on one elbow, looking round the room.

Turcifel prayed. But as her fingers rolled each bead on the necklace, the air between them glimmered, as though wet with dew. The tattoo running down her neck undulated like ink in water, and the temperature dropped.

'What is this?' murmured Voltas, growing even paler. 'What are you...?' His words faltered as he saw Turcifel's necklace. It had changed. Rather than linked beads, it was now the edge of a ragged wound. A wound in the air, glistening and steaming.

Coteaz gripped his bolt pistol. 'Turcifel?'

'Not me,' she managed to whisper, her eyes straining.

The air inside the wound congealed, and colours blossomed like oily water. The colours streaked and rolled, forming shapes that looked, at first, to be random.

Voltas rose from the gurney and reached around for his weapons, knocking over trays and scattering needles.

Turcifel prayed harder as the temperature continued to drop. Frost crept over the tables and shelves, glittering in the barrels of syringes and on the surface of jars.

Coteaz cursed his foolishness. He had ordered Turcifel to employ her powers on Voltas, to try to repair the damage in his lungs. Her skill was in the manipulation of inanimate matter, but she had managed to help, driving the fumes from his airways and healing most of the damage. But now something had gone dangerously wrong.

Coteaz took out his gun and aimed at her head.

He caught a glimpse of the shape forming on the other side of the wound in the air. He could only half see it from where he was standing, but there was something familiar about it. Curiosity stayed his hand.

There was a moist *pop*, like the smacking of lips, and a face emerged from the wound. Its skin was viscid, billowing around yolk-like eyes. Voltas backed away as the face slid further from the wound, streaked with blood and pus, looking cheerfully around the room. It spread its mouth in an unnaturally wide grin, revealing a line of pale grubs where there should have been teeth. A stench filled the space, making it hard to breathe.

Long, spindly fingers reached through the hole, too numerous to belong to a single pair of hands. They rippled like insect legs, then began pulling the gap wider. As the hole stretched, a mumbled chorus filled the air – hundreds of voices, all speaking gibberish and rising quickly to a crescendo.

Voltas finally found his weapons and grabbed a pistol. He took aim at Turcifel.

'Wait,' ordered Coteaz.

Turcifel's eyes had rolled back and her head sagged limply on her shoulders.

'Traitor.'

The word hung in the air. The voice was no more than a whisper, but it caused Coteaz's breath to catch. It was a voice and a word that had long haunted him. Finally, he saw beyond the bulging features and recognised the face. He gripped his hammer tighter.

'Laredian.'

Turcifel fell backwards and slid down the wall, dropping her prayer beads. The wound in the air vanished, along with the face. The voices faded and the temperature started to rise. The only sound came from Voltas, breathing heavily and quickly. He was slumped against the wall, gripping his pistol, muttering frantically.

Coteaz stared at the space where the face had been. 'Laredian,' he whispered again, feeling as if someone had stripped him of his armour. For decades, his faith had hinged on a single fulcrum: that he earned his role as High Protector by ridding the galaxy of Laredian.

Turcifel looked up at him from the floor, her face white. 'What did I do?'

As Coteaz reached down to help her up, he realised that his hand was shaking. 'You did not harm anyone.'

Turcifel nodded, but when she noticed his tremor she looked even more concerned.

'Say nothing of what happened.' Coteaz glanced at Voltas and Turcifel as he led them into the depot's hangar. Turcifel nodded without looking at him, examining her prayer beads carefully, as though looking for flaws. In truth, neither of them *knew* what had just happened. Coteaz had given Turcifel several powerful talismans, taken from reliquary boxes on his armour, and the three of them had prayed together before leaving the room. She had no recollection of the warp spawn, but there was still a chance he might have to eliminate her if the same thing happened again. Or the suppressed memory of it might emerge at some point and render her insane. Turcifel's presence had always been a risk. Sanctioned or not, her psychic powers were incredibly dangerous. And, since landing on Novalis, her control seemed to be slipping. He would have to monitor her even more closely from now on.

Voltas seemed less troubling. Like everyone else, he was now wearing a new envirosuit, and while he was not walking with his usual swagger, he was managing to stay in control of his emotions. As an Ordo interrogator, Voltas knew far more than most of Coteaz's retainers about the nature of the threat they faced. He, too, would need to be closely watched, however. What did he think he had just seen?

'Lord inquisitor,' said Captain Malevich. He was standing on the far side of the hangar with the rest of the group. They were all wearing the grubby yellow envirosuits that the colonists wore and had gathered round a rusty old air hauler. The Scions were working on the vehicle and Korov was helping, using several of his mechanical limbs. The gloom filled with sparks as they welded armour to the chassis and repaired damaged wings. The flyer looked like a mechanical insect, with a chain of hexagonal cargo holds for a thorax. Crystals caked its fuselage and there was a tear in one of its canvas wings. Sato and the abhuman were standing a little way off, talking urgently in the shadows and casting glances at Coteaz as he approached.

Coteaz was still dazed from hearing Laredian's voice. Everything felt off kilter, as if at any moment his old mentor might return to tell him that his entire life had been a sham. He had not had time to process what had happened, but various theories vied for his attention. Laredian might actually be alive. His heresy might have somehow enabled him to survive the destruction of his flesh. Perhaps he had made a bargain with the Ruinous Powers that granted him immortality. Or perhaps the voice Coteaz heard belonged to the daemon he had seen, all those years ago, in Laredian's crystal – the crystal he'd smashed when he denounced his former master. Perhaps that act of violence had released the daemon and it was now masquerading as Laredian, trying to confuse him, or distract him from its real purpose.

Other possibilities filled his thoughts, but however shocked Coteaz was feeling, he had decades of experience when it came to hiding his emotions and, as he approached his retainers, he gave no sign that anything untoward had happened.

'We can make it fly, Lord Coteaz,' said Malevich, as his men continued to work. 'There is not much fuel, though.'

'We are close to Vespertinus,' replied Coteaz. 'Besides, Thula should have reached the governor by now. They may already be heading this way to meet us.' He studied Malevich. The captain saluted, but his movements were stiff and he was keeping the weight off his injured leg. 'There's morphia in the medicae chamber,' he said. 'You can't fight if you can't stand.'

Malevich saluted again and hobbled away in the direction of the medicae room, barking orders at Scions as he went.

'Something happened in there,' said Sato, looking closely at Turcifel.

Coteaz was about to reply when he heard Laredian again. *Traitor.* The word echoed round his mind. It was *him.* But daemons were infinitely devious. There was a chance the voice had come from a being that had no idea who Laredian was. The creatures of the warp could peer into a soul and root out its darkest fears.

He called out to Malevich as he limped back into the hangar. 'How long until we can leave?'

'Ten minutes, my lord. Fifteen at most.'

Coteaz nodded. 'Then we will soon be back on track. Once we reach Vespertinus Governor Aldrov will need to explain why he has allowed Chaos worshippers to roam at will.' It occurred to him that Aldrov might even be the *source* of the heresy, which would complicate matters further.

'But we didn't come here to chase mutants.' Sato gave Coteaz a pointed look, though she was wise enough not to mention the soul glass by name. 'Vespertinus is *not* our destination.'

'It is now.' Coteaz nodded at the air hauler, gesturing for people to climb aboard.

Voltas and Sato were watching him with a kind of hunger, like stimm abusers eyeing up a fix. Under normal circumstances, their fervour would not have bothered him. But today, with Laredian's voice echoing round his skull, he felt like an actor who had rehearsed his lines too often. He gripped the ladder and began to climb, battling thoughts that had not troubled him since childhood.

Anamnesis

'How did you know?'

The Hall of Assembly on Varoth is a triumph of Imperial architecture. A vast auditorium carved with a host of saints and warriors, grand enough even for the mighty daemonhunters who are gathered beneath its vaults. Cowled figures stand in alcoves, heads bowed and hands resting on ceremonial weapons, while above them, vast stone eagles crouch on pillars, gripping rods and axes in their monolithic talons. Vat-grown cherubim whirl overhead, trailing banners through the censer smoke and singing mournful hymns. This is a place of beginnings and endings. A place where deceit is uncovered and treachery uprooted. There can be no half-measures here.

'How did you know?' repeats the inquisitor standing nearest to me as we look down at Laredian's ruined corpse. 'How could you be so sure?'

I study shards of the broken crystal, remembering the abomination I saw in its facets. And I struggle to answer. Pain grips me – not physical but intellectual. Being proved right is not always a victory.

I have killed the one I trusted.

Where does that leave me now?

'I was sure because I learned from him.' I kneel by the body of my former saviour, watching the blood spread. 'Because he taught me how to sort truth from lies.' I speak fiercely, conscious that the conclave are gathering around me, staring at the corpse. But my thoughts are troubled. Could I have *saved* Laredian? If so, why did I not?

Laredian's eyes, once filled with such insight and determination, are now dull and sightless. The fire has gone. But I cannot shake the memory of how he looked at me in those final moments.

I turn to face the assembly. The die is cast, and I can no longer allow myself the luxury of hesitation. There can be no weakness. I must become worthy of He who dwells on Terra.

That which proceeds from Him cannot be false.

That which does not proceed from Him is a lie.

I summon the rage that drove me to slay my master. Laredian betrayed me. He betrayed all of us. And now I must succeed where Laredian could not.

I hold my hammer aloft and pour faith through the metal. Light erupts from the filigree, dazzling and pure. 'Let fires be lit! Let diabolists recoil! Let the sinners beg! Let the abominations flee! It will avail them not!

'I *am* the Emperor's wrath!

'I *am* the hammer of daemons!

'I *am* judgement!'

The figures in the alcoves step forwards, lifting their weapons. Weapons that are not so ceremonial after all. There is blood yet to be spilled this night. There are many in the assembly who would never accept my judgement of Laredian. And there are many others who will need to see that I have the strength to replace him.

I study the conclave.

'Retribution!'

I slam the hammer down.

'Has!'

I strike again, as guns start to bark.

'Begun!'

CHAPTER EIGHTEEN

The weather grew worse and the air hauler lurched as it fluttered over the slopes of the pinnacle. Coteaz thought that *pinnacle* was too unimpressive a name for such a vast edifice. It was too regular and slender in shape to be called a mountain, but it was thousands of feet tall. Novalis was like no other world he had visited. He wondered how far the pinnacles plunged until they reached a solid surface, but as he tried to look down, red rain washed against the armaglass hull, dissolving the view into pools of gore.

'No sign of a welcoming party,' said Malevich.

Sato was up in the cockpit and she turned to face him. 'Could Thula be lost in the storm?'

He looked at her pale face, silhouetted by the ferocious weather. How strange to hear her speak of the eagle with such familiarity. It dragged him back, back to the time before she broke his trust. He felt the need to say something, to demand something, but he could not decide what. As he thought, the rain spiralled around them in monstrous columns, caught in a crosswind, whipping against the rocks.

'She's endured worse than this,' he said, finally, unsure if he meant Thula or Sato.

'Perhaps the weather's too severe for them to leave their complex,' suggested Voltas. His voice was strong and clear. There did not seem to be any permanent damage to his lungs. Employing Turcifel's powers had been a mistake, but it had probably saved the interrogator's life.

Sato shook her head. 'I've seen scavenger rigs out in worse than this. And Governor Aldrov is hardly likely to ignore a request from an inquisitor.'

'Unless he has something to hide,' said Voltas, echoing Coteaz's earlier thoughts.

'You might want to look at this,' said Sato, nodding to the rocks below.

He leant forwards and looked out at the landscape, struggling to see clearly through the storm. Then the wind changed direction and he saw what Sato meant. They had reached another broad plateau cut into the side of the pinnacle, and there was a bright, orange circle at its centre, flickering and dancing around darker shapes.

'The governor's complex,' he said. 'Burning.'

'I'll fly lower,' said Sato.

Again, Coteaz had the disorienting sense of their relationship slipping back into old shapes. 'No,' he said. 'We've been shot down once already today. Move away from the buildings first.'

She did as instructed, flying the hauler in a wide loop and bringing it down near the edge of the plateau. The rotors screamed as she hovered briefly then let the wheels crunch down onto rocks.

Malevich rushed to the exit hatch and opened it, hurrying down the ladder with his Scions following close behind. 'Fan out!' he barked, as they all clambered from the hauler into the storm.

Coteaz paused to check the seals on his helmet and take out

his bolt pistol, then clattered down the ladder after the others. Rain and wind hit him with such force it rocked him back on his heels, and it took him a moment to steady himself and start walking. The others followed, battling against the weather.

Coteaz used his armour's auto-senses to filter the atmosphere, and data spooled down his retina. He signalled for the others to pause as he studied the reports. 'Combat. Large scale. Artillery.' He squinted into the rain but struggled to see very far.

'Who could be attacking the governor in such large numbers?' asked Voltas.

'This *is* more than just riots,' said Coteaz. 'Think of what we saw in the trench. Those people were not just agitators, they were heretics. Blasphemers. Followers of false gods. And they were well armed.' He studied his helm display again. 'Heavy munitions have been employed here. Advance in small groups. Malevich, take half the Scions. Approach the buildings from the north. Voltas, take Korov, Sixtus and Turcifel and approach from the south with the other Scions. Sato and I will approach head-on.'

'Coteaz,' said Sato as they headed off. 'We didn't come north to rescue besieged governors.'

Coteaz nodded to the 'I' emblazoned on her chest. 'Does that mean *anything* to you? What would you have us do, continue with our business and leave this situation to fester?'

She glared back at him but clearly had no answer.

More data filled Coteaz's vision as he strode across the rocks, but he wondered if his suit was malfunctioning. The screed spoke of combat on the kind of scale he would associate with a planetary invasion. And that could not be the case. He would know if Novalis had been invaded.

He came to a stop as he reached an overturned vehicle. The chassis had been blasted open and the whole thing was warped out of shape, but he recognised the silhouette of the vehicle. It was an armoured personnel carrier. The kind used by Militarum regiments in major campaigns.

He peered through the hole in the chassis and saw movement inside. As his visor adjusted to the gloom he saw body parts, caked in scabs and pus.

Coteaz took aim, looking for an attacker under the remains.

Then he realised the remains were not being shoved or jostled; they were moving of their own volition.

'He walketh in judgement,' he muttered.

The body parts were trying to reassemble themselves.

'Keep clear,' he said, stepping back and rolling a grenade inside. He led the other two on and did not stop to look back as flames erupted behind him.

There were corpses sprawled across the rocks. Some wore the tattered remnants of envirosuits, but most were in rags, their clothes torn apart by mutations. Coteaz noticed a consistency to the transformations. Several of the corpses had a single eye that dominated the top half of their face.

'Do not trust your eyes,' he said. 'These dead are still dangerous.'

Sato was nearby, watching him closely. 'You knew.'

'What?'

'That there was a Chaos threat here.' She studied the mutated bodies. 'I thought you only came here for the soul glass, but your purpose must have been to deal with this.' She shook her head and hacked at the air with one of her sickles, hurling its weighted chain through the rain.

'I didn't know until you showed me,' he replied.

'What are you talking about? Genetor Glycon said there was unrest up here. He made no mention of a heretical cult.'

'Think of the images you showed me. The map.'

She frowned. 'Someone's using a quietus tablet to plot a route to the soul glass.'

'And with every murder, every time they add more detail, they are doing something else. Those tablets are more than just maps. Perhaps the murderer doesn't even realise what else they're doing.' He was conscious that he had fallen back into his role as mentor, but, despite everything that had happened between them, he felt disappointed that Sato had missed a key point. 'Look again,' he said.

She unfolded her data-slate, peering at the images.

'How many locations will it describe?' prompted Coteaz. 'How many points will there be on the map, once it is complete?'

She tapped the screen. 'Seven.' She shrugged. Then her expression hardened. 'I'm a fool.'

'You are many things, but not that. Which is why I'm surprised you missed it.'

'What's he talking about?' asked the abhuman.

'Seven,' she replied. 'The sacred number of a false god.'

'And the seven points form three circles,' said Coteaz. 'Do you see? The Onogal Fly.'

'An occult symbol,' explained Sato to the abhuman, 'used in sacrilegious rites.'

Coteaz marched on into the rain, his pistol held before him as he picked his way through the bodies.

'We need support,' said Sato as she followed. 'If we're dealing with large numbers of cultists, a few Scions isn't going to be enough. And Malevich is wounded.' She waved at the mounds of bodies and vehicles. 'We can't take on an army. We should summon Domus Alpha or send a message to a relay station. We need to alert the fleet.'

'And shine a spotlight on Novalis?'

'But we can't keep this situation secret. It has to be dealt with quickly.' She looked at the ground, frowning and clicking her joints. 'And you know that. So there must be something you're not telling me.'

Coteaz heard movement in the rain and came to a stop. He peered into the storm. It could have been rocks settling, but he doubted it.

Sato gripped her chain-sickles and lowered herself into a crouch.

Coteaz stepped towards her and fired.

There was a hiss from behind Sato. A heretic flipped back through the rain with crimson spray where his head should have been.

Coteaz fired again and the man stopped moving.

Sato snapped her arm, causing the chain on one of her sickles to uncoil and whip through the rain. The barbed weight slammed into the face of another heretic, crunching bone and locking into flesh. Sato tugged on the chain, and as the man stumbled towards her, she used her other sickle to behead him. As he fell at her feet, she pointed the bloody blade at Coteaz.

'I understood you. You were worried that I might treat you the way you treated Laredian. That's why you always held me back, even once I became an interrogator. You'll do exactly the same with Voltas.'

Figures began rushing at them from every direction, lunging and twitching and raising weapons.

Coteaz holstered his pistol and took the daemonhammer from his back as a figure rushed towards him. The heretic's body was rolling and bubbling like liquid. Faces were slipping in and out of his skin. 'Back to the abyss!' Coteaz howled, thrusting the daemonhammer forwards. The weapon lit up like a beacon. The heretic faltered at the sight of the blazing weapon and the faces in his skin screamed.

'Burn in the unyielding light!' Coteaz brought the daemonhammer down with such force that the heretic exploded, hurling bile and skin through the rain.

He turned to Sato, pointing the smouldering hammer at her. 'I keep secrets from you because you failed me. And then, when I hear that a good man like Agent Krasner has died, who do I find waiting at the murder scene?'

Sato sidestepped as a rusty blade was thrust at her throat. She moved with the peculiar, liquid grace that Coteaz had noticed the first time they met. It was as if she inhabited a different environment. She turned on her heel and brought both her sickles down into the face of another heretic, tearing his skull apart and sending him flailing back through the air.

'You know I'm the one,' she called.

Coteaz could see another mutant shambling towards them, but he paused to look at Sato. 'What?'

She waved the abhuman towards the approaching heretic while she faced Coteaz. 'You have never found an acolyte who understands you as well as I do. You've never found anyone else who could continue your work.'

Coteaz brought his hammer round with thunderbolt force, blasting a mutant across the rocks. He was vaguely aware that a group was gathering around them, but he was curious about what Sato had said. Did she really still want to serve him? To become his protégé? Or was this just another ploy to distract him from her true motives?

'Those weapons you carry,' he said. 'They are a blemish on the name of the Ordo. I don't know what you've been doing in Domus Alpha, but I know you have blood on your hands.'

Coteaz flattened two mutants with one swing, and Sato sliced the others apart with a flurry of chains and blades. Once their attackers had stopped moving, the two inquisitors stood in silence, struggling to catch their breath. Then Coteaz faced Sato again.

'The truth is that I shared too much with you,' he said. 'I knew it the day you left the *Pilgrim's Wrath*.'

She shook her head. 'I left because you forced me to. And now I know why. You were afraid of what I was becoming.'

Coteaz was about to reply when his helmet's vox-bead crackled into life.

'Lord Coteaz,' said Captain Malevich. *'We have reached the main entrance. We were attacked as we approached but we have sustained no injuries. I am tracking movement in every direction.'*

'We have also encountered resistance. The situation here is clearly out of control. The governor may be dead. Is the entrance barred?'

'The doors are down. Demolished. Shall we enter?'

'Hold your position. I will join you there.'

Coteaz ran on into the storm with Sato rushing behind. Shapes loomed out of the rain ahead of them – vast gates approached by a colonnaded portico. The gates were set into a tall, windowless rockcrete wall, pitted and scarred and covered in the same patches of red crystal that clad everything else on the planet. The place had the utilitarian feel of a detention block or a waste containment facility. The rest of the group stood waiting at the end of the portico. The Scions were scanning their surroundings down the barrels of lasguns, while the others watched the gates. The gates were dozens of feet tall, but artillery fire had ripped one of them apart.

As Coteaz approached the entrance he saw that there was a courtyard on the other side, heaped with even more bodies than the surrounding rocks. A smell rushed out to greet him – the same rotten stench that had accompanied all the other corpses. And there was a low buzzing sound as swarms of flies boiled over the dead. At first he had mistaken them for mist or rain, but as he entered the portico, the flies seemed to sense his presence and they billowed across the courtyard towards him.

'Scatter,' he said, raising his voice over the sound of the insects.

Some of the bodies were still burning and the red smog was even heavier than usual. Coteaz watched the corpses for movement as he approached a raised dais at the centre of the courtyard. The overseers he was stepping over had been well equipped with flak armour and lasguns, but they had still been overwhelmed. The dead mutants were just as well armoured and they had attacked with a whole array of different weapons.

'These people were armed to the teeth,' said Sato, as she picked her way through the bodies beside him.

He looked at her, filled with conflicting emotions. If she had remained loyal to him, if she had followed the rules he set her, she could have become living proof that he was not like Laredian. She could have picked up his mantle. She *could* have been the one.

'What game are you playing?' he said. 'Tell me the truth and then perhaps...'

'Perhaps what? You might give me a chance to be another one of your shackled slaves? I don't want it, Coteaz. You're too afraid of exposing yourself, of opening yourself to attack. It makes you weak. All you can think about is not becoming Laredian.' She waved one of her chain-sickles. 'I found these on a drifting void hulk and I saw their worth. You would have burned them in holy fire.'

'"The tools of the alien,"' he said, quoting a religious tract, '"are poison to the soul."'

'They're dangerous.' She waved the blade at him. 'But I have the *strength* to manage that danger. And thanks to these blades, I was able to terminate the coven on Plusidae Minor.'

Coteaz felt a flicker of pride. When he took her in, she could barely speak; now she was a lethal weapon. The situation on Plusidae had festered for months and several inquisitors had failed to dismantle the coven.

As they had been talking, they had reached the dais. Coteaz climbed the steps and looked around, with Sato and the abhuman following his lead. The courtyard was so heavy with fumes that he could only just make out the rest of the group, picking their way through the bodies.

'Interrogator Voltas?' he said, speaking into the vox. 'Do you see anything from where you are?'

'No, lord inquisitor.'

'Captain Malevich?'

'No, lord inquisitor.'

'There's another doorway up ahead,' said Sato. 'Looks like it leads into the main complex.'

Coteaz strode across the dais.

Las-fire flashed through the smoke, kicking up shrapnel at his feet. He dropped into a crouch and returned fire, targeting the source of the shots. There was a crump of breaking stone as Malevich and the Scions also opened up.

After the echoes of the gunfire had faded, Coteaz called out, 'I am Lord Inquisitor Coteaz, High Protector of Formosa. Declare yourselves now and your lives may not be forfeit.'

He heard low voices and the distinctive, rattled tone of people encountering an inquisitor for the first time.

'How can we believe you?' called out a defiant voice. 'How do we know this isn't another trick?'

Coteaz rose to his feet, heedless of the danger. 'I am an instrument of the God-Emperor's will!' As he shouted the words he lifted the daemonhammer from his back and held it aloft, willing his faith into the metal. The weapon bathed him in light and drove back the red rain, forming a column like a miniature tornado that whirled and danced around him as he crossed the dais. 'Let faith answer your question. Listen to the fear in your soul. You *know* what I am.'

It only took a few moments for the figures to appear, weapons lowered as they trudged from the ruins, staring at Coteaz as if he were the Emperor Himself.

CHAPTER NINETEEN

Governor Aldrov was a good man. Coteaz saw it the moment he laid eyes on him. He was lying on a bloodstained bunk, his head wrapped in dark, sodden bandages, but as Coteaz entered his room, Aldrov struggled to his feet and saluted, making the sign of the eagle across his chest. He guessed the man was in his mid-forties and, until recently, must have been in good health. His face was marred by crystals, but not as badly as some of the aides who gathered around him. He was tall and powerfully built, with a short ginger beard and broad, open features, and his head was shaved in a tonsure. He had a gleam in his eye that seemed to be a mixture of pride, hope and shame, but it was not his expression that told Coteaz Aldrov was impressive; it was the expressions of those around him.

There were a dozen or so officers flanking the man, wearing uniforms that marked them out as colonial militia. All of them had the same look in their eyes. They were terrified of Coteaz, but they were also prepared to die for the governor. It was always easy to spot officers who maintained their position through fear and nothing else. Their subordinates tended to make themselves scarce when Coteaz arrived. But these soldiers looked utterly loyal to Aldrov. Coteaz sensed that whoever was behind the heresy on Novalis, it was *not* the governor.

'I can imagine what you must think of me,' said Aldrov, his face growing paler as he struggled to stay on his feet. 'And you're right. I have failed in my duties. Vespertinus is the biggest mine on Novalis and I've lost it. I didn't see any of this coming. When the heretics arrived, they begged for help, saying they had been attacked. It was only once we'd opened the gates that they opened fire. I'm a fool. But, before you do your duty' – he raised his chain and spoke louder than the small room required – 'you should know that my troops did nothing wrong.' His face was rigid. 'This was my failure, not theirs. They should not be punished on my behalf. They did all that could be–'

Coteaz silenced him with a raised hand and looked around the group. All of them were wounded, but none bore any signs of contagion. Some exhibited mutations, but it was only the influence of Novalis' smog. Others were entirely covered by a layer of crystals, with only their eyes visible.

'Forgive me,' said Aldrov, his words strained. 'I did not presume… High Protector, I just want you to know that the things you saw outside are not the fault of my men.'

Coteaz looked around the room. Malevich stood at one of his shoulders, Sato at the other, and Voltas was waiting near the door. He had ordered the abhuman to remain outside with the others. Thula was in the room, perched on an empty crate, glaring at Aldrov. She had delivered Coteaz's message then waited patiently, with such fierce expressions on her faces that no one had dared try to move her.

'I did not come here to punish you,' said Coteaz. 'I did not intend to come here at all. I have business in the north. We were shot down by insurgents. And when I saw the nature of our attackers, I was forced to investigate.'

Aldrov struggled to digest this. He had obviously been so prepared for his impending execution that he had not considered Coteaz might not be here for him.

'Do you understand what happened to those miners?' asked Coteaz. 'Do you understand why they attacked you?'

'Forgive me, lord inquisitor, I don't think I do. Perhaps if I had, I could have…' His words trailed off and he stared at the floor. 'The entire garrison has been wiped out. Every miner who remained loyal and nearly all of my overseers. All dead.' He waved at the six men standing around him. 'This is all I have left. Out of over eight hundred souls. There were so many of those… of those things. I don't understand where they all came from. A group of my miners went missing from Vespertinus about a month ago, but there were a hundred at most. I would say there were thousands who attacked us. They must have come from every mine on Novalis.' He gripped the edge of the bunk, his arms trembling. 'But the strangest thing was how heavily armed they were. Where did they find such weapons? They were better equipped than we were.'

Aldrov gestured for one of his men to pour a pair of drinks. 'They slaughtered everyone and then left of their own accord. It was as if they were answering a summons.'

'They left knowing you were still alive?' asked Voltas.

'They butchered everyone they could find and trashed all the mining equipment, then they went. I was holed up in here, waiting to die. They knew where I was, but they all just left. They fuelled up the biggest scavenger engines we had and headed south. I've been trying to get word to Port Gomera or Domus Alpha, but it's been impossible in this damned weather. I finally managed to contact the tech-priests this morning but only for a few minutes.' He grimaced, massaging his scalp. 'And they said they are unable to aid us because they are already on their way to another location.'

Coteaz refused the drink he was offered. 'You spoke to Magos Xylothek?'

'No, her second-in-command, Glycon – the one with the...' He waved vaguely at his face, indicating the lenses that covered the genetor's head. 'He seemed uninterested in my situation.'

'Did he say any more?'

'He said, and these were his exact words, that they are pursuing a matter that is central to their purpose on Novalis.' He frowned at Coteaz. 'But surely they should be more concerned about what's happening up here. Why don't they come? Is it because they don't want to be infected by whatever made those people outside look like...' He shook his head, and lowered his voice. 'What exactly *is* wrong with them? I shot a man and he got back up. I shot him here' – he tapped his forehead – 'and he just kept moving.'

Coteaz pitied the governor. The man thought he had seen a form of illness. But if he lived, his mind would keep returning to the memory of those mutants, worrying at it, questioning what he had seen, starting to guess at the truth, until finally his sanity would fold.

'What you saw *was* a kind of disease. I've seen it many times before,' said Coteaz.

Aldrov closed his eyes, looking visibly relieved. Then he finished his drink. 'I thought so. It was just... They were such *strange* symptoms.'

Coteaz studied Aldrov and his remaining men. They still looked resolute. It was possible that Malevich could find a use for them. Afterwards he could employ a meta-cleansing ritual to remove their memories. A full mind-wipe might not be required. He would need to consider the options properly later.

'You will come with me,' he said. 'Report to Captain Malevich.'

The governor saluted and seemed pleased. 'It will be an honour, Lord Coteaz. But what will you do now? You said you didn't intend to come here. Will you pursue the heretics?'

'I have to stop them before they reach wherever they're headed.'

Sato shook her head. 'We need to continue north to Taphos.'

'Taphos?' Aldrov frowned. 'It's strange that you should mention that place. That was where Glycon said the Mechanicus facility was heading. But it's a hellhole. The smog is particularly bad up there. Even envirosuits wouldn't be much use.'

'Coteaz,' said Sato. 'We have to move fast. If we go south after the heretics while the Mechanicus explore Taphos, this entire journey will have been for nothing.'

'How quickly could we reach Taphos?' Coteaz asked Aldrov.

'We have aircars left. You could get there in two hours. Three, at the very most.'

'We came here in an air hauler,' said Voltas. 'We could use that.'

'Only if we want to draw attention to ourselves,' said Sato. 'That hauler is huge.'

'The aircars are small and fast,' said Aldrov. 'I don't know who you're trying to avoid, but no one would see the aircars coming in this weather. As long as you fly low and land on the lower slopes, beneath the ruins, to evade any auspex returns.'

'Two to three hours.' Coteaz considered this.

Sato was knotting and unknotting her arms as she watched him. 'We *have* to reach Taphos. Xylothek might already have overtaken us. We can't chase those heretics south.'

'We will do both,' said Coteaz. 'You and I will continue north to the ruins at Taphos, while Interrogator Voltas heads south and tracks the heretics.' He looked at Voltas. 'Take Malevich and half the Scions.'

Voltas nodded his head in a bow.

'Track the heretics down, plot their course, and then rendezvous with us at Taphos. Do not engage them. This is reconnaissance only. Find out where they are headed and estimate their numbers.'

'Understood.'

Sato gave Coteaz an unreadable look, but it was only later when they were about to board the aircars that she spoke up. She checked that the others were out of earshot and leant close. 'Are you sending Voltas into danger just to prove me wrong? Are you risking his life just to prove that you can place trust in people?'

Coteaz shook his head. 'Voltas is a capable interrogator.'

It was an absurd suggestion. Voltas *was* capable. But her words still rankled. *Was* he trying to prove something? Had Sato got under his skin to that extent? Or was she just trying to impair his judgement?

As Coteaz climbed aboard the flyer, he recalled Laredian's face, sliding from Turcifel's necklace, spitting his venomous accusation. *Traitor.*

CHAPTER TWENTY

'The trail is getting clearer,' said Sato as turbulence battered the flyer. 'We just need to keep on the–' Her voice was drowned out by a scream of feedback from the aircar's control panel.

'Repeat that,' said Coteaz, as the craft lurched again and their new pilot battled with the controls.

'Keep on past the next pinnacle.' She was blindfolded again and holding the piece of quietus tablet in her hands, gripping it tightly as ash drifted from between her fingers.

Coteaz had made detailed studies of her voidborn psychic ability. It had taken years and much suffering on Sato's part before he was sure he could let her live. But in the end, he had fought her cause. When others in the Ordo demanded that she die, calling her an inhuman voidborn, he had refused to yield. She had absolute faith in the Emperor and the institutions of the Imperium. She had strayed, long ago, into radicalism, but he had never once seen her psychic grasp slip. Watching her work, he was reminded of just how useful she could be. As the storm grew more violent, the navigation controls became worthless, but she guided the pilot with confidence. Every few minutes she would hold her fists to streamers around her head, pressing the vellum into her eye sockets, but beyond that and the ash, there was no sign that she was using her inner sight.

They had been travelling like this for nearly an hour when the weather became even worse. Alarmed calls came in from the governor's other pilots, and Coteaz's flyer lurched so violently that he thought the wings might be torn away.

'Should we turn back, Lord Coteaz?' asked the pilot.

Coteaz shook his head, analysing the data that was scrolling down his helm display. 'It would serve no purpose. This storm covers the entire region. It is just as severe over Vespertinus. Besides, we have to reach–'

A tremor rocked the aircar, and the world tilted on its axis.

The craft flipped, end over end. Warning sounds howled from the control panel. Wind screamed through the hull as the flyer began to dive, hurtling down through the rain and the smoke. The pilot grappled with the controls, but the aircar only fell faster. It dropped with stomach-wrenching speed, falling for several minutes. Finally, he managed to bring the yoke back and the flyer climbed, skimming just a dozen feet away from the surface of the pinnacle.

The wind continued to howl, but a deeper, rumbling sound grew even clearer.

'This is more than just a storm.' Coteaz adjusted the runes on his helm display, analysing the information gathered by his power armour. 'There is something else happening. Seismic tremors.'

He opened the vox-channel. 'Report. Are you still airborne?' There was a chorus of distorted replies.

'My lord,' said the pilot, glancing back at him. 'I see something up ahead, on the next pinnacle.'

'Taphos?'

'No,' said Sato. 'Too soon.'

'It looks like there are buildings down there,' said the pilot. 'But there shouldn't be.'

The auto-senses in Coteaz's armour struggled to give him clear data until they had flown closer, then he recognised the signals. 'Domus Alpha.'

'Xylothek is here ahead of us,' said Sato.

'But she has landed. Or crashed. Take us closer.'

Sato removed her blindfold. 'What if she has already laid her hands on the thing we seek?'

Coteaz did not reply.

As the aircar raced past the surface of the pinnacle, they saw that the landscape beneath them was being transformed. Storms had lashed the planet unceasingly since Coteaz landed, but this was different. The towers of rock were juddering and splitting, and as they came apart, shapes were emerging from the holes, like pus from an infected wound. It was impossible to make out the details at this distance, but they were pallid and gleaming, a shocking contrast to the dark, bloody hue of the pinnacles.

'It has begun,' said Coteaz.

Sato glanced at him. 'What do you mean?'

Coteaz shook his head. The situation had worsened even faster than he had anticipated. 'Novalis is damned.'

CHAPTER TWENTY-ONE

Until they left Vespertinus, Voltas had only seen scavenger engines from a distance. It was only now, as he looked out from the cabin of one, that he realised just how vast they were. The thing resembled an enormous, armoured flea, with a bulky middle section, small head-like cabin, and dangling drill cables that resembled legs; but where fleas were flightless, the scavenger engine was held aloft by rotor blades that howled and hacked at the storm. The cabin alone was large enough to hold dozens of miners and cutting servitors, but the passenger compartment behind it could hold hundreds. There were currently only a dozen people in the cabin with Voltas. As well as Malevich and Korov, six Scions, one of Aldrov's pilots, and three of his colonial militiamen had joined the party. The viewport was at the front of the cabin, like a domed eye, and Voltas was seated before it, strapped securely into a chair, watching the storm hit the armaglass.

The scavenger engine looked as old as the *Pilgrim's Wrath*, but unlike Coteaz's flagship, it had not been revered and polished daily by legions of servitors. Everything was coated in rust and crystals. Split pipes dangled from a broken ceiling, leaking steam and hissing, and Voltas' seat was a badly taped mess of torn synthleather, oily rags and buckled plasteel. Such slovenliness made his jaw clench, and he imagined what his father would say if he saw a vessel left in such a disgusting state. Thinking of his father reminded him of home. He pictured the gleaming palaces where he was raised and tutored. They were the staging ground that had prepared him for a life of leadership. He could see, now, that some of it was decadent, but he still found merit in much of what he was taught. Highborn families *should* live well. They *should* be proud. They *should* set a good example to those of lesser birth.

'The weather is growing worse,' said the pilot. She was seated just behind Voltas in a command throne that looked on the verge of collapse. The vehicle's other controls were operated by mono-function servitors – cadaverous, eyeless lumps, welded into wall-mounted logic engines. The pilot communicated with them by means of a plasteel skull cap sewn to her scalp and linked to a control panel by a quivering mane of cables and wires. 'Do we keep heading south?' Her face was anxious and lit from beneath by the viewscreens.

'The heretics left in engines even larger than this one,' said Malevich. 'Our auspexes will pick them up soon.'

'Only if we're heading in the right direction,' said Voltas. 'Governor Aldrov was only guessing when he said they might be headed to Port Gomera. They could just as easily be making for one of the other mines. They may be planning another attack. We don't know which sites have fallen yet.'

Malevich nodded. 'You have a point, interrogator. What do you suggest?'

Voltas thought back over the military treatises he had read, recalling descriptions of similar insurrections. 'They're mustering heretics. Governor Aldrov told Coteaz that the people who attacked Vespertinus came from many different mines, places right across the northern hemisphere. Whoever's leading them must be summoning them somehow. They must have sent out some kind of call to arms. A beacon.

'Widen your search,' he said to the pilot. 'Use your auspexes to look in every direction for as far as you can. Even behind us.'

The pilot muttered to herself, looking panicked as she clicked activation runes on her console. A servitor in the wall responded, groaning and shifting position. The pilot's viewscreens flickered as she stared at the displays. She inflated her cheeks as she frowned at the data, running a finger over the digits. She looked closer at the viewscreens.

'There are quite a few faint signals,' she said. 'Groups of aircars, by the look of them. Most of them are coming from the Xema hub.'

'A mine?'

'A small one. We haven't heard anything from them for months.'

'Plot all the routes and calculate their intended destination. See if they match.'

The pilot looked back down at her controls, touching levers and causing the servitors to move again. 'The course is erratic because, well… The storm makes it hard to be sure, but I think… If they stayed on the same route, it looks like they're all headed for a point to the north-east of Port Gomera. Pinnacle 12:33:48F.'

'They might be mustering for an attack on the port,' said Voltas.

'We should alert Lord Coteaz and await his instructions,' said Malevich.

'No. We have to be sure. I won't go to Coteaz with an unproven theory. We need to see them land.'

Malevich tried to reply, but Voltas spoke over him. 'I'm not suggesting we engage them in combat. We simply need visual confirmation that they're congregating near the port. Otherwise, I might send Coteaz misinformation. We're in a mining rig. If the heretics spot us, they will think we're just answering their call.'

Doubt flashed in Malevich's eyes, but he nodded. 'As you command, interrogator. We should maintain a safe distance, though.' He waved at the cabin. 'I examined this rig before we left Vespertinus. It would be little use in a fight. The underslung drills are adapted from lascannon technology. They could be used as makeshift weapons, but not with any accuracy.'

'Head for the pinnacle,' said Voltas, 'but keep checking your auspex returns for any sign of smaller vessels. Tell me when we're a few miles away.'

The pilot nodded and whispered something, working furiously at the controls. Then the cabin tilted as the scavenger engine banked, eliciting another howl from the rotors.

No one spoke for a long while after that. The only sound came from Korov, who prayed relentlessly, adding more words to the scrawl that covered his rags. Nearly an hour passed before the pilot spoke up again.

'We're nearing our destination. And the auspex is picking up more signals. Larger masses. It must be other scavenger engines. They're static. It looks like they've landed on Pinnacle 12:33:48F.'

'You were right,' said Malevich.

Voltas nodded. 'Land us on the pinnacle, but keep a safe distance from the heretics.'

'Forgive me, Interrogator Voltas,' said the pilot, 'but how will I know what a safe distance is?'

'The nearest rigs will have picked us up on their auspex returns, but no one has shown any interest in us. We're just another scavenger engine, as far as the heretics are concerned. Just keep out of sight. Land us a mile or two from any of the other flyers. If they approach us, move on.'

The scavenger engine swayed and howled again, the noise of its rotors reverberating through the battered hull. Voltas noticed that Korov had stopped writing on his rags and sealed his envirosuit back up.

The rotors screamed as the vehicle dropped, and Voltas saw a shape emerging from the rain, directly beneath them. The pinnacle was as vast as all the others, and as the storm crashed around it, he could make out no sign of the heretics.

'Secure your envirosuits,' said Malevich as retro thrusters shook the floor.

Voltas waited for the engines to die then unfastened his harness and rose from his seat, wishing he could reach inside his hood to wipe the sweat from his face. The temperature and the crimson rain made him feel like he was bubbling through an artery. He resisted the urge to remove his suit and nodded to the access hatch that led out of the cabin. 'Arm yourselves.' He shook his head as the pilot began removing her harness. 'Remain here. Be ready to take off.'

She sat down again, looking even more troubled by having to remain alone than she had been by leaving with the others. A militiaman yanked the access hatch open. A shaft of red rain poured up into the cabin, splashing across the crooked ceiling panels and causing them to rattle and flap.

Voltas strode down the ladder, gesturing for the others to follow, then gave hand signals, directing the group to spread out in the shadow of the scavenger engine, spilling across the rocks. Korov was gripping a heavy lasweapon in his tendrils as he advanced, and the soldiers all raised guns as they deployed through the rain.

Voltas saw that the rocks ended not far ahead of where they were all standing. Waving the party forward, he walked on, shouldering his way through the atrocious weather, wiping treacly liquid from his hood as he climbed carefully over the hard terrain.

He unsheathed his rapier, holding it before him like a torch, using the fizzling current to protect the blade.

Eventually, the rocks sloped down to a ledge, which abutted an ocean of red fumes.

'Some of the surface will be crystal rather than rock,' said a yellow-clad militiaman, holding up his hand in warning. 'And the crystals give way sometimes.'

Voltas came to a halt near the edge of the precipice, then, conscious of the wind, crawled the last few feet. 'Magnoculars,' he called, glancing back, and one of the Scions passed him a pair. He clicked the activation rune and the lenses whirred. On the far side of the abyss, rising from the storm, there was a tower of darkness. He could tell immediately that it was not just another pinnacle. It was swaying in the wind like smoke, but it was symmetrical in shape, with plumes rising from either side that resembled wings. And right at the centre of the darkness was something that caused him to curse.

'Is that a face?' he muttered. He handed the magnoculars back to Malevich, who had just crouched next to him.

Malevich looked and frowned. 'A statue?'

Voltas took the magnoculars back and looked again. Something about the shape reminded him of the face that had slid from Turcifel's prayer beads. He could tell, by the way it was drifting and billowing, that it was not a solid mass, but Malevich was right – it did resemble an enormous statue, like a dark, ragged angel, rising from the storm. He tried to look at its face again but found that he could not make out the details. He stared harder, but then he was gripped by a nausea so violent that he had to avert his gaze. He looked down instead, remembering his original reason for approaching the ledge. The clouds rushed past, giving him a clear view of another ledge, a mile or so below.

'I see them,' he said, keeping his voice hushed, even though there was no way he could have been heard by the figures he had spotted. 'Scavenger engines. At least ten of them. Bigger than ours. And aircars. The heretics have all disembarked by the looks of it. There are hundreds of them down there.'

'What are they doing?' asked Malevich.

The heretics had formed a rough semicircle and it looked as if they were facing the column of darkness.

'Praying?' Voltas suggested. He adjusted the lenses, trying to get a closer view. 'They're on their knees, heads bowed. I think I was right about them being heliocultists. It looks like they're just–'

'Leave,' said Korov.

Voltas and Malevich looked round at him in surprise. It sounded like he had clawed the word from behind his muzzle.

'Now,' the man added.

'Control yourself,' replied Voltas. 'It is not your place to give orders.' He kept his voice level, but something was wrong with him. Cramps were tightening in his stomach. He felt like doubling over and retching. And there was a sense of dread growing in him. The face he had seen in the darkness filled his thoughts. It *was* similar to the face he had seen in Turcifel's prayer beads.

'We leave when I say,' he said. As the ominous feeling grew, he almost felt like doing as Korov suggested, but where would that leave him? What chance would he have to shine if he departed now? *Be bold.* His mother's words gave him fresh resolve. He would not return to Coteaz with half a report.

He scanned the scene again, spending several painful minutes trying to gather more accurate information as Korov gasped prayers.

He kept coming back to the dark shape. It was the size of one of the pinnacles, bigger than a mountain.

Like a god.

Where had that thought come from? It was almost as if someone else had deposited it in his thoughts.

'Leave!' snarled Korov again.

Voltas thought his legs were shaking. Then he realised it was the ground. The rocks were shifting beneath his feet as a tremor rumbled through the pinnacle.

'Earthquake,' said Malevich, backing away.

Still, Voltas wanted to stay. To leave like this, with nothing, would make him look ineffectual and weak.

Finally, the tremors grew so bad he had to relent.

'Back to the mining rig,' he said, turning and striding away from the ledge, still battling the urge to vomit.

A jet of liquid burst up into the air, hissing angrily, causing Voltas to sidestep and jump back. The tremors redoubled in force, and as rock and crystal broke all around him, a terrible smell wafted through the storm. It was the same stink he remembered from the ambush in the trench but much more powerful. A mixture of infected meat and faeces. More columns of dark liquid burst from the ground, hurling rocks.

Most of the group began to run.

They had only gone a few paces when a militiaman's hood filled with bright-green vomit. He stumbled to a halt, gripping his head, turning to look at Voltas with a shocked expression.

Everyone halted as he staggered, groaning, and wrenched the hood off, flinging vomit through the air. He looked panicked as he shook the hood, holding his breath. He was about to put the hood back on, when the smell grew even worse and he vomited again, so violently that he let go of the hood and it was whipped away by the storm.

As the man cried out and stumbled off into the rain, another militiaman doubled over, groaning and coughing and clutching his stomach. Even some of the Scions were coughing and weaving from side to side.

'Keep moving!' cried Voltas, still striding as the others ran.

They had almost reached the scavenger engine when the ground split, tearing like sodden rags.

A thunderous roar shook the air as a wall of sulphurous liquid juddered up in front of them, blocking their way and showering the rock with yellow spume. The stench intensified and the ground shook so hard that Voltas struggled to keep a grip on his pistols. Then he heard screaming. It was such a shrill, deranged sound that it seemed inhuman, but it was coming from the Scion nearest to the eruption. He was backing away, shaking his head as his lasgun fell from his hands and clattered onto the rocks.

'Throne...' snarled Korov.

Another vast shape heaved itself from the ground, but this time it was not rock or liquid. Intestines were bubbling up from beneath the surface – the intestines of a leviathan, glistening and vast, steaming as they boiled into the rain.

Voltas took aim at the shape with his pistol, struggling to identify the best place to shoot it. Then he realised it was not *it* but *they.* The shapes were enormous invertebrates – larvae as big as hab-units, writhing in silence as they spilled out across the rocks.

The Scion nearest to him was still screaming, his voice hoarse and hitching as he dropped to his knees. An enormous, worm-like thing turned its eyeless head on the trooper. It paused, as though sniffing him, then lurched forwards and swallowed the top half of his body. The man continued screaming as the grub ingested him. Voltas heard his muffled cries as his legs kicked and convulsed. Then the grub jerked backwards and consumed the rest of him.

Voltas stared, unable to look away as the grub swallowed, its ridged body undulating, the lump made by the Scion still visible as it sank lower. The screams finally ended and the scene became eerily quiet. As Voltas watched the tide of pale, bloated shapes, he felt his mind starting to strain. They were not natural. These things were not normal predators. He could feel it instinctively. The sight of them made his pulse hammer. They did not belong in this world. In *any* world. They were warp spawn. This was sorcery.

'Recant!' boomed Korov. Bright fire spewed from his flamer, engulfing the monsters as he switched it back and forth. He repeated the word until it became incomprehensible, but the grubs remained silent, even as they blackened and burst, though they did recoil, scattering across the rocks like waves breaking on a beach. As they split, they poured other shapes into the air – clouds of bluebottles that bloomed up into the smoke and rain.

Voltas ran to Korov's side, sheathed his rapier and fired his pistols, one after the other. It was impossible to know which part of the creatures to target, so he fired wildly, howling a prayer.

Malevich appeared at his side, shooting with a calm that looked surreal in the face of such lunacy.

The barrage of shots was so ferocious that the monstrous shapes fell away, rolling and spreading further across the top of the pinnacle.

'We're driving them back,' said one of the militiamen, sounding hysterical.

Voltas looked around and saw how wrong the man was. There were shapes snaking into view everywhere he looked. It was as if the whole pinnacle had become rotten meat, rupturing as parasites coiled up from beneath its skin.

'Now! cried Voltas, rushing forwards and waving for everyone else to follow. Korov had managed to burn a path through the monsters. The scavenger engine was up ahead and looked to be undamaged. But it would only be a matter of seconds before the warp entities surged over it.

Flies drummed into his visor as he ran, settling over his

envirosuit, buzzing at the seams and trying to find a way in. Some were grotesquely large, as big as his fist and heavy enough to hurt as they thudded against him, tearing at his suit. He batted them away, fighting the urge to vomit as the stink grew.

Voltas and the others had almost reached the access ladder when Malevich cried out a warning. Voltas turned and looked back to see that Korov had stopped. The monsters he had ignited were detonating, hurling toxic-looking liquid through the air.

Another shape juddered up through the ground.

Korov fired a projectile. There was an ear-splitting boom and a fresh wave of slop sprayed towards them, followed by a series of moist popping sounds as more of the warp spawn erupted.

Voltas spotted a route through the tide of filth and ran on.

As he approached the scavenger engine, one of the creatures loomed up ahead of him.

He fired and there was a roar of heat and noise.

Agony ripped through his face and he fell back to the ground.

He could feel his skin bubbling beneath his suit. Malevich was rushing to help him, calling out his name, but his attention was fixed on something else. He had fallen near a precipice, and from where he lay, he could see that he had misunderstood something fundamental about Novalis. Something his reports had all failed to mention.

The pinnacles were not the planet's only feature. Rising between them was something even larger.

'Tell Coteaz,' he gasped, as Malevich's face loomed into view. Then smoke robbed him of consciousness, dragging him into velvet darkness.

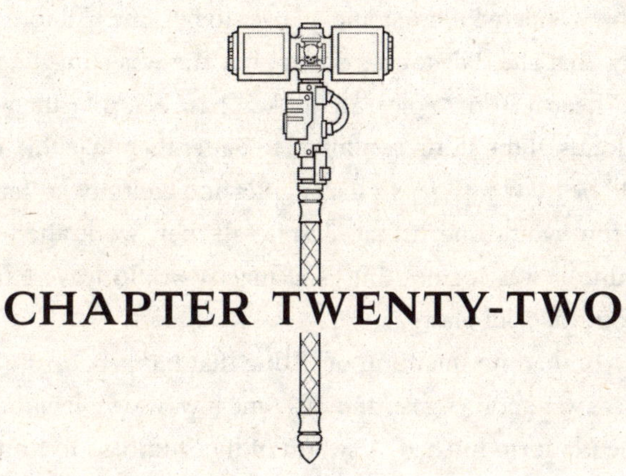

CHAPTER TWENTY-TWO

Glycon watched Magos Xylothek as she worked, waiting for any sign that she needed his assistance. They were standing on Domus Alpha's landing platform as adepts and servitors attempted to repair the engines. The crash landing had torn large holes in the enviro-baffle and the wind was now attempting to make them even larger, wrenching the canvas back and forth and screaming, banshee-like, through the seams.

Most of the adepts were praying furiously to the platform's machine spirit. Some were kneeling, heads bowed, hands and mechadendrites splayed on the grilled floor. One was swinging a pair of copper censers and surrounding herself with perfumed smoke as she called out to the Omnissiah. Another had severed one of his fingers and was using it to draw zeros and ones on the floor, shouting, 'The Spirit is the spark!' as he bled onto the metal. With the bulk of the tech-priests praying, only a few were available to attempt repairs. And even those paused every few seconds to lend their voices to the chorus.

Magos Xylothek was praying too, but she was clearly in pain, grimacing and clutching at her side. Every time she stumbled, Glycon wondered if he should go over to her. She had told him, firmly, that she did not need help, but she was struggling. He could hear it in her voice. He looked past her, into the whirling clouds. If the storm continued to batter them like this, there would be no way to repair the engines and continue to Taphos. And that would mean that, despite all their work, the whole expedition was for nothing. The magos would leave Novalis without the soul glass.

Glycon had no intention of letting that happen.

There was another gust, and this time it was so violent that the whole platform lurched. A swarm of flies tumbled in from the darkness outside. The flies had begun congregating on Domus Alpha a few hours ago, when the storm worsened; before that, Glycon had not realised flies even lived in the planet's northern hemisphere. To his surprise, they gathered around him, settling on his robes and his lenses, clogging the mechanisms and obscuring his vision.

A tremor shook the platform, throwing Xylothek to the floor. Her skirt of legs scrabbled uselessly across rain-slick metal and her face blanched.

Glycon batted away the flies and rushed over to her, taking one of her arms as a tech-thrall took another. <We have to go back inside, magos,> he canted, addressing her in voiceless, binharic code. She was about to refuse, but then, seeing that some of her legs had buckled and snapped, gave a grudging nod and allowed them to lead her into the facility.

Once the airlock was sealed, she shrugged off their grip and dusted herself down, shaking her head. <The damage is repairable. The Omnissiah will find a way.> Her eyes clicked as she waved the thrall back into the storm. Once the thrall was gone, she reached down to examine her damaged legs, snapping broken struts and tightening others. Then she limped off down the passageway.

Glycon whispered a prayer of thanks as he watched her go, inspired, as always, by her resolve. When the Omnissiah created Magos Xylothek, he poured all his ingenuity and wisdom into her. There were people, even within the Martian priesthood itself, who spread doubt and cynicism, but in Xylothek the Machine God had provided incontrovertible proof that humanity, in its improved form, was bound for glory.

He studied her as she hobbled away from him. She seemed unharmed, apart from the minor damage to her legs, but Glycon was not fooled. He had seen the pain in her eyes grow worse over recent weeks. She had confided in him, as soon as she heard of the malignancy in her lungs. The disease had spread so quickly that even replacing organs with machine parts had been unable to slow it. It was in her blood and in her bones. The weakness of her flesh had betrayed her. On the night she told him, Glycon had taken the news in stoic silence, but when he was alone, he had felt despair. How could it be that she would die? How could that be the Omnissiah's will? Then, to his amazement, as he prayed, Glycon heard the Omnissiah answering him. The voice had entered his thoughts robed in beautifully elegant binharic.

Bring her to Novalis. There is soul glass here. The magos need not die.

To Glycon's delight, when he suggested the idea to Xylothek, it had struck a chord with her. Rather than dismissing it as irrational, as he thought she might, she had been delighted with him, revealing that Novalis was one of the worlds she had suspected of being home to soul glass. He had given her the missing piece to a puzzle she had spent her whole life grappling with. And now, as the storm raged outside, he was close to giving her everything she ever wanted. He wished he could tell her, but he had sworn not to.

She must not know I have spoken to you, the Omnissiah had warned. ***She must think this was your idea. Imagine the uproar if you reveal that I am working through you directly. Xylothek and the other magi would have to examine the nature of this miracle. Months would be lost in needless debates and fruitless research. And while the arguments raged, the soul glass would be taken by another. Inquisitor Coteaz. He is already on his way.***

Glycon had seen the sense of the argument immediately and the magos never learned where his idea came from.

She paused and looked back, as though sensing that he was thinking of her. <Ensure that they work fast. None of the previous storms have lasted this long. The statistics imply it will end soon. We must be ready to launch. Or I will remain stranded here while Inquisitor Coteaz secures that which we have…> She shook her head. <Or perhaps not even Coteaz. It may even be Sato. She has withheld many truths from us.>

<Of course, magos.>

She turned and lurched back towards her chambers, looking like she was carrying a heavy weight.

He waited until she was out of sight, then he checked the chronometer blinking in his lenses. Perfect timing. If she had not dismissed him at that particular moment, he would have excused himself anyway. The timings were very specific. They had been all along. He patted his robes to check he had everything he needed, then, rather than going back out onto the platform, he set off in a different direction, heading through a door and down a narrow corridor, making for the facility's suite of laboratoriums. He passed servitors, menials and tech-thralls, but they were all rushing to the exit, racing to help with the engine repairs.

'Lexmechanic Keuper?' he called, tapping at a door.

There was a shuffling sound from the other side and the sound of void-crates being dragged across the floor. Then the door rattled open to reveal a small, hunched-looking tech-priest. He was wearing the same crimson robes as Glycon, but rather than a nest of metal-cased lenses, he still wore his original, human face. He was old, with jowly features and rheumy, protruding eyes.

<Genetor Glycon.> He peered myopically up at Glycon for a moment, then shuffled back into his room, leaving the door open.

Glycon followed him in, closing the door behind him. The room was as small and cluttered as the rest of the facility. Keuper's job was to analyse data and reports, and the room was crowded with datascreeds – mounds of anointed parchment, filled with inky, handwritten columns of binary. There was a workbench at one end of the room, heaped with a variety of logic engines, chronometers and measuring devices, and the floor was mostly covered by stacks of books and discarded scrolls. It looked like utter chaos, but Glycon had worked with Keuper for decades and he knew the old man would be able to lay his hands on any information that was requested by Magos Xylothek or any of the adepts.

Keuper returned to his work, hunching over the workbench and continuing to write on a half-completed parchment. <There is no logic to any of this. The storm is not following the usual pattern. It should be calming by now.>

Glycon quietly bolted the door, then walked over to the workbench to look at Keuper's work. He was no lexmechanic, but even he could see the picture Keuper was painting with data. The storm had seven focal points, though three were much larger than the others. One was near Port Gomera, one was over their heads, and the largest of all was above the ruined tower at Taphos. The three points formed a triangle.

<Very peculiar,> continued Keuper. <Triple-eyed hurricane. Not a concentric eyewall cycle but three distinct eyes, working as one. And if you include those other areas of concentration, it forms a seven-pointed symbol.> He picked up another scroll and peered at the numbers, holding it so close to his face his nose was almost touching the vellum. <And have you seen this?> He looked up at Glycon, passing him the scroll. <Flies. A plague of flies. On a world made of lifeless rock. Where are they coming from?> He paused, frowning as he noticed the small, flat plate of metal Glycon was holding. <Is that…> He looked closer, eyes widening in surprise. <What *is* that?>

Glycon turned the metal so that Keuper could see the designs engraved into it. <A quietus tablet.>

Keuper licked his lips as though eyeing up a choice cut of meat. <I have never heard of one surviving in such good condition. Almost like new. How did you acquire it? Is it part of Magos Xylothek's collection?>

Pride washed through Glycon; if he'd had a mouth, he would have smiled. <The Omnissiah grants us different ways to serve.> He held the metal up, so that it glimmered in the light of the strip lumen dangling from the ceiling. <I have been given the chance to complete this map. The lines you see show the location of something called soul glass. And the seven points form a key that will reveal the exact location. But, as you can see, the seventh point is yet to appear. It is all I need to complete the map.>

Keuper frowned. <Quietus tablets are heretical, Glycon. You know that. Forbidden.>

At the last moment his eyes filled with fear and he tried to back away, bumping against the table. But Glycon was too fast. Keuper was old and clumsy, and Glycon had performed six sacrifices prior to this one. He had discovered that he had an unexpected aptitude for murder. He brought the quietus tablet down in a chopping motion.

The metal sliced neatly through Keuper's skull.

Keuper stared at Glycon, blood rushing from his nostrils, then he toppled back against the workbench.

Glycon worked quickly, using a knife to lever the man's skull open so he could press the metal plate onto the exposed brain. There was an immediate surge of power, just like on the previous occasions, just as the Omnissiah had told him there would be. This time it was even more powerful. The metal glowed with inner fire as Keuper's life force rushed into it.

Glycon felt drunk as he backed away, letting Keuper drop to the floor. The map was drawing itself before his eyes, smouldering lines snaking across its surface and connecting the seventh point on the symbol. He whispered a prayer of thanks. It had worked. Everything had worked, just as it had been promised. With the seven points complete he could see the exact part of Taphos where the soul glass was stored. For a moment, all he could do was stare at the blood-drenched map, his heart racing. Then he remembered how little time he had left. The storm *would* abate. The Omnissiah had been clear on that. Domus Alpha would reach the soul glass. All he had to do was show the map to Xylothek and explain what he had done. She would be free to transfer her soul into a new, healthy body. Perhaps *his* body, if she thought him worthy.

He wiped the metal down with a rag and resecured it under his robes. He paused at the door, looking back at the corpse, wondering if he should hide it somehow. No, he decided. It made no difference now. Xylothek would never forgive him for the murders. Or for using the quietus tablet. He had known that all along. Even though he was giving her the prize she had sought all her life, it was inevitable that she would have him executed for what he had done. But he was going to save her life. Perhaps, in years to come, she would understand. All he had to do was make sure he placed the map in her hand and explained what it was. After that, nothing else mattered. The soul glass would be hers.

He unlocked the door and rushed out into the corridor, heading towards Xylothek's chamber, but he had only been walking for a few minutes when he noticed something odd. Something was moving under his robes. It felt, bizarrely, as if something was crawling across his skin.

He pulled his robes open, half expecting to see a rodent. Then he saw that the quietus tablet was being absorbed into his organic body. It looked like a raft, sinking beneath the surface of a pool. Half of the metal was already hidden, embedded in his stomach. He pawed at it with his fingers, panicked. He had to hand it to Xylothek. Once he was revealed as the murderer, he would be killed. He had to make sure the tablet was in her possession before he died. He sank his fingernails into his skin, drawing blood, but it was useless. Within a few seconds the entire piece of metal was inside his body. He could see its shape, dark beneath his pale skin, like a rectangular bruise.

He drew the knife he had used on Keuper, wondering if he could cut the thing out, but to his horror he realised it was already too deep. He would have to cut his stomach apart to reach it. He might bleed to death before he could tell Xylothek what he had done for her.

He looked back the way he had come, wondering if he should return to the laboratorium and hide Keuper's body to buy himself some time, but quickly rejected the idea. He had to reach Xylothek. Whatever happened, he should have time to inform her about the map. Even if they gunned him down, he could tell her that she needed to look in his corpse – that he contained her salvation. There was a kind of strange poetry to the idea that he was carrying her future life. He tried to grasp what was happening. Perhaps the map needed one last surge of soul matter? But it was complete. He had seen the location of the soul glass.

He clutched his head as he ran on, still determined to reach Xylothek. The strangeness was not over, however. As he ran, he was overcome by the sudden need to vomit. It was not liquid that emerged, but a torrent of pale grubs. He stood there, slumped against the wall, focusing lenses trained on the larvae as they crawled around his boots.

Curious, he thought, spilling maggots from his respirator grille.

<Genetor Glycon?> An adept rushed from a doorway, looking at Glycon in concern. <You are unwell. Let me...> His words trailed off as he saw the pile of glistening grubs. <What is...?> He shook his head, backing away, confused.

Glycon took a phosphor pistol from his robes and fired, engulfing the adept in a sphere of white light. The adept convulsed on the floor for a few seconds then lay still, with currents scintillating over his corpse.

Glycon slammed the door then slumped against the wall again, battling the urge to vomit. He could no longer feel the map in his stomach, but there was a strange vigour washing through him, as though he had drunk an energising tonic. Despite the horror of what had just happened, he had to resist the urge to laugh. He realised, as bizarre as it seemed, that he felt pleased. He wondered if he was losing his grasp on sanity. The quietus tablet had dissolved in his stomach, he was a murderer, and there were maggots fidgeting in his mouth, but he felt elated. He dismissed the issue. Only one thing mattered. He had to reach Magos Xylothek.

He continued down the corridor, and even when he realised

his body was swelling and changing he did not falter. 'I am coming, magos,' he said, speaking aloud in a moist growl.

CHAPTER TWENTY-THREE

Light filtered into Voltas' consciousness like sun through curtains, diffuse and mesmerising. He lay still for a while, eyes closed but sensing movement through his lids. Delicate shapes flitted past and he heard birdsong, some of it nearby but some distant enough to summon an image of far-off leafy groves. It all seemed so familiar and pleasing. Voltas was filled with such a feeling of wellbeing that, for a long time, he could not bring himself to move, but gradually he became more aware of his surroundings. There was short, springy turf under his hands and a warm breeze caressing his face. There were painful memories waiting to pounce on him, the moment he opened his eyes, so he battled the urge to look, cherishing the moment of peace. But the memories came anyway. He pictured the flames that engulfed his body. Was he dead, then? Was this his reward? No, it could not be. This could not be his fate. He would not accept it.

He opened his eyes to find he was lying in an ornamental garden. There were flowerbeds, shrubs, and ponds everywhere he looked, arranged in such a harmonious design that one shape led to another and every plant and fountain seemed to be engaged in a graceful dance. It was the garden he had trained in as a child, fencing and riding, but at the same time it was not. It was something far more wonderful. It was more perfect than any real garden could ever be.

Voltas knew none of this made sense, but the dream was so intriguing that he played along, climbing to his feet and walking across the sun-dappled lawn. He trailed his fingers in wonderfully cold pools and looked up at the sky through sun-drenched canopies. Everything was so perfectly arranged. Every leaf had been placed with care. As he walked, he realised he was not alone – there were people tending to the plants, watering and pruning in silence, their faces hidden in deep green and brown hoods. They were doing more than tending to the plants; they were counting and cataloguing them, keeping tallies of every stem and leaf, filling the columns of ledgers with exhaustive notes and calculations. They were keeping track of everything that lived and grew. He did not even consider speaking to them. They radiated a sense of timelessness, as though they had been working at this garden since the dawn of the cosmos. But then he spotted another figure. This one was different. Rather than working, it was striding down an avenue of trees, heading away from him. The sun was low, casting long shadows, but Voltas could see that it was a large, powerfully built man in bulky, golden armour.

'Coteaz?' He was right. He wasn't dead. Coteaz had saved him somehow.

Voltas crossed the lawn and headed down the avenue of trees. 'Coteaz?'

The figure reached a leafy arbour, turning to face Voltas as he sat on a bench under an arch of knotted branches. It was not Coteaz. He was wearing armour that looked almost identical, but his features were cruder and more brutish than the High Protector's. Also, rather than wisps of white at his temples, this man had thick black hair, tied back in a plait. There was something barbaric about him. He was an inquisitor though, that much was clear from the rosette on his armour. And he was dressed for war, with a beautifully worked bolt pistol at his belt and a sword at his other hip. He gave Voltas a smile that was so warm and unaffected that it made the situation seem perfectly ordinary. He nodded to the stone bench he was sitting on, indicating that Voltas should join him.

Voltas was about to do so when he noticed something about the man's golden armour and the beautiful scene behind him. It seemed, for a fraction of a second, too vivid, too saturated with colour. The feeling passed as quickly as it came, but it was enough for Voltas to remember that he should not be here. He could not really be strolling in a beautiful garden.

'Who are you?' he asked. He half expected his words to emerge as petals or sunlight, but his voice sounded normal.

The man gestured to the seat again, but when Voltas continued standing, he shrugged cheerfully. When he spoke, his words sounded intimate, as if they were registering in Voltas' mind, rather than in his ears.

'My name is Laredian. High Protector of the Formosa Sector.'

Again, Voltas had the odd sensation that the grass was too green and the flowers smelled too sweet, but he was keen to hear the man out. Perhaps this was only a dream, but dreams could be illuminating.

'You are dead,' he said.

The man seemed untroubled by the suggestion. He looked around at the garden. ***'All a matter of perspective.'*** He adopted a more serious expression. ***'We don't have long. Listen to me while you can. Coteaz is a threat. I should know, I created him.***

I taught him, when he was still a child, that only one thing matters – to know more than anyone else. What a poor teacher. A few words, spoken without thought, can do a lot of damage. Coteaz grasped my words but not my meaning. He thinks knowledge is a thing to be hoarded and hidden. He has a genius for acquiring it, but then, once he has it, he's afraid someone might put it to better use than him.'

Even in such an idyllic location, the words rankled. It reminded Voltas of when Inquisitor Sato had tried to poison him against Coteaz. But he sensed that this conversation had more riding on it than his talk with Sato.

'Why are you telling me this?'

Laredian, if it was Laredian, smiled again. There was no bitterness in his face. *'Because there will come a time, Nicolas Voltas, very soon, when you will see him for what he really is. He has power. I know that better than anyone. It's the reason I trusted him when I should have known better. If I had left him where he was, or if I had left him to become a simple warrior, he might have become a great man. But as he is, with his grip on all of Formosa, he is a threat.'*

Voltas was about to reply, but the man held up a hand, still smiling.

'I understand. You are suspicious of me. You don't believe me. Which is all as it should be. Your loyalty is commendable. I just want you to know something. I am going to destroy Coteaz. I think it will happen in a matter of hours, but I have not seen every eventuality. There's a small chance he might escape his fate for a while. He's nothing if not cunning. And if that happens, if his end is postponed, you will have a chance to ensure your future. If Coteaz survives, if he finds a way to leave Novalis, remember our conversation. And when you realise I spoke the truth, all you need to do is pray to me – pray with all your

heart and I will find a way to reach you. And, together, we will stop him. Together we will give you your due. Remember that.'

The smile faltered on his face as he looked at something behind Voltas.

Voltas' sense of foreboding increased and he looked back down the avenue of trees. He gasped as he saw flames rushing through the garden, ripping through it as though the whole scene was a burning canvas. It was terrifying and beautiful. He looked back towards the arbour, but the man was gone and flames were rushing from that direction, too. He tried to run, sprinting away from the arbour, but the fire pressed in on him from every direction, surrounding him with unbearable heat. Burning branches crashed down around him, and he coughed on smoke and embers as the garden collapsed.

As the scene burned away, it revealed a peculiar sight: a sea of inky colours, whirling like a kaleidoscope, but Voltas was only half aware of it. All he could think about was the agony washing over his skin and the stranger's words. *Ensure your future.* What did that mean?

He tumbled to the ground, gasping as heat devoured him.

CHAPTER TWENTY-FOUR

'What *is* that?' gasped the pilot, hammering at the aircar's controls.

Coteaz studied the pilot, wondering how long the man's sanity would hold.

The shape rushed at them again, but this time it halted in mid-air, a dozen feet away, hovering. The thing was grotesque. It looked like a hunched, sickle-shaped fly, but it was obscenely large, as big as the aircar, with flesh that was grey and rotten, leaking black, tacky blood into the rain. It flew closer, moving in glitchy bursts like damaged pict footage, slipping in and out of focus, vanishing and reappearing, its foothold in reality not yet fully established.

'Warp spawn,' said Coteaz and Sato simultaneously.

Coteaz felt a familiar tingle in the air. Etheric currents caressed his skin and throbbed in his bones, gnawing at him like an ague. The pilot banked again, avoiding another winged shape. It was either the same monster or an identical one, and as the aircar rushed past it, Coteaz saw it in sickening detail. Its hide was so corrupted it had split in many places, trailing knots of wet viscera. There were other shapes in the holes, faces staring out from the insect's abdomen: terrified and half-digested, calling to him for help. The souls of the damned. This was the fate of everyone who strayed from the light of the God-Emperor. Their faces were scored with runes like those Coteaz had seen as a child, cut into the bodies of his family.

Bile filled his mouth, his muscles tensed. 'Open fire.'

The pilot was shaking, but his sanity continued to hold. He grabbed a control and the cabin shook as he fired a hull-mounted stubber. The gun rattled noisily, spewing bullets through rotten hide, spraying blood and pus into the air. The warp spawn juddered, pounding its decayed wings and managing to hold its position, then it tumbled from view.

'Thank the Throne,' whispered the pilot.

'I need to know why Domus Alpha has come down here,' said Coteaz. 'I need to speak with Xylothek. Find a place to land.'

Sato shook her head. 'The mapmaker is not here. They're at Taphos.'

'But the magos arrived ahead of us. She may already have the glass. Take us down.'

As the flyer plunged towards the rocks, Coteaz saw other shapes starting to materialise around them, all as grotesque as the first.

'Stay close,' he said into the vox, addressing the other aircars. 'We are going to attempt a landing.'

Below, they saw Domus Alpha, but much of the research facility was hidden from view. A rotating column of darkness enshrouded the whole pinnacle. Coteaz leant forwards in his seat, studying the storm. It looked like a cyclone, but it was clearly no natural weather phenomenon. It was black rather than the red common to most of the storms on Novalis, and there was something odd about its texture. As they flew lower, he saw it was made of flies, the insects swarming and frenzied, as though they were fighting for rotten meat. Some of the flies were normal in appearance, but others were huge and grotesquely deformed, like the one that had just attacked them.

The other thing that was odd about the cyclone was its shape. It seemed to have been designed, rather than forming naturally. Two protrusions rose from its sides like enormous wings, and at its centre, there was the half-formed outline of a face.

Coteaz had spent his whole career confronting things that might stop another man's heart, but despite the surgeries Albaro had performed on him, he was still mortal. He was not a genetically engineered being, like the Emperor's Angels of Death. And when he faced a vision like the one forming over Domus Alpha, he felt the same revulsion any sane individual would feel. But unlike most sane individuals, he could parcel his emotions away, handling them as if they were irradiated rock and placing them in the deepest recesses of his thoughts. The fear was present, but it did not debilitate him.

'Xylothek is here,' he said, watching the glyph flickering across his retina.

'Could she have done this?' said Sato, grimacing at the shapes forming in the clouds. 'Could it be her who has weakened the veil?'

'Perhaps. But when I spoke with her I detected no trace of heresy.'

She stared at him. 'What about in the medicae room, with Turcifel and Voltas? What did you see then?'

'My old master,' he said, watching her closely to see how she would respond.

She frowned. 'You fired his corpse into the heart of a sun.'

Coteaz remembered the ceremony on the *Pilgrim's Wrath* when Laredian's corpse was interred in a boarding torpedo. The air had been so thick with censer smoke that the slain inquisitor had looked like a ghost. As the tech-priests sang they anointed the missile with ink, oil and wax.

He shrugged. 'Sometimes the past refuses to stay in the past.'

Flies drummed against the hull. Some sounded like hail, but others struck with the force of hurled bricks, slamming against the plasteel and causing it to buckle and split.

'This is the right altitude,' gasped the pilot, swinging the flyer back and forth through the darkness. The cloud of insects was too dense for them to see anything and the flight controls were juddering in his grip. 'But there's no landing platform.'

Coteaz leant forwards in his seat, peering out into the storm. 'Loop around. Keep looking.'

The pilot did as he was ordered, and a few minutes of stomach-lurching flight later, Sato pointed. 'There. Fly lower.'

As the aircar dived, Coteaz saw that Domus Alpha was beyond saving. The baffle had been torn away, exposing the buildings and equipment to the elements and the flies. Several of the structures had collapsed and pieces of wreckage were whirling around the platform, caught in the tornado. There were a pair of skitarii on the platform, the cybernetic Mechanicus soldiers struggling to stay upright despite their mechanised legs. They were both firing rifles into the storm of insects.

The Mechanicus troops looked up as the aircar lurched and tumbled down towards them, but then they returned to firing at the mutated insects. The aircar clattered onto the landing platform, but just as the pilot was about to kill the engine, the wind lifted the vehicle up again, hurling it towards the buildings.

'Damn!' he cried, jolting the controls back and narrowly missing a roof as he flew them up into the storm.

'Bring her round again!' demanded Coteaz.

The pilot brought the flyer down onto the platform a second time, and as its landing gear clattered on the surface, Sato and the abhuman leapt from the vehicle and grabbed cables, lashing them around the wheels.

'To me!' bellowed Coteaz as he exited the flyer, looking at the two skitarii troopers. They hesitated, then lowered their rifles and rushed over to help, hurling more cables over the landing gear and fixing them to the columns at the front of the building. Finally, with the flyer anchored to the ground, the pilot killed the engine and leapt out to help tie the aircar down. Thula launched herself into the storm, both heads screeching as she battled to hold her position, thrashing her enormous wings.

Once he was sure the vehicle was secure, Coteaz looked skyward for the other aircars. They were banking and lurching as clouds of flies drummed into them.

The pinnacle shook violently, rocked by another massive tremor. Coteaz was hurled sideways with such force that he almost fell from the edge of the platform.

The quake lasted longer than the previous ones, and he could do nothing but lie there as the flyer was thrown sideways and slammed into a cliff face on the side of the pinnacle. It exploded, filling the storm with flames and heat.

Coteaz had to shield his face as pieces of burning debris clattered down around him. There was a scream of broken rotors, then the flyer rolled onto its side and plunged into the abyss, trailing smoke and embers.

As the tremor started to lessen, he climbed to his feet, grabbing ropes with one hand and holding up the other one for Thula. She soared through the flies and latched on to his wrist as he hauled himself towards the door, calling for the others to follow him.

'Abort!' he ordered into the vox. 'Do not attempt to land. Back away from the pinnacle. It is too dangerous. Withdraw and await further instructions.'

The replies were distorted and jumbled, but as the aircars banked away into the storm, Coteaz saw that he had been understood.

He waited until Sato, Turcifel, and the others were in the airlock, then hauled the door shut. The noise of the storm was muffled but not silenced, and Coteaz could tell it was growing in violence. The chamber's floor slanted at an angle, like the deck of a listing ship. The whole station was close to collapse. There were klaxons barking in the distance, and the place was drenched in blinking red light.

He turned to the two tech-guards. Like most Mechanicus troops, they appeared more mechanical than human, but Coteaz knew that was misleading. Their legs were robotic, but the rest of them was simply encased in so much armour and diagnostic equipment as to appear inorganic. Beneath their combat helms there would be human faces, watching him with the same fear as anyone else who stood before an inquisitor.

'Where's the magos?' he demanded.

They shook their heads. 'Our orders were to guard the platform,' replied one of them, her voice like knives on metal. 'The order has not been countermanded.'

'Are you still in contact with your superiors?'

'The noosphere is compromised,' she replied, referring to the communications network used by the Adeptus Mechanicus. 'There was an attack on the magos' private chambers, but Genetor Glycon ordered us to hold our position.'

'An attack? By whom?'

'My lord, I do not have that information. Genetor Glycon ordered us to hold our position.'

Sato was about to reply, but Coteaz raised a hand for silence. Above the sound of the storm outside, he could make out the crackle of Mechanicus radium weapons.

'The attack is still in progress,' he said. He opened the airlock's other door and strode into the corridor beyond, lifting the daemonhammer from his back as he met a wall of smoke. 'Which way?' he snapped, looking back at the skitarii. They hesitated, then one of them gestured to a door.

Coteaz marched on into the facility, breaking into a run as the noise of fighting grew louder. As they approached Xylothek's chambers, a deep droning sound reverberated through the walls. At first, he thought it was the sound of the superstructure starting to collapse, but when he paused to listen, he realised it was something stranger.

'Sato. Do you hear words?'

Sato frowned as she listened to the rumbling sound. 'Perhaps,' she replied. 'Distorted, though. Someone speaking through an emitter? It's like a looped recording.'

Coteaz shook his head. It did not sound like an emitter. He could feel it in his stomach. He looked at Thula, wondering whether to send her ahead, but decided against it and rushed on, slamming the next door open with his hammer and passing into a large storeroom. He stumbled to a halt again after a few paces. The air felt viscous and treacly, as if he were pushing through liquid. His footfalls sounded muffled, adding to the sense he had entered a different environment. It was all too familiar. The moment Sato showed him her images of the quietus tablet, he had known this was coming, but things were moving faster than expected. The damnation of Novalis had been accelerated. Perhaps in response to his arrival.

He waded on through the thick, greasy air, ignoring the stench spilling out of the doorway ahead.

They had almost reached the doorway when the emergency lumens failed, plunging the research facility into darkness. The droning grew louder, booming with such force that void-crates tumbled from shelves, scattering ration packs and bedrolls across the tilted floor. The words were now unmistakeable as they roared through the darkness.

'Life eternal! Life eternal! Life eternal!'

The cry was too loud and resonant to have emerged from the throat of a natural creature.

The rest of the group triggered lumens and followed Coteaz as he waded towards the doorway and out into the corridor beyond. As he stepped over the threshold, Coteaz sank into knee-deep, steaming liquid. The floor looked stable in the dark but had actually been replaced by a thick, bituminous slurry. As he disturbed the surface, the stench increased, causing all of them to gag and cough. There was movement at the far end of the corridor, and as Sato shone her lumen that way, Coteaz saw figures moving near an open doorway. It was hard to make them out, but there was clearly a fight taking place. Above the subterranean rumble of the voice, he could still hear gunfire.

'Lord inquisitor,' said Turcifel. 'The hate, the anger I sensed when we were up on the shuttle. It's rising.'

Coteaz blinked through his retinal display grid, looking for the signals, and saw a glyph drifting into view. 'Voltas,' he muttered, adjusting the display and zooming in on the signal. 'He may be close enough to vox.' He opened a channel, ignoring the squall of feedback. 'Interrogator. Proceed to Alpha Domus. Prepare for extraction.'

There was a bang and the viscous liquid surged down the corridor, causing Coteaz and the others to stagger. Red-robed adepts and metal-clad skitarii backed towards them, firing blue-white energy into the darkness. The air crackled and seethed. Magos Xylothek appeared at the centre of the group, leaning on an adept and firing a radium pistol.

The doorway beyond them cracked and exploded, flinging plasteel through the air.

A colossal shape swelled through the gap, surging into the barrage of shots.

No sane man faced a daemon without fear. Coteaz had seen more than most, but this one was so big that it filled the corridor, rippling towards them like a sack of grey blubber. It looked like something excreted from the bowels of a leviathan, pale and boneless, with no discernible limbs. It boiled, sagged, and slapped towards them, oblivious to the shots striking it.

'Daemon of the abyss!' cried Coteaz, marching forwards as everyone else fled from the creature. 'You have no dominion here!' As he shouted, he held the daemonhammer aloft, spilling ether-light from the metal. Faith rose from his chest and the hammer responded, burning even brighter, magnifying his words, shaking the air. 'By the light of the Emperor! I *abjure* you!'

'Life eternal!' groaned the daemon in reply.

As its nauseating voice boomed out, Coteaz saw that the thing was not entirely featureless. There was a cluster of eyes blinking at its centre – dull, black orbs, like rotten berries pressed into animal fat, and near the eyes was an atrophied arm, holding something out. It looked like a piece of metal, but where the daemon had touched it, it was rusting and bubbling with corrosion. Wherever the daemon's flesh brushed against the walls or ceiling the same rot spread, washing over the metal like accelerated pict footage, corroding and infecting at incredible speed.

'Keep away from it!' he cried, calling back over his shoulder as he advanced. If the daemon touched the Scions or the Mechanicus adepts, he would find himself facing multiple enemies rather than one. He had seen many times how fast plague daemons could infect people, creating legions of zombie-like killers.

'Life eternal,' repeated the daemon, holding the lump of rusted metal towards Magos Xylothek.

Xylothek forced her way back towards Coteaz. 'It was birthed through Genetor Glycon's body. It emerged through him.' Her face was splashed with blood and her eyes were rolling. 'And he was the, ah, murderer. He was killing adepts as he came to find me.'

'He was looking for the soul glass,' said Coteaz, looking at the piece of metal the daemon was holding. 'To give it to you.'

She stiffened as he finally spoke the words out loud, but then she abandoned all thought of secrecy. 'Is that soul glass? Is that it?' Her voice was strained; she looked at the thing slumping towards them and the object it was holding with a sudden hunger in her eyes, and stepped towards it.

Coteaz shoved her back and shook his head, looking at the dripping lump of rust. 'It is not the glass. It is a quietus tablet. And it is poison.' The daemon had almost reached him. 'Get the magos out of here!' he ordered, before drawing back his hammer and charging.

The daemonhammer flashed as he swung it at the nest of eyes. He prayed as it landed, and it detonated, hurling noxious flesh through the air and forcing the daemon back. A lesser weapon would have rusted and crumbled, or mutated into something hellish, but the daemonhammer only blazed brighter. Coteaz drew it back for another blow.

'I *abjure* you!' he roared, bringing it down again and again.

Black, tar-like blood splashed across his armour and flies erupted from the wounds, but he was calm now. This was the Emperor's work. He was face to face with the enemy of all life. At these moments, more than any other, he felt truly alive. A mouth opened in the daemon's flesh, a foot-wide gash stuffed with wet intestines, and it tried to lunge at Coteaz, to devour him. But, by this point, he was incandescent, both physically and spiritually, his faith burning as bright as his armour. He was vaguely aware that another tremor was shaking through the facility, but his attention was fixed on the daemonhammer as it rose and fell. Pummelling the madness. Splitting the dark.

The daemon collapsed under the storm of blows until only its face remained – the cluster of ink-dark eyes and the grotesque, flaccid mouth. Coteaz drew back his hammer, but before he could strike the killing blow, the daemon grinned, spilling more flies from its mouth.

'Novalis will rise.'

It started to repeat the phrase, but Coteaz silenced it with a final blow, spattering the walls with muck. 'I abjure you,' he said.

As the daemon sizzled and dissolved into the slurry, Coteaz realised how bad the current tremor was. The whole structure was shaking, while outside it sounded like someone was using Novalis as a drum, pounding it with such force that the planet might collapse.

'Coteaz,' said a strangled voice. He whirled around to see who had spoken. It was Xylothek and she looked panicked. The rust that was spreading across the walls had washed up over her jumble of needle-thin legs. Where it met her robes, it had become a white mould, and where it had reached the skin of her forearms, it was an infection, causing her skin to fester and split. She held up one of her arms, staring at flies that were crawling from beneath the scabs.

The other tech-priests had retreated, but it was too late; as they looked down at their own bodies, they saw disease and decay rushing over them.

Now that the daemon had been silenced, the corridor was oddly quiet. The tremors had ceased for the moment and Coteaz could hear Xylothek's panicked breathing and the buzzing of insects. She stared at her hands as they curved and hardened, forming into talons.

'Wait,' she said, looking up at Coteaz. 'We can–'

Coteaz and Sato fired as one. Coteaz loosed silver-tipped psybolts, slugs of etheric power that flashed as they punched through metal, flesh and bone, purifying as they killed and filling the air with the scent of holy oil.

Once the killing was over, Sato lowered her gun but Coteaz remained as he was, staring at Xylothek's broken body, pistol raised, smoke trailing from the muzzle. When at last he looked away, he turned to Sato.

'We must continue to Taphos,' he said.

'We can't go back the way we came.' She gestured to the corrupted corpses.

Coteaz nodded at the doorway the daemon had emerged through. It was a festering hole, draped with threads of lemon-yellow pus. The metal bubbled and seethed, as though about to melt completely. 'Xylothek's chambers look even more toxic. But we need to reach the aircar before this facility collapses.'

He pictured the layout of the building. Voltas had shown him schematics while they were still on the *Pilgrim's Wrath* and he could roughly remember the location of the various rooms. If he was right, they were near the small chamber he had used when he interviewed Sato. And that backed onto an antechamber with a window in the exterior wall. He stepped back and studied the plasteel. It was slumped and bowed, and the daemon's rust was gradually spreading across it.

'Turcifel,' he said, nodding to the wall.

She obeyed without hesitation, praying furiously and gripping her beads.

The temperature dropped and the air around Turcifel became opaque. She yelled, the cords in her neck bulging, but no sound emerged from her mouth.

Then the wall ballooned away from her with a deep, grinding sound. Rivets spat through the air and supports buckled. A moment later the metal parted, melting away to form a circular opening.

They leapt through the gap and Coteaz saw that he had almost been right. The hole made by Turcifel actually straddled two rooms. One was a storeroom, heaped with esoteric devices and engine parts. The other was where he met Sato.

They crossed the room and entered the antechamber, looking out through a rain-lashed wall of armaglass at the scene outside. The building was almost entirely shrouded in darkness as flies swirled around it, but they caught glimpses of other pinnacles in the distance. As Coteaz tried to focus on them, he saw that something new was happening – clouds were rising up their sides like a flood tide, surging over the rocks towards the summits.

'Voltas,' he said, speaking into the vox.

There was no response, even though Coteaz could see on his helm display that Voltas was near the pinnacle.

He switched to a different channel. 'Malevich?'

After a brief pause Malevich's stiff tones filled the room. *'Lord Coteaz. We need to evacuate the planet. There is some kind of flood. Sixtus has analysed the liquid. It is highly toxic.'*

Coteaz peered out through the wall of flies, trying to catch a glimpse of the horizon. The swarm of insects parted for a moment and he saw the surrounding pinnacles again. What he had taken for clouds, boiling from the abyss, was actually a filthy ocean, rushing up to engulf the towers of rock. It was rising fast and it was boiling with corruption, hissing and rolling with pale shapes.

'Novalis will rise,' he said.

'What?' cried Sato, struggling to see what Coteaz was looking at.

'Novalis will rise,' repeated Coteaz more loudly, angry at himself for missing something so obvious. 'Those words didn't refer to a military uprising. It's not a metaphor. The *sea levels* are rising. Everything is going to be washed away.'

CHAPTER TWENTY-FIVE

'Lord inquisitor,' barked Malevich into the vox. 'We're approaching Domus Alpha now. Are you near the landing platform?'

The storm was booming all around them and the rig was shaking so violently that Coteaz's reply was lost beneath the noise of the rain, his static-fuzzed voice barely audible.

'Repeat, my lord,' said Malevich. 'I lost you.'

'Avoid the landing platform.' Coteaz's voice battled against the din. *'The superstructure is compromised. Approach from the north-east. Look for my signal.'*

The turbulence intensified as they reached the column of darkness. Objects slammed into the hull. Malevich watched in disgust as bloated shapes detonated across the armaglass, but he was more concerned by the scene below. The flood was rising so fast he could see it climbing up the sides of the pinnacle. It looked like a butcher's slop – dark and treacly and filled with lumps of pale meat. And there were things moving in it. He could not tell if he was seeing tails or serpents, but all of it was coated in the same tacky, mucal gunk.

These things were all vaguely familiar to him, as if he had dreamt about them or faced this moment before. He experienced this sense of deja vu often when serving Coteaz, but the inquisitor's silence on the matter had told him not to press the issue further. There were things Malevich would never know about his life with Coteaz – he sensed his memories only showed him a glimpse of his true career – but he was sure of one thing: serving the High Protector was an honour that was worthy of sacrifice. He glanced at Voltas, unconscious and bound to a chair. *Any* sacrifice.

The sea had almost covered the pinnacle and the small cluster of Mechanicus buildings at the top. The buildings were being torn open by the storm and there were insects crawling over the wreckage, flies as big as a grox and pale, eyeless pupae that were even larger, all tearing through the rockcrete and pulling the place apart. Close by, other, even more disturbing things clambered from the rubble: hunched, humanoid figures that were clearly *not* human. They were clad in the same mottled flesh as the grubs, but they had scrawny arms and legs and sagging guts. The weather was too bad for Malevich to see them in any detail, but again he felt a sense of recognition. They carried rusty metal cleavers and, despite the mayhem surrounding them, worked with slow, methodical purpose, trudging through the flies and scanning the buildings with the single boil-bright eye embedded in each creature's forehead. They were clearly in no hurry. Around them, smaller shapes, like bloated infants, cavorted and gambolled through the fumes.

'What *are* they?' said the pilot, looking over at him. Her face was white and her hands were shaking on the flight controls.

'The enemy,' said Malevich. 'Take us lower.'

There was a flash near one of the upper windows. Malevich recognised the dazzling quality of the light. 'That's the High Protector. Get us as close to that window as you can.'

The pilot nodded. She was made of sterner stuff than Malevich had expected. As they flew closer, the air began vibrating with a low, droning hum. It was a tuneless, monotonous dirge. It sounded like the warp entities were counting or reciting a list.

'No closer!' gasped the pilot as the rig hovered a dozen yards or so from the top of the building. She peered out of a viewport. 'Are those people?'

'Keep your eyes on the research facility,' he replied.

The pilot looked from Korov to Malevich, then back at the storm. 'And what then? What if Port Gomera is flooded too?'

No one answered.

'The High Protector,' said one of the Scions, pointing out into the storm.

Coteaz had emerged from the collapsing building, his golden armour flashing, even in the miserable pall. He had climbed through a broken window, gripping a crumbling piece of rockcrete as he reached his hand towards Turcifel, who was climbing out after him, followed by Sato and the abhuman. Pieces of masonry flew past them, thrown by the storm, and flies rushed towards them in their thousands.

The flood was rising at shocking speed and the surface was only ten or eleven feet from Coteaz's position. One slip and they would tumble into it. As the liquid rose, it bubbled and popped, spawning grey tendrils that stretched towards the inquisitor, snaking lazily across the rocks.

Coteaz looked up towards the scavenger engine and gestured for them to come closer.

'Madness,' muttered the pilot, but she was staring at Coteaz intently, and Malevich could imagine what she was feeling. Her world was falling apart and she was pinning all her hope on the inquisitor. He had seen it happen before. The pilot had no idea what was happening to Novalis, but she knew, by instinct, that Coteaz was her chance of surviving it.

'We will need to get him aboard,' said Malevich.

'The cargo bay,' replied the pilot. 'It's directly behind us. There are loading doors with grappling ramps. And winches and rotary drills if that won't work.' She nodded at one of the colonial militiamen.

The man looked like he wanted to scream, but he nodded and left his seat, gesturing for Malevich and Korov to follow as he clambered through an access hatch and left the cabin. He led them down a narrow, hexagonal corridor heaped with upended crates and discarded equipment. They all halted as another tremor hit, rocking the drill rig with such force that Malevich had to plant his hands on the walls to stay upright. Then, as the tremors faded, they hurried on and emerged into a cavernous cargo hold, big enough to contain several smaller, wheeled rigs and crammed with pallets and equipment. The air was hazy with red dust; even through his rebreather, Malevich could taste an acrid, chemical tang.

The noise of the rotors was louder here and the militiaman had to raise his voice. 'This way!' he yelled, leading them to a row of circular doors in the wall. The vehicle was still being battered by the storm and the three of them staggered as they approached a hatch. He tapped it. 'They have extendable grappling ramps. They can latch on to pretty much anything. They're big enough to walk down.'

The man turned a wheel handle. Then, after bracing himself, he yanked a lever and the door dropped away from him, opening onto the storm. Flies, wind, and rain rushed in, causing the three of them to stagger backwards, shielding their faces. Malevich grabbed a handle at the side of the door until he was able to see. The drill rig was dangerously close to the building and it was swaying wildly in the wind.

'Send out the ramp!' he cried, and the man pulled another

lever, prompting a thick sheet of metal to rattle out from beneath the opening. Bundles of claws at the far end crunched into the rockcrete wall, holding it fast and steadying the scavenger engine.

'The warp,' snarled Korov.

The surface had risen even higher and was now only a few feet beneath them. Malevich was still staring at it in shock when a glistening shape lurched from the depths and latched on to the doorway, drowning them all in a dreadful stink. He staggered backwards, whipping out his pistol and firing. The thing looked like a bloated tree, with rotten meat for bark and boils for buds. It juddered as his shots hit home but continued gripping the doorframe. As it leant closer, a teeth-filled hole opened in its side and it began squeezing its bulk through the doorway.

Fire filled the opening as Korov stomped forwards, gripping a heavy flamer with his mechadendrites. The tree made a low, grinding noise as it burned, as if someone were tearing wet material, then it disintegrated in the heat, dropping back into the fast-rising sea. Some of the limbs gripped on for a moment longer before they fell away too.

The militiaman staggered back from the doorway, his face pale and his eyes straining. Then he bolted for the cabin.

'Is he there?' cried Malevich as Korov stood on the threshold, staring out into the tumult.

He rushed to his side, pistol still raised as they looked at the wind-lashed ramp.

Coteaz and the others were clambering down the outside of the building and firing into the sea. Shapes were erupting in every direction as the surface boiled.

Malevich and Korov opened fire on the sea as Coteaz dropped onto the ramp, quickly followed by Turcifel, Sato and the abhuman. The group began walking towards the doorway, treading carefully with the liquid sloshing right below them. They were only halfway across when a shape hauled itself from the deluge and clambered onto the ramp, blocking their way. From where Malevich was standing, the thing looked like a lump of animal fat – white and glabrous and veined with black mould. As it settled into position, faces formed on its surface, giggling and bestial as they launched into bowel-juddering song.

It continued laughing and singing even as it collapsed under a barrage of shots, and as the pieces slid back into the water, Malevich saw human remains in the gloop – severed, half-digested heads and black, rotten bones.

Coteaz rushed to the doorway and Korov hauled him inside, whispering furious prayers as Malevich helped the others aboard.

Once they were in, Malevich wrenched the lever that retracted the grappling ramp. Another shape swelled up from the depths at the last, but their hail of fire dismembered it before it even broke the surface, and they never saw what it was.

The door closed with a slam but something banged against the outside, hitting the rig with such force that the vehicle jolted sideways.

Coteaz addressed the pilot over the vox. 'Get us out of here.'

'Yes, my lord,' came the relieved-sounding reply, and the scavenger engine tilted as it lifted away from the pinnacle, causing Coteaz and the others to stagger and grab on to railings. *'What heading?'*

'Sato,' said Coteaz. 'Do you still have the trail?'

She nodded, taking out her fragment of quietus tablet. 'Get us to Taphos. I can direct you from there.'

'We're almost out of fuel,' replied the pilot.

'Can we reach Taphos?' demanded Coteaz.

'Yes. But we couldn't make it anywhere after that.' She sounded numb. *'That would be our last stop.'*

'Sixtus,' said Coteaz. 'Are the ruins at Taphos still above sea level?'

Sixtus gargled before replying. *'Are the ruins still above sea level? Yes, the ruins are still above sea level.'*

'What about Vespertinus and Port Gomera? Are they still intact?'

'Are they still intact? Impossible to say if they are still intact. Vespertinus is submerged. As is Port Gomera. No life signs.'

Malevich heard panicked voices in the cabin as the pilot and the militiamen realised there was no longer a way to leave Novalis.

Coteaz nodded. 'Continue to the ruins.' Then he killed the vox and turned to Malevich. 'Could you fly this thing? The pilot may no longer be any use to us once she sees what's waiting at Taphos.'

'I can keep us airborne,' replied Malevich.

Coteaz rolled his shoulders, causing the joints of his battle plate to clank. Then he looked around at the group. 'Ready yourselves. It is time to do the Emperor's work.'

CHAPTER TWENTY-SIX

Voltas lay in blissful silence. The agony had ceased. His body felt wonderfully strong, filled with an odd sense of vigour. It was as though someone had bathed him in healing balm.

'They'll call you a monster.'

The voice was different this time and Voltas opened his eyes. The garden was the same, even more beautiful, if anything, with no trace of disorder or confusion. As he sat up and looked around, he saw dozens of the hooded gardeners, keeping tallies and examining the profusion of leaves and vines. The speaker stood close by. It was not Inquisitor Laredian this time, but a man who was a strange mixture of young and old. Voltas guessed he was no more than thirty, but his skin was lined and his eyes stared out from sunken pits. He looked proud though, and determined. He was wearing a grubby miner's envirosuit and his face was unshaven, but he radiated confidence, despite his slovenly appearance.

'Monster?' Voltas muttered, looking down at his body, and understood. His once beautiful clothes were charred and, in some places, had bonded with his skin, creating an angry, shiny mess.

'They'll call you a heretic.' The man looked at Voltas with pity.

Voltas climbed to his feet. 'I'm a servant of the Holy Throne. I serve the Lord Inquisitor Coteaz.'

'You *did*.'

'I still do. I did not fail him.'

The man looked pained. 'You were consumed by plague-fire. And it did more than burn you. Your wounds are deeper than you realise. The changes are more profound. More ruinous. That fire was tainted by Chaos.'

'Why are they keeping me alive if they no longer value me? If they consider me tainted, they would already have executed me.'

'Lord Coteaz will not wish to appear hasty. But how long do you think you have? Do you think he'll want you at his side when he leaves Novalis to be amongst his peers? Do you think he'll want to be seen at a conclave with a ruined, Chaos-scarred cripple?'

There was no malice or mockery in the man's voice, just sympathy, but that only made the words more offensive. Voltas pictured his parents' faces when they had learned Coteaz wanted to recruit him. Despite all their success and power, he had never seen them look so proud.

The man looked even more sympathetic. 'He won't let you leave Novalis. You'd be a symbol of his incompetence. He allows his witch to live, knowing how dangerous she is, but there are those who use that as ammunition against him. They say he is being reckless. If he lets you live, you would be living proof that he *is* reckless. More reckless than Laredian ever was. If you leave Novalis, there would be too many questions.

'The time will come soon,' said the man. 'When you reach the ruins at Taphos, Coteaz will deal with you. He'll make sure you don't leave that place.' He leant forwards, looking intently at Voltas. 'But you should know that there is a chance for you. I will also be there. You will recognise my face. And if you help me, at the crucial moment, the power you have always dreamt of will be yours – power far greater than anything Coteaz would ever have offered.'

Voltas slumped back onto the grass. 'You are wasting your time, whoever you are, I am no traitor.'

'My name is Elias and I can save you.' The man still looked eager rather than angry or offended. 'Coteaz will kill you because you are an indicator of his failings. He will rob you of your destiny, but there *is* another way.'

Voltas was on the verge of an angry reply, but his words stalled on his tongue. Much as he hated to admit it, the stranger might be right: Coteaz *would* execute him if the fire really had transformed him in some way. He thought of the shapes he had seen rising from the rocks. They were warp spawn. The flames they spilled would be warpfire. He tried to block out the thought but he could not. Coteaz *might* kill him. He could not let that happen. That was not the destiny he deserved.

'You're a liar,' he said, but there was no conviction in his voice.

Elias shrugged and looked around the garden. 'So many lies. They spring up like weeds, don't they? I've realised that it's impossible to root them all out. You could send yourself mad trying. I think many people do. The lies are too numerous and the liars are too clever. I've decided that all I can do is fight cruelty where I see it. And when I see that Coteaz is going to murder you because you embarrass him, I know that's wrong. If you want my help, I can keep you on a different path. A path to power and influence. The path you have always been on.'

He stood up to go. 'Remember me, Nicolas Voltas, when the time comes. When it's time for you to die, remember my words.

If you think it's right that Coteaz should murder you, then remain loyal to him and make your peace. If all you ever desired was to be a loyal servant, then you need do nothing.' He turned, then paused and looked back. 'But if you want something more than that – if you want to fulfil your potential, the potential you know you have always had – then remember my warning.' With that, he walked away.

Voltas wanted to denounce him, but he could not bring himself to do it. He recalled the blast that had washed over him and knew the man was right. He would never leave Novalis. At least, not in the company of Coteaz. He pressed his hands down into the grass and found he was gripping battered synthleather. He felt a rush of certainty. When he saw Coteaz, he would know the truth. Either way, he would know.

CHAPTER TWENTY-SEVEN

'We are approaching the ruins, Lord Coteaz.'

Voltas was surprised to hear Captain Malevich's voice. He opened his eyes and looked around the cabin of the scavenger engine. He had been slipping in and out of fever dreams since being wounded, and he struggled to understand how everyone could be back together in one place. Malevich was at the flight controls, working furiously to steer the drill rig through the storm. Turcifel was seated on one side of him and Korov was on the other, praying. Sato and the abhuman sat behind them, and directly in front of him was Coteaz, staring out through the viewport at the fore of the cabin. He was silhouetted by a hellish scene. Waves of crimson were colliding all around them, filling a sky edged with lightning. Coteaz noticed that Voltas was awake and turned to look at him. His expression was cold and distant. A heavy weight settled over Voltas.

'Fly past without slowing,' said Coteaz, looking away again. 'Governor Aldrov. Maintain your current altitude. Keep your aircars close to us.'

Aldrov's voice crackled through a vox-caster. *'As you command, lord inquisitor.'*

Voltas shifted his position, relieved to find his injuries were not as debilitating as he had expected. The conversations in his dreams had left him with the idea he would be unable to even move, but when he flexed his fingers and stretched his legs he found that he was able to move as normal. The blast had scarred him horribly, but the damage was mostly superficial. He looked horrific, though. He could see his reflection in a viewscreen and large areas of his skin were blackened and blistered. Most of his face was hidden by bloodstained bandages, but glimpses of the mess beneath were clearly visible. A memory surfaced to torment him. He looked like the members of his father's household who were burned on his orders – like one of the corpses that had earned him his place in Lord Coteaz's entourage. He crushed the thought. He was *nothing* like those people.

Turcifel heard him and looked back. Her expression was hard to read. Pity? Disappointment? Suspicion? He struggled to tell. 'Captain Malevich has morphia,' she said. 'Let him know if you need more.'

He could think of nothing to say. He could feel the presence of Coteaz, ahead of him, *judging* him, an axe waiting to fall. He knew the garden was a morphia-induced dream, but it had dredged an undeniable truth from his subconscious: Coteaz would never let him live, not after he had been burned by warp-fire. He would consider him tainted. Then he thought of the memento mori in his breast pocket and wondered if he might be mistaken. When they spoke that day on the *Pilgrim's Wrath*, Coteaz had seemed to believe in him. Perhaps the morphia was muddying his thoughts?

'Throne,' grunted the abhuman, as the clouds parted over the pinnacle.

Voltas lifted himself up on his elbows to look out at the scene. The pinnacle was a lone point of stability, surrounded by a seething ocean. There was a rocky, rounded hill at the top, roughly circular in shape, and at the top of the hill sat an object Voltas struggled to understand. At first glance he thought it was a rotten plant, like a carrion flower, with a stem that was hundreds of feet tall and leathery petals hanging from a sagging orifice. But then he realised that the *stem* had architectural features and must once have been a stone tower. It was a ruin, part of a processing hive that had been consumed by wet, decomposing growths. There were spores drifting from the orifice, floating out across the sea.

As his gaze slipped lower, Voltas was even more disgusted. Pouring from the building, tumbling over the rocks in their thousands, were all the legions of the warp. It looked as if every hell in the cosmos had been emptied. If Voltas had not been so dazed by the morphia he would have been appalled, but as it was, the whole thing just seemed absurd. The swarms of flies gave some respite, blurring the shapes of the figures, but not enough to fully shield Voltas from the madness. Some of the figures were humanoid, rotten and hunched, trailing black innards from blue-white flesh. They had long, gangly limbs, pot bellies and solitary, lurid eyes. Many possessed tusks that jutted from their brows or antlers that coiled around their slack-jawed faces. Most were gripping shards of rusted metal – virulent swords that steamed as they swayed back and forth.

As well as the humanoid figures, there were things that looked, to Voltas, like a kind of sentient viscera: translucent, pulsing organs, sporting limbs and mouths, that wound between the legs of the human-sized daemons or, in some cases, towered over them like pillars of festering meat. Their appearance was made all the more disturbing by the way in which they moved.

Rather than charging or running they plodded methodically, spilling flies and bile with every leaden step. And as their faces oozed they sang dirges, serenading the mucal sea.

'Four to five thousand warriors,' said Sixtus, clicking dials on his chest.

Warriors. Voltas thought the word too sane for the things he could see trudging from the tower.

'Highest concentration?' replied Coteaz as he stroked the psyber-eagle perched at his side.

'Highest concentration,' Sixtus whined atonally. 'Beneath the tower. Catacombs. Or crypts. A large empyric entity.'

'Exterminatus may be unavoidable now.' Coteaz announced the destruction of a world as calmly as if he were contemplating cleaning his armour.

Sato glanced at him.

'Once I have what I came for,' said Coteaz.

'Another flypast?' asked Malevich as the rig flew back out into the storm, leaving the madness of the rock behind.

'Higher this time. We have to handle this carefully.'

'More contacts approaching from the west,' droned Sixtus. 'Large. Travelling on approach vector two-four-A. Ten of them.'

Coteaz nodded but gave no reply.

Voltas could not understand why Coteaz was not troubled by Sixtus' warning.

'Should we take evasive action?' asked Sato.

The High Protector stroked Thula again, ignoring Sato and speaking to Malevich. 'Hold this position.'

'Lord Coteaz?' said Turcifel. She was trying to sound calm, but her lips were trembling slightly. 'Should we not–'

He silenced her with a glance.

Shapes glided towards them through the rain. Whatever they were, they were so big they made the air vibrate, shaking Voltas in his seat. They were no more than shadows at first, vast slabs of darkness, thundering through the clouds. Then, as they came closer, Voltas began to make out details: broad, low-slung wings and bulky silhouettes, heavy with guns and ornate, gilded buttresses.

'Drop-ships,' he breathed. Of course. Coteaz had planned this in advance.

'Thank the Throne,' muttered Turcifel, and even Malevich looked relieved. Only Korov seemed uninterested, muttering prayers into his mask.

'Orbit-to-surface landers,' clarified Sixtus. 'Vyrtus class. Each carrying a company of Tempestus Scions, plus ancillary staff and airborne assault carriers.'

'Give me exact numbers,' said Coteaz as the enormous aircraft rumbled closer.

'No accurate data. Ten drop-ships, each carrying a company. Companies averaging around three hundred Scions. So, approximately three thousand troops, plus ancillaries. The *Pilgrim's Wrath* came directly. And covertly, as you ordered. So there would not have been any opportunity to sequester other regiments.'

'How did you do this?' asked Sato.

Coteaz turned to face her. 'I summoned the *Wrath* when we first reached Domus Alpha. When you unwittingly showed me evidence of a Chaos presence on Novalis. The *Wrath* is currently anchored in low orbit.'

Malevich hailed the drop-ships over the vox and pulled the drill rig onto the same trajectory, heading back towards the pinnacle flanked by the enormous aircraft. The landers were so vast that Voltas felt as if the vibrations from their engines were going to tear him apart. Even through his mind-fug, he felt a stab of pain. He could understand why Coteaz would keep this move secret from the others but not *him*. He was his interrogator. He touched the coin in his pocket. He thought Coteaz had made him a confidant, someone he could trust with things he might not even share with his other retainers. But he had not even shared the basic facts of the mission with him. Coteaz had *lied* to him.

He recalled words from his dream. *The lies are too numerous and the liars are too clever.* Anger writhed in his stomach as he watched the others readying their weapons. Coteaz did not value him. Perhaps he never had. Perhaps he only ever saw him as a witless lackey, like that oaf Korov. The idea was maddening. Voltas was aware that pain and trauma were twisting his thoughts, but he could not shake a growing sense of betrayal.

CHAPTER TWENTY-EIGHT

Coteaz sprinted across the rocks, gripping the daemonhammer in one hand and his bolt pistol in the other. The drill rig had barely touched down, but he had leapt out before any of the others, eager to lead the ground assault from the very front. The Emperor had granted him another opportunity to serve, another opportunity to scourge the madness. He would treasure every moment. The years fell from his limbs and his muscles surged with vigour, powering him up the hill. The pain fell away and he could feel every fibre of his body, potent and alive.

'We are the blood of the Throne!' he cried. 'We are the light in the abyss!'

Assault carriers screamed overhead, spilling black-clad Scions with grav-chutes, flamers and hellguns. They were firing even before they hit the ground, slicing through the downpour and gouging holes in the enemy lines. The drop-ships had landed above the southern face of the pinnacle and disgorged infantry and ordnance with impressive speed. The artillery was already taking up positions on the rocks, preparing to unleash hell. Coteaz had an army at his back and the Emperor in his blood.

'In the name of the Emperor!' he roared, charging up the slope that led to the ruins. This close, and hazed by the rain, the tower looked like a rotten tumour, bursting through diseased flesh, rearing from the darkness and looming over the crowds below. Fumes leaked from gashes in its sides, and it radiated a powerful stench of infection and decay.

The daemons plodded slowly and calmly down the hill towards Coteaz. There were humans mixed in with them, malformed wretches wearing the tattered yellow remains of envirosuits and gripping an impressive assortment of guns. As the daemons stomped and slithered down the incline, the mutants opened fire, shooting in unison, as if responding to an unspoken command.

Shots screamed past Coteaz, tearing into the Scions running alongside him. Some of the stormtroopers did little more than stumble, protected by their carapace armour, but others tumbled back down the hill, spilling blood that flew skywards, snatched up by the crimson rain.

Carriers boomed through the clouds, multi-lasers flashing as they burned through the crowds of daemons and mutants. Rocks and bodies detonated, but as Coteaz ran on, he found his mind slipping. *Traitor.* The word snaked into his thoughts, summoning Laredian's face. What was he going to find when he reached the tower and entered the tomb beneath? Was his past waiting down there to reclaim him? He tried to rid himself of distracting thoughts. He *had* to find the soul glass; nothing could get in the way of that.

'All troops are now in range,' said Malevich over the vox.

'Open fire,' replied Coteaz.

Malevich relayed the order and light tore into the enemy lines. Daemons and mutants dropped in their hundreds. Coteaz doubted Malevich's troops would have missed a single target. But the enemy still showed no sign of a response, trudging on down the slope, droning their dirge as the ground split before them. Their song swelled, merging with the fury of the storm. Some of the Scions shook their heads, grimacing at the inhuman din, but they charged on despite it, firing again and again.

Coteaz was the first to reach the enemy. He barely registered the first few kills, swinging the daemonhammer in wide arcs as he barrelled through the crush. Prayers tore through him, exploding from his lungs as the hammer ignited, spilling a silver halo across the pall. Every time he faced the beasts of the warp, he recalled the murder of his family. And every time he recalled those corpses, his flesh burned, lit up with wrath – not merely an emotional response but a psychic blast that radiated from his core. And, with every howl of denunciation and banishment, the Emperor granted him more strength. In his youth he had struggled to harness it, but when the Sisters of the Sacred Throne blessed the daemonhammer, they gave him a conduit worthy of his wrath. Now, as he fought, he felt all the hope and belief of humankind radiating through its consecrated metal.

Artillery shells rained down along the enemy flanks as Coteaz led a charge through the middle, running without pause as he dealt out blow after blow. The prayers came thicker and faster, morphing into an archaic form of High Gothic that he did not recognise. The words came from somewhere beyond his body. The God-Emperor was reaching out, all the way from the Golden Throne of Terra, meting out judgement via Coteaz's willing flesh. Coteaz's faith was not an obscure, intangible hope; it was a visceral bond with his lord. He heard the Emperor's voice in every cracking bone. As he fought, he was only vaguely aware of the Scions landing around him, trusting to Malevich that his plans would be carried out to the letter.

He slowed a little as he reached a shattered slab of rockcrete, upended by the tremors. As he crested the top, a bloated figure clambered into view, blocking his way. It was a hybrid of the daemonic and mechanical – a rusting carapace, studded with metal tusks, carried on a cluster of oozing, muscular legs. Its arms ended in serrated claws and there was a sagging, leering face protruding from the centre of its torso. The thing was larger than the daemons Coteaz had faced so far, nearly three times as tall as he was, and as it jerked towards him, he was put in mind of an enormous, rotten crustacean. It swung a claw and he saw that there was a muzzle jutting from the metal.

He ducked bolter rounds then leapt into the air and hammered the daemon's face.

Liquid hissed from the creature as the face disintegrated, but the daemon did not seem to notice. It locked another claw around Coteaz's waist and lifted him off the ground. As Coteaz struggled to free himself, the daemon engine raised a third arm and revved a chainsword.

Coteaz brought his hammer round to parry the blow. Teeth screamed against the haft, filling the air with sparks. He pressed the muzzle of his bolt pistol against the corrupted limb and fired, severing it in a shower of yellow blood. Then he holstered his pistol and took out a grenade, jamming it in the wound, before dropping back to the ground.

The daemon engine exploded behind him, hurling meat and metal through the air as Coteaz walked on, his armour drenched in filth. Lesser creatures leapt at him, but he flattened them with the daemonhammer and sprinted on through crowds of reeling figures.

He took out his pistol and loosed off more shots, then, spotting a vantage point on a fallen wall, he raced up onto it and paused to survey the battle. The Scions had crossed half the distance to the tower. It had taken minutes, and from what he could make out through the fumes and the storm, they had suffered only minimal losses.

'Malevich?'

'Approaching from the east, as ordered. Close to the tower. Two, three minutes at most.'

He nodded and looked through Thula's eyes. She was soaring through the rain-slashed smoke, high above the fighting. All of the Tempestus companies had now disembarked, and in most places, the daemons were being cut down. As artillery shells shook the ground and the assault carriers returned for another strafing run, large gaps were appearing in the enemy lines. Not all the gains were due to the Scions though, he noticed. As Thula circled, he saw that holes had opened in the ruins, consuming whichever troops happened to be standing on the spot, whether human or daemonic. There were cracks in the ground everywhere, caused by the tremors, but these were different – gloopy and viscous, glistening like weeping sores.

As his battle fervour faded, Coteaz realised that the whole pinnacle was unstable. No, he decided, unstable was not the right word; it was in flux. There was such an intense concentration of warp energy that it was mutating the ground. He looked down at the rock beneath his boots. It seemed to be melting, the jagged, angular lines becoming smooth and yielding. He stamped and the surface tore like skin, revealing a bloody pulp beneath.

'We need to reach the mapmaker,' he said, addressing Sato over the vox.

'What if it's not here, Torquemada? What if we find the mapmaker and they say the soul glass is somewhere else?'

Coteaz had already considered this. 'The Mechanicus had a completed map in their possession and they were trying to reach *this* point. Prior to that, your psychic trail indicated that the mapmaker was here at Taphos. Sixtus tells me this location is also the centre of all the seismic disruption. All the Chaos activity is emanating from this point. And this is the only place that is still above the waves. The soul glass is here, or it is lost to us.'

Coteaz tapped his hammer against his chest armour, then leapt back into the fight. 'The glass is here, Castra. And I *will* find it.'

CHAPTER TWENTY-NINE

Voltas raced after Malevich and the others. He had been given too much morphia to feel the pain of his burns and he had enough strength to grip a gun. His own, beautifully crafted House Voltas weapons were ruined, but he had demanded a laspistol from the captain.

They were surrounded by black-armoured Scions, but the warp spawn were so numerous that, as Voltas stumbled down an incline, one of them burst through the ranks and lashed out at him with a cleaver. It was a gangrel, one-eyed thing, with pus oozing from its bruise-purple flesh. He sidestepped and fired, sending it reeling backwards. It laughed as it lay bleeding at his feet, maggots tumbling from the hole in its head, and then, as he aimed at its face, its rotten gash of a mouth slurred words.

'Tainted.' It giggled, pointing at him. 'He will... not... forgive you.'

Voltas fired, furiously, until the thing was still. He looked around, horrified by the idea that someone might have seen what had happened. The thing had addressed him with cheerful familiarity, as if they were old friends. Malevich looked back briefly at him but did not break his stride, rushing on with the squads of Scions.

Voltas hurried after them, unable to rid himself of the warp spawn's words. They seethed under his skull as if they were alive. He was wearing an envirosuit, but he could still picture how charred and grotesque he was. How did the thing name his fear so accurately? Coteaz was going to kill him. He could not escape that one, dreadful thought. Just as he had killed Laredian. Just as he was going to kill Sato. But when? Would he do it now, in the heat of battle? Would he gun him down when no one was looking, so he appeared just another casualty of the battle? Or would he denounce him as a heretic in some public fashion? If that happened, if everyone saw what transpired, the Voltas name would be ruined. Voltas had sentenced half the royal household to death so that his family could not be accused of heresy. And now it was all going to be torn down by a scandal resulting from *his* failure.

The tower loomed up ahead, rotten and stinking of carrion, and as they crested a rise, he saw the battle spread out below. Scions were driving wedges through the daemons, rushing into the spaces opened by the assault carriers, but in other places the daemons were growing in numbers, washing over their attackers like an unstoppable fungus.

'There!' cried Malevich, pointing out a group who had almost reached the base of the tower. The two command groups had been approaching the structure from different directions, but they were about to be reunited. For a moment Coteaz was obscured by rows of hunched, festering daemons, then he broke through, knocking them aside with his hammer as the Scions behind him opened fire, hurling the daemons away from their master with a barrage of shots. Coteaz was even more magnificent than the last time Voltas had seen him fight, but rather than filling Voltas with hope, it now filled him with bitterness.

Malevich led his squads on until they reached the High Protector. Sato was at his side and their armour was covered in soot, blood and pus. They looked almost as inhuman as the things they were fighting.

Malevich stared up at the tower. 'Is there a way in?'

Scions were firing on the surrounding daemons, buying them time to think, as Coteaz and the others looked at the structure that crowned the hill. It was pulsing slightly, as though breathing.

'Is it alive?' wondered Voltas aloud.

'The Great Enemy does not live,' replied Coteaz, 'not truly, even when it pierces the veil. This is nightmare masquerading as truth.'

'There,' said Sato, pointing at the base of the tower. There was a cluster of vein-like roots, formed into an arch around a patch of darkness. 'The mapmaker is that way. We're close now.'

The ground shifted beneath them as another tremor hit. They all stumbled and some of the Scions dropped to their knees as they fired.

Coteaz looked back towards the drop-ships. There was a great wall of steam where the waves were crashing onto the rocks. Parts of the pinnacle were already vanishing from view, and the liquid was pooling around the landing gear of the aircraft. Their time was almost up.

'Captain!' cried a Scion sergeant, scrambling up the slope towards Malevich. 'The enemy are holding their ground. And growing in numbers.'

Coteaz nodded and raced off towards the tower with the others rushing after.

Voltas was still feeling dazed, but he managed to keep up

as they charged across the top of the hill and approached the opening in the tower wall. There were no warp entities here; they were all further down the slopes, locked in battle around the drop-ships. A few turned and tried to rush back up, but the Scions gunned them down with unhurried precision.

Coteaz did not hesitate as he reached the opening, marching on into the darkness with Thula swooping in after him.

Voltas tried to hold his breath as he followed the others inside. It was like climbing into a month-old corpse. The floor was fibrous and wet, and grubs bubbled over his boots. Scions triggered gun-mounted lumens, revealing a broad passageway that looked like the throat of a great beast. Coteaz had ordered the bulk of his troops to remain outside, holding the daemons at bay, so only fifty or so accompanied him into the darkness, along with his retainers.

They entered a large space that must once have been a hall. The walls were so bloated with organic matter that it resembled a flesh-lined grotto. Voltas realised why the floor was so uneven. There were bodies sunk into the rock and soil. He could see faces with sightless eyes and wasted, diseased limbs. They had merged with the ground, glued together by filth. It was like congealed soup. As he ran on, he saw that some of the faces were moving, their mouths opening and closing.

Scions gathered in a circle at the centre of the hall, facing outwards, guns raised, their lumens splashing over sagging walls. As Voltas joined Turcifel, Korov, and Malevich at Coteaz's side, he realised that the morphia was starting to wear off. He could feel a warmth spreading all over his ruined skin that was nothing to do with the temperature in the tower. As the pain grew he felt that his time was running out. If he grew delirious, he would have no way to defend himself. No way to defend the Voltas name. He looked at Coteaz, who was staring into the darkness, deciding his route. He had to act quickly. He had to *do* something.

'Sato?' said Coteaz.

'We need to go down,' she replied, emerging from the shadows. Her eyes were closed and there was ash drifting around her clenched fist. 'There are tombs. The steps are that way.'

Coteaz nodded and set off once more with the others trailing after.

'There's something not right about this,' said Coteaz as they ran, glancing at Malevich.

Malevich frowned and looked back the way they had come. 'No guards.'

'They're probably all out on the hillside,' said Sato. 'Trying to reach the drop-ships.'

Coteaz did not look convinced.

They descended a series of slumped, reeking corridors before finally emerging at another mouth-like opening.

'The mapmaker is on this level,' said Sato as they all came to a halt at the doorway. 'We're very close.'

Korov stepped in front of Coteaz so that he could go first.

Voltas stumbled and wanted to cry out. The pain was growing fast now, urging him to curl up on the floor, but he remained quiet, determined not to draw attention to himself. The end was in sight. And he knew, now, what he had to do.

CHAPTER THIRTY

Elzevyr looked up at Elias and smiled. She was kneeling in the grass, carefully planting a sapling in the soil, placing it so that it was in line with the others that bordered the grove. He smiled back at her and took a deep, nourishing breath.

'I never wished for this,' she said, turning back to her work, patting the soil down. 'I never dreamt of immortality.' She waved at the immaculate garden. 'But it's because I never imagined what it would mean to live forever, what I could achieve.'

Elias planted a kiss on her head. 'That's because the preachers kept the truth so well hidden. They didn't want us to escape our mortality – they wanted us to work in those mines until we fell apart. We were just another tool to them, less valuable than the drills.'

When Elias spoke, now, he spoke without doubt or hesitation. When he joined his future self in the bathing pool, all his uncertainty fell away. He saw everything so clearly: illness and old age need not be the end. It was possible to exist and grow, for all eternity. Novalis had taught him that; the old gods and spirits beneath the tower existed beyond the reach of overseers and priests, and they had never lost the ability to truly live. He strolled on, watching the others as they worked, enjoying the sense of timeless, perpetual peace. The voice no longer spoke to him, but that was because its knowledge was now his knowledge; its voice was now *his* voice.

He knew that Coteaz was near, rushing towards the garden. The garden had been hidden for so many years beneath the ancient tower, but the inquisitor wanted to tear it down, to destroy it so he could unearth the soul glass hidden beneath. Elias smiled at the irony. Immortality was real, here, in this garden, and it was for everyone, but Coteaz would destroy it to buy immortality for himself. Could there be a greater illustration of the Imperium's rotten heart? He felt no fear. Battle was moments away, but the old gods of Novalis had seen all of this. They had engineered Coteaz's coming. And, when Coteaz arrived, he would find Elias armoured with a faith deeper than the Imperial lie. He looked at the blade in his hand. It was simple and functional, crude in comparison to the finery Coteaz would be wielding, but it was enough, because it was wielded by a believer.

As Elias neared the edge of the garden, he saw the gates beyond which lay his mortal life. The gates were broad and ornate, threaded with living vines that merged seamlessly with the metalwork. He could see nothing through them, but he knew where they led: they led to pain and frailty and death; they led to the Imperium of Man and the craven corpse-god of Terra. Memories of his old life threatened to disturb his equilibrium, but he calmed himself by looking at the blade in his hand. Once Inquisitor Coteaz was gone, the garden would be forgotten by the Imperium. He and Elzevyr would live in eternal peace.

He heard them before he saw them, their boots clattering on old stone and their guns rattling against their armour. This must be how Novalis' original inhabitants felt, he realised, in the days of the Great Crusade, when they were dragged under the yoke of the Emperor. The people who built wonders like soul glass must have despaired when they saw Terran ships gliding from orbit.

Fast-moving soldiers raced towards the garden. Most of them were dressed in dark, utilitarian armour, so it was an easy matter to pick out Inquisitor Coteaz. He was clad in absurd gilded battle plate that only the most vainglorious narcissist would consider wearing. There was light pulsing from the hammer he was carrying, and it gave Elias an unexpected stab of fear. The light dazzled him, distorting his vision, and for a moment, the garden seemed to lose it shape, darkening and sagging. Then he blinked and everything returned to normal. He sensed the others behind him, looking up from their work, placing their trust in him. Helk and Sturm stepped to his side, gripping weapons, their eyes bright with pride and determination.

'No more death,' he whispered, picturing Elzevyr's face and gripping his knife tighter. 'No more pain.'

As Coteaz came closer, Elias saw that his absurd armour was splattered with blood and that the stormtroopers in his wake were equally filthy, as if they had fought some kind of battle to reach this point. The inquisitor did not pause as he reached the beautiful gates, booting them open, buckling the ornate metal and cracking the hinges.

As the gates swung inwards, Coteaz and his soldiers stumbled to a halt at the edge of the garden. Some of them grimaced in disgust as they looked around at the orchards and hedges, and some even retched, as though the flowers were repugnant.

'Are you so poisoned that you can't look upon beauty?' said

Elias, filled with hate. 'I pity you almost as much as I...' His words trailed off as a pressure built in his stomach. Something turned in his guts, jostling his innards. Something was moving in his body.

'Elias?' said Helk, frowning.

'It's *him,*' said Coteaz calmly, raising a gun and pointing it at Elias. 'He's the host.'

A green-brown torrent burst from Elias' stomach, tearing his skin like water exploding from a cracked dam. The wonderful vigour dropped from his muscles and he felt as if a great weight were pressing down on him.

He reached out to grip Sturm's shoulder. 'I can't...' he began, but a violent nausea made it impossible for him to finish the sentence.

'What's happening?' asked Sturm, trying to pull away, his eyes wide.

Elias convulsed and arched his back as liquid filled the air, blocking his view of Coteaz and the others. As it spewed from his guts it formed a solid, quivering mass. Then the torrent ceased and he collapsed to the ground, clutching feebly at his exposed organs, blood pouring from the hole in his stomach. When he hit the ground he did not land on grass, as he expected, but something wet and giving. He lay in the muck and looked around to find that the garden had vanished. In its place, there was something obscene – a charnel house filled with decaying matter. It was hard to distinguish putrefying meat from rotten branches. As Elias teetered on the brink of oblivion, he saw that the nearest shapes had faces and bodies. They were so diseased that it took him a moment to realise they were Helk and Sturm. Their mouths were opening and closing, but no words emerged from their misshapen heads, only a drain-like gurgling sound.

'No,' he whispered, finally seeing the depth of the lie.

CHAPTER THIRTY-ONE

Coteaz and the others fired into the shape forming in front of them – a hill-sized sack of pustulant meat that absorbed their shots without so much as a shudder. The plague daemon discarded its host, leaving the man slumped on the ground. Waves of etheric power radiated from its blubber, hitting Coteaz so hard he felt as if he were leaning into a storm.

'That was him!' cried Sato over the din, pointing at the bloody remains of the man who spawned the daemon. 'That was the mapmaker!'

Coteaz had no time to consider the implications of the mapmaker's death. As the daemon's power lashed into him he was assailed by visions. They clawed at his mind, trying to muddy his thoughts, trying to break his resolve, but he raised the daemonhammer, wielding it like a standard, drawing on the decades of prayer he had poured into its rune-scored metal.

'He walketh in fire and blood!' he cried. 'He walketh in judgement!'

The hammer's light met the power of the daemon, creating

a thunderclap of colliding energy fields. The blast lifted Coteaz from his feet and hurled him back against the wall of the crypt. The wall gave, enveloping him with grasping fronds and snaring him in place.

Coteaz strained and realised he was trapped. The wall was slowly absorbing him. Digestive acids sizzled across his armour as warm fat oozed over his battle helm, obscuring his view. Warnings chimed in his suit as the joints began to buckle under the pressure. He bellowed a prayer and the Emperor's light blazed through him, burning the flesh that was consuming him, but it was not enough. The weight of the wall bore down on him until he could no longer breathe. *Traitor.* The word resonated through the blubber, filled with revolting mirth, laughing as Coteaz suffocated.

If the accusation was intended to demoralise him, it had the opposite effect.

Coteaz rammed his head forwards, breaking his face free of the filth. *'And so it was written!'* He freed his hammer in a shower of pus and ligaments. *'The beast and the idolator will be cast down!'* He swung the weapon in a murderous arc, pounding the wall, triggering another dazzling blast. *'There will be no mercy!'* He struck again. *'No quarter! No repentance!'* He staggered free from the wall, light searing his eyes as he attacked without cease. *'Only judgement!'* Daemons rushed at him, but he sent them tumbling to the floor, crying out again, *'Only judgement!'*

As Coteaz faced the wall, it reared up like an animal preparing to pounce. Columns became talons and balustrades became maws as its surface boiled, towering over his blazing form. He turned to face a tsunami of corruption, incandescent with faith and purpose.

A new source of power rushed over him and the wall shuddered, then recoiled.

Turcifel strode past him, head thrown back and prayer beads held before her. Her mouth was gaping as though she was yelling, her face contorted, but no sound came from her throat. As she neared the wall it recoiled, spilling rivers of gore as she drove it back. Mouths opened across its surface, all of them screaming in outrage, but Turcifel stood firm, waving the necklace as if it were a burning torch.

As Turcifel forced the wall of meat away, Coteaz strode towards the daemon. It was fully formed now, towering over him. Its skin was puckered and mottled, like the surface of a rotting apple. Its head was a malignant tumour, dark and glistening and crowned by gnarled antlers. Coteaz and the others reloaded their weapons and spread out in a semicircle as the creature's eyes opened, the lids splitting to reveal orbs like egg sacs, cloudy and teeming with pupae. It raised a three-fingered claw and shoved it through a wound in its gut, parting intestines to spill ink-dark blood. Then it raised its sword – a slab of corroded iron the size of an ancient oak.

'I knew you'd come.'

The words were like meat slops rushing up a throat.

'I knew you'd follow them here.'

Scions howled and dropped to their knees, vomiting and clawing at their necks.

Follow them here? What did that mean? He *had* followed Magos Xylothek, knowing she would be seeking the soul glass. And he had followed Sato for the same reason. But what exactly was the daemon implying?

All around the chamber, figures were rising from offal, shrugging off gore as they got to their feet. Many of them were humans – miners who had been corrupted and deformed by Chaos, their bodies distorted by mutations and their eyes rolling with madness. The rest were lesser daemons, much smaller than the one that had spoken – scrawny, cyclopean things, like the creatures out on the hillside – but there were a *lot* of them. Hundreds, Coteaz estimated.

'Stay back,' he warned, glancing at Malevich and the other Scions.

He stepped forwards, staring up at the grinning daemon. 'Abomination!' he cried. 'You will not have this world!'

The daemon laughed. The sound was even more repugnant than its voice, a rancid belch that drove Coteaz back a few paces. ***'I did not come for Novalis.'***

Coteaz was used to the hubris of daemons. And he had learned how to capitalise on it. As the daemon laughed he used the time to his advantage, nodding silent orders to his acolytes, positioning them around the creature's bulk so they could attack it from as many directions as possible.

Sato climbed some ruined architecture, gripping her chain-sickles and readying herself for a leap. Korov approached from the opposite side of the daemon, a heavy flamer resting on his hip. Turcifel was still at the wall, head bowed, her prayer beads gripped in her fists, still holding the deluge of meat at bay. Voltas looked distracted, muttering to himself, but he raised his pistol and came to stand at Coteaz's side. Most of the Scions had withdrawn, as he commanded, but some were left crawling in the muck, sobbing and vomiting, staring up at the daemon and clawing at their armour as if it were suffocating them.

The daemon planted its sword in the ground and rested its elbow on the pommel, giving Coteaz a friendly smile. ***'Don't pretend you don't know me, Torquemada. I made you.'*** It leant closer, spilling more slops from its gut.

Coteaz had been lied to by daemons so many times that he rarely engaged in discourse with them. They had countless methods of disguise, countless ways to masquerade as something they were not. He gave no answer.

The daemon laughed and shifted position again. Mustard-yellow spores leaked from its skin, and as they whirled through the darkness, the walls of the chamber began to fade, revealing a forested landscape. Wherever the forest was, it was not Novalis. Sodden, miserable-looking glades rolled off into the distance, the trees as diseased and rotten as the daemons, bowed by cankers and decay, leaning over stagnant, fly-hazed pools.

'You will join me eventually, Torquemada, whether you realise it or not. But I brought you here to offer you a chance.' The daemon lowered its voice, speaking in a conspiratorial tone. *'The glass is here, not far from where you now stand, but let me share a secret with you: it is worthless.'*

The daemon waved at the landscape surrounding them. The walls had now completely vanished, revealing a vista of despondent groves and tumorous buildings.

'Entropy awaits. You're coming here, Torquemada, to me. It doesn't matter how many transfusions you endure or how many bodies you steal, this is where your journey will eventually terminate. But the real secret is this – the thing you need to understand is that there are two paths to the garden. There is the one taken by souls who are brought here, fighting with their last breath, but there is another path, a higher path, that is taken by those who choose to come. And that path, Torquemada, is the path of power.'

Coteaz had heard such threats and boasts before. But he could not rid himself of the suspicion that this might really be Laredian, or at least some echo of him. And that idea chilled him. Executing Laredian was the most hard-won of all his victories. If that was for nothing, if his greatest victory had been meaningless, what did that mean for the rest?

Coteaz sensed that the daemon was playing for time. He looked back and saw that the passageway behind him was now as crowded as the hall they were standing in. Daemons were shuffling towards them from every direction, all wearing the same asinine grin and wielding the same pestilent blades, but they were holding back, waiting for a sign.

'I sense that you won't come willingly,' said the daemon, moving backwards with a sudden lurch. At the same moment, the crowd of smaller daemons attacked, loping forwards and raising their swords.

Coteaz strode forwards, lifting his hammer.

Gunfire erupted around him. Scions filled the air with las-beams while Korov advanced like a one-man army, spewing fire with some of his limbs as others spat bullets or hacked with rotary saws.

Sato leapt acrobatically, whirling her sickles, stabbing and wrenching at the massive daemon and slowing its retreat.

The Scions and retainers worked together to cut a path to the creature. Coteaz stormed down it. He spotted a raised area ahead. It was the plinth of a long-forgotten statue and he leapt up onto it, buying himself time to reload his bolt pistol as the daemons recovered and tried to scramble up after him. Opening fire, he cleared a circle around the pedestal. Simultaneously, he studied the fight through the eyes of Thula, who was circling in the darkness overhead, trying to spot a route to the daemon who had been taunting him. The fight was illuminated by a flurry of las-fire and he saw his route. He was almost through.

Elias lay still, afraid to move. He was surrounded by noise and light, and for several minutes he thought he had died. He could remember the pain he felt as the monster erupted from his body, but now, as his blood rushed through his fingers, he felt only a terrible numbness. The disease that had consumed his flesh had inured him to pain. Before, that had seemed liberating, but with the truth unveiled before him, it was horrific.

He could hear the monster talking to someone with the voice he had thought was only for him. But the voice was not in his mind. It was not the voice of his future. It was the voice of the thing that had grown from his stomach. The thought crushed him. How could he have believed in the idea of hope? How could he have been so deluded? The galaxy was filled with tyrants and despots on the one hand, while on the other there was only madness and ruin. He could see people trying to fight the monster he had spawned, bathing it in las-fire, but he could not bring himself to care. Everything was lost.

Slowly, he dragged himself into a sitting position, leaning against the wall and looking around. The scale of the lie was staggering. There was no garden, at least, not the beautiful haven he had imagined. The bathhouse was full of ponderous growths, but they were all as grotesque as the monster: decomposing, distended stems and leaves like blackened lungs. As he looked around, he saw what he had done to his people. Tears filled his eyes. Helk and Sturm lay nearby. They had been transformed by disease. It had altered them beyond all recognition. They looked like pathetic, wizened versions of the monster who had betrayed him. He thought at first that they were dead, but then he saw that it was worse than that – they were grasping at their innards and gurgling some kind of awful song.

He groaned in horror as he saw something else familiar, resting on one of the corpses. A flash of gold. He dragged himself closer and held it in his hands. It was the medallion he had given Elzevyr. The mutated, pox-riddled mess lying before him was all that remained of that beautiful, kind woman. She must have been dead for days – no, he realised, *weeks*. Cold with shock, he turned the medallion over in his fingers. It was only now that he saw it was not a winged sun. Surrounded by so much disease and decay, it was clear: the image was a fly.

He dropped the medallion and put his head in his hands, willing death to take him. Death did not come, but a memory did. He remembered what Elzevyr had said when he gave her the medallion. *Stay true.* The words cut into him. He had done worse than become like the overseers. He had betrayed his own people and birthed a monster. *No,* he thought, as anger quickened his pulse. *I wasn't the traitor. I wasn't the one who betrayed us.* Elias looked up from Elzevyr's body at the monster on the far side of the chamber. *It was that. That thing. It did this.*

Shame and fear fell away from him, replaced with a searing rage. He looked around for a weapon. Munitions crates and guns were still lying on the ground, half sunk in the filth. There was a missile launcher a few feet away, and he knew, suddenly, what Elzevyr would want him to do. He knew what staying true meant. His diseased flesh was still free of pain. He grabbed the weapon and, despite his wounds, began dragging it across the hall. As he moved, he felt his mind slipping away from him, his sense of self fading as the rot ate deeper.

He summoned Elzevyr's face, carrying it before him like a talisman, and crawled on.

Voltas felt oddly calm as he followed Turcifel through the carnage. His decision was made. The stranger in the garden had been right. Coteaz did not care about him or about the Voltas family name. The High Protector of Formosa was only really interested in protecting himself. The inquisitor would murder anyone to save his own reputation without a moment's consideration of what it meant for others. He would not care that he was tearing down centuries of proud history. Voltas could see the faces of his parents watching over him, filled with pride, confident he was destined to preserve their legacy, not destroy it. There was a voice at the back of his mind that tried to challenge this belief – that suggested Coteaz was doing what was right – but the voice grew smaller with every step Voltas took. His limbs were now trembling with the pain of his wounds, however. He would have to handle this very carefully. He had to wait until exactly the right moment.

Coteaz had cleared a space through the centre of the hall, and the others capitalised on this, launching another barrage of shots and allowing the High Protector to rush towards the enormous daemon. Voltas could not bear to look at the thing, so he kept his gaze locked on Korov's rag-shrouded back as he stomped through the crush, tearing daemons apart as he went, howling the word 'Recant!' with every kill. Sato and the abhuman had been hurled across the chamber and were now fending off attacks, but Malevich was leading the surviving Scions forwards, barking orders and keeping his troops in orderly ranks.

Voltas fired a few half-hearted shots to give the impression that he was under the same delusion as the rest of Coteaz's retainers, but when they all reached the inquisitor and joined their shots to his, firing up at the bellowing daemon, he held back. He knew, now, what his life had been building to. Finally, he saw the path to greatness.

Coteaz saw several things at once. First, he saw that the daemon was grinning even wider, stepping back to reveal that even more daemons were flooding into the hall, rushing from hidden doorways and clogging the vast chamber with ranks of leering horrors.

The second thing he saw was that Sato had rushed back towards him and aimed her pistol at his face.

He shifted his aim, targeted Sato, and opened fire.

* * *

Damn you, thought Sato, leaping sideways as she fired. Coteaz's rounds screamed past her face, missing by inches, but despite the fact that she was mid-jump, her aim was true.

Pain exploded in Voltas' side and he tumbled backwards, crying out. He slammed to the ground, filling the air with blood as Sato sprinted towards him, preparing to shoot him again. The abhuman was with her, drawing back its chainaxe to behead him. Voltas was about to fire back at them but immediately realised that would be a mistake. He had one chance left to get this right. He slumped onto the ground, rolling his eyes back in their sockets.

'Castra!' roared Coteaz.

Sato stopped and looked over at him, her expression furious, but she held her fire and shoved the abhuman, preventing it from decapitating Voltas. Instead of lowering the chainaxe, Khull redirected the blow, running past Voltas' prone form and crashing back into the daemons.

Coteaz stormed over to her, wiping blood from his face. 'What in the name of the Throne are you doing?'

'Saving your life.'

Coteaz shook his head. 'I do not need your–'

Voltas rolled onto his back and took aim at Coteaz's face.

Coteaz was ready. He slammed the daemonhammer down and Voltas' head exploded under the weight of the blow, filling the air with blood, teeth and fragments of bone.

Voltas convulsed once, then lay still.

Coteaz wrenched the hammer free and stared at the corpse.

'Learn who to trust,' said Sato, struggling to catch her breath.

Coteaz had no time to process Voltas' betrayal, or to argue with Sato. 'Korov!' he cried, pointing to a scrum of lesser daemons blocking their way.

Korov poured flame onto the mob, engulfing them in burning promethium. Coteaz marched through the burning mess and Sato jogged at his side, ducking and weaving like a pit fighter, casting her billhooks into the fray.

Daemons attacked from every direction, swinging swords and spitting bile, but Coteaz and Sato fought seamlessly. Where he pummelled and smashed, she stabbed and lunged, killing with almost inhuman speed, moving in a peculiar, loose-limbed manner that confounded the eye. He was the hammer, she was the blade. Together, they were unstoppable.

The others tried to keep pace, but Coteaz and Sato were soon alone, surrounded by waves of grisly faces. He and Sato looped around each other, performing a perfectly timed dance, and for a while it was enough to know he was doing the God-Emperor's work.

Slowly, however, Coteaz's muscles began to tire and his blows began to slow. He could hear Sato's breath becoming ragged as she wrenched and kicked.

The daemon calling itself Laredian was no longer fighting or even directing the smaller warp spawn. It had raised its sword and was belching incantations to the fumes.

Malevich and the remaining Scions were being butchered, torn to the floor by a storm of blades. The sea might have already swamped the drop-ships; the daemons outside might have overwhelmed the other troops. It might already be too late, he realised.

He glanced at Sato and her expression hardened. She knew him well. She saw the frustration in his face and guessed his thoughts. She backed away, lowering her chains. She could see what he saw, could see it was impossible, but she still nodded at him, preparing to leap back into the fight.

'In the name of the Emperor,' she said, locking her eyes on his, her voice shaking with emotion.

She had betrayed his trust and deceived him, but here she was, preparing to die at his side. Coteaz still could not fathom her. But in her eyes he saw a faith as unshakeable as his own.

'In the name of the Emperor,' he replied, and they charged forwards again, tearing into the ranks of daemons.

Korov was still pouring flames into the enemy, his head thrown back as he howled prayers and tore limbs. Turcifel was now holding the weight of the whole bathhouse, her face locked in a silent scream as the ceiling rained down upon her. Malevich was on the floor, crouching near Voltas' corpse, firing and bellowing orders even though Coteaz could see no Scions standing. The blood of the Throne was in every one of them. They were the light in the abyss. They *must* not fail.

'Coteaz!' gasped Sato as she fought, pointing one of her blades. 'The mapmaker is still alive.'

The man who spawned the daemon was dragging himself through the battle. His stomach had been torn open and his body was bloated by tumours, but he was still managing, somehow, to move. As he crawled across the floor, he kept his eyes fixed on the daemon with a determination so powerful that it was almost physical. He was dragging a missile launcher that looked far too heavy for him.

When Coteaz saw the man, he felt a rush of religious fervour. He carried the light of the Emperor in him, Coteaz could sense it. Whatever the man had done before, the Emperor was working through him now.

Daemons were loping towards the man from every direction, grinning and moaning. *Keep him alive,* thought Coteaz, willing Thula down from her safe vantage point.

The eagle dived and Coteaz felt her relief at finally being allowed to join the battle. She circled the mapmaker like a cyclone, tearing throats and ripping chests. Daemons tried to retaliate, but they were too slow for Thula. She cut through them like a phantom, creating space for the mapmaker to keep crawling. If he was aware of his winged protector he did not show it, dragging his weapon through pools of bloody water, his eyes streaming tears.

Stay true, thought Elias as blood loss started to overwhelm him. He felt a brief moment of panic as his arms trembled, unable to drag him the last few feet, but then he found a final reserve of strength and crawled on. He felt Elzevyr willing him forward, helping him, whirling through the monsters and holding them at bay, giving him this chance to undo what he had done.

Finally, he reached a vantage point that would give him a clear shot. He lay back against a corpse and managed to prop the missile launcher up on another body. The missile was already loaded, but even aiming the thing was almost too much for him. His arms shook as he tried to move it into position.

Is that all you think it would take? The voice spoke clearly in his thoughts, just as before, but its tone was utterly changed. Where it had been jovial and kind, it was now sneering and cruel. ***You did this, Elias. You created this. Do you think one missile can divert the will of the Plaguefather?*** The voice laughed. ***Take your shot, Elias.***

'Novalis will rise.' The phrase had a new resonance. Elias was no longer thinking of insurrection but of survival. The survival of sane, real, human life. Before the monster could realise what he was doing, he shifted aim and fired.

Coteaz staggered as the krak missile hit, detonating somewhere behind the daemon. The explosion filled the hall with light, and he cursed as he saw how wide of the mark the shot was. It had hit a stone structure built in the shape of a chalice, a kind of bathing pool. The blast ripped through the pedestal with such force that the daemon paused to look back. As the plinth crumbled, the pool it held tilted sideways, spilling a torrent of dark liquid. It crashed down over the daemons below, increasing the stench. Then the whole structure collapsed, hurling stone and spray.

Then Coteaz understood. 'He didn't miss,' he whispered. The daemon was still grinning, still holding its sword aloft, but its skin was stretching back towards the stone bowl, as though dragged by invisible talons.

'The Emperor is here,' said Coteaz, raising his voice. 'He did not forsake us. He has given us a chance.'

The lesser warp spawn attacked again, but as the daemon claiming to be Laredian was wrenched out of shape, the smaller ones began to alter too. It was like watching someone smear a painting across a canvas. The humans who had been fighting alongside the daemons finally succumbed to their afflictions and tumbled to the ground, choking on fluid-filled lungs and sobbing as they died. Behind them, the daemon finally noticed what was happening to its body. It bellowed. The cry was so loud the walls shook. It rose up over its toppling army and surged forwards, crossing the chamber with impossible speed, raising its sword and swinging at Coteaz.

'He walketh in fire and blood!' cried Coteaz, parrying with the daemonhammer.

The weapons collided with another explosion of light, but the daemon no longer had the strength to defy Coteaz's wrath. The blade jolted back, then rippled like oil in water, dissolving into shadow.

'He walketh in judgement!' cried Coteaz, slamming his hammer into the daemon's contorted face.

The daemon roared, trying to drag itself away from the chalice, but it was pulled inexorably backwards.

'Judgement!' cried Coteaz, following and landing a flurry of pummelling blows.

The daemon fragmented, as if Coteaz were hitting liquid. It regained its shape for a moment, gave one last roar, then flew backwards and vanished from view, leaving Coteaz to stagger in its wake.

The room filled with wails and screams as the lesser daemons were pulled in the same direction, smudged across the darkness, stretched into abstraction. The chamber shook. A column toppled with a crash, hurling pieces of rock, and cracks began snaking through the flagstones.

The adamantine spirit of man, thought Coteaz, thinking of the miner who had fired the missile. 'We need the mapmaker,' he said, staggering back through the mounds of dead, trying to locate him.

'There,' said Sato, clambering over corpses and leading Coteaz to the man. His body was so horribly torn it was incredible he was still alive, and again Coteaz felt the Emperor's gaze watching over them. He wished Salmasius could be there to see it. The old man would have wept to see such a miracle.

'Tell me of the map,' said Coteaz. 'Now.'

The man's eyes were rolling wildly and it took him a moment to focus on Coteaz. He looked afraid, then defiant. 'It lied to me. Whatever that thing was, it lied. That thing told me the map would save us, but–'

'Where did the map lead?' demanded Coteaz.

'I know what you want,' whispered the man, his defiance crumbling as he looked around at the carnage. His eyes began rolling again and his mouth filled with blood. 'The soul glass is minutes from here.'

The chamber juddered again, shedding more masonry and throwing up dust.

'Tell me,' snarled Coteaz.

The miner's words were growing weaker, but he managed to tell them which of the surrounding chambers they needed. Then he tried to rise. The two inquisitors watched in silence as he struggled, their expressions hard. At last he slumped back to the floor, his final breaths wheezing from his ruined chest. A moment later, his gaze grew dull and the breaths stopped coming.

Coteaz whispered a prayer. Then he unloaded his pistol into the man's remains, firing until there was nothing left that could re-form or endure.

When he was done, Coteaz looked up from the corpse and saw how badly the tremors were shaking the hall. The air was full of dust and noise as the walls shed lumps of masonry across the floor.

'The warp was the only thing holding this place together,' he said.

'My lord,' called Malevich, approaching through the dust clouds, leaning on Korov's shoulder. 'Turcifel is weakening. We do not have long.'

Turcifel was barely visible in the gloom, surrounded by a haze of distorted air. Coteaz allowed his consciousness to touch hers and he felt her pain. Malevich was right. She was near to collapse.

'Get everyone back to the drop-ships,' he said.

Malevich saluted and hurried away. Korov hesitated, then followed.

Coteaz felt Turcifel's pain like thorns under his skin. The air around her was icy and the colour had drained from her face. She was standing upright and rigid, like a statue, with her necklace held above her head and blood running from the corner of her mouth. The ground beneath her was bucking and shaking.

She looked as inert as the architecture, but he could feel her despair. Her grip on the tower was slipping.

He went to her side and grasped her shoulder, holding the daemonhammer aloft with his other hand. Sharing her consciousness was like bathing in acid. The pain in his temples doubled.

He poured all his faith into her, praying furiously. More and more pillars were slamming down, and the subterranean rumbling sound swelled around them. With his thoughts locked to hers, Coteaz could sense the vast, unstable weight of the ruins, straining and heaving, ready to crash to the ground.

'The soul glass,' said Sato, looking round at the storm of rocks. 'We have to go now.'

'I cannot leave her,' said Coteaz, his voice strained. 'We would be buried alive. I must stay here.'

Sato looked at the doorway the miner had directed them to, then back at Coteaz. They both knew the answer.

Coteaz stared at her in silence. Rubble struck the rock around them. It was only a matter of time before one of them was killed. The abhuman was snorting and pacing, but Sato did not move, holding Coteaz's gaze, waiting for him to speak. *Did* he trust her? He remembered something Laredian said once, when he was still a boy. *While we're alive, we tend our fires, but once we die they run free, Coteaz, for good or for ill*. What would Sato become if she outlived him? Had he filled her with doubt or with faith? What kind of fire had he lit?

Turcifel gasped in pain. More cracks opened across the walls.

Sato took something from beneath her armour – a metal disc, hung round her neck on a chain. It was the coin he had given her, all those years ago. She had kept it. Emotions flashed across her face – a mixture of pride, shame and hope.

Coteaz stared at the coin, studying the ruined face and the healthy one. Then, almost imperceptibly, he nodded.

Sato sprinted away without a word, dodging tumbling rocks as she raced for the distant door with the abhuman rushing after her. He could see them for a while, then the clouds of dust billowed across the room and they vanished from his sight.

Turcifel was jerking as if a current was passing through her, and he had to focus all his attention on helping her. He had made his choice. All he could do now was live long enough to see if it was the right one.

Turcifel gripped his shoulder. Blood was streaming from her eyes, pouring down her cheeks. She tried to speak but could not.

There was a deafening *boom* as a chasm opened across the floor of the chamber. Statues, bodies, and pillars tumbled into it, smashing and falling from sight.

Turcifel screamed.

'Lord Coteaz.' Malevich sounded short of breath. *'We have to leave. Are you clear of the ruins?'*

Coteaz tried to reply, but he was exerting too much effort to help Turcifel; the words would not come.

'Lord inquisitor. Are you there? The tower is falling. The whole pinnacle is collapsing. We cannot reach you.'

'Soon,' he managed to gasp as sweat poured down his face and his muscles started to spasm. 'Be... ready.'

'Yes, lord inquisitor.'

Turcifel turned to face him. Her skin was becoming translucent, revealing the pulsing blood vessels beneath.

A section of wall landed a few feet away, hurling rubble at them. Coteaz managed to shield Turcifel, his armour's refractor field crackling as it absorbed the impact.

'Here it comes,' he gasped.

A wound opened across the span of the ceiling, tearing the vaults apart, spilling stone, blood and flies.

Coteaz felt Turcifel's power start to fail. 'We are the light in the abyss,' he whispered.

'We... are...' Turcifel could not finish. Her mouth was full of blood and she was shaking furiously.

'Run!' howled Sato, sprinting towards him across the shattered stone. The abhuman was at her side, scowling. 'I have it!' she said. 'Go!'

Coteaz lifted Turcifel up and stumbled towards the exit. Empyric force burned through him. He cried out but managed to break into a run, still cradling Turcifel. He felt her battling to stay conscious, still forcing the walls to hold.

They raced through doorways and antechambers and, finally, out onto rain-spewing slopes.

Behind them, the ruins juddered as Turcifel's hold on them finally gave way.

They ran on until they reached a safe distance. Then they watched in silence as the tower fell in on itself, hurling up a column of dust and smoke.

Coteaz lowered Turcifel to the ground and looked around. The immediate danger had passed. The sea was already retreating from the rocks, and while the stench of death still filled the air, it was nothing more than the charnel stench that covered any battlefield. At the bottom of the hill his troops were marching up ramps back onto the landers, and he could see Malevich leading the squads through the drizzle. There were signs of heavy casualties – mounds of corpses littered the slopes and many of the troops boarding the ships were badly wounded.

He turned to Sato and held out his hand.

It was only now that he saw how many cuts and bruises she had sustained since she left him. There was blood flowing freely from a gash on her head and more rushing from one of her ears. But, despite her injuries, she looked elated.

There was a tense pause, then she took a small, battered containment unit from inside her jacket. She hesitated, then held it out to him, her eyes full of reverence. Her hand trembled as she dropped it into his palm.

Coteaz peered at it. The case was intricately engraved, and through a diamond-shaped window in the lid, he saw a faceted shape floating in a clear solution. He looked her in the eye. 'Did you come to Novalis so you could give this to me?'

Her expression grew rigid. She looked pained. 'Whether it's what I planned or not, I *am* giving it to you. What difference do my original motives make now? You have it. Nothing else matters. This is it. This is thing you've dreamed of for all these years. Your path to immortality.' She was about to say more, but the strength seemed to go out of her and she reeled away from him. The abhuman caught her before she fell and helped her sit on a piece of broken masonry. Then they both stared at him in silence.

Coteaz studied the tiny crystal. It looked just as he had known it would. With this he could elude the oldest enemy. He could defeat time itself. There would be no need to trust anyone with his half-completed plans. Albaro would use it to stop the sand falling through the hourglass. Finally, after all these decades, he could escape the trap Laredian had explained at the archdeacon's funeral. He would no longer have to live in the shadow of death.

Very carefully, Coteaz placed the case on a piece of fallen masonry, wedging it into place so that it would not be shaken loose by a tremor. He looked up at the sky and whispered a prayer of thanks. Then he raised the daemonhammer and smashed the containment unit, hitting it so hard that the crystal inside it was vaporised.

Sato stood slowly, watching glittering dust float away from the rock.

'What have you *done*?' She pawed at her bloody scalp. 'You had it. Immortality. It was in your grasp. I handed it to you. This is what you've searched for all these years.'

'I have searched for soul glass many times,' replied Coteaz. 'And this is not the first time I have found it. But my intention was *never* to use it.'

Sato gripped the handles of her billhooks. 'After everything we went through to get here. After everything I've *done*.'

'What did I teach you? Know everything before you act. Know all the facts. Why is soul glass significant?'

Sato sounded numb, but she frowned and looked into the middle distance, trying to grasp his meaning. 'It grants immortality.'

'No. That is the *least* of its power. Soul glass is a talisman. A symbol of faith. For whom?'

Sato shrugged, looking at the floor. 'Resurrection cults. Lunatics. People who think they could take the soul of the Emperor out of the Golden Throne. People who believe they could place Him into a new body and make a new Emperor. Fanatics who spout heretical nonsense about reincarnation.'

'Lunatics,' agreed Coteaz. 'A wide range of them. And for some of them, the cornerstone of their madness is soul glass. They can't agree, of course, on whether it's real or not. Which is why they butcher each other and never become a threat.' He lowered his voice, stepping closer to Sato. 'What do you think might happen if the existence of soul glass was proven? What if people knew that the article of their faith was not a fantasy but reality? What if those misguided fanatics knew that it might *actually* be possible to transpose the Emperor's soul into a new body?'

Sato nodded slowly. 'There would be a groundswell of support.'

'And then?'

'Schisms. Holy wars.'

'*Sector-wide* holy wars. Formosa, already attacked from all sides, would wage war on itself. It would threaten everything I have tried to build. That is the *true* power of the soul glass. The power to destroy. The power to tear Formosa apart.'

She nodded again, looking back at the ruined tower. There was still anger in her eyes, but there was understanding there, too. She knew he was right.

'Do you have a way off this planet?' he asked. 'Do you have a ship waiting in orbit?'

She frowned, looking at his hourglass. 'What are we to each other now, Coteaz?'

'You have betrayed me.' He looked at her weapons and at the abhuman. 'With everything you do and everything you believe. You are a disgrace to the Ordo.'

She raised her chin in defiance but said nothing, waiting for him to finish.

'But,' he continued, 'you could have taken that glass and fled. And, instead, you came back.'

'I told you before,' she said. 'I will not beg for mercy.'

They studied each other in silence.

Coteaz was about to say more, but she turned her back on him and walked away. She was tense, clearly conscious that he could gun her down, but she did not glance back. Then she paused to look at the remains of the containment unit.

'I was never convinced,' she said. 'Immortality is not a gift. We're meant to die. It's what gives us purpose. Death is the thing that makes us live.'

Coteaz watched her disappear into the rain, his hand locked tightly around the handle of his gun. After a moment he looked down at Turcifel. She had slipped into unconsciousness but the agony had left her face. She would survive. He had seen her endure much worse. The pinnacle trembled again, as if reminding him to leave, so he lifted Turcifel and began carrying her down the hillside, whispering prayers as he picked his way through the dead.

Later, as the drop-ships banked away from Novalis, heading back up to low orbit to join the *Pilgrim's Wrath*, Sixtus pointed out a signal on the augur returns.

'A shuttle,' he said. 'Heading away from us, to the far side of the planet.'

Coteaz watched the surface of Novalis spreading out beneath him. The seas were dropping; from this height it looked almost as if nothing had happened.

He pictured Sato's face.

'Let it go.'

CHAPTER THIRTY-TWO

'The rogue psyker,' said Coteaz, raising his chin as straps were lashed around his throat. 'The one your agents tracked to Ruelant Secundus. Sobala, was it?'

'Terminated,' replied Interrogator Lycus. 'Along with everyone else on the bonded transport.' He was a big, heavyset man with strong, bullish features and an air of unshakeable confidence. Since being brought into Coteaz's inner circle, he had become even more self-assured. He looked like he could stop las-fire with the force of his stare. 'We suffered zero casualties,' he boomed.

Coteaz tried to nod, but his head was now fixed securely in place. Serfs bustled around him, fixing straps to his arms and legs and flicking the needles of syringes. Turcifel was looking away into cable-crowded shadows, clicking her beads. Korov had bowed his head, clearly uncomfortable, wearing his muscles like an ill-fitting suit.

'My lord,' said Malevich. 'You recall the problems we had last time with the restituta.'

Albaro's face slid from the ceiling, pallid and oily, grinning down at Malevich, blinking gunk and chewing furiously.

'My lord,' said Lycus. 'You have not shared any details with me regarding the insurrection on Tricala. And I know nothing of the retrieve-and-purge mission on Drimargo. Agent Zaum has left the *Wrath* and I have no idea what his objectives are.' He paused. 'And there are the other matters we discussed. The ones you promised to elucidate me on.'

'Elucidate,' sniggered Albaro as he pulled a lever, firing up the chair's engine.

Currents fizzled over Coteaz's skin as the machine's gears rattled and locked into place. Serfs slid needles under his scarred skin. He recalled his exchange with Sato on Domus Alpha, when she had accused him of *wanting* his protégés to fail. He found himself arguing with a memory of her. If he had wanted Voltas to fail he would never have taken him to Novalis. He took him on a crucial mission and gave him every possible chance to prove his worth. Every possible chance to succeed.

He thought of the last time he had seen Voltas. He recalled the moment, just before he died, when the confidence fell from the interrogator's eyes. The moment he knew he had failed. It was the same look Coteaz had seen in Laredian's face all those years before.

'You know enough, for now,' said Coteaz, glancing at Lycus.

'My lord,' began Lycus, 'if you could just let me know which–'

'Begin,' said Coteaz.

'Beginning,' said Albaro, baring his tabac-blackened teeth in a grin.

Coteaz convulsed as chemicals flooded his veins.

He took a deep, agonising breath.

And held it.

ABOUT THE AUTHOR

Darius Hinks is the author of the Warhammer 40,000 novels *Leviathan*, *Blackstone Fortress*, *Blackstone Fortress: Ascension* and the accompanying audio drama *The Beast Inside.* He also wrote three novels in the Mephiston series: *Blood of Sanguinius*, *Revenant Crusade* and *City of Light*, as well as the Space Marine Battles novella *Sanctus.* His work for Age of Sigmar includes *Dominion*, *Hammers of Sigmar*, *Warqueen* and the Gotrek Gurnisson novels *Ghoulslayer*, *Gitslayer* and *Soulslayer.* For Warhammer, he wrote *Warrior Priest*, which won the David Gemmell Morningstar Award for best newcomer, as well as the Orion trilogy, *Sigvald* and several novellas.

YOUR NEXT READ

EISENHORN: THE OMNIBUS
by Dan Abnett

Charting the career of Inquisitor Gregor Eisenhorn as he transitions from zealous upholder of the truth to collaborating with the very powers he once swore to destroy, this omnibus brings together the novels *Xenos*, *Malleus*, *Hereticus* and *The Magos*, as well as four short stories.

An extract from
Xenos found in *Eisenhorn: The Omnibus*
by Dan Abnett

Hunting the recidivist Murdin Eyclone, I came to Hubris in the Dormant of 240.M41, as the Imperial sidereal calendar has it.

Dormant lasted eleven months of Hubris's twenty-nine month lunar year, and the only signs of life were the custodians with their lighted poles and heat-gowns, patrolling the precincts of the hibernation tombs.

Within those sulking basalt and ceramite vaults, the grandees of Hubris slept, dreaming in crypts of aching ice, awaiting Thaw, the middle season between Dormant and Vital.

Even the air was frigid. Frost encrusted the tombs, and a thick cake of ice covered the featureless land. Above, star patterns twinkled in the curious, permanent night. One of them was Hubris's sun, so far away now. Come Thaw, Hubris would spin into the warm embrace of its star again.

Then it would become a blazing globe. Now it was just a fuzz of light.

As my gun-cutter set down on the landing cross at Tomb Point, I had pulled on an internally heated bodyskin and swathes of sturdy, insulated foul weather gear, but still the perilous cold cut through me now. My eyes watered, and the tears froze on my lashes and cheeks. I remembered the details of the cultural brief my savant had prepared, and quickly lowered my frost visor, trembling as warm air began to circulate under the plastic mask.

Custodians, alerted to my arrival by astropathic hails, stood waiting for me at the base of the landing cross. Their lighted poles dipped in obeisance in the frozen night and the air steamed with the heat that bled from their cloaks. I nodded to them, showing their leader my badge of office. An ice-car awaited: a rust-coloured arrowhead twenty metres long, mounted on ski-blade runners and spiked tracks.

It carried me away from the landing cross and I left the winking signal lights and the serrated dagger-shape of my gun-cutter behind in the perpetual winter night.

The spiked tracks kicked up blizzards of rime behind us. Ahead, despite the lamps, the landscape was black and impenetrable. I rode with Lores Vibben and three custodians in a cabin lit only by the amber glow of the craft's control panel. Heating vents recessed in the leather seats breathed out warm, stale air.

A custodian handed back a data-slate to Vibben. She looked at it cursorily and passed it on to me. I realised my frost visor was still down. I raised it and began to search my pockets for my eye glasses.

With a smile, Vibben produced them from within her own swaddled, insulated garb. I nodded thanks, put them on my nose and began to read.

I was just calling up the last plates of text when the ice-car halted.

'Processional Two-Twelve,' announced one of the custodians.

We dismounted, sliding our visors down into place.

Jewels of frost-flakes fluttered in the blackness about us, sparkling as they crossed through the ice-car's lamp beams. I've heard of bitter cold. Emperor grace me I never feel it again. Biting, crippling, actually bitter to taste on the tongue. Every joint in my frame protested and creaked.

My hands and my mind were numb.

That was not good.

Processional Two-Twelve was a hibernation tomb at the west end of the great Imperial Avenue. It housed twelve thousand, one hundred and forty-two members of the Hubris ruling elite.

We approached the great monument, crunching up the black, frost-coated steps.

I halted. 'Where are the tomb's custodians?'

'Making their rounds,' I was told.

I glanced at Vibben and shook my head. She slid her hand into her fur-edged robes.

'Knowing we approach?' I urged, addressing the custodian again. 'Knowing we expect to meet them?'

'I will check,' said the custodian, the one who had circulated the slate. He pushed on up the steps, the phosphor light on his pole bobbing.

The other two seemed ill at ease.

I beckoned to Vibben, so she would follow me up after the leader.

We found him on a lower terrace, gazing at the strewn bodies of four custodians, their light poles fizzling out around them.

'H-how?' he stammered.

'Stay back,' Vibben told him and drew her weapon. Its tiny amber Armed rune glowed in the darkness.

I took out my blade, igniting it. It hummed.

The south entry of the tombs was open. Shafts of golden light shone out. All my fears were rapidly being confirmed.

We entered, Vibben sweeping the place from side to side with her handgun. The hall was narrow and high, lit by chemical glow-globes. Intruding frost was beginning to mark the polished basalt walls.

A few metres inside, another custodian lay dead in a stiffening mirror of blood. We stepped over him. To each side, hallways opened up, admitting us to the hibernation stacks. In every direction, rows and rows of ice-berths ranged down the smoothed basalt chambers.

It was like walking into the Imperium's grandest morgue.

Vibben swept soundlessly to the right and I went left.

I admit I was excited by now, eager to close and conclude a business that had lasted six years. Eyclone had evaded me for six whole years! I studied his methods every day and dreamed of him every night.

Now I could smell him.

I raised my visor.

Water was pattering from the roof. Thaw water. It was growing warmer in here. In their ice-berths, some of the dim figures were stirring.

Too early! Far too early!

Eyclone's first man came at me from the west as I crossed a trunk-junction corridor. I spun, the power sword in my hand, and cut through his neck before his ice-axe could land.

The second came from the south, the third from the east. And then more. More.

A blur.

As I fought, I heard furious shooting from the vaults away to my right. Vibben was in trouble.

I could hear her over the vox-link in our hoods: 'Eisenhorn! Eisenhorn!'

I wheeled and cut. My opponents were all dressed in heat-gowns, and carried ice-tools that made proficient weapons. Their eyes were dark and unforthcoming. Though they were fast, there was something in them that suggested they were doing this mindlessly, by order.

The power sword, an antique and graceful weapon, blessed by the Provost of Inx himself, spun in my hand. With five abrupt moves I made corpses out of them and left their blood vapour drifting in the air.

'Eisenhorn!'

I turned and ran. I splashed heavily down a corridor sluiced with melt water. More shots from ahead. A sucking cry.

I found Vibben face down across a freezer tube, frozen blood gluing her to the sub-zero plastic. Eight of Eyclone's servants lay sprawled around her. Her weapon lay just out of reach of her clawing hand, the spent cell ejected from the grip.

I am forty-two standard years old, in my prime by Imperial standards, young by those of the Inquisition. All my life, I have had a reputation for being cold, unfeeling. Some have called me heartless, ruthless, even cruel. I am not. I am not beyond emotional response or compassion. But I possess – and my masters count this as perhaps my paramount virtue – a singular force of will. Throughout my career it has served me well to draw on this facility and steel myself, unflinching, at all that this wretched galaxy can throw at me. To feel pain or fear or grief is to allow myself a luxury I cannot afford.

Lores Vibben had served with me for five and a half years. In that period she had saved my life twice. She saw herself as my aide and my bodyguard, yet in truth she was more a companion and a fellow warrior. When I recruited her from the clan-slums of Tornish, it was for her combat skills and brutal vigour. But I came to value her just as much for her sharp mind, soft wit and clear head.

I stared down at her body for a moment. I believe I may have uttered her name.

I extinguished my power sword and, sliding it into its scabbard, moved back into the shadows on the far side of the hibernation gallery. I could hear nothing except the increasingly persistent thaw-drip. Freeing my sidearm from its leather rig under my left armpit, I checked its load and opened a vox link. Eyclone was undoubtedly monitoring all traffic in and out of Processional Two-Twelve, so I used Glossia, an informal verbal cipher known only to myself and my immediate colleagues. Most inquisitors develop their own private languages for confidential communication, some more sophisticated than others. Glossia, the basics of which I had designed ten years before, was reasonably complex and had evolved, organically, with use.

'Thorn wishes aegis, rapturous beasts below.'

'Aegis, arising, the colours of space,' Betancore responded immediately and correctly.

'Rose thorn, abundant, by flame light crescent.'

A pause. 'By flame light crescent? Confirm.'

'Confirm.'

'Razor delphus pathway! Pattern ivory!'

'Pattern denied. Pattern crucible.'

'Aegis, arising.'

The link broke. He was on his way. He had taken the news of Vibben's death as hard as I expected. I trusted that would not affect his performance. Midas Betancore was a hot-blooded, impetuous man, which was partly why I liked him. And used him.

I moved out of the shadows again, my sidearm raised. A Scipio-pattern naval pistol, finished in dull chrome with inlaid ivory grips, it felt reassuringly heavy in my gloved hand. Ten rounds, every one a fat, blunt man-stopper, were spring-loaded into the slide inside the grip. I had four more armed slides just like it in my hip pocket.

I forget where I acquired the Scipio. It had been mine for a few years. One night, three years before, Vibben had prised off the ceramite grip plates with their touch-worn, machined-stamped engravings of the Imperial aquila and the Navy motto, and replaced them with ivory grips she had etched herself. A common practice on Tornish, she informed me, handing the weapon back the next day. The new grips were like crude scrimshaw, showing on each side a poorly executed human skull through which a thorny rose entwined, emerging through an eye socket, shedding cartoon droplets of blood. She'd inlaid carmine gems into the droplets to emphasise their nature. Below the skull, my name was scratched in a clumsy scroll.

I had laughed. There had been times when I'd almost been too embarrassed to draw the gang-marked weapon in a fight.

Now, now she was dead, I realise what an honour had been paid to me through that devoted work.

I made a promise to myself: I would kill Eyclone with this gun.

As a devoted member of his high majesty the God-Emperor's Inquisition, I find my philosophy bends towards that of the Amalathians. To the outside galaxy, members of our orders appear much alike: an inquisitor is an inquisitor, a being of fear and persecution. It surprises many that internally, we are riven with clashing ideologies.

I know it surprised Vibben. I spent one long afternoon trying to explain the differences. I failed.

To express it in simple terms, some inquisitors are puritans and some are radicals. Puritans believe in and enforce the traditional station of the Inquisition, working to purge our galactic community of any criminal or malevolent element: the triumvirate of evil – alien, mutant and daemon. Anything that clashes with the pure rule of mankind, the preachings of the Ministorum and the letter of Imperial Law is subject to a puritan inquisitor's attention. Hard-line, traditional, merciless... that is the puritan way.

Radicals believe that any methods are allowable if they accomplish the Inquisitorial task. Some, as I understand it, actually embrace and use forbidden resources, such as the Warp itself, as weapons against the enemies of mankind.

I have heard the arguments often enough. They appal me. Radical belief is heretical.

I am a puritan by calling and an Amalathian by choice. The ferociously strict ways of the monodominant philosophy oft-times entices me, but there is precious little subtlety in their ways and thus it is not for me.

Amalathians take our name from the conclave at Mount Amalath. Our endeavour is to maintain the status quo of the Imperium, and we work to identify and destroy any persons or agencies that might destabilise the power of the Imperium from without or within. We believe in strength through unity. Change is the greatest enemy. We believe the God-Emperor has a divine plan, and we work to sustain the Imperium in stability until that plan is made known. We deplore factions and in-fighting... Indeed, it is sometimes a painful irony that our beliefs mark us as a faction within the political helix of the Inquisition.

We are the steadfast spine of the Imperium, its antibodies, fighting disease, insanity, injury, invasion.

I can think of no better way to serve, no better way to be an inquisitor.

So you have me then, pictured. Gregor Eisenhorn, inquisitor, puritan, Amalathian, forty-two years old standard, an inquisitor for the past eighteen years. I am tall and broad at the shoulders, strong, resolute. I have already told you of my force of will, and you will have noted my prowess with a blade.

What else is there? Am I clean-shaven? Yes! My eyes are dark, my hair darker and thick. These things matter little.

Come and let me show you how I killed Eyclone.